COSETTE'S Tribe

LEAH GRIFFITH

Nonpareil PRESS
Port Charlotte, Florida

Cosette's Tribe
Copyright © 2012 by Leah Griffith

Published by Nonpareil Press
(Associated logos are trademarks of Nonpareil Press)

Cosette's Tribe is a work of fiction. While, as in all fiction, the literary perceptions and insights are based on experience, all names, characters, places, and incidents are either products of the author's imagination or are used fictitiously.

LIBRARY OF CONGRESS CATALOGING-IN-PUBLICATION DATA

Griffith, Leah
Cosette's Tribe / Leah Griffith. — 1st U.S. ed.

ISBN 978-0-9853066-0-1 (paperback)
ISBN 978-0-9853066-2-5 (e-book)

1. Coming of age — Fiction. 2. Child sexual abuse — Fiction. 3. Friendship — Fiction. 4. New England — Fiction. 5. 1960s – 20th century — Fiction. I. Title

813.54 –dc22

First Edition
March 2012
Printed in the United States of America

Book design and cover art by
Fran Murphy

Acknowledgements

I would like to express my thanks to some very special people, who without their unique and loving assistance, *Cosette's Tribe* may never have found its way into your hands.

I extend sincerest thanks to Fran Murphy, for being there for me in the early years of my life...and once again - presently. I am forever grateful for his artistic genius, his stunning cover art and galley layout, without which, *Cosette's Tribe* would not be what it has become in content and design. I cherish his contributions to my work.

Thank you to my ardent confidant, Beth Castrati, for never doubting my abilities and for providing me with the shelter of her friendship as I explored the dark places; to my sister, Patricia Caricchio, for her loyal support and the endless phone hours spent together deleting pages. I never could have done that by myself. Thanks go out to my sister, Joyce Carlton, for believing that nothing is impossible; to my late brother Michael Lynn who sits with me daily; to Laine Cunningham, for her tireless coaching through the novel birthing process. To Kathy Grey, for her inspiring friendship, meticulous editing skills, and for keeping me laughing.

My deep appreciation goes to Rebecca DeSimone and Jean Mirabile, for those early edits when Cosette's Tribe was still untitled.

I would also like to thank my friends who volunteered to read the manuscript early on and provided me with valuable input and honest feedback.

Sincere thanks go to my treasured children, Ben, Stephanie and Lacey, for being my most zealous cheerleaders, and to my son-in-law Charles, for his generous support; and finally, to my precious granddaughter Mallory, because I see the future in her eyes.

For Ma,
her stubborn genius will forever inspire me

and

for my husband, Mike, whose love leads me home

COSETTE'S Tribe

LEAH GRIFFITH

1965

Sometimes I feel like there's too much room inside of me, and that things are knocking around in there. I got a lot of secrets knocking around inside of me for a kid. Things I can't tell anyone. Ma would die if she knew some of the stuff I've been up to. I wish I could feel happy again like when I was little. I didn't have any worries back then because my soul was still white like the truth.

The Mother's Day Card

I wouldn't be in this big mess if my dad was around but he's been gone for so long that I can't even remember him. Ma likes to tell me stories about what he was like. She says that he was movie-star handsome and a great dancer. I dream about him sometimes but I can never see his face. We used to have a little picture of him but my big sister tore it up because she was mad at Ma. I never did get to see that picture, so I'm still kind of sore at her for that.

Ma says that I have my dad's brown eyes. Everyone else in my family has got Ma's blue ones. Whenever I ask Ma what my dad looks like she always tells me to go look in the mirror... but all I see is me.

I wish my dad was here so he could see how much I look like him. I want him to dance with me too, like he did with Ma, and teach me all those fancy steps, and I'll show him that I'm smart and can read better than most of the kids my age. I'm almost ten, and I want him to be sorry that he hasn't been around for all those Christmases and birthdays. Boy, he owes me tons of presents. If he ever comes back here I'm going to hold his hand and walk right down the middle of my street so I can show him off to everyone. I don't think he's coming back though.

Ma has a boyfriend named Ken and it's because of me that she got him. I knew Ken first because my best friend Jimmy Elliot (he lives on the first floor of our apartment building) dragged me into his grandmother's apartment to meet his uncle Ken. I guess Jimmy wanted to show off his uncle's Air Force uniform.

I was kind of shy when I first met him, because of his important job and how handsome he was, but he talked to me and Jimmy like we were grown-ups and told us some good stories. Then he said he'd give us each a quarter if we took his kid, Tommy, to the store. Ken said that he got Tommy in the divorce but his wife kept the three girls. It made me feel sorry for Tommy, his mother not wanting him anymore, and now all he got is his Grammy Green for a mother. Grammy looks like a big round hen and stays worried about germs all the time. I'm glad I got my mother; she's young and pretty, and likes to do lots of fun stuff with me and my two sisters.

Me and Jimmy hauled Tommy off to the store and bought a bag full of penny candy. Then we ate all of it while we were swinging at the side of the house so we wouldn't have to share it with anyone else. Tommy's seven and looks just like Ken with his squinty brown eyes, dark hair, and no lips; just a skinny line of pink skin under his nose.

One day I decided to invite Ken upstairs to meet my mother. I guess I was thinking that he could join my tribe seeing that my dad hit the road a long time ago. Tribes are sort of like big families, and I saw in a magazine how the people get to choose who lives in their tribes and who gets kicked out. So I figured because he was really nice to me, and he had a good job, him being in the Air Force and all, that my mother would like him and then maybe they would fall in love and he could be my father.

That day Ken had on his blue uniform and looked really handsome in it. My mother was washing the floor when I brought him into the house and her face twisted up when she saw him. I could tell that she was mad at me for bringing him over without telling her, but she didn't say anything right then. She just pushed her hair out of her face and said "hi" to him like she knew he was coming. She started talking really fast about how sorry she was for looking a mess and that she didn't know that he was coming, but Ken didn't seem to care about her washing the floor and her hair being all messy, because he said that he thought she looked pretty just the way she was. Ma turned as red as a raspberry when he said that. I was feeling really proud because I could tell that they both liked each other. When he left, Ma yelled at me and called me a little shit for not telling her that he was coming, but she didn't smack me so I knew that she liked him.

Ken comes by all the time now and Ma acts different around him, laughing at stuff he says even if it's not funny, and wearing lipstick around the house, just in case he stops by. She used to only wear lipstick when she was going out somewhere.

Having Ken around was really a blast at first because he took us places in his blue Cadillac. We never had a car of our own because they cost too much and Ma says that her welfare check can only go so far. One time Ken took us all out to eat at a Chinese restaurant and we each got little cups of tea and cookies with fortunes in them. My fortune was the best. It said that I was going on a great journey. Ken told us to eat as much as we wanted and then he paid for the whole thing. Ma was so happy she couldn't stop smiling.

Another time Ken brought us swimming at Mooney Lake. It's way out in the country and it took forever for us to get there. He even let our dog, Crumbs, come along. Mooney Lake is humongous and there are lots of places to swim. We went down a tiny dirt road to a place where there were no other cars around. Tommy spotted an old rope swing tied to a big branch so we took turns jumping off of it into the cold water. Me, my sister Janice, and Tommy, kept doing the Tarzan yell every time we swung because we were pretending that we were in the jungle, but my oldest sister, Diana, told us to can it because it was irritating her. Everything irritates her.

Me and Tommy don't know how to swim yet, so Diana kept a big black tire tube in the water for us to hold onto when we landed. Ken said that he promised he would teach Tommy and me how to swim some day.

I used to want Ken to be my dad because I liked how he would always talk to me like I was a grown-up and act like what I said was important. We spent lots of time sitting on the front stoop together and sometimes he would take me for walks and I would hold his hand like he was my dad. He gave me lots of stuff too, mostly money, but once he gave me a little red knife that had all kinds of parts, like arms, stuck inside of it. I still have that knife.

I liked sitting on his lap, so I could get a good whiff of his after-shave. He smelled really handsome, like a father on TV would smell. I could see all his little black whiskers popping up like those seeds on the rolls at the Jewish deli, and he let me feel his whiskers too. They felt like my cat, Ranger's, tongue, all prickly and rough. I really wanted him to be my father and take me to carnivals and the movies, and vacations far away, but now I don't want Ken to be in my tribe anymore and I wish that I never brought him around my mother. But Ma likes him more than ever.

Things turned bad when Ken invited me into Grammy Green's apartment when nobody else was there. I didn't want to go with him because I wanted to go upstairs and show Ma the Mother's Day card that I made for her at school. I went with Ken anyways because I didn't want to hurt his feelings.

The house seemed different without Grammy in it. The lights were all out, like a store after it's closed, and I felt like I wasn't supposed to be in there. Ken said to follow him so I walked behind him through Grammy's kitchen, with her cute little elf salt and pepper shakers sitting on a doily on her table, and down the hall to a bedroom. There were two small beds in the room, one was for Ken, and I could tell the other one was Tommy's because it had cowboy sheets on it. There was a bunch of stuff on the bureau, all boring men's stuff, and a bottle of that after-shave that smelled so good on Ken's face.

Ken smiled and told me to sit on the bed. I felt nervous being by myself in Grammy's quiet house with him. The blanket on his bed was green and scratchy but I sat there anyway. I could hear my sisters. They were in the side yard swinging and talking about buying some new magazines. Ken closed the window and then pulled the shade down so I couldn't hear Diana and Janice any more. Then Ken looked at me for a long time, but I kept looking at a pair of worn out slippers on the floor. They were lined up nice and neat under the bureau, like he was proud of them.

Ken told me that he loved me, and I told him I loved him right back, and that he was kind of like a dad to me. Then he sat beside me and put his hand on my knee and said that he really loved me. He moved his hand up under my dress and asked me if I loved him, but I didn't answer him because I felt like I was falling into a deep hole where no one would ever find me.

Ken's eyes looked dead black, and his hands were shaking while he touched me. He laid me down on the itchy bed and pulled down my underpants, but I kept my eyes shut tight like I do at the horror movies. I could hear his belt buckle clanging and his zipper going down. Then he climbed on top of me and put his thing on my stomach and started moving around. His chest was rubbing against my face and I could taste the salt from his sweat. Warm spit filled my mouth and I felt like I was going to throw up. I asked him to stop but he kept moving around, and making noises in his throat like a growling dog.

I thought about Ma upstairs waiting for me, thinking that I was outside playing, and I wished that I was safe at home giving her that card that I made for her. There was a big picture of the Virgin Mary on Ken's wall. Her face looked long and sad with her black shawl over her head and her watery eyes staring down at me. I turned my head away because I couldn't look at her any more, and then I closed my eyes and prayed for Ken to stop, and promised God that I would never do it again.

Ma was fixing the kitchen faucet when I walked in, and she asked me why it took me so long to get home. I told her that I was out playing in the yard. I was going to throw the Mother's Day card away but Ma saw it in my hand and asked to see it. She made a big fuss over the card and then she taped it to the refrigerator for the whole wide world to see. It was a big red heart with her smiling face in the middle of it. When I drew that card in school I could smile in Ma's face true blue. Now I feel like a faker because of the secret I'm carrying. I just want to go back to being the way I used to be.

Ma gave me a bear hug, and a kiss, for making her that card, like I was the best kid in the world. But that just made me feel curled up inside, like a traitor, because of what Ken and me did under that big picture of the Virgin Mary. I don't want Ken in my tribe any more. I want him to move back to California and leave us all alone. As soon as Mother's Day was over I tore that card to pieces and threw it away.

He's Always Here

I haven't seen my Uncle Richie for a long time. He's my favorite, and only, uncle, and Ma's little brother. He has no wife and kids yet, so he acts like we're his kids. He's a ton of fun to be around and he always buys us the best presents ever. One year he got us all brand new bicycles for Christmas. It was too snowy to ride them outside so Ma let us ride them up and down the long hallway in our apartment.

Uncle Richie is a butcher and has to wear a white coat, like a doctor, and a clean white shirt with a tie to work every day. Sometimes he comes to see us straight from work and still has blood all over his white coat so it looks like he just murdered somebody. I don't care though because I know that he didn't kill anybody.

We're Catholic, and we can't eat meat on Fridays, so Uncle Richie brings us fish almost every Friday. I don't really like fish, but Ma fries it up so that it doesn't taste like fish any more, and then she makes crunchy corn fritters and French fries to go with it. I love Fridays!

Last time Uncle Richie came over he had a new girlfriend named Carla with him. She had blond hair piled high on her head like an ice cream cone, and her eyes looked catty with heavy black lines traced around them. She's a little fat, but I think that she's pretty. She was nice to us but Uncle Richie acted kind of funny. When I ran up to him for a big hug he only gave me a half of a hug because his other arm was wrapped around Carla's chubby waist. He wasn't paying attention to me like he used to do. My sisters said the same thing. Diana said that Carla doesn't like us because we're poor and our house isn't nice like Uncle Richie's. He has a three story house with an attic and a cellar with nice furniture and stuff.

Things are boring around here without Uncle Richie stopping by every week. I miss him playing with us and taking us for rides in his car with the top down. I wish he never met Carla and that my dad would come back and move us all far away from here.

Ken comes by all the time now and I'm so sick of him that I could gag. Sometimes he eats supper at our house and hogs all of Ma's attention. After supper they sit in front of the TV and watch everything that Ken likes. Ma shushes us so that he can hear his stupid cowboy shows. He sits there and picks at his fingers and drops the little pieces of skin all over our couch. My sister Diana calls him a snake because snakes shed their skin every year. He watches me all the time too, and winks at me because we have a secret. I want to tell Ma what happened, but I can't.

My sister Diana says that Ken is trying to steal Ma away from us and that she hates his guts. Diana is nearly fourteen, and is Ma's big helper. But now Ma treats her like a little kid again because she has Ken to help her with stuff. When Ma goes out with Ken she still leaves Diana in charge of me and Janice, and Diana smacks us when we talk back to her, just like Ma does. I hate that about her because she's a lot stronger than we are so we can't fight her off. Sometimes when Diana gets real bossy we say that we're going to tell Ma on her, and she quits. We never tell on her though.

Last night Ken made Diana madder than a wet wasp. She was going to have some cereal before bed, but Ken saw her digging around in the refrigerator and said, "Isn't it kind of late for cereal?"

Diana told Ken that Ma always let her eat cereal at night because it helped her sleep. Ken swallowed hard and looked at Ma, and then Ma looked over at Diana and told her to put the cereal away and go to bed. I could tell that Ma didn't really care if Diana had the stupid cereal because Ma's eyes were smiling like she was hoping that Diana would go right along with her. But Diana didn't go along with Ma's little game and she got stiff like a soldier and said, "He's not my father," and then she threw her spoon across the kitchen. Ma jumped up and slapped Diana across the face and screamed "Don't you ever talk to me like that again!" So Diana ran into her room and slammed the door. Ken smiled at Ma and said "You did the right thing; a kid needs to know their place." I think Ken knows that Diana doesn't like him so he's trying to make her life torture.

When all the yelling was over I tiptoed down the hall to Diana's room and peeked in. She was crying so hard that she couldn't talk to me. I went in anyways and sat on the end of her bed, waiting for her to stop, but I didn't say anything because I didn't want to get her mad at me too.

Pretty soon my sister Janice came in and sat on the floor and all three of us whispered about what a jerk Ken was, and how we hoped that Ma would ditch him. I almost told them about my secret, but I couldn't do it because it was too awful to say out loud.

After a while Ma came into Diana's room and caught us all up whispering and told us to get to bed. When Ma came into my room later, to give me a kiss goodnight, she smelled good, like Ivory soap, and it reminded me of when I was little and she used to stick me in the kitchen sink for my bath. I liked playing with the soap because it floated like a boat. We were happy back then. I cried a lot last night and today Diana is still in a sour mood.

"Cosette! Will you go get me some cigarettes?"

"Sure," I said, stuffing my bare feet into my sneakers. Ma usually asks my older sisters to go to the store for her, but Diana is still mad about last night, and Janice is in Diana's room trying to cheer her up. Ma handed me the money and asked, "Where's your socks?" I lied. "They're all dirty, Ma."

Ma folded her arms into a pretzel and said, "Go get a pair of Janice's socks or you can't go to the store for me."

I ran back to my room and I grabbed a dirty pair of socks off the floor and put them on. I like going without socks because all mine are gray, like old snow, and I hate gray socks because they make me feel poor.

"I'll be right back," I shouted out to Ma, letting the screen door slam behind me. I cringed, waiting for Ma to yell at me for slamming the door, but she didn't, so I climbed onto the shiny wooden banister in the hall, like I was sitting backwards on a horse, and then I let go... swooosh! At the end of the ride I bumped my butt on a big wooden ball, but it didn't hurt a bit.

I was just about ready to slide down the next banister when I heard a man's voice floating up to me from the first floor. I knew right off that it was Ken's voice because of the way that it made my stomach twist up. I stood as still as a statue hoping that Ken wouldn't hear me. Ken's always watching me, and smiling at me, like he wants to do that nasty stuff to me again. Ken went back into his apartment, so I snuck down the rest of the stairs and ran out the front door.

I looked around to see if Jimmy was outside, but he wasn't. I didn't see any other kids hanging around either so I walked by myself with Ma's money in my fist.

We have a bunch of three deckers on our street and all kinds of people live in them. Ma calls our neighborhood a melting pot. When I walk to school in the morning sometimes I hear other mothers calling their kids in different languages. It seems to me that the people who can't speak English are extra careful about how they do things. Like they want to be the best so that nobody can tell that they're different. Nikko, the Greek kid, pops out of his house every day with his hair plastered down like Alfalfa's, and a spit shine on his shoes.

Ma says that I'm a mongrel; a bunch of nationalities mixed together like the mutts at the pound. That's where we got our dog, Crumbs. She is part German Shepherd and some other stuff too. My Uncle Richie says that mutts make the best dogs because there's no inbreeding. We got our cat, Ranger, from the pound too, but I don't think that cats can be mutts.

The big metal bell clanged when I opened the store door and Mr. Mancini looked up and smiled at me. I think Mr. Mancini is about a hundred years old. He's missing three fingers and wears thick glasses that make his eyes look owly. Ma says that Mr. Mancini is a war hero. I don't know about that. It's hard to picture him trying to shoot at anything with those weak eyes and no fingers.

"How's the family?" he asked, smiling up at me with his big eyes.

I looked away and told him that the family was good, (big fat lie) and then I asked him for Ma's cigarettes. Mr. Mancini put the cigarettes on the counter and then laid three tiny Tootsie Rolls on top of them. I handed over the money, smiled, and said, "Thanks Mr. Mancini." Mr. Mancini's a nice old man and I bet he doesn't pull down little girl's underpants.

Back at the house, Diana was crying again so I asked Janice what was wrong. Janice pulled me aside and said, "Ma's downstairs at Ken's house inviting him for supper, and Diana is crying because Ma smacked her in the face for mouthing off about Ken being here all the time." Ma always goes for the face. My stomach felt like it was full of wet dirt because of all this fighting that I caused by bringing Ken home to meet Ma.

I didn't want Ken coming over tonight either. On Saturday night Ma usually makes us a picnic on the parlor floor and we eat it right in front of the TV. It seems like we never get to have fun with Ma any more because Ken is always butting in. And tonight we'll be watching his corny Westerns instead of what we want to watch.

I went to my room, grabbed my stack of Archie comics, and started reading. I like Betty the best. She's pretty and nice too. Veronica is nothing but a snob. Ma came in the back door calling my name. "I'm in here!" I said, in my best normal voice. Ma peeked in and asked me where her cigarettes were. "They're on the kitchen table." I said, pointing like she didn't know the way to the kitchen.

I tried putting on my sad eyes, hoping that she could tell that I was unhappy, and maybe ask me what was wrong. But she didn't. Instead she tossed me a fake smile and then she told me that creepy Ken was coming over for dinner. I guess she could tell that I wasn't happy about Ken coming over because I wasn't smiling, and her million dollar smile melted into her mean face and she snapped, "You better not act up tonight either young lady; I've had about enough of that shit from Diana."

"What? I didn't say anything!"

"Well, you better not."

Ma stomped off to the kitchen. I could hear her clanging the pots around and slamming the cupboard doors. It seems like everyone stays mad lately. It's too late to ever tell Ma about Ken because she likes him too much. My nose started tingling, so I let myself cry while I read my comic book, and watched my tears drop all over Archie's face.

3

I Love Ice Cream

Ken was banging on the door, making Crumbs bark like crazy. Ma shouted "Somebody get the door," but I stayed in my room. Ken kept knocking, and Crumbs kept on barking, so I finally got up to answer it.

Ken was there with a big brown grocery bag in his arms. Tommy was there too, but he scooted right past me so that he could go pet Crumbs. I don't know why they bother knocking any more seeing that they almost live here. Ken smiled down at me, "Hi sunshine," he said, and then he winked at me. Whenever Ken winks at me I feel like he's thinking about all that stuff we did. I looked away from Ken's eyes.

"Come on in," I said. "Ma's in the kitchen."

Walking in front of him, I could feel him watching me, giving me the creeps, like he could see through my clothes.

"Ken's here!" I hollered, and then I tried sneaking back into my room, but Ma stopped me and asked, "Where are your manners? You need to stay out here and visit with our guests." Guests? Guests sounds like too good a word to use for Ken and Tommy. Tommy isn't a guest because he's always sleeping over, and Ken isn't a guest because he goes in our refrigerator without asking, and bosses us around. I didn't bother telling Ma that I would rather take worm medicine than sit and talk to Ken.

I asked Tommy if he wanted to play with my Fort Apache set and he started bouncing up and down like he was on a pogo stick saying, "Yeah, yeah yeah." I love my Fort Apache set. Ma got it for me when I was eight and it's my next favorite toy. My favorite toy is my doll, Blabby. When I squeeze her stomach her mouth opens and she cries. It doesn't really sound like she's crying though; it sounds like she's yelling and everyone thinks she's funny. I sat at the kitchen table while Tommy played on the floor. Ken started unloading the grocery bag. There was ice cream, chocolate sauce, nuts, whipped cream in a can and some soda.

"How about some sundaes for dessert?" Ken asked, looking at Ma and grinning.

Ma rubbed her hands together like a fly, and said, "Yummy" and then Janice came running in and did a twirl when she saw all that stuff on the table.

"Don't you like ice cream?" Ken asked, messing my hair with his big hand. I moved my head away, but Ma gave me the eye. So I smiled at Ken and said, "I love ice cream." Ma smiled over at me and put the ice cream in the freezer. All this fake smiling was giving me a nervous twitch.

Ma let Diana stay in her room for most of the night. I guess she was afraid that Diana might start up again and spoil the ice cream party. Me and Janice played games with Tommy while Ma and Ken watched TV. Sometimes Ken can be fun and I forget about what we did, and then I start wanting him to be my dad again.

I brought my Indian blanket out and spread it on the floor, so that we could eat on it, but it wasn't as fun as when we did it with Ma. Ma made sundaes but Diana said that she didn't want one. I knew Diana was only saying that because she was still mad, so I gave her all three of the Tootsie Rolls that Mr. Mancini gave me.

The next morning I woke up on the floor under a sheet with Crumbs. I didn't even hear Ken and Tommy leave last night.

I remembered that it was Sunday morning and that we had to go to church with Meme. Meme is my mother's mother and she takes us to church sometimes because we don't have a car. I like church, most of the time, because I get to light the candles. They come in different colors but the red ones are my favorite because they remind me of Christmas. I think if you have a special prayer, and light a candle, that God will answer it because he knows that you really mean business.

I crawled over to the parlor window to look outside. Pushing my nose flat on the screen I could see that nobody was out there yet. I figured I'd go outside so that I could be alone and think about stuff for a while. I like going out early in the morning when everything is quiet. I put on my shoes and then Crumbs came over and stuck her pointy head on my lap. I gave her a good pat and she followed me out the back door.

Outside the sun was hiding behind the clouds but it was still warm out. I crossed the street and sat on the curb under my favorite tree. A couple of blue jays started squawking and fluttering through the tree making little twigs and things fall onto the road. I didn't know that birds could fight like that. They reminded me of Diana and Ma.

I grabbed a twig and started writing my name in the sandy dirt. C O S E T T E   O R M O N D. I don't know any other kids with the name Cosette. My mother said that she named me that, after the little girl in a book called *Les Miserables*. She read that book when I was still in her stomach and she said that she loved the little girl in it so much that she named me after her. Some day I'm going to read that book and find out for myself why Ma loved her so much.

The front door slammed shut and Jimmy Elliot came running down the stairs, still in his pajamas, and wearing a big grin on his face. I rubbed my name out of the sand so he wouldn't think that I was in love with myself or something. Jimmy plopped down next to me and started yapping about how his father was buying a brand new car. I fake smiled and told Jimmy that I was happy for them, and then I said that I had to go upstairs to get ready for church. I didn't really have to go, but I could tell that he was going to brag, brag, brag and I didn't want to hear it. We never had a car and Jimmy's old car still looked good to me. I felt like crying because I had to go back upstairs when all I really wanted to do was sit on the curb, by myself, and think about stuff before I went to church.

Swimming Lessons 4

Meme almost hit a car in the church parking lot and then she swore at the old lady driving it. "Stupid son of a bitch!" she said, with her face snarled up like a witch's. The old lady didn't hear her but God sure did. Diana looked at me and raised her eyebrows and then we both burst out laughing. I spotted Meme's evil eyes in the rear view mirror staring at me, so I elbowed Diana to stop laughing.

"What's so funny back there?" Meme asked. But we knew better than to say anything because she was just looking for a reason to smack us good. We put on our church faces and got out of the car. This was Meme's church. It's a lot bigger than our neighborhood church and looks a lot like a scary stone castle from a storybook.

Meme dug into her purse to fish out our mantillas. They look like little black doilies and we wear them on our heads at church. I felt like Jesus' mother Mary when I put on mine, all holy and quiet. Meme found us a pew and I sat between her and Ma. Diana got to sit on the end where Ma or Meme couldn't pinch her from that far away. The only good thing about sitting next to Meme is that sometimes, when her throat gets dry during mass, she eats a cough drop and then passes one to the kid sitting next to her.

I looked around at the white statues standing against the walls. Everyone was there: all twelve apostles, Mary, Jesus, and even Joseph. They looked like ice ghosts with dead eyes. I pushed my back into the hard seat and closed my eyes. I pretended that I was praying but I was really daydreaming. The priest's voice sounded far away and I could feel my body getting all heavy. I tried staying awake but I couldn't.

My eyes popped open, and my stomach flipped, because of a bad dream I was having right in the middle of the Gospel of John. It was like I was watching a scary movie in my head with Ken and me on his bed and the Virgin Mary tsk-tsking me. Meme looked down and pinched me for fidgeting, so I sat up straight. I didn't want to be thinking about stuff like that in God's house. I bet there were no other kids in church thinking about stuff like that. I asked Meme if she had a cough drop but she just shushed me and kept her eyes on the priest.

Mass seemed like it was lasting extra long today. I wasn't going to ask to light a candle, or take communion, because I didn't go to confession yesterday. Ma forgot to remind us because she was too busy cooking for Ken.

I'll never tell the priest about Ken and me. I'd rather die with a black spot on my soul and stay in purgatory for a while with all those un-baptized babies. Janice will take communion because she never does anything wrong and her soul is still squeaky clean. She'll hold Meme's hand on the way up there, and then when she comes back, with the host stuck to the roof of her mouth, she'll walk down the aisle with her prayer hands together like a little angel. Sometimes I wish I was Janice.

After church Meme said that she was dropping us off at our house because she had a bunch of work to do. She makes wedding gowns and sells them in her store downtown. All three of us groaned at the same time but Ma said not to worry because

18

Ken was taking us swimming out at Mooney Lake. Diana looked over at me and rolled her eyes because she didn't want to go any where with Ken.

The lake felt really cold and my teeth were chattering, but when I got out of the water the sun warmed me up right away. I laid on a big rock squinting my eyes, because it was so sunny, and it looked like there were a million diamonds dancing on top of the lake. Diana and Janice were trying to teach Tommy to swim. I could hear Diana telling him "Move your arms like this and kick with your legs straight."

I'm tired of learning how to swim. I try hard but I get scared when I'm in the deep water, so I sink. Ma can swim like Esther Williams and does all kinds of dives. My favorite is her jackknife. She does it perfectly, and hardly makes a splash.

I felt a tug on my big toe but I ignored it. I figured it was Janice trying to get my attention. Then I felt something crawling up my leg, but it was only Ken with a pine needle in his hand dragging it over my skin. "What?" I said, trying to sound tired so he would leave me alone.

"I want to teach you how to swim."

He looked really young in his swimming trunks with his hair all wet, and I could see little dots of sunshine in his eyes.

"I don't feel like it. I'm cold."

"Aw c'mon, you big baby," he said, and then he held onto my leg and dragged me over the rock onto the grass. I yelled, "You're going to rip my bathing suit!" and I tried not to laugh, but I couldn't help it. He looked so funny. Like a big kid. He ignored my yelling and pulled on both my arms until I was standing up, and then he pushed on my back until he had me down by the water. I wasn't in the mood to go in but part of me kind of wanted to. Sometimes I think of Ken the old way I used to before he messed with me, and it makes me miss him. I keep hoping that he won't try anything else with me.

The tire tube was at the edge of the water and Ken plopped me right into the middle of it. Tommy was begging to come with us, but Ken said, "No. Go play with the dog." Then he put one arm through the tube and swam me out into the deep water. I could see Ma sitting on the blanket reading. Crumbs was lying next to her, and Tommy was standing on the shore, with his arms folded like an Indian's, watching us fade away. I wasn't scared because Ma was right there and Ken wouldn't dare try anything with Ma watching.

I was way out in the deep water floating around in the tube but I couldn't see Ken any where. I looked for some bubbles coming up from Ken's breath but there weren't any. Then I heard some splashing behind me and felt myself going up into the air. The tube tipped over and I hit the cold-water face first. Water went up my nose and my head was burning. I could see the sun coming through the water in wavy lines, so I tried to swim up to the sun for some air, but Ken grabbed my foot and pulled me down deeper. I kicked hard, trying to get loose, but he wouldn't let go of me. I had no air left so I took a breath and felt the cold water coming into my mouth and down my throat. That's when Ken pushed me up above the water and held onto me. I started choking and couldn't catch my breath, but Ken just laughed and said, "You're supposed to hold your breath you dummy."

I started crying. "MA!" But she was so far away that she couldn't hear me.

"MA!"

"Shut up!" Ken said, moving the muscles in his jaw around the words.

"Bring me back," I said. "I don't want you to teach me how to swim any more. You almost drowned me!"

Ken's voice got soft and he said, "It's okay Cozy, just sit here a minute and rest. I'm sorry. I didn't think you would try to swallow the whole lake."

I choked some more and spit over the side of the tube. I was shivering and my chest was burning. I could see Ma talking to Tommy, showing him something on the shore. Diana and Janice were throwing a stick into the water for Crumbs to fetch. I wished that I was with them, and not way out in the deep water with Ken.

"You feel better now?" he asked.

I did feel better, but I still wanted to go back to the blanket with Ma.

"I'll teach you how to kick on the way to shore," he said. "Just drop your legs over the tube, and keep them straight behind you, and then kick like this."

Ken started kicking his legs straight up and down. His feet were pointed and he moved back and forth in the water like a shark.

"I don't want to," I said, staying in the tube.

"C'mon Cozy, you have to learn to swim," he said, moving up close to me and wiping my bangs out of my eyes. "You want to drown some day?"

I thought about what he was saying, and he was right. I almost drowned ten minutes ago. And if I knew how to swim I'd head back to Ma right now and I wouldn't be stuck out here with him. Besides, most of my friends know how to swim. Jimmy Elliot took lessons at the YMCA and now he can dive and everything.

"Okay," I said. "But just the kicking part and I'm not letting go of the tube."

I dropped over the side and grabbed onto the tube with my arms. Then I started to kick like Ken showed me.

"Not like that," he said. "Your legs look like noodles. They have to be straight like this."

He held my feet in his hands and pumped my legs up and down.

"Okay, you can let go now," I said, copying what he told me to do.

"No, you're doing it too fast." Ken grabbed my legs and lifted them up and down like scissors. His hands were way up high and I felt his fingers hitting between my legs.

"Stop!" I shouted. "That's enough. I can do it myself."

"What? Don't you like me anymore?" he asked, and then he swam around and put his face up real close to mine. I could see the water dripping off his hair, little clear drops, rolling onto his eyelashes and cheeks, hanging from his nose and running into his mouth like teardrops.

"I thought we were friends?" he said.

I started feeling bad for him because of how I had been treating him like he had the plague or something. And I figured that he wasn't really trying to touch my crotch or anything. He must have just bumped it by mistake.

"We are friends," I said. "I just want to go back to the blanket because I'm hungry."

"Okay," Ken said, dropping down low into the water. "Let's forget about the lesson and I'll swim you back."

I got back in the tube and Ken slowly swam me towards shore. "Can't you go any faster?" I asked. He didn't answer me though. He kept creeping through the water like an old turtle. My butt was stuck in the middle of the tube, hanging down into the water, and I could feel his fingers pulling at my bathing suit bottom, trying to find a way under it. I looked over and saw Ma. She was under the tree reading her book. She couldn't see anything that Ken was doing to me because we were under a great big blanket of black water.

Today is the last day of summer vacation. It's Monday but it feels like Saturday because Ma's suppose to take us downtown to pick out shoes. I'm going into the fifth grade but it doesn't sound so big because my sisters are both in junior high now. I'm used to Diana being in junior high but it's going to be weird without Janice going to school with me any more. I bet Ma asks me to walk with Tommy because he's only in third grade. It will be like I'm the big sister now, even though he's not my brother.

"Cozy, hurry up! Ma said that we're leaving in ten minutes," Janice announces, like she's a TV newsman or something, and then she heads out of the room to go give Ma an update on what I'm up to. Ma likes to send Janice on spy missions. I pulled my shoes out from under my bed and put them on, and then went looking for Ma.

I found her in the bathroom putting on her lipstick. I sat on the tub and watched, while she twisted the bottom of the silver tube until the lipstick popped up like a red bullet. She looked so serious, like the school nurse giving a kid a shot. She made an "O" with her mouth and traced her lips with red, and then she colored them in. I handed her a little square of toilet paper and she put it in her mouth, pressing down hard until her lips disappeared. "Perfect," she said, and then she dropped the paper into the toilet bowl. And there it was…Ma's pretty red kiss floating on top of the toilet water. I didn't want to flush the toilet with her kiss in there because it made me feel like a part of her would disappear forever, so I sat and watched it float around while Ma finished getting ready. Looking in the mirror, Ma fluffed her hair, and then reached over and flushed the toilet. I watched her kiss twirl around like a tiny tornado, until it went down the drain and the bowl filled with new water.

Shoe shopping went pretty good today. I got a pair of Keds, and a shiny pair of black Mary Janes. They were a smidge tight but the store guy said that they would fit fine after I broke them in. We visited Meme at her dress shop and she paid me a dollar to pick up all the pins and threads off of the rugs in her fitting rooms. Ma said that we have to go to bed early tonight because of school in the morning. Part of me can't wait to go, but the other part doesn't want summer to ever end.

Two 5 Digits

Today is my birthday and tonight Meme and Uncle Richie are coming over to celebrate. Ma is making spaghetti for supper and then chocolate cake with coffee frosting for dessert. I love Ma's chocolate cake and I bet I get to lick the bowl by myself because it's my birthday.

I have to go to school today but I don't care because I know everyone will be wishing me a happy birthday. Phyllis Garrett will be really jealous because I'm ten and she's not. She's always trying to act older than me but she won't be ten until April. Phyllis is okay, but she's really pretty and likes the same boy that I like. His name is Steven Swenson, and he's dreamy cute! He has pretty blue eyes. Blue enough to swim in, and he always laughs when I tell him jokes. His mother lets him grow his hair long so it hangs down over his eyes like the Beatles. Long hair looks good on him. I think he likes Phyllis better than me because she's prettier and already wears a bra. I'm still flat like a pancake.

At school Mrs. Foley said that she was going to read us a story. I looked up at the big clock sitting over the "M" on the alphabet strip that runs across the top of the black board. Its three o'clock so this will make the last half-hour of school go by faster. I like it when she reads to us because she lets us put our heads down and sometimes I fall asleep.

I closed my eyes while she read. She used different voices for each person, just like Ma does when she reads to us, and I can picture how the people look. I see the little boy in the story riding a wooden raft that he made himself. I pretend that I'm on the raft with him getting ready to push off into the dark swirly river. I was waiting to hear what came next but Mrs. Foley stopped reading and told us to look out the window. We all looked over and saw that it was snowing big fat flakes! Everyone ran to the window to watch, and Mrs. Foley didn't yell at us to go back to our seats. She came to the window with us and stood right next me.

I never saw such big snowflakes before. They looked like pieces of pretty white lace floating around in the sky. I tried to watch a real big one but it kept getting mixed up with the other ones and disappearing. Ma says that snowflakes are like people, no two are the same. I wonder how God makes so many different snowflakes and then lets them melt away forever. If I made a snowflake I would keep it in my freezer so I could show it to my friends. I hope there's no school tomorrow. I want to go sliding, or maybe go shoveling with Janice.

Walking home from school, it was still snowing. I opened my mouth to catch a big one and it landed smack on my tongue. I could feel it melting, like the host at church does, and it was like God just gave me communion straight from heaven. Tommy spotted me, and came running over. His nose was running clear, like water, right into his mouth. "Wipe your nose!" I told him, so he took his jacket sleeve and wiped. "Yuck!" I said. "Look at your sleeve now; it's all shiny with snot."

"Grammy will wash it," He said, and then he tried catching some more flakes on his tongue. I think that boys are different from girls. They don't mind disgusting stuff as much. I'm definitely not holding his hand to cross the street, and I don't care if I get into a world of trouble for it either.

When I got upstairs there was a big glass-mixing bowl full of chocolate batter sitting on the kitchen table. I yelled for Ma, but she didn't answer. I saw her lit cigarette sitting in the ashtray, with the smoke curling up like a genie coming out of a bottle, so I knew that she was around somewhere. I stuck my finger in the bowl of batter and put it into my mouth...Mmmm. I didn't feel bad about tasting the batter because it was my birthday cake. I was about to get some more but then I heard Ma coming in the back door so I moved away from the bowl.

"Hi birthday girl," she said, hugging me tight. I breathed in her smell. I love how Ma smells, like food, soap, and cigarettes all mixed into one. I held onto her for a long time, and then she tipped my chin up and looked in my eyes, "I can't believe that my baby is ten years old today, and look, you're almost as tall as me."

"Yup," I said. "Two digits now."

I felt empty, like an old tin can, and my stupid bottom lip started quivering. "Don't cry honey," Ma said, hugging me tighter, but that just made me cry even harder.

"Ma, I don't want to grow up and move away from you. I want to live with you forever."

She pushed me back a little and looked at me, and then she wiped my face with her hands. Her eyes were wet too. She swallowed hard and said, "Some day you'll feel differently, Cosette, but for now you're not going anywhere." Then she squeezed my shoulders and said, "You want some cake batter?"

I said yes, but I didn't really feel like eating it any more. I wanted to sit on Ma's lap and have her rock me back and forth, and make that humming noise in her throat like she used to do to stop me from crying when I was little.

Ma got a big wooden spoon out of the drawer and put it in my hand. "Go ahead and dig in," she said, standing there watching and waiting like she did when she wanted me to take a pill. I knew that she was trying to make me feel better, so I scooped out a huge drippy spoonful of batter and stuck the whole thing in my mouth at once. Ma started laughing, so I did too. I was laughing but my insides felt like mud. I wanted to beg Ma to move us all away from Blaine Street, so that Ken couldn't find us, and we could be a regular family again like we used to be. But I couldn't tell her none of that stuff because then she would ask me why, and I would have to tell her about me and Ken and all the nasty stuff we did.

"That's my girl!" Ma said, watching me lick the last streaks of batter off the spoon. She turned and opened the bottom drawer to the stove and pulled out 3 round cake pans.

"You want to grease and dust these for me Cozy?"

"Sure," I said, tossing the batter spoon into the sink and grabbing the pans. While I greased and floured the pans, I pretended that Ken didn't really exist and that things in our family were back to the good old days.

It's already dark out even though it's still early. When I look at the streetlights I can see the snow is still falling, making the ground all white and soft like a bubble bath. Me and Janice are waiting at the window for Uncle Richie and Meme to get here and we're guessing what number car they will be that rides down our street. I guessed number ten because I'm ten today and Janice guessed number sixteen because she can't wait until she turns sweet sixteen, even though she's still only twelve. Finally Uncle Richie's car pulled up, but he was only car number five.

"We both lose!" Janice shouted, and then she ran to beat me to the door. I let her win because I know that it's me that they are coming to see.

I gave Meme a big hug and kiss and I could smell the fresh air sticking to her coat. It was a really fancy coat with a fur collar, and she was wearing a matching fur hat with it. She looked beautiful.

"How old are you now?" Meme asked, handing her coat to Ma.

"I'm ten."

"Hmmm…" she said, "you're getting old Cozy. From now on never tell a man your real age." And then she winked at me like a movie star.

Uncle Richie snuck up behind me and hit me behind my knees, making me fall backwards into his arms, so he could lay me on the floor. Grabbing both of my ankles, he tipped me upside down and said, "You're not too big to do this to." I tried holding my shirt up, so that my flat-as-a-pancake boobs wouldn't show, but I was laughing too hard and my head kept bonking on the floor. Uncle Richie plunged me up and down a bunch of times, and then he laid me straight out flat on my back like a piece of bacon in a frying pan. I was glad that Uncle Richie's girlfriend Carla wasn't there and that I had him all to myself.

Uncle Richie looked at his watch and said, "We can't stay too long. The snow is starting to pile up and driving is going to get rough."

"Can you eat supper here?" I asked.

"You betcha!" he said, peeling off his coat. "My sister makes the best spaghetti sauce in the world!" He turned and gave Ma a big bear hug. "Stop!" she yelled, using both hands to push him away, but I could tell that she liked it because her smile kept going.

Meme placed a shiny red bag on top of the refrigerator and said, "No peeking."

I couldn't wait to see what was in it!

Ma set up a little table for the kids, because our kitchen table was way too small to fit everyone, but I got to sit at the grown-up's table because it was my birthday. I just wanted supper to be over with so I could open my presents. Even Tommy brought me something.

Uncle Richie heaped his plate with a second helping of spaghetti while Ma put the coffee on to go with the cake. Diana and Janice were in charge of putting the candles on my cake and Ma shooed me and Tommy into the parlor until they were ready for me. I had jumping beans in my stomach and I kept sending Tommy to peek in the kitchen to see what they were up to. Tommy came back and told me to shut my eyes because they were ready for me in the kitchen. When I opened my eyes the kitchen was dark except for the glowing candles on my birthday cake. Everyone started singing to me and I loved the part when they all sang my name "Happy Birthday dear Co-sette..." I counted the candles and all ten of them were there. Janice held my hand and said, "Make a wish Cozy," so I closed my eyes and wished that Ma would never marry Ken. Then I blew as hard as I could and all the candles went out at once! Everybody clapped.

Ma gave me a pink diary with a little lock and key and my sisters gave me some black ink pens to go with it. I always wanted a diary so that I could write important private stuff in it. I'd have to find a good hiding place though, so that nobody else could read it.

Uncle Richie gave me a small orange transistor radio with earplugs so that I could listen to it without anyone else hearing it, and Meme gave me a real gold chain necklace with a pearl drop. I never had anything that expensive and grown-up before. Tommy even gave me a present; some pretty white knee-socks wrapped in Christmas paper.

Because of the snow, Meme and Uncle Richie had to leave right after I opened my presents. Ma sent Tommy home with some cake for everyone, and then she let us stay up and watch TV until the late news came on.

I opened my eyes; it was still dark outside. I felt like I should be excited about something but I couldn't remember what it was. And then I remembered the snow. The bathroom light was on, shining across the hall and into my room. I spotted my radio on my bed table so I put the earplugs in and turned it on to see if there was any school today. The DJ was yammering on about a sale at some stupid car place but then he said "Happy Snow Day! If you can hear me then it's you're lucky day.... School's been cancelled throughout our entire listening area!"

Janice was sleeping beside me. She was curled into a little ball and buried under the covers. I gave her a good shake and told her that there was no school today. "Huh?" She said, sitting up and rubbing her eyes.

"There's no school today!" I said louder this time so that she could hear me past all those potatoes in her ears, and it was like I shot her out of a cannon because she jumped up and ran to go look out the window.

"Did you tell Diana yet?" She asked.

"No."

Janice made a dash to Diana's room and I chased behind her. We jumped up and down on Diana's bed singing "There's no school today, there's no school today."

Diana rolled over and screamed, "Get out!"

"But there's no school today," we said again, softer this time so we wouldn't tick her off more than she already was, but this time she screamed at us even louder, "OKAY, NOW GET OUT!"

We knew that Diana would probably sleep until noon so we headed for Ma's room so we could tell her too, but she was already up, sitting at the kitchen table, drinking her coffee. When she saw us she smiled. "No school today," I said, and she said, "I know, but it's really early so why don't you girls try to go back to sleep?"

Sleep? There was no way that we were going to be able to fall back asleep, but we could tell that Ma wanted to drink her coffee in peace so Janice and me went back to our room to plan something fun for the day. I'm glad that I have Janice to hang out with. It would be so boring without her.

We decided to ask Ma if we could go shoveling to earn some money. The guy on the radio said that we got nine inches of snow, the heavy wet kind, and there were lots of people who would pay us to shovel. I went into the kitchen and Ma was still sitting at the table working on her crossword puzzle. I can't wait until I get smart enough to do crosswords. Sometimes Ma gets stuck and asks us kids if we know the answer. I got the answer right once and I couldn't help but smile in front of everyone.

"Pour me some more coffee, Cozy." Ma held her cup up but kept her eyes on her puzzle. "Sure," I said, bringing her cup over to the percolator. I put my finger on the glass knob, to hold the top on, and tipped the pot until the coffee poured out, and then I remembered to leave enough room in her cup for the milk. I set the cup in front of her, without spilling a drop, and waited for her to notice me.

"Thanks honey," she said, but she still didn't look up at me. I sat at the table and watched while she put some milk in, stirred, and then took a sip. "Ah, good," she said, and then she winked at me with both of her eyes at the same time. Ma was pretty, even in the morning with her hair all messed up, and I wondered what she would look like when she got old. I couldn't picture it no matter how hard I tried.

Ma caught me staring at her so she asked, "Did you want something?"

Without thinking I blurted out, "Can we go shoveling?" because I was still stuck on trying to picture Ma old.

"Whose we?"

"Me and Janice."

"Where?"

"The rich neighborhood."

Ma stared past me looking like she was in a trance, but I knew that she was only sorting things out in her head before she gave me an answer, so I kept my mouth shut and waited.

"I guess so," she finally said, "But dress warm and be back in time for lunch."

I gave Ma a hug and bounced back to my room to tell Janice the good news.

When we got outside things seemed really quiet because of all of the snow everywhere. We couldn't even hear our footsteps. It was like walking through piles of wet feathers. I spotted a bunch of black birds flying right above me in the white sky. They reminded me of my dot-to-dot books and I pretended that I had a pencil and tried connecting the birds to find a picture in them.

We lugged our shovels up Cherry Street where there were big stone houses on both sides of the road. Some of them were three floors high, and looked like little castles, with fancy diamond windows and high walls around them. I wished I lived in one of those houses. I bet the girls who live in those houses never have to wear stained socks or worry about their mom's boyfriends getting fresh with them.

"There's a guy shoveling!" Janice shouted, pointing to an old guy across the street clearing his sidewalk. His coat was unbuttoned and he was throwing the snow around like he was mad at it.

"You ask him," I told her.

33

"Okay, but you have to ask the next one."

I stood back while Janice went to talk to him. His house was pretty big but his driveway didn't go back too far. The old guy started pointing at the steps and the driveway like he was telling her what he wanted shoveled. I was getting cold from standing still for so long so I stomped my feet on the ground to keep them warm.

We never tell people how much we charge when we shovel for them because we're afraid that it will be too much – or too little. Most people pay us pretty good though. Janice ran back to me and sang, "We goooot it!"

It took us all morning to finish shoveling the house out. We usually do two or three houses in one morning but this one was big and the old man had us do the back path and steps too. Then, when we were all done, the stupid snowplow came by and pushed a bunch of snow back onto the end of the driveway so we had to shovel it out all over again.

I was feeling really hungry, and I had to pee, plus I had little clumps of snow, like pompoms, stuck all over me that shook when I moved and made my clothes feel heavy.

We rang the doorbell to get our money and an old lady opened the door. She had a bright pink see-thru robe on over a long black nightgown. Her chest was so big that it had a crease in it so it looked like she had an extra fanny under her chin. I didn't dare look at Janice because I knew that she'd make me laugh.

The heat from their house was warming up my face, and smelled like coffee and apples, making me hope that she would ask us in for hot chocolate or something. I tried to see past her but all I could see was the hallway. Janice announced, "We're all done shoveling." And then we both stood there, at attention, waiting for the old bird to say something.

"Nice, nice, very nice," she mumbled, and then she looked behind herself and shouted, "HOWARD, THE GIRLS ARE ALL DONE!"

Howard came to the door with a pipe in his mouth and a little black change purse in his hand. He snapped it open and stirred the coins around for a while with his crooked old man finger. Janice looked over at me with her uh-oh face. A change purse wasn't a good sign. We wanted paper money for all the hard work that we did. Howard looked up and grinned at us, like he was waiting for us to say something, but we kept our traps shut, so he snapped the purse closed, and said, "I'll be right back."

The cold air was blowing into the house so Mrs. Howard told us to come inside, but to stay on the mat, and then she stood there, leaning against the doorframe, staring at us like a jail guard. I figured she was probably thinking that she better keep an eye on us poor kids because we might try to steal something. I looked down and could see the polka dotted bread bags coming up out of my boots. Ma always makes us put bread bags over our socks to help keep our feet dry. I hate wearing bread bags.

Howard came back with a roll of green bills in his hand. He asked if we had change for a ten and we both said "No" at the same time. The smoke from his pipe twirled up, like a little chimney, and went into his eye, so he squinted it shut and held out the ten-dollar bill. "Here you go then. Who do I pay?" Janice went to grab for the money but he snatched it back and laughed like a pirate at Janice for being too slow.

"HOWARD!" His wife yelled, "GIVE THE GIRLS THEIR MONEY."

"Cripes Eunice, don't have a stroke." Howard said, putting the money in Janice's hand, "I was just kidding with them."

Me and Janice stood there staring at the piece of green paper in her hand. It was only a piece of paper but it would buy us lots of stuff downtown. She closed her skinny fist around the money while Eunice shooed us out the door.

We headed home with the ten dollars stuffed inside Janice's mitten. "We each get five," she said. And then we didn't say anything else because we were both thinking about all the things that we could buy with five dollars. I wanted to buy Ma something really nice, and my sisters too. But I wasn't going to be getting Ken anything because I didn't want him thinking that he was a part of my tribe.

Having all that money made me feel so good that I wasn't even hungry or cold anymore. And the pee feeling disappeared too.

We took our wet clothes off in the hallway and put them on a rack made of crisscrossed wooden poles. When I was little I was afraid of that rack because it looked like a fish skeleton to me. Ma handed us our dry clothes and asked, "Did you make any money?" Janice showed her the ten and Ma whistled. "Wow! You did well!"

"Yup," I said. "Five for Janice and five for me."

"Good job girls," Ma said, pulling the bread bags out of our boots. "Now get in the kitchen and eat before it gets cold."

I could smell the grilled cheese sandwiches and spotted the tomato soup already in the bowls. Ma shoveled the sandwiches out onto our plates and we dug in.

I was working up the courage to ask Ma if she would let Janice and me take a walk to High Street and spend some of our shoveling money. High Street is right down the road from us, and Ray's Five & Dime is on it. Ray's has gobs of neat toys and candy in it. The store kind of looks like a long hallway with stuff piled high to the ceiling. When Ray walks down the aisle he fills it up and you have to stand sideways to let him go by. He wears red suspenders on the outside of his shirt and a little bowtie under his chin; plus he's as bald as a mountaintop and wears little kid glasses on the end of his nose. He kind of reminds me of Mr. Potato Head, but he's really nice.

Mrs. Green, Ma's friend who lives downstairs, came over after lunch. She was still in her pajamas, but I could tell that she brushed her hair because it was in a fat red pony tail and her puffy bangs were curled under. She was sitting at the kitchen table, with a cup of coffee in her hand, whispering to Ma like she had some big secret. Pretty soon Mrs. Snively, Ma's other friend, was at the table too. Mrs. Snively reminds me of a pencil with a wig on. She's really tall and skinny. I went into the kitchen so that I could ask Ma about going to High Street, but Ma nearly snapped my head off.

"Get out of here and go play in your room!"

I went to Diana's room and tapped on her door. Then I waited for her to let me in.

"WHO IS IT?" She asked in her bossy voice.

"It's me, Cozy."

"Come on in."

I was surprised that she let me in without yelling, so I opened the door and saw that she was looking at a *True Story* magazine. That magazine has all kinds of juicy stories in it about girls getting into trouble. Ma says that that magazine is nothing but trash and doesn't like Diana looking at them. But Diana keeps them hidden under her mattress and only reads them when Ma won't catch her.

Crumbs was lying on the bed with Diana. Her head was on her paws, and she looked up at me without moving her head, showing the white around her chocolaty eyes. She looked really cute so I went over to pet her.

"What do you want?" Diana asked.

"I think something is going on."

"Like what?"

"I don't know. Ma and her friends are in the kitchen whispering about something and Ma kicked me out."

"So what, they always kick us out when they get to yapping," Diana said, without taking her eyes off of her magazine.

"Yeah but Ma yelled at me right away. She usually tells me to get out a couple of times before she yells at me. Plus they're whispering in a big clump at the kitchen table and peeking over their shoulders to see if anyone can hear them."

Diana finally looked up at me. But she wasn't really looking at me; she was looking past me just like Ma does when she's thinking of something.

"I'll find out what they're talking about. You stay here," Diana said, dropping her magazine on the bed, then throwing her coat and shoes on. She left and Crumbs followed behind her.

Janice came in the room and asked me where Diana took off to, so I told her all about Mrs. Snively and Mrs. Green sitting in the kitchen with Ma, whispering like witches in a circle, and that Diana was going to try and find out what they're yapping about.

"It's probably nothing," Janice said. Then she sat on the bed with me and opened up Diana's magazine. There was a picture of a girl on the cover of the magazine with a mini skirt on and black eye make-up. She was leaning up against a car and there was a boy in front of her looking like he was about to kiss her. She must be the one who was in trouble. I know that being in trouble means getting pregnant before you get married because Diana told me that. I know how babies are made too, because Jimmy's big brother Rick told him and then Jimmy told me. He said that two people had to fuck. I didn't know what fucking was until Jimmy told me about it. At first I couldn't believe that Ma did something that disgusting, and I got mad at Jimmy for saying it, but now I know that everyone's mother has to do it if they ever want to have any kids.

Diana came back in the room and plopped down on the bed. I was waiting for her to spit out the news but I knew she was going to make me wait and ask her.

"Well, what did she say?"

Diana looked at me like she didn't know what I was talking about, and then she said, "Oh, she won't tell me anything right now. I have to wait for her friends to leave, and then I'll get it out of her."

I could tell that Diana felt a little embarrassed that she couldn't get it out of Ma because Ma usually tells her everything. Diana picked up another magazine and started reading. I couldn't stop thinking that they were talking about Ma marrying Ken. He would be here all the time and I would never be able to get away from him.

"What if they're planning Ma and Ken's wedding?" I asked out loud, but Janice and Diana kept reading those juicy magazines and ignored me. I bet they're worried about that too and now I wished I hadn't said it out loud.

Crumbs was on the floor sleeping on her side, so I scooted down to sit next to her and rubbed her soft stomach. There was hardly any hair on it, just little baby hairs, and a bunch of pink nipples. I counted eleven of them and said, "Crumbs can have eleven puppies." But Diana and Janice just kept on reading.

Janice and me forgot all about asking Ma to go to High Street to spend our shoveling money. Today feels like it's lasting forever. Mrs. Snively and Mrs. Green finally left, but Ma's been in a sour mood all afternoon, snapping at us for nothing, and complaining about the house being a pigsty. She even made us empty our drawers out on our beds and fold everything. Diana isn't asking her any questions either; she said it was important to wait for the right time to ask her. It's already dark out and Ma hasn't even started supper yet. I'm starving.

Me and Janice sat on our bed combing out our dolls' hair. After a while Ma popped her head into our room and said, "I'm going down to Mrs. Snively's to call Uncle Richie. I'll be back in five minutes." We've never had a phone of our own so we always have to borrow a neighbor's. The only phone number I know is Meme's because Ma makes me call her sometimes to see if she's left to pick us up for church yet.

As soon as Ma left I headed for the refrigerator to look for something to pick at. There wasn't much in there, mostly "to go with" stuff, like margarine, ketchup, and mustard, so I grabbed a carrot and headed back to my room.

Janice saw me eating my carrot and jumped up off the bed. I knew that she was going to grab a carrot for herself too. Ma came back and saw us eating our carrots, but she didn't yell at us for snooping in the fridge because she knew that it was way past our suppertime.

"I forgot to thaw something out for supper," Ma said, "so Uncle Richie is coming over with some pizza."

Janice shouted "YIPPIE!" and wrapped her spaghetti arms around my neck. I was happy because we hardly ever get to eat pizza, but Uncle Richie was just here last night, and now he was coming over again with pizza – on a school night. I figured that there was something fishy going on. I peeled Janice off of my neck and went into Diana's room to tell her that Ma called Uncle Richie and that he was bringing us some pizza for supper.

"So," I asked her, "Now do you believe me when I say that something big is up?"

Diana rolled her eyes and said, "No shit, Sherlock! When does Uncle Richie ever come over two nights in a row?" Sometimes I'm afraid to ask Diana anything because she likes to make me feel dumb.

I sat at the kitchen table and pulled up the shade so I could look over at Mr. Robard's windows. He's our bachelor neighbor who lives in the house next door. Ever since we were little he's been taping holiday decorations to his windows for us kids to look at, but tonight his windows were dark and boring. Ma shouted over to me, "Pull the shade down Cosette, I don't want all the neighbors gawking in our windows." I pictured all the neighbors standing on the road, with their eyes poking out of their heads like bullets, gawking up at our window. All they would see is me sitting here at the table looking down at them. That's all. I didn't think that the neighbors cared about our window but I pulled the shade down so that Ma wouldn't have a cow.

Uncle Richie brought us pizza with tons of stuff on it. Ma told us to go in the parlor and eat our pizza while she and Uncle Richie had a talk. Diana turned on the TV and clicked the channel to some stupid scary show that she liked. The music sounded like pointy needles, and it made my stomach hurt. I sat at the end of the couch, closest to the kitchen door. I wanted to go in the kitchen but I didn't dare try it because Ma and Uncle Richie were in there yapping.

The show was about a big blond doll that came alive at night and walked around the house with a knife in her hand looking for people to stab. I tried stuffing my fingers in my ears and shutting my eyes but I could still hear the doll's creepy voice. Diana looked over at me and sucked her teeth, "Big Baby" she said, and then she laughed at me. Janice joined in too, making fake crying sounds like a little baby, "Wah, wah, wah," she said, and then she looked over at Diana and they both laughed some more. I wanted to run to my room but I was too scared to be alone so I stayed put and made myself think about good stuff, like Crumbs when she was a puppy.

Ma came in and shut the TV off. "Hey!" Diana shouted, but then she shut up because she knew better than to say "hey" to Ma. I was glad that Ma turned it off, so I looked over at Diana and Janice and smiled a big ha-ha smile at them.

Ma stood in front of the TV set like she was about to do a Show and Tell, and said, "Me and Uncle Richie have something exciting to tell you guys; so I want you to keep quiet and listen." Then she went and sat in the green chair near the parlor heater, like her turn was over.

Uncle Richie plopped down on the sofa, still chewing on his pizza. He folded his arms across his belly and his legs around each other so he looked all tangled up. I snuck over and sat next to him. I was still feeling scared from that creepy TV show; plus I was afraid of what the exciting news was going to be. I was praying really hard inside; "Please don't say that you're marrying Ken."

Uncle Richie wrapped his arm around me, so I snuggled in next to him. Sometimes I like to pretend that Uncle Richie is my dad, and that I'm his one and only kid who he spoils rotten. I wish I could tell him about my secret with Ken but I don't dare because its way too icky and he would probably never be able to look at me again. I would die if that ever happened.

Ma leaned forward with a big smile on her face, like she was going to tell us a joke or something. "I got a letter today from the housing authority," she said, and then her smile got even bigger.

I don't know who the housing authority is, or why they're sending Ma a letter, but she seemed pretty happy about it. Ma kept her smile going and swallowed hard.

"They said that they're going to be building a new school in our neighborhood."

I'm thinking that a new school sounded good. Our school is ancient like the pyramids.

"In order to build the school," Ma said, "they are going to have to tear down some houses, and a lot of people in the neighborhood will have to move."

"Whose houses are getting torn down?" Janice asked, with her eyes getting as big as meatballs.

"A lot of people's houses," Ma said.

"Like whose?" Diana asked.

Ma didn't say anything but looked over at Uncle Richie. We all looked at him too. Uncle Richie sat up strait and coughed a little.

"Well," he said, "most of the old houses are going; like Mr. Robard's, and the Cat Lady's."

"NO!" Janice shouted, "We love Mr. Robard. Where will he live?" Then she started squirting out tears and howling. I looked over at Diana and it looked like she was crying too but she wasn't making any noise about it. I felt bad because I wasn't crying. They were just teasing me for being a big cry baby and now I couldn't even drop a tear. I felt really bad for Mr. Robard, and the Cat Lady, but I was just glad that Ma wasn't marrying Ken. God must have heard my prayers.

We don't know the Cat Lady's real name. We just call her that because she walks her cat on a long skinny rope, like it's a dog. It's a fluffy orange cat, and fat too, so it looks like a pumpkin on a leash. Her gray hair is really long for an old lady's, and it's messy, and blows around in the wind like thick smoke. Some kids say that she's a witch. But I know that witches only like black cats. I am kind of scared of her, though.

Uncle Richie kept on talking about houses being torn down, and the new school, and how grand it would all be, but I got this funny feeling inside, like Uncle Richie and Ma weren't telling us something, so I piped up and asked, "Is our house going to be torn down too?" Uncle Richie looked over at Ma and then looked down at the floor and said, "Yes honey, your house is being torn down too."

Now I was crying right along with Janice and Diana. Ma and Uncle Richie didn't even try to calm us down; they just sat there and let us cry it out all at once.

I can't sleep, and all I can hear is our old refrigerator humming. I bet it's about three o'clock in the morning. I can't stop thinking about my house getting torn down. I looked over at the doorframe and I could see where the paint was flaking from us kids climbing up the sides of it, like monkeys, to hang from the top of it and then drop down again. I tried to picture it broken to pieces, and lying in a big pile, like house bones.

Pretty soon it would be time to get up for school and I wondered if any of the other kids knew about all the houses being torn down. I thought about Warren Measley. He has stubby blond hair and Coke bottle glasses. His parents don't let him go out to play very much. I think that they're afraid that he'll get hurt or something, so he's always sitting in his window looking down at the rest of us kids playing in the street. When I was six, he bought me a ring from a gumball machine, and asked if I'd marry him when we grew up. I told him okay, but I'm not really going to marry him. I was too little to know what I was saying so it's not really a lie. I like having Warren live across the street from me though because it kind of makes me feel special knowing that he wants to marry me. He's the smartest kid in my class.

Jimmy Elliot is my best "boy" friend, but not in a mushy sort of way, and Rosemarie Jarvis is my best girlfriend. She's short and has a puffy face, like a bee stung her and things swelled up a bit. Her skin is as dark as Ma's chocolate cake and her hair stays where you put it without using bobby pins. I sleep over at her house sometimes and we take turns playing with each other's hair. My hair's always a rat's nest so she takes her time and brushes it out, without hurting me a bit, and then she lets me make her hair into all kinds of shapes. One time I made her hair into the Statue of Liberty's crown and we laughed so hard we almost peed our pants. I can always tell when Rosemarie is going to smile before her mouth even moves. All I have to do is look at the little shiny spots in her eyes; they get bigger and bigger until her mouth joins in. She has the best smile in the world with teeth as white as milk.

Rosemarie told me that her step-dad likes to drink a lot and acts like a fool. She doesn't like him a bit and sometimes I see him winking at her like Ken does to me. The last time I slept over her house her stepfather came into our room and tried to get in the bed with us. The streetlights were shining through our window and I could see his shadow sneaking around our room, all smooth and skinny, like an hungry ghost, and when he bent over to get into our bed I could tell that he had no clothes on. My heart pounded so hard that I thought my head was going to blow off. I didn't know what to do so I sat straight up and started fake coughing, really hard, like I was choking to death. I was hoping that he would get scared that Rosemarie's mom might come in to check on me, and then catch him in there with us. Sure enough, he jumped up and ran out of our room.

We didn't sleep any more that night, because we were afraid that he would come back, but we never did say another word about it. We just sat up reading comics and stuff. Me and Rosemarie don't need to talk about every little thing. Sometimes we'll sit on the curb in front of my house and say nothing at all. I wish she was my sister and she could move away with us.

A Regular Family

At school today everyone was talking about the housing authority tearing down our neighborhood. We had to have indoor recess because the snow was still too deep to play outside. Steven Swenson sat at the desk next to me for a while. He said that he didn't have to move because he lived on the other side of the neighborhood where they weren't tearing any houses down. He's so cute I could die. He kept talking to me but I didn't hear too much of what he was saying because all I could do was look at his pretty eyes and that sweet smile.

Big boob Phyllis Garrett came up to me while I was talking to Steven and asked me if I had to move. I already told her that I had to move so I knew that she was only asking again to make me feel bad. I didn't say anything, but she grinned and told Steven that she didn't have to move, and then he told her that he didn't have to move either, and then they both smiled at each other like they were madly in love. It was nauseating. They'll probably get married someday and live happily ever after and I'll end up living far away in some crappy apartment and have Ken for my stepfather. School was the pits today.

Mrs. Green, my mother's friend who always stays in her pajamas until after lunch, came up after school today and asked me if I would sleep over her house with her daughter Pam because Pam was really sad about having to move. I didn't really want to sleep over Pam's house, but I said I would because I knew that it would make her feel better. Pam's father is Ken's brother, Steve Green. It seems like everyone in this house is related to Ken. Pam is a little older than me but she still acts like a little kid. I used to play with her all the time; but not any more because she still wants to do little kid stuff.

Pam's hair is orange, like a rusty nail, and it stays tangled up because she won't let her mom brush it. Sometimes Mrs. Green asks me to brush it for her. I always try, but Pam gets mad if I pull it, and peels the skin back on my arms with those long fingernails of hers. I'm not allowed to hit her back because Pam is kind of slow and in a special class at school. So, I mostly just let her hit me. But sometimes, when her mom ain't looking, I whack her back real good.

When I get to Pam's she's already sitting on the floor in her room with Barbie stuff tossed everywhere. I sit down and grab the black haired Barbie with the ponytail because she looks a little like me.

I poked through the clothes until I found a pretty black dress, some matching high heels, and a matching hat. I think I'm going to miss coming here and playing with Pam. We're kind of like sisters. When we were little we would sit on a scatter rug and Mrs. Green would pull us around the house until her floors shined liked a mirror. We're way too big for that now – plus, Mrs. Green is going to have a baby so she can't be straining herself.

I went to get a drink of water and Mrs. Green was sitting at the kitchen table with a little night-light on. Her pregnant belly was poking out of the bottom of her pajama top like Humpty Dumpty's head. The way she was just sitting there, listening to the radio, and looking out that dark window, made me feel bad for her. She didn't even turn around to say hi to me. She just kept on staring out that black window, with her chin in her hand, like she was watching a shut off TV.

I figured she was waiting for Pam's father to come home. He's more handsome than his brother Ken. He has thick black hair and a dimple in his chin. He's a lot taller than Ken too. I bet he could be a movie star if he tried. I got my water and went back to Pam's bedroom.

In the morning me and Pam were sitting at the table, still in our pajamas, waiting for a mouth-watering breakfast. Mrs. Green brought us some tea in fancy flowered cups, with saucers under them, and matching glass plates piled high with peanut butter toast. It makes me feel like a rich kid eating toast this way. I tried making peanut butter toast and tea at home, but it always tastes better at Pam's house.

Pam's father finally got up and came into the kitchen to say good morning to us.

"Did you girls have fun last night?" he asked.

I never know what to say to him. I feel like he's real important so I better say my words right. Pam sat up straight in her chair and said, "We played Barbie, and then mom let us paint our fingernails." She held out her fingers for her dad to see. I painted her long fingernails pink, and they looked nice, like a glamour girl's fingernails.

"They look beautiful!" he said, and then he held her fingers up to his mouth and kissed them. Next he looked over at me.

"Let's see yours," he said, but I didn't want to show him mine. I bite my fingernails so they're all stubby, and Pam painted them and got red polish all over the ends of my fingers. I held out my hands anyways and he bent in close to see them, and said, "Very pretty."

My face felt hot, and I looked down at the floor.

"Thank you," I said, even though I knew that they weren't pretty. Some day I'm going to stop biting my nails and have pretty ones like Pam's.

After breakfast we went into the parlor to watch Saturday morning cartoons. Pam's dad sat on a fancy yellow chair and put his coffee cup on the little polished end table next to it. Mrs. Green ran in and put a coaster under his cup. Mrs. Green fusses over her husband like he's a king or something, always chasing behind him with his newspaper and coffee. Mr. Green put his feet up on the hassock and opened his newspaper. I could see the bottoms of his white socks. They were still store-bought clean. I liked watching TV with Pam's dad sitting in his chair. I could hear him, turning the pages of his newspaper and humming, and it felt like I was in a regular family.

I wondered if he knew some of the stuff his brother Ken was up to, messing with me and all, and if he did stuff like that to Pam. Thinking about it made me want to wash my brain out with soap.

When I got home Ma had the washing machine rolled out into the kitchen.

"Did you have fun?" she asked, and then she fed my pink dress through the wringer rollers. I watched it come out the other side, flat, like run over bubble gum.

"It was okay," I said, and then I went into my room and threw my dirty clothes in a pile on my closet floor. I knew the best thing to do was to stay clear of Ma on Saturdays or she would be sure to find some house cleaning for me to do. Janice was fake sleeping in the bed. I could tell because her eyelashes were twitching like centipede legs. All I had to do was tempt her with something fun and she'd wake right up.

"You want to go downtown today and spend our shoveling money?"

Janice opened her eyes and said, "I was going to ask you the same thing!"

"I knew you were faking," I said, and pulled the covers off of her. "I was just laying here until you got home. I was afraid if I got up Ma would make me help her clean the house."

"We better clean our room or she won't let us do anything," I said, and then I picked up a pile of my comic books off of the floor.

"We'll clean it really good, white glove clean, then Ma will definitely let us go," Janice said, and then she ran to get the broom.

When she got back with the broom she used it to push everything out from under our bed. I looked down and saw dusty socks, shoes, cups, candy wrappers from Halloween, and little toys all in a pile. I picked out the good stuff and Janice put the rest in the trash.

When we were done the room looked pretty good. I arranged the things on our dressers in rows and then lined up my Wishnik collection on the windowsill. I put my diary on my bed table with my transistor radio. I haven't written anything in my diary yet. But I don't know what to write in it. I don't need to be putting my big secrets in there because someone else might read it. Maybe I'll just write the juicy gossip that I hear about other people.

Crumbs was walking way behind us, following us like a spy. We couldn't get on the bus to downtown because she would have chased it. The walk seems extra long today because it's freezing out, and Janice keeps stopping to pull up her saggy socks. The shortest way to downtown is down the steepest hill in town, Frank Street. Walking down the hill isn't too bad but climbing back up it is a killer.

"I'm going to do all my Christmas shopping today," Janice said, in an important voice, like she was trying to sound like Ma or something. I told Janice that I was going to do some Christmas shopping too, and started thinking about what I could get everyone.

We turned onto Main Street and saw Russell Jenkins gawking at the stuff in the joke shop window. Russell is really tall, and skinny as a zipper. He wears beatnik glasses, plus his mom always makes him wear a white shirt and tie so he looks like a business man. He moved here from Virginia and is in the same grade as Janice. He has a bunch of sisters and brothers, and they're all tall and skinny, and talk with Beverly Hillbilly accents. His sister Sandy and me are pretty good friends and sometimes she sleeps over my house.

We stopped and stood with Russell, staring at the plastic dog doo, fake puke, and trick gum in the store window. The whole place was full of great pranks to play on people. Russell straightened up and said that he was going to buy a stink bomb, when he gets some money, and set it off in gym class. I didn't think the he'd do it but I went along with his story anyway.

"How much is the stink bomb?" I asked.

Russell stuck his hand in his pocket and jingled some change around like my Uncle Richie does when he wants to get me begging for a quarter.

"More than I have," Russell said.

"Won't you get in trouble for doing that?" Janice asked.

"Not if I don't get caught."

I knew that Russell was too chicken to set off a stink bomb in school, so I said, "Your mom would croak if you did something like that."

Everyone calls Russell's mom "Miss Winnie." She carries a big black bible around with her and talks about the Lord like he's her best friend. She's always saying stuff like, "The Lord told me this, and the Lord told me that." Russell must have known what I was thinking because he piped up and said, "My mom's been a little crazy ever since my dad choked to death at a church dinner."

We stood there staring at Russell. We never heard this story before and I think that his sister Sandy would have told me about it because of her being my friend and all. Russell kept on talking.

"Yup, he was eating a nice thick slice of ham and a chunk of it got stuck in his throat when he went to laughing at a joke that his best friend Shorty told him. He died in the church hall right there in front of everybody."

Things got really quiet. I wasn't saying anything; because if he was lying then I'd look stupid for falling for his story, and if he was telling the truth then there was nothing to say because of it being so sad. Janice looked like she was about to start crying and said, "That's awful Russell. I'm sorry you're dad died like that right in front of everybody."

Russell looked away; I could see his shoulders shaking like he was crying really hard, and I was feeling like that fake dog doo in the store window for not telling him that I was sorry for his loss too. Russell turned back around and took off his glasses, then wiped his eyes with his coat sleeve. Janice touched his shoulder; the way Father White does at church when he wants you to feel extra special. Putting his glasses back on, Russell bent down a little and put his skinny face right up close to Janice's, and said, "Gottcha!!"

Janice pushed hard on his chest, shoving him backwards, and said, "Russell Jenkins! That's a rotten thing to lie about!" Then she grabbed me by the arm and pulled me down Main Street. I was feeling pretty good because I didn't fall for it all the way, like Janice did, and when I looked back I could see Russell standing in front of the joke store still laughing at us.

"Boys are so stupid!"

"I know," I said, but I was thinking that Russell was pretty clever for coming up with a doozy of a story like that one.

Woolworth's was the first store we hit. Crumbs had to wait outside in the cold, and I felt bad for her. She was sitting there on the wet cement shivering and her eyes were saying, "don't leave me out here in the cold." but Janice told me that dogs didn't get cold like people do, because they have fur coats on. That made me feel much better, so I went into the toasty warm store and started my Christmas shopping.

This was my first time Christmas shopping on my own. I looked at tons of stuff but couldn't find the right thing for Ma. Ma's not a fancy mother, like some of my friend's mothers who wear gobs of make-up and fancy jewelry, and look like they belong in a magazine. Ma is more of a tom boy kind of mother, like she belongs in the Sears catalog.

I looked at the nylons and found some real pretty black ones for only 49 cents. Ma liked to wear black nylons in the winter to church. That would leave me plenty of money left for a garter belt to go with them.

I hummed along with the Christmas music, and figured I'd ask Janice if she knew what size nylons Ma wore. Looking around I couldn't see her anywhere, and I was just about to check the pet section (Janice loves to look at the birds and hamsters) when I saw Mean Carlene walking toward me. We call her that because she can take every kid in the neighborhood. Even the boys! She got special permission to quit school when she was only fourteen because she was such a troublemaker.

Carlene has bleached orange hair, with black roots, and keeps it cut really short like a boy's. She wears way too much face make-up so it looks like she's wearing a rusty mask; plus she has gobs of mascara on her lashes so they look like hairy spider legs. But the scariest part of Carlene is her teeth. Her front teeth look like little black pegs and it's hard not to stare at them when she talks to you. I looked around again for Janice but couldn't find her.

"What are you doing in here?" Carlene asked, like she owned the store or something. Her sweater was way too small, making her boobs pop out of the top of it like bread dough. I kept my eyes down and said, "Just looking at stuff with my sister." Carlene snatched the nylons out of my hand and said, "I don't see no sister."

"Oh," I said, trying to think up something fast, "She just went to get my Uncle Richie. He's supposed to meet us here and help us with some Christmas shopping for my mom."

"Yeah, right," she said, and slipped the nylons under the back of her jacket.

"You're here all alone, and you're making up that stupid Uncle Richie story so I'll go away."

"No sir," I said, trying to keep a plain face so she wouldn't catch me in a lie.

Carlene pulled a wrinkled pack of Old Gold's out of her jacket pocket and lit one up. I tried walking away, but she stayed right behind me and kept stepping on the backs of my boots. I walked a little faster and prayed that Janice wouldn't show up because she might blow my whole Uncle Richie story. I stopped at the busy perfume counter, figuring that she'll leave me alone because of all the people around, and stood near the sales lady. She was yapping away to old lady LaPrade trying to sell her some lipstick. I felt braver there so I looked at Carlene and said, "What do you want with me?"

Mean Carlene looked down at me, dragged on her cigarette so hard that her cheeks caved in, then she blew a smelly cloud of smoke right into my face. I fanned it away and stepped back, looking to see if the sales lady was noticing that Carlene was being mean to me, but she was too busy ringing up Mrs. Laprade's order to notice anything.

"I need you to cover for me," Carlene said, flicking her ashes on my head like I was an ashtray.

I tipped my head forward and brushed off the ashes, watching them fall like little gray snowflakes. Carlene was getting on my last nerve and I wanted to ditch her before I got beat up... or arrested for stealing.

"What do you mean, cover for you?"

Carlene leaned forward to whisper in my ear. She smelled like smoke and hair spray.

"You know," she said "be a lookout so nobody sees me getting my five finger discount."

"No way Jose! My mother would kill me if she caught me stealing." I must have said it too loudly because all of a sudden Carlene went on red alert looking around to see if anyone heard me and then she hissed in my ear, "Shut the fuck up, big mouth. You're not stealing anything. I'm doing the taking, you're just looking out."

I cringed because her breath was tickling my ear, but there was no way I was going to laugh and really tick her off.

"I can't," I said, and then I tried walking away from her again. Carlene blocked my way, and said, "Oh really, then I guess I'll just have to kill you. It's your choice chicken shit, be afraid that mommy might kill you, or have me definitely kill you!"

I was feeling like I couldn't breathe. There was no way I wanted to help Carlene steal anything. I got caught stealing candy when I was six and my mother took out her paddle, the kind that comes with that little ball on an elastic string, and beat my butt red, and then she threatened to turn me in to the cops. I swore I would never do it again. I needed to ditch Carlene...somehow.

I told Carlene that I needed to go to the bathroom and that I would be right back, but she didn't fall for it, and said, "You must think I'm an idiot. I know you're planning to run."

"No I'm not," I said, trying not to blink when I said it. "I really do have to pee. Just wait here and I'll be right back."

Carlene stomped her cigarette out on the tile floor, like she was outside on the street, and then she looked at me with her spidery black eyes. "You better not be screwing with me or I'll kick your ass."

"I'll be right back. I swear!"

I wanted to run, but I walked like I was still browsing the store, hoping that she wouldn't follow me. The bathroom was in the pet section, so I headed that way hoping not to bump into Janice. I walked for a while and couldn't hear anything behind me, so I turned to see if she was following me and I slammed smack into Carlene's big boobs.

"Looking for someone?" she asked, with a witchy sneer pulled across her face.

"I was just checking to see if my sister was around."

"Right, and I'm a chimpanzee."

My heart was racing, but I smiled like she was being silly and said, "No, really, that's all I was doing."

I opened the ladies' room door and saw that it cost ten cents to pee, so I started digging for a dime. Carlene dove under one of the stalls and called me a sucker for paying. I flew out of the ladies' room and called her a sucker (under my breath) for giving me a chance to get away. I tore out of Woolworth's back door, because it was right next to the pet section, and then I ran around the block to the front door of Woolworth's to get Crumbs and find Janice.

When I got around front Crumbs was gone. She would never leave unless she followed Janice somewhere else, so I crossed the street and headed for Kresge's, because Janice likes to shop there sometimes.

The sidewalk was crowded with people Christmas shopping so I zig-zagged through the crowd, praying that Carlene wouldn't see me. Looking ahead, I spotted Crumbs sitting up pretty, waiting by Kresge's front door for Janice. When she saw me she came running.

I rubbed her head, saying, "Good girl!" so she started licking my face with her slimy tongue. Ma says that a dog's tongue is cleaner than a human's, so I wasn't worried about germs, but I couldn't stand the slipperiness of her spit, so I pushed Crumbs away and told her to "sit and stay."

I got into Kresge's and it was toasty warm and smelled like new toys and perfume. I walked past the cash registers toward the toy department and caught Janice playing with a Slinky.

"Look at this!" she shouted over to me, holding the Slinky up with one hand and letting it fall so it bounced up and down like a big spring. I ran up to her and snatched the Slinky out of her hand.

"Hey! I was playing with that."

"Hey, nothing," I said. "We got to get out of here. Mean Carlene is after me!"

"Mean Carlene? What's she after you for?"

"Never mind, I'll tell you later, but we got to go. NOW."

"But I haven't finished shopping yet."

"Mean Carlene is going to kill me, Janice! WE GOT TO GO NOW!"

"Alright already," she said, picking up her bags and following me out of the store.

"C'mon Crumbs," I hollered, walking fast down the street. I was way ahead of Janice because she was lugging two shopping bags full of stuff that she bought; plus her stupid socks kept falling down into her boots, so she had to stop and pull them up every two minutes. I grabbed a bag from her and told her to forget about her socks.

"But they get bunched up under my feet if I don't pull them up."

"I'm gonna bunch you up if you don't start running faster," I told her, and then I grabbed her hand and turned up Bancroft Street. It's a pretty big hill and St. Paul's Church is on it. This was the long way, and I figured Carlene wouldn't come this way because she was too lazy. We ran up the hill, as best we could, and when we got to the top I pulled Janice across the street and into the old church.

We were both standing in front of the holy water and prayer candles panting like thirsty dogs. There were a ton of pretty red candles, all in rows, like a little choir of light, and I was thinking of lighting one, and asking God to help me with Mean Carlene and Ken, but I didn't want Janice to see me getting all mushy with God.

"Should we go in?" Janice asked softly, like we might wake up baby Jesus or something.

"Sure, God's house is open all the time," I said, and then I blessed myself with the holy water and walked down the aisle like I owned the joint. Janice followed behind me, looking up at the lights hanging from the ceiling on long chains. Janice thinks that she knows everything about churches, so she says; "This church is smaller than Meme's, but I like the lights," like the whole world was waiting for her opinion. I bowed at the end of a pew and sat down. Janice sat next to me with her noisy bags crinkling.

"Shhh!" I whispered, but then I figured I better keep her in a good mood because I needed to tell her to take off her socks.

"Take off your socks."

"What? No. My feet will freeze!"

"Look," I said, "you can't run fast if you're wearing those saggy punks, so take them off."

Janice held her bags close to her and stared straight ahead and said, "No," like that was the final word on it. But I knew how to get to her so I put on my pitiful face and said,

"Come on Janice, you want Carlene to kill me?"

I sat quietly, watching Janice squirm in the pew like she had a bad case of the worms. Finally she said, "Oh, alright, but if I catch a cold you got to be my slave for a whole month."

Janice pulled off her boots, and Wonder Bread bags, and then she peeled her green socks off.

"P U!" I said, pinching my nose. "When was the last time you changed your socks?"

"You want me to put my socks back on so you don't have to smell them?"

I figured I better leave Janice alone so I sat still until things got buzzy quiet. Janice's face went soft again and she looked pretty sitting there with her cheeks red as apples from the wind biting at them. Ma says that Janice has the prettiest blue eyes in the family and right now they looked shiny, like a saint's would look if they saw God or something.

There was no one else in the church but us so I told Janice about how Carlene told me that she would kill me if I didn't help her steal, and how I escaped out of the bathroom and now she was after me. Janice didn't say anything for a while; she just sat there peeking into her shopping bags. Every time she opened the big bag I could smell her socks again and it was making me feel sick.

"Shut that bag, you're stinking up the whole church," I said, covering my face with my hands.

"Fine. I was just going to say a prayer so that Carlene doesn't kill you," she said, loud enough so any priest that might be hanging around could see what a good Catholic she was, even though her feet smelled like a garbage truck. I almost said something smart back to her, but I needed a prayer, so I said, "Thanks Janice," and sat back in the hard pew to plan my escape home.

I figured we could go around the big field, cut through the alley at the top of John Street, and then home. Carlene lives at the other end of the neighborhood, so she probably wouldn't think to go that way.

Janice was still praying, with her eyes closed and her lips moving, like Ma does when she's thinking out loud. I didn't want to interrupt her when she was talking to God and all, but we had to go before Carlene caught up with us. I tapped Janice on her shoulder and whispered, "Lets go."

"Shhhh! You should never disturb a person while they're praying," Janice said, and then she blessed herself, bowed, and walked down the aisle with her polka dotted bread bags sticking out of her boots.

The wind was blowing so hard that it took my breath away.

"We got to go by the big field," I told Janice, and then I kept walking as fast as I could, with my head down. Janice yelled out to me, "My feet are freezing!" I felt bad for her but there was nothing that I could do about her cold feet.

"We're almost there," I told her, but she knew we still had a long way to go.

I kept stomping forward, by myself, making sure that Mean Carlene wasn't hiding around any corners.

We started through the alley on John Street and stopped for a while to rest. Janice was crying because her feet were numb. I felt bad for her so I took off my boots and gave her my socks. Janice smiled while she held onto me so she could pull them on, saying,

"Mmmm, your socks are still warm, Cozy. Thanks."

I was glad that I gave my socks to Janice even though my toes were already turning into ice cubes.

"This time we're really almost home," I told Janice, as we finally made it to our street.

"When I get home I'm going to put my feet in the oven," Janice said, grabbing her shopping bag out of my hand and running ahead of me.

I'd been walking fast the whole way, but now I was dead dog tired, and it hurt when I walked because of my toes being so frozen. Crumbs hung back with me while Janice ran past the Armenian Church to our house.

Janice and me always hang around on the steps of the Armenian Church. It's a little wooden church that's near our house but it's far enough away so that Ma doesn't see everything that we're up to. Someone had cleared off the church steps for church tomorrow, so I figured I'd sit down for a second to catch my breath.

I felt something hit me on the head, so I touched at it, thinking maybe a bird crapped in my hair, but I couldn't feel anything. Then something stung me on the cheek, like a bee, but I knew there were no bees around in the wintertime, so I rubbed my face and stood up to see what was going on.

"Did you miss me sweetie?"

"Huh?"

I turned around and Mean Carlene was leaning against Mrs. Jones's fence with a straw in her mouth and a cheek full of spitballs.

"Oh shit."

Carlene marched up to me and grabbed me by the coat. I knew she was going to bash me so I tried pulling away from her; she gave me a shove, and I fell and hit my head on the cement stairs. My head was stinging and I could hear a loud humming in my ears. Carlene grabbed my coat again and stood me back on my feet, and then she lifted her fist high enough to get a good punch in. Her face looked all screwed up with her lips stretched tight showing all those black teeth clenching down against each other. I caught her punch with my hand and pushed it away... and then Carlene fell backwards like a bowling pin! I was feeling pretty proud of myself until I saw Crumbs, dragging Carlene by the seat of her pants.

"Get this fucken mutt off me!" she shouted, but Crumbs kept on growling and pulling.

I couldn't help laughing because Mean Carlene looked so silly with Crumbs hanging off of her ass.

"I'm going to kill you…and your dog!"

"That's what you get for hitting me!" I shouted back, feeling safe because Crumbs had things under control. Crumbs let go for a second, and then grabbed on again to get a better hold of her. This time she got a pinch of Carlene cheek in with the pants and Carlene started howling like a big fat baby.

I stood there watching and I was thinking that Mean Carlene didn't look so mean any more, so I shouted, "Screw you Carlene!" and then I called my dog off. Crumbs let go of Carlene and came running up to me. "Good girl! Good girl!" I said, and let Crumbs wash my face with her wet tongue. Carlene was busy trying to peek around herself to see if she had a boo-boo on her butt cheek.

It took me a little while to get up all the stairs to my house. My head was killing me and my feet felt like I had a thousand little needles sticking in them. I opened the door and Ma was busy in the hallway lining up all the boots and stuff. She told me to give her my coat and to line my boots up with the rest of them. I handed over my coat, and when she looked at me she screamed, "OH MY GOD!……. YOU'RE BLEEDING!"

I didn't even notice that my head was bleeding because I was feeling so good about watching Carlene get her butt chewed off. Ma grabbed my arm and walked me into the kitchen and then she sat me down near the window. Tipping my head toward the light she said, "My God, you got a big gash right here behind your ear Cosette. What in the world happened?"

I told her about Mean Carlene, and how she wanted me to help her steal, but I wouldn't. Then I told her how Crumbs came to my rescue. Ma cleaned the blood off of my head then she got some white tape out of the medicine cabinet and cut it into little bow-ties. "You need at least three butterfly stitches." she said, and then she called Carlene a mean son of a bitch.

"Never throw the first punch, Cozy, or you'll always lose the fight," Ma told me, while she was stitching up my head. "You see, if they hit you first it makes you extra mad and that gives you a big dose of adrenaline."

"What's adrenaline?" I asked, while I scrunched my eyes shut because she was pinching my skin together.

"It's a kind of strength that God gives you when you need it," she said, kissing me on the top of my head. That was Ma's way of saying that she was done stitching me up.

Janice and Diana made a big fuss over Crumbs, and me, and for the rest of the night everybody waited on me like I was a hero or something. Crumbs pulling Mean Carlene off of me was like a miracle. I thought I was a goner for sure, and then PRESTO! Crumbs jumped in and saved my hide at the last minute, just like Lassie always does for Timmy.

I thought about being in that old church today, and Janice praying for me, and how I poked fun at her for acting so holy. It made me feel ashamed; so for now on I wasn't going to tease her about that anymore. And maybe God will jump in and save me from Ken just like he did with Mean Carlene.

A Bad Move

Ma and Mrs. Green have been driving around the neighborhood looking for a new place for us to live. They finally found an empty three decker right on the other side of our neighborhood, and the landlord said that they could move in by June if they helped him fix it up. So Ma's been painting walls and sanding the wooden floors, while Mrs. Green's been mostly watching Ma do all the work, and making a big fuss over her brand new baby, Steve Jr. He's got black fluffy hair that stands up straight. I like blowing on it because it lays down flat and then bounces back up again. He used to just lie in his playpen, like a basket of buns, and make ugly faces, but now he smiles a lot because he can see better. Ma says that babies can't see much when they're first born.

We're going to be living in the first floor apartment this time. It's going to be weird because you never know when a peeping Tom might be peeking in your windows, or even climbing in if he wanted to. I like the third floor because we never have to lock our windows. I'll be locking my windows every night at the new house.

We've been moving boxes all day. All our stuff is mixed up like a thousand piece jigsaw puzzle. I saw one of my shirts in with some towels and dishes. It's like our home is in Purgatory, just floating around in the middle of everything. I don't think we'll ever be able to put things back the way they were.

Ma and Ken got a big truck and put our furniture in it, but us kids had to load up all the boxes. The new apartment is on Pike Street. It's only a block away from my old school, and there are no big hills to climb, so I'll be able to walk to school in five minutes. I'm really happy that I don't have to go to a new school, and that Phyllis Garrett won't have Steven Swenson all to herself. When I told her I wasn't moving away she puckered her face up like she was looking into bucket of worms and said, "Oh that's nice Cozy." What a liar. She was hoping that I was gone for good.

Ken's not wearing a shirt today because he's trying to show off his muscles. He's got birds tattooed on his chest; one on each side. He likes to move his muscles to make it look like the birds are going to fly into each other. "Hey Cozy, watch this," he says, and then I got to stand there and look all amazed at what his birds can do. Ma thinks that he's fantastic; but me and my sisters think he's a jerk. I still haven't told anybody about Ken and me. He hasn't tried anything in a long time so maybe I won't ever have to say a word to anyone.

Grammy Green and Ken moved into an apartment right across the street from our new house. Grammy is still on the first floor, and Jimmy Elliot moved into the second floor, so some of our old neighborhood moved near us.

Every time I went into my old room to grab a box I kept my eyes closed so I wouldn't have to see how sad it looked without all my stuff in it. I peeked a little bit, just to see where I was going, but that's all. Mr. Robard already moved to New York to live near his sister. He gave us all his holiday decorations before he left. Ma let me keep the witch with the wart on her nose for my own, she's my favorite, and I'm going to hang her in my new room; even if it's not Halloween.

No one has seen the Cat Lady all week. Ma said that she must have moved away without telling anyone. I wish I could have seen her just one more time so I could take a picture of her in my head. Now she's gone, and I already forgot what her face looked like. She wasn't my friend or anything, but I'm still going to miss seeing her walking with her fat cat.

Me and Janice have to share a room again, but Diana, the queen, gets to have her own room. Our new apartment has four bedrooms, so I asked Ma why we couldn't all have our own bedroom. Ma told me that she had plans for the extra bedroom and didn't want to hear another word about it. When Ma says she doesn't want to hear another word about it, she means it, so I kept on carrying boxes with my mouth shut tight so I wouldn't tick her off.

We were all done moving boxes, but nothing was in the right place. I headed for my new room to look at it again, now that some of my stuff was in there, but it didn't look like a bedroom because our beds weren't built yet, and it still smelled like paint, but it was bigger than my old room. Janice and me already picked our sides. We each have a tall window that goes right out onto the front porch, but Janice has an extra window right beside her bed. I didn't want a window right over my bed on account of the peeping Toms that might be prowling between the houses. I opened my window up wide, closed my eyes, and took a deep breath. The air on Pike Street smelled the same as it did on Blaine Street – fresh with fun sprinkled in it. I turned my radio on and set it on the window sill.

Help me Rhonda was playing, so I blasted it right out the window. I could see a teenage boy sitting on his porch across the street. He had shaggy brown hair and he was holding onto a yellow Frisbee while a little brown and white dog was tugging on the other end of it like Crumbs does with our socks sometimes. He heard my music and looked over. I felt frozen, like he caught me spying on him, but he smiled and waved at me, so I waved back, like he was already my friend. Maybe this neighborhood won't be so bad after all.

"Time for a talk," Ma said, while we were all taking a break and munching on hamburgers on the back porch. Everyone was sitting around on crates, and boxes, trying not to drop their food or tip their sodas. Tommy dropped most of his fries on the floor, and some got stuck between the floor boards, so Crumbs was busy trying to lick them loose. Ken was sitting in a real chair and had his food on a TV tray that Ma set up for him. I was trying to wash down my burger with a big swallow of soda when Ma said that the extra bedroom was for Tommy. I started choking on my burger, and could feel little chunks of food flying out of my nose. Ma jumped up and slapped me on the back while Crumbs tried licking the disgusting mess off of my face. I pushed Crumbs away and stood up.

"I told you to chew your food or you'd choke," Ma said, slapping me on my back, but I didn't care a bit about choking. I wanted to die because I figured I knew what Ma was going to say next. I looked over at Janice and Diana and they were looking at me. They both looked frozen with their mouths hanging open and their sodas in their hands, and I knew that they were thinking the same thing as me.

Ma brushed off her shirt, fixed her hair, and announced, "Today Ken asked me to marry him and I said yes."

Then she pulled a little box out of a black velvet bag and opened it up really slowly, like it had the moon in it or something, and passed it around for all of us to see. I held the box in front of me, and stared at the tiny diamond ring that was telling me my future like the gypsies do on TV. My life was going around and around, and then down the toilet like one of Ma's lipstick kisses.

Ma's marrying Ken right after school gets out in two weeks, but Tommy is going to move in as soon as Ma sets his bed and stuff up. I sat on the toilet crying until Janice nearly broke the door down knocking because she had to go. I wanted to hide in my old room, under my Indian blanket, but all I had was a new room full of boxes. I went out and sat on the front porch by myself, but then Tommy came out and sat on the step below me. He was grinning like he was expecting a parade to come marching down the street at any minute, and then he looked up at me, squinting his brown eyes, and said, "I can't wait to move in!" But I didn't say anything back to him. I just sat there waiting for him to get bored and leave.

Today Ken and Ma are fussing over their new bedroom. They went out and bought some new furniture and then arranged it just the way Ken likes it. They got a big brown bed that my sister Diana says looks like a Spanish fighting ship, and two dressers to go with it. One of the dressers has tall mirrors with points on top of it like a fence. It reminds me of haunted house furniture. Ken brought that picture of the Virgin Mary from his room at Grammy Green's and hung it on the wall over the bed. I get a rock in my stomach every time I look at that picture.

It didn't look like Ma's room anymore. I couldn't find anything big that was hers. I only found little stuff, like her pillow and her lipstick and hairbrushes lined up on the dresser. Even the blankets on the bed were different and Ken had one of those Army blankets lying on the chair in the corner. Ma came in while I was looking at her room and asked how I liked it. I told her that it was really nice, especially the new furniture. She smiled at me like she just got a star on her paper for drawing a nice picture.

Ma and Ken got married downtown at city hall. None of us kids got to go, but we didn't want to go anyways. Instead we went to Meme's house and helped her set up some tables for the fancy sandwiches and food that she made for everyone. She even had champagne and little plastic glasses to pour it in. Meme said it was to toast the bride and groom, and that someone had to toast to them or they would have bad luck. She invited a bunch of people over to eat all the food and make a big fuss over Ma and Ken for getting married.

At the reception all of the adults were drinking champagne and beer; except for Grammy Green who was drinking tea because of her stomach troubles. Ma looked beautiful in her flowery yellow dress that she made just for her wedding day. She kept looking at Ken and smiling, but she never once looked my way.

I kept finding little plastic glasses around the house with bits of leftover champagne in them, so I drank them down. It was kind of sweet and looked just like ginger ale. Janice and me even had our own little toast when nobody was looking. We filled our glasses up with champagne and beer from all the leftovers, then we went into the back hallway, stuck our pinky fingers out like the snooty ladies on TV do, and toasted to Ken getting lost forever.

We laughed really hard for a while, but pretty soon I saw that Janice wasn't laughing anymore, but was crying so hard that she got the hiccups. "I hate his guts," she said, and then she blew a humongous bubble out of her nose that stuck there for a while, like a bubble gum bubble, and then it popped when she hiccupped. She looked so silly that I started to laugh again and Janice couldn't help but laugh either, so we both laughed until our stomachs hurt.

After all that toasting with Janice I felt tip top dizzy and went and sat on the floor in the corner of the kitchen watching Ken drink and laugh with everyone, like he was one of them. But he didn't fool me because I knew what he looked like naked, and a grown-up shouldn't pull their pants down and do nasty stuff to kids. I wanted to make everyone stop talking, and toast to Ken, telling everyone what a big fat pig he was, but I knew it would ruin Ma's party, so I just sat there and kept my toast in my head.

Things got really mixed-up after that, and the next thing I remember was me sitting in the gutter out in front of Meme's house crying, and throwing up all those fancy little sandwiches. Uncle Richie found me out there and carried me back into the house and put me on the bed in Meme's extra bedroom, and then he put a trashcan next to it for me to puke in. That's all I remember about it; I don't even remember Ma leaving or anything.

The next day no one said a word to me about being drunk. I had a sore headache and a weak stomach all day long. Meme said I had a bug and not to get too close to her, or my sisters, and she let me lay on the couch with a pillow and blanket while everyone else cleaned up after the party.

Ma and Ken went on a honeymoon for three days to a hotel and we got to stay with Meme the whole time. Tommy stayed at his Grammy Green's. When the honeymoon was over Meme drove us home. She didn't bother coming in because she said we needed time to be alone as a new family. I think that Meme's glad Ma married Ken so she doesn't have to help us out with everything any more.

When we got in the house Ken was sitting at our kitchen table with no shirt on, chewing on a bologna sandwich. He didn't smile or anything, he just kept chewing on that sandwich like an old cow; then he took a big slurp of soda and told us that our mother was upstairs at Mrs. Green's and for us to go put our clothes away. I got that feeling inside, like I couldn't wait for him to go home, but then I remembered that he was never going home again, so I went to my bedroom, and while I was putting my clothes away, I cried without making a sound.

So, tonight's the first night with Ken sleeping over and I want to kiss Ma goodnight, but their bedroom door is already shut and it isn't even dark out yet. I can hear the TV through their door but I don't dare knock because then I'd have to kiss Ken goodnight too. I figure I'll catch Ma when she comes out to go to the bathroom or something.

71

I went back to the kitchen and sat on the floor with Crumbs. She was knocked out on her side and her legs were twitching like she was trying to run away. It doesn't feel like summer vacation. Usually we all stay up late and watch TV together and Ma makes us snacks. But now the house is boring. Diana is in her room listening to her new Simon and Garfunkle album with the door closed tight, and Janice is sitting with Pam, and baby Steve, upstairs until her parents get back from grocery shopping. She said I could go with her but I wasn't in a Pam mood. I wanted to be with Ma a little. Tommy is sleeping on the couch in his underwear and tee shirt because it's way too hot for pajamas. It's weird seeing a boy sleeping on the couch. Our couch is used to girls. I head into the parlor and kneel in front of the window. Across the street there is a yellow house with an open window in the attic apartment. The wind kept sucking the curtains in and out of the window, so it looked like the house was breathing. I tried to see if anyone was in there but I couldn't see a thing.

Diana said that she thought a hippie lived up there because she saw a guy with long curly hair, and bell-bottom pants, park his van and go into that house. I've never met a real hippie before; Ken says they're all dope heads, queers, and draft dodgers, and that this country is going to hell in a hand basket.

I heard Ma's bedroom door open so I looked to see if it was her, but it was Ken in nothing but his skivvies, heading for the kitchen. He didn't see me, so I stayed really quiet until he was gone, and then I snuck over and stood in Ma's doorway looking in at her. I was hoping that she would tell me to come in, but she was under the covers with her back at me, so I faked a cough. But that didn't make her move; she just lay there, knocked out, just like Crumbs. Her bed looked really soft and comfy, with the white sheets and puffy pillows piled high around her like little hills. I was thinking about snuggling in with her, like I used to do, but then I felt a hand on my shoulder and I knew who it was. I turned around and Ken was there looking down at me like he caught me robbing a bank or something. I was about to tell him that I was going to kiss Ma goodnight but he clenched his teeth and said, "You better not wake her up. She needs her sleep!" He looked like a growling guard dog ready to bite me, so I backed up a little and said, "I was just going to give her a kiss goodnight."

"Well, you can kiss her good morning instead," he said, and then he shut the door in my face. I could hear Ma's voice behind the closed door so I kept standing there, hoping that she would come out and kiss me goodnight. But she never came out and after a while I got a little scared that Ken might catch me standing there, so I went to bed and hid under my Indian blanket to wait for Janice to come home and keep me company.

It's Just A Scratch

I just cut my own bangs. Chopped them off and watched them fall into the sink, all fluffy and separate, like eye lashes. I was trying to take just a smidge off so they would be even to my eyebrows, like Ma does them, but I couldn't get them straight enough, and now they're way up on my big white forehead. I was going to ask Ma to cut them but she was still in bed with Ken and I got tired of waiting for her to wake up. Now I'm afraid to leave the bathroom because I know how stupid I look and Ma is probably going to kill me.

I was still playing with my bangs, wishing that I never chopped them off, when I heard Tommy whining like a little girl at the bathroom door.

"I gotta pee!"

"Stop your whining you big tit, I'll be right out!"

I knew that Tommy was doing the pee-pee dance outside the bathroom door so I pulled most of my hairs out of the sink and washed the rest down the drain. Then I wrapped my head in a big white towel and ran to my room. Janice was still sleeping, but it was late enough to wake her up without her getting too mad at me.

I leaned over and blew on her face then sat back and waited. She rubbed her eyes, because that's where I mostly blew, but she stayed sleeping. I gave her another blow, but this time in her ear, and she jumped up rubbing her ear like a spider might be in it or something.

"What'd you do that for, you idiot?"

"I was just trying to wake you up."

Janice looked at me and a big grin spread across her face. "What the heck did you do to your bangs? You look like a retard!" She started laughing, and holding her crotch, like she was ready to wet her pants, but I didn't think it was funny at all so I sat and waited for her laughing fit to end and said,"Go ahead and laugh you idiot, but it won't be so funny when Ma kills me."

Janice tried to straighten out her face and said, "Sorry Cozy," but she was still grinning at me and said, "I can't help it; your bangs are wicked short. You'd laugh too."

Janice started with another roll of ha-ha's, so I waited for her to stop, and was a little tempted to laugh too, but I held it in because I wanted her to feel bad for laughing at me.

Finally, she stopped laughing, and brushed my bangs backwards. Then she pulled them down straight like she was trying to stretch them out. Janice always acts like she can fix everything, but she is pretty smart, so I waited for her to figure it out.

"How about you wear a hat for a while?"

"Yeah, right, like I can wear a hat all the time. All I have is my Easter hat and that's way too fancy to wear around the house."

"How about an Indian head band right across your forehead like Cher wears? I think I got one. It's not really a headband; it's just a strip of brown suede that Meme gave me from her scraps, but I bet it's long enough to tie around your head."

Janice went into the closet and came out with a big clear bag stuffed full of colorful scraps, and started digging through it. I sat with her and felt all the different materials. Some were rough and bumpy and some were shiny and smooth. They were beautiful. Janice pulled out a long strip of dark brown suede and put it aside.

"Come here," she said. So I stood in front of her while she fixed my bangs. I could tell she liked doing it because her tongue was hanging half out of her mouth.

"Turn around so I can tie it in the back."

Janice tied it so tight that my brain felt like it was going to pop, and it was pulling my hair, but I didn't say anything because I figured it was better than having Ma kick my butt.

"There! You look cute, Cozy. Go look."

I looked in the dresser mirror and smiled because it looked pretty good. "Thanks, Janice," I said. "It looks really nice. Do you really think I look like Cher?"

"Yeah, you even have that bump on your nose like hers." I felt the bump on my nose, remembering that Ma told me that my father had the same bump. I loved my bump, and my brown eyes, because they were proof that I had a real father. Somewhere.

I went into the kitchen feeling better. I liked the headband, even if it hurt a little. Tommy came into the kitchen and said, "You playing Cowboys and Indians or something?"

"No," I said. " I'm just wearing a head band because they're in style now."

I went into the pantry and grabbed a bowl and box of Cheerios. I was slurping down the last of the milk in my bowl when I got cuffed off the head really hard. The bowl smashed into my lip and milk spilt all down the front of my pajama top.

"You look like a goddamn hippie in that thing. Take it off!"

I wiped off my mouth with my sleeve and saw the pink stain from my blood mixed up with the milk. Ken turned and put his face right up to mine and said, "Are you deaf or just stupid? Take that friggen thing off your head NOW!" I jumped up off the chair and ran to my mother's room. The door was open and I could see her making her bed. I was crying inside but not out. It was all stuck behind my eyes and I felt like I couldn't breathe. Ma looked up and smiled but then she spotted my bloody mouth and said, "What happened to you?" I still couldn't catch my breath, and I was trying to tell her what happened, but then Ken came marching in and snatched the headband off my head. Ma stood there staring at my bangs with her mouth in a big O.

"Who cut your bangs?" she asked, but I still couldn't talk. I didn't care about my bangs anymore. All I wanted was for Ma to yell at Ken for making my mouth bleed.

"I asked who cut your bangs?"

"Will you look at that," Ken said, "What the hell kind of hair cut is that supposed to be?"

Now they were both up in my face asking me questions, but my voice was gone because I was all clogged up inside.

"She had that head band on like one of those hippies from down on High Street," Ken said, and then he threw Janice's headband in the little metal trashcan right next to the ugly bed he bought. I started crying really hard, and Ma must have been feeling sorry for me because she pulled me into her and started rubbing my back up and down and humming to calm me down.

"Go ahead and baby her," Ken said. "Screw me and what I have to say about anything around here." Then he stormed out of the room.

I told Ma what Ken did, and showed her my bloody lip, but Ma said it was just a scratch and that I should know better than to cut my own hair. I was thinking that she figured I deserved what Ken did to me, because I cut my bangs, and that things were even, so I went back to my room, with my retarded bangs, and a fat lip. Janice was there and so was Diana. They both inspected my lip and hugged me. We sat around and called Ken the worst swears words that we could think up. Diana's was the best; she called him a fucken coward because he hit little girls. I wanted to tell her what else he did to little girls but I didn't. He hadn't tried anything with me for a long time and I didn't want to think about it anymore. I'd rather have the fat lip any day.

Alex

"Ken's in there putting a lock on Ma's bedroom door," Diana said, taking a big swig of her soda. She was sitting outside on the side steps drinking a Pepsi with her new best friend Kelly Richmond. We'd only been living at the new house for a month and Diana already had a friend. I still had some of my old ones but I didn't see them much so it was mostly boring. I miss Rosemarie.

Kelly lives upstairs with her mother. They have all those bedrooms for only two people. Kelly's 18 years old and has short yellow hair that she teases into a beehive every day. Right now she's got curlers all over the top of her head and she's smoking Tareyton cigarettes. Diana has a cigarette too, and she's smoking it just like Ma does, flicking the ashes off and letting the smoke come out of her nose.

"Does Ma know you're smoking?" I asked, looking around to see if anyone was watching. Diana took a long drag and blew the smoke out hard, like she wanted the world to see her smoking.

"She doesn't care if I smoke."

I ignored the smoking and asked, "Why is Ken putting a lock on the bedroom door?"

"Because he's a dick," Diana said, like there was no question about it.

I went into the house and Ma was in there helping Ken put a lock on. It was a big lock, the kind you needed a real key to open.

"Why are you putting a lock on your door?" I asked, because I figured maybe someone tried to steal their stuff or something, but Ken said it was because they didn't want us kids in there.

"This is our room, not yours," he said, like I didn't know that already.

I watched while he worked on the lock, turning the screwdriver while Ma handed him the screws. "Geesh." I said, "All you had to do is tell us not to go in there."

"Smart Ass! You think I don't know that you kids snoop around in there when we're not around?"

"We do not!"

Ma looked over at me with hard eyes that were trying to tell me to shut up. But then her words pushed out of her mouth loud enough for the Eskimos to hear.

"Cozy, you better get your ass outside and go play or you're going to get a smack across the face for being a fresh little shit!"

"Sorry," I said, but I wasn't. I could feel the anger growling in my chest and climbing up my throat, so I headed back out to sit with Diana and Kelly. "Ma and Ken are both dicks," I said, half quiet and half loud.

I sat next to Diana but Kelly was gone.

"Where's Kelly?"

"She went to get her radio," Diana said, and then she took another puff off her Tareyton.

"Can I have a puff?"

Diana looked over at me like I was crazy, but then she handed the cigarette over. I turned my head and took a drag, just a teensy one, and blew the smoke out the way Diana did.

"This isn't the first time that I've tried a cigarette," I tell Diana, "Sometimes when Ma leaves one burning in the ashtray I sneak a puff. Her's tastes different though because they're menthol.

This one tastes funny, like burnt leaves." I handed the butt back to Diana but she didn't say anything back to me. I wanted to ask if Janice smoked too, but I figured Diana didn't feel like yapping.

Kelly came back with two more Pepsis, and her transistor radio. It was hot out, and the cold bottles of soda looked so good. I could see the sweaty little drops of water all over them, and I wanted a swig really bad. But I knew better than to bug them, so I sat and listened while they did all the talking.

Kelly likes to dance to her favorite songs right in front of the house. She blasts the radio and dances liked she's on stage. People always watch her, but she doesn't care a bit because she keeps right on dancing no matter who's looking. Diana doesn't dance like that, but sometimes at night she'll get up and dance a little. Diana dances like a lady but Kelly dances like she's on fire. I was hoping that Kelly would dance today because it would be fun to watch. She has big boobs and shimmies them like Jell-O to the fast songs. That always cracks us up.

Pretty soon Janice came out to sit with us. I don't even know what day it is because in the summer it doesn't matter. I'm thinking its Thursday, but it could be Wednesday. Janice and me sat on the bottom step and we were all listening to *Love Potion #9*, when a junky blue van pulled up and the hippie from across the street climbed out of it and waved to us. I've seen him a lot – nearly every day, and he always waves and then goes right into his house. He's kind of wacky looking, real long and skinny with a head full of wild curly hair, and he wears a long black scarf that goes all the way down to his feet even though it's hot outside. Diana says he's cute, and so does Janice, but I can't tell yet because all I can see is that hair. Today he's not wearing his scarf, probably too hot even for him, but he has his hair in a ponytail and he looks like an ugly girl to me. I'm waiting for him to go in his house but instead he starts walking across the street toward us. Diana kicks me in the back and sits up real straight but Janice and me just stare.

"Hi, I'm Alex," he says, and then he takes Diana's hand and kisses the top of it. She turns purple and smiles, but doesn't say anything else, so he says, "And you are?"

"I'm Diana."

Kelly puts her hand under his face and says, "I'm Kelly." And I know she's looking for a smooch on the hand too. He kisses Kelly's hand and then looks down at me. I'm not looking up. I got an interesting crack in the sidewalk that I'm keeping my eye on.

"What's your name?" he asks, and touches my head so I can't ignore him anymore. Diana pipes up and says, "That's my baby sister, Cosette. She's ten."

"That's a cool name," he says, and then he asks me how I spell it. I spell it out for him, but I'm still not looking up.

"You're a shy little thing," he says, but that kind of ticks me off because I'm not little or very shy. I just got to get used to people, that's all. So I look square into his eyes without blinking or saying a peep. But he keeps looking right back at me. His eyes are blue with green dots in them, and his lashes are heavy and black. I can see the smile in his eyes, that little light, like my girlfriend Rosemary gets when she's about to smile, so I smile, just a tad, and put my head back down. Diana smacks me in the head and says, "Cosette! The man is talking to you." But I just get up and leave because I don't have any words. I can hear him talking to Janice now. I guess it was her turn for hand kisses.

Ma and Ken are arguing again. It's always the same fight. He says he's sick of Ma defending us girls instead of sticking up for him. I don't think Ma sticks up for us too much. She lets him get away with everything. Right in the middle of the fight, Diana decides to tell Ma that she wants a lock on her bedroom door too. I can't believe she's doing it because she taught us not to ask for stuff when Ma's in a bad mood. I'm waiting for Ma to pop and spin, but she just stands there staring at Diana.

Things get so quiet we can hear the birds singing outside. Then Ken smiles at Diana, not a happy smile, more like an I'm going to eat you and pick my teeth with your bones smile, and says, "No friggen way!" Diana looks red hot, but all she does is smile back at Ken and stomp off to her room. Ma runs in after her and we all chase behind them. Ma starts smacking the crap out of Diana. They're rolling around, tipping over stuff, and yelling, and I bet the whole neighborhood can hear them screaming because it sounds like they're getting the Chinese torture. Ken is standing there, watching with his arms folded like he paid to get in, but Janice and me try breaking them up. Ma pushes Janice backward and she falls against the doorframe. I hear her head hit the wood, like a rock landing in the sand, and I can tell it hurt her because she's getting ready to cry. Ken grabs me and holds my arms behind me so I can't move. All I can do is watch.

Diana got scratches and welts all over, and Janice got a good sized goose egg on the back of her head. I didn't get anything, but my stomach hurts. My insides feel mushy like mud, but with glass all mixed up in it, and the glass keeps hitting the sides of my stomach and hurting really bad. I think Ma beat up Diana to show Ken that she doesn't stick up for us kids too much. Diana didn't do anything too bad, she just lipped off a little. Ma came in afterwards and tried making up with Diana, but I could tell that Diana wasn't buying it because when Ma hugged her, Diana didn't hug back. She just stared ahead like she couldn't wait to get the hug over with. I don't see what the big deal is for Diana to want a lock on her door too. I figure she wanted the lock to give her more privacy now that there are men in the house. She's nearly sixteen and has plenty of boobs and hair to hide. She's been using a chair for a lock. She jams it under the doorknob, but if Ken knew that he would take her chair away.

Ever since Ma and Ken got married all we do is fight around here. Ma doesn't smile like she used to, Diana stays locked up in her room, and Janice reads all the time. Tommy seems the same to me, but I don't know him so well yet.

Ken is never happy about anything. He's the biggest sour puss in the world. Sometimes he asks me to pop the zits on his back. I don't dare say no to him or he'll stay in a bad mood all day and make us all pay for it. So I do it just to keep him in a good mood for a while. I'm finding all sorts of ways to keep him in a good mood. One day I cleaned his car, inside and out. Another day I sat on his lap, like I used to do, because I wanted him to be in a good mood. If I never brought him home to meet Ma we wouldn't be in this big mess.

Uncle Richie is marrying Carla. I'm kind of glad that he's getting married because Ma says that he's getting old and needs a wife to take care of him. We haven't seen him for a while. I guess he figures that Ken is here now so we don't need him anymore. When Uncle Richie does come over Ken goes into his bedroom and ignores him. I can tell that Uncle Richie feels funny being at our house because he always checks his watch and only stays for a few minutes. I wish Uncle Richie would take me with him for a ride around the city streets with the top down, and the radio blasting, like he used to.

A Good Day

Things have been pretty B O R I N G around here. I spend most of my time sitting on the porch steps with my sisters. I help Dewey Sloan with his paper route on Fridays because that's collection day and he shares his tips with me. Dewey used to go to my school but I never hung around with him because he lived too far away. Now I hang around with him because I live closer to him. Dewey is twelve, and nice once you get to know him. I used to think that he was slow because of the way he talks, but Ma says he has a slight lisp because his tongue gets stuck against his teeth when he tries to say an "S" word. But that doesn't mean he's slow. I'm used to it now, but sometimes kids poke fun at him. He doesn't seem to mind too much though because he just laughs right along with them until they get bored and go away.

Dewey is pretty tall, and has some muscles on him too, so I figure he could take any of those boys if he really wanted to. My sisters like to tease me about Dewey, saying that he's my boyfriend, but we're just regular friends. Ken teases me about Dewey too, and it really ticks me off because he raises his eyebrows and says stuff like, "I know what you two have been up to." He's so disgusting.

Ma's been working at Meme's store sewing wedding gowns for her, so she's gone all day. The store is downtown and Meme drives her to work in the morning, but Ma has to walk home every night and then cook us all supper. We're having crumpled hamburger and mashed potatoes tonight for supper.

Us kids have to clean the house now because of Ma working. This week I have to do dishes. I hate dishes. I'd rather sweep and vacuum, but Janice gets to do that this week. Tommy has to feed the animals, and Diana has to set the table and dust stuff. Ken never does anything except inspect our cleaning. He takes out a white cloth and rubs it over stuff to see if it's military clean. If it's not clean enough he makes us do it over again. He always makes Diana do her chores over again even if the cloth is still clean.

Ma's in a good mood tonight. I can tell because she's joking around with us and humming while she cooks. I'm in a good mood too because Ken is working the night shift this week and I'm going to plop my butt in his chair so I can sit at the head of the table right next to Ma. Plus I love crumpled hamburger because Ma drowns it in gravy and then pours it all over our mashed potatoes. I mix my green beans right in with it so I can't taste them.

"Come eat!" Ma yells, and all of us run for the kitchen, but when I get in there Diana has already planted her butt in Ken's chair, where I wanted to sit. I go and sit on the other side of Ma and don't argue with Diana. I figure she took enough slapping to earn that seat.

Tommy starts gulping his food down like he's never had a bite in his life. He has potatoes on the end of his nose and I can hear him smacking when he chews. I want to elbow him, because it's so irritating, but it's too late because Ma is sitting there with her fork full of food but she's not eating it. She's just staring at Tommy like he came to the table naked. I kick Tommy to try to clue him in, but he doesn't get it, and Ma yells, "Eat with your mouth shut, and wipe your face!"

Tommy looks up, shuts his mouth, and then wipes his gooey face on his sleeve.

"USE A NAPKIN!" Ma shouts, and then mumbles something about having Tommy do his own laundry. Janice and me are being quiet because we're hoping for one fight-free night in this house, but Diana is sticking her two cents in so she can show Ma that she's on her side.

Then Tommy does something that I would never have the guts to do. He looks over at Diana, with his head up high like he means it, and says to her, "Shut up, you're not my mother." Ma keeps on eating, like he said nothing special, but Diana's face is turning red and her cheeks are puffing out like she's ready to pop. She doesn't say anything back to him, not with her mouth anyway, but I can tell she's talking to Tommy through her eyes, and the way he has his head way down low, I can tell he knows what Diana's saying to him.

I'm washing my last pan when someone knocks at the door. I don't move because my hands are all wet, plus I figure Diana will get it seeing her room is right next to the door, but she doesn't. I yell, "DOOR!" but still no one goes to get it so I open it myself. There's a girl standing there with big brown eyes and a face whiter than Ma's mashed potatoes. She's wearing a prissy plaid skirt, and clunky shoes, and asks me if my mother's home, so I turn my head and yell, "Ma!" And then I tell the girl to come in.

I can tell that she doesn't really want to come in because she stands in the doorway, halfway in and out. Ma finally comes to the door and the girl asks her if she wants to buy some candy that she's selling for her school. Ma asks the girl her name and she says, "Peggy."

"How much is your candy, Peggy?" Ma asks, and Peggy tells her $1.00 for a big candy bar. Ma says she'll be right back , leaving Peggy and me standing there with the door wide open and her half in and half out.

"What school do you go to?" I ask, figuring it's probably a Catholic one because of her uniform, and she tells me South Prep.

"What grade are you in?"

"I'm going into the eighth," she says, staring at her candy paper.

"Why do you have school clothes on in the summer?" I ask, trying to get her to look at me. But she doesn't take her eyes off of her important paper, and says that she has to wear her uniform when she's selling candy.

She looks too little to be in the eighth grade but I don't think she's lying because she looks like a goody-goody in that plaid skirt and all, and she probably isn't too good at lying.

Ma pays her a dollar for a huge Hershey bar with nuts and tells Peggy that it was nice meeting her. Peggy says that she'll bring the candy by next week and smiles at Ma, a peep of a smile, and then runs out to the street. I walk out to the porch to see which way she's walking. I watch her run up the hill to where all the one family houses are. They have big front porches and pretty fences around them. Peggy goes into the green house without knocking, so I know she lives there. I figure she must have a la-te-da life because she lives in such a nice house and goes to that fancy prep school and all. I bet she thinks she's better than us because of it too.

I decide to sit on the steps by myself for a while. I miss sitting with Jimmy. He hangs around with some boys from the new neighborhood and never asks me to come along with them. He told me that my friend Rosemarie wouldn't be going to my school any more because she moved so far away. That's cruddy because I didn't even get to say goodbye to her, or get her new address, and I wonder if I'll ever see her again. It takes a long time to find a good friend like Rosemarie, and then she disappears like she was never really here at all. I'm glad I have Dewey to hang around with, and my sister Janice, but I still miss Rosemarie a lot.

I hear a noisy car coming and see that it's that hippie, Alex in his junkie van. This time I'm going to say hi first because I want to show him that I'm not "a shy little thing" like he says I am. The minute he gets out of the van I blurt out "hi" before he can say it first. He sees me and smiles.

I wasn't counting on him coming over to talk, but here he comes. His curly hair is bouncing up and down when he walks like its one big clump, and he has that stupid scarf on again today. I can feel my stomach jumping because I have to talk to him all by myself, and I don't know what to say to a hippie. Boy, am I glad that Ken isn't home because he would throw a fit if he caught me talking to him. Every time Ken sees Alex get out of his van he has something mean to say, like, "Look at that, you can't tell if it's a boy or a girl."

Alex sits down beside me like he's my best friend or something. I can smell him, and he smells different. Nice. Like perfume, but not lady perfume and not that stuff that Ken rubs all over his face. It smells friendly, like the woods at Mooney Lake. He starts yapping and tells me that he's a student art teacher at the art museum. I didn't think teachers were allowed to look like him. All my man teachers wear ties and stuff. I tell him that I never met an artist before and that I like to draw sometimes. And then he offers to teach me to paint if I want, but I don't answer him, I just stare at his feet. His bell-bottom pants cover up most of his sneakers. I can tell they used to be white but now they're all covered with little sprinkles of colored paint. They remind me of the jimmies I put on my ice cream cones. He asks me if I'm getting shy on him again, and I say, "No, I was just thinking, that's all."

"Thinking about what?"

"Nothing." I say, because I don't know what I'm thinking about. I only know I like sitting with him and he smells good.

"You want to see one of my paintings? I have one in the van."

"Sure!" I say, and walk beside him across the street to his van. It feels weird to be walking with Alex because I remember when

I used to poke fun at him with Ken. If Diana saw me with him she would be jealous because she thinks he's such a doll, but Ken would kill me.

Alex opens the back doors to the van. There are no seats in there, except the front ones, and the back is full of boxes. I can see some jars with brushes in them and tubes of paint that look like toothpaste. There's a white sheet covering something big and square but I can't tell what it is, but then Alex lifts up the sheet and pulls out a big painting. It's of a lady sitting down on the floor like an Indian. She has long red hair and a headband on, like the one Janice made for me, and bell-bottom pants like Alex's.

"Is this your girlfriend?" I ask.

"Nah," He says. "She's just a student who posed for me."

"You did a good job. She's so pretty and real looking, like a picture from a camera."

"Thanks," Alex says, "But it wasn't that hard. I've been painting since I was ten years old."

"I'm ten." I tell him, and then my face gets hot and I don't know what to say next.

"I hear my mother calling me," I say, but it's a big fat lie. I just want to get away from him so I can think about things for a while.

"Thanks for showing me your painting," I shout, running back across the street, into the house, and straight to my bedroom where I plop myself on my bed. I feel like a bunch of butterflies are loose in my stomach, but I like it. I like the way he treats me like I'm one of his grownup friends. I might even let him teach me how to paint some day.

I'm waiting for Janice to come home because I want her to go have a cigarette with me. I've been smoking all summer but I don't ever get caught. I can inhale and everything without even getting sick. I didn't even know that Janice smoked until I caught her puffing off a cigarette that Ma left burning in the ashtray and she begged me not to tell on her. I didn't say anything back. Instead I picked up the cigarette and took a long drag off of it, and inhaled just like Ma does. Janice's eyes got big, but her mouth was smiling.

"You smoke?" she said. Then she hugged me and said she wouldn't tell if I didn't. So now us three girls all smoke, and we keep clipping Ma's butts but she hasn't said a word about it.

Janice comes into the room and asks me if I want to go have a cigarette with her.

"I was just going to ask you that!" I tell her.

"Do you have any cigs?" she asks me.

"No. Don't you have any?"

"No."

"Then how are we supposed to go smoke without any cigarettes?"

"I'll swipe one of Ma's," she says, and then she disappears out the door.

On Fridays I usually get a whole pack of butts. Dewey and me take our tip money from his paper route and head to the store to get them, and then we go to the top of the Carver building and sit on the roof and smoke. But Dewey doesn't inhale like me so he's not really smoking.

From the top of the Carver building you can see the whole city; it's fourteen stories tall, so it's kind of like standing on the top of a mountain. The cars and people all look really small, like you could pick them up between your fingers and flick them around. Sometimes we spit over the side at people and then crouch down and laugh until our faces hurt.

Dewey and me spend lots of time hanging around lately. I didn't use to think he was cute, but now I do. I like the way his top lip gets stuck to his tooth when he smiles, and how his hair looks when the sun is on it, all yellow and shiny, like the Beach Boys.

I'm not saying he's my boyfriend or anything, but sometimes I try to think of what it would be like to be married to him. I picture him coming home from work and me cooking supper for him and wearing pretty dresses with my hair done up really nice, from a real hairdresser.

I like to think of what our kids would look like, and what kind of a house we would have. I want a real house, like the ones on Cherry Street, with an upstairs and a yard with flowers and I want pretty trimmed hedges around it too. Ma could come and visit me and maybe someday she'll divorce Ken and come and live with us in our big house.

Dewey is poor now but I bet he gets a good job some day because he's really smart and can fix anything. Once he found an old red wagon, the kind with the wooden sides. He fixed it up and painted it red so now it looks almost like new. He uses it all the time to deliver his newspapers and sometimes he takes his little sister Tina with him. He plops her in the wagon with all his newspapers and pulls her up and down the hills. Tina's only four and the youngest out of eleven kids. Dewey's mom fusses over her because she's the baby, so Dewey takes extra good care of her when he takes her out.

Dewey's mom is really skinny and looks all worn out, like she's a hundred years old. I bet it's because of picking up after all those kids. I've never seen Dewey's dad because he works the night shift in a factory and has to sleep all day, so he's never around. Dewey only sees him on the weekends but says that he's always sitting in front of the TV with his beer grumbling about being tired. Dewey's not going to work in a factory, like his dad, because he says that he can't make any money doing that. He wants to build things, like bridges and buildings, and put his name on them, like old man Carver's name is on the front of the Carver building. I bet he does it too.

Janice comes back in the room and says, "No luck. Ma's got her cigarettes in her dress pocket, and there's no big clinchers in any of the ashtrays."

"I don't care," I tell her. "Let's go watch TV before Tommy hogs it."

Ozzie and Harriet is on. I like this show because I get to see Ricky Nelson. He's a dreamboat. Janice writes his name on her forehead at night with her finger so she'll dream about him. I tried it but it didn't work for me.

Pretty soon Diana comes in and sits on the couch. She pulls a squished pack of Winstons out of her bra and lights up a cigarette, right there in the house.

"Aren't you afraid that you'll get caught?" Janice asks.

"Ma gave me permission."

"Lucky duck! Can I have one?" Janice asks.

Diana pulls a bent up butt out of the wrinkled pack and hands it over to Janice.

"Come on!" Janice says, so we run out to the back porch to smoke and gab.

"I met a new girl tonight named Peggy," I tell Janice. "She came to our door wearing a uniform from her la-te-da prep school, and sold Ma a candy bar."

"How old was she?" Janice asks.

"Fourteen, but she looks twelve. She's going into the eighth grade."

"Was she pretty?"

"Not really. She had nice brown eyes but she was really pale, like a vampire had gotten to her or something. She lives up the hill in that green house before the alley and she's coming back next week to bring Ma her candy bar."

"I've seen that girl before," Janice says. "I talked to her once when I was sitting on the wall waiting for Ma to come home. She was nice to me, and she had her sister Sue with her. Sue's eleven and kind of cute."

Janice squished the cigarette out on the step and kicked it to the side and then headed back to the parlor to watch TV with Diana and Tommy. Janice sits in the chair, but I keep on walking because I'm going to try to visit Ma for a while in her room. We're not allowed in there because Ken says we snoop around, but when he works late Ma sometimes lets us lie on her bed and watch TV with her. The bedroom door is cracked open and I can hear her TV, so I knock, a little knock, and wait.

"Come in."

I open the door and see Ma lying on top of the covers with her arms behind her head watching *The Virginian*.

"Can I watch TV with you?"

"Sure," Ma says, patting the bed beside her. I lay down next to her, staying really quiet so I don't tick her off by gabbing in the middle of her show. She has a bag of candy open and she hands me a few and says, "Don't tell the others or you'll never get another piece of candy from me for as long as you live."

I slip the candy into my mouth, letting the chocolate melt on my tongue, like an ice cube in the sun. Ma and me don't talk much anymore.

Not since she married Ken. It seems like she doesn't want to hear nothing bad about him so I keep my trap shut.

A commercial comes on and Ma lights up a cigarette. I want to say tons of stuff to her, but I have to be careful not to make her mad, so I tell her that I miss her. Ma takes a long drag off her cigarette, and I can tell that she's stalling, trying to think of what to say about me missing her. "Don't be silly," she finally says, swiping at the air. Then she puts her hand on mine and holds it there. I know Ma doesn't want to talk about any mushy stuff, so I lie there with her hand on mine and *The Virginian* comes back on.

"Cozy, will you get me a drink of water?"

"Sure," I say, even though I don't want to break the spell of Ma holding my hand. I run to the kitchen, grab a tall glass and fill it up to the top, and then head back to her room. Ma tells me to set the glass on the bed table and then she tells me to go get ready for bed. That's Ma's nice way of kicking me out of her room. I don't bother getting ready for bed though; instead, I sit in the parlor with everyone else and watch *The Beverly Hillbillies*. After that we all go to bed.

I'm almost sleeping, but then Crumbs wakes me up barking at Ken coming in from work. I hear Ken say, "Aw, shut up!" to Crumbs, and then walk to his room and lock the door. Crumbs walks low and skulky around Ken, the way a kid does when they're afraid of getting smacked.

Now it's really quiet in the house again and I'm bored. I hate it when I wake up like this because it's really hard to fall back asleep. I turn on the little lamp by my bed and look over at Janice, hoping it doesn't wake her up, but she doesn't even blink. I figure I'll look at one of her magazines for a while, so I grab a *True Story* from Janice's table and climb back into bed. There's a girl on the cover with a black beehive hairdo, smiling, like she knows all the secrets. Beside her it says, "Never Say No To A Man." It makes me feel funny inside, kind of excited like I have something special to look forward to when I grow up. I wonder what it's like to go all the way with a boy. Diana says that it supposed to hurt the first time but after that it gets better. I don't know any boys that I want to go all the way with. It all seems so grown-up, like eating fried clams with the bellies on them. Yuck! But I like reading about it anyway.

I'm reading some pretty juicy stuff when I hear somebody coming. I want to hide the magazine but it's too late because my door opens and Ken pops his head in.

"Do you know what time it is?" he asks, but then he sees the magazine on my lap and comes and snatches it away from me.

"Never say no to a man, huh? What kind of trash are you reading anyway?"

"I was just looking at it because I was bored and couldn't sleep."

Ken drops the magazine on the floor and moves around my bed and clicks the light off. Now it's dark but I can still hear him breathing. I keep waiting to hear him leave, but instead I feel my bed go down, the way it does when Crumbs climbs in with me. Ken's hands are under the covers pulling at my pajama bottoms. I try pushing him away. But he doesn't go away. He'll never go away.

It's Saturday morning and I can hear Ma in the kitchen making us a big breakfast. I remember last night with Ken's hands everywhere, and how he climbed on top of me like he owned me. I don't want to get up and sit out there with everyone because I'm scared that they'll be able to tell what I've been up to. I look over at Janice's bed but it's empty, and I wonder if she heard Ken last night.

"Get up Cozy, it's time for breakfast."

It's Ma coming into my room. I turn my back to her and pretend that I'm still sleeping. She sits on my bed and plays with my hair. It feels good, so I keep my eyes closed so it will last longer.

"I made pancakes with bacon and eggs."

"I don't feel good Ma. Can you save me some for later?"

Ma puts her lips on my forehead, and says, "You're as cool as a cuke, Cozy. C'mon get up." Then she peels my blanket off of me and tosses it onto Janice's bed.

"MA!"

"MA NOTHING! Get up NOW. The food's getting cold." That settles it. I have to go face Ken at the breakfast table.

Everyone is busy chomping away at their food and the only one who looks up at me when I sit at the table is Ken.

"Well look who finally decided to join us," he says, putting a big forkful of pancakes in his mouth and smiling all big and goofy at me while he chews. Everyone laughs at Ken because they want to keep him smiling all day long. I don't though. I pour some syrup on my pancakes and watch it spread, like lava, down the cakes and onto my plate. I picture little people running away from it, trying to find a safe place to hide. They jump off my plate and onto the table. I pretend to put them in my pocket so I can take them to a nice home someplace far away from the volcano.

"We're going to the carnival today!" Tommy says. "Aren't we dad?"

Everyone stops eating and looks over at Ken, waiting for his highness to open his mouth and say something, but all he does is raise his eyebrows up and down like an idiot.

"Yippee!" Janice shouts, planting a bony hug on me.

"Will you go on the Scrambler with me Cozy?"

"Sure," I tell her, but I don't care if I do or don't.

Everyone is in a good mood today because Ken's taking us to the carnival. Janice says that I'm going to spoil it because I'm being a sour puss. Even Diana and Tommy made up, and Diana promised not to get him back for sassing her at the dinner table. Ma told me that I better wipe the scowl off my face or she'd wipe it off for me. If they knew why Ken was in a good mood they wouldn't be smiling no more, but I'll never tell them a thing. I figure it's my fault for bringing Ken around here anyway.

At the carnival Ma told Janice and Diana to stick together, but I got stuck staying with Tommy and them. I told Ma that I wanted to ride the Scrambler with Janice, but she gave me the "eye" so I simmered down and followed way behind them. Tommy hung back with me. He looked so little and excited, like I used to get when I didn't have any worries, so I let him walk with me. I figure he can't help it if he's Ken's kid.

"You want to go on the Scrambler with me?" he asked, looking up at me with his winky little eyes.

"Sure," I told him, and then I looked around to see if I could spot Janice and Diana anywhere.

"There's Janice!" Tommy shouts. I look over and see Diana and Janice standing in a clump of people looking like they don't know where to go next. I head toward them, pulling Tommy by the arm so I don't lose him in the crowd.

"You guys want to come on the Scrambler with me and Tommy?"

"There's no way we're all going to fit in one seat," Diana says, with her hands on her hips like she means business. But I don't let her bossy look scare me and I say, "Yes we can because we're all really skinny."

Diana says that she'll try it, but not to blame her if they don't let us on.

"Three per car," the carnival guy says, without even looking at us. He's got bumps all over his face like a naked chicken, and long greasy blond hair. Diana looks over at me and grins.

"Excuse me," she says, "but I'm watching my brother and sisters so I can't go on the ride without them. They're really skinny and we'll fit in fine. Please?" Then Diana smiles, showing all those sparkly white teeth, and he can't take his eyes off her.

"Okay," he says, tucking his T-shirt in like he's being inspected, mumbling, "Man, I hope I don't get canned for this."

He lets us through and we race for a blue car. We click our door shut and then Mr. Greasy Hair comes by and locks it for us. He looks up at Diana and smiles really big, so all his teeth are showing, but he has more empty spaces than teeth, and I have to look away because I feel like laughing – but I don't want to hurt his feelings.

We're all squeezed into the seat waiting for the ride to start. *I Get Around* by the Beach Boys is playing on the loud speaker, and I can feel my stomach jumping up in my throat. The ride starts slowly, so I look around until I spot Ma and Ken standing by the gate. Ma is waving at us like we're leaving on a long trip. I wave back and then hold on tight because the ride is getting faster. I can't see anything anymore because things are swooshing by too fast. Diana keeps squishing into me, and it hurts, but I'm laughing because I can't tell her to stop and I'm stuck on this ride that's killing me. Every time we swing out, Diana slams into me, and then when we go in, Janice slams into Tommy. Poor Tommy is crying, but we can't do anything about it because we're all screaming, the music is blaring, and even though it hurts, I never want the ride to end.

I don't think Tommy will ever go on the Scrambler again. Ma yelled at us for sticking him on the end, but we didn't know he was going to get squished. Ken bought Tommy a blue snow cone to calm him down, and then he let me go off with my sisters to ride more rides.

On the way home I got that empty feeling in my stomach, because I had nothing to look forward to anymore. I knew that we were going to go home, eat, clean up, and then hang around the stupid house, bored like we always do.

When we got home I went into my room, took off my shoes and socks, and tossed them into the closet. My closet was a mess so I figured I better shut the closet door so Ma wouldn't see it. That's when I spotted a box way up on the top shelf, and I couldn't remember what was in it. I couldn't reach the box, so I dragged our desk chair into the closet, and stood on it. It was way too heavy and when I pulled on it I lost my balance and fell backwards off the chair. I grabbed at the clothes that were hanging up, but the whole pole came down and all the clothes landed on top of me.

Janice came running into the room and when she spotted me sitting on the floor covered in clothes she said, "Ma's going to kill you!"

"Shhhh! She'll hear you! Help me pick this mess up."

Janice stuck the pole back onto the holders and asked, "What the heck were you doing, Cozy?"

"I found this box up there and I wanted to see what was in it."

"What box?"

"This one right here, "I said, brushing the clothes off the top of it.

Janice grabbed the box from me and tore into it. There was a bunch of old socks and school papers in it so she said, "This is just a bunch of junk. I fixed the pole. You can hang all the clothes up yourself. "

"I was going to anyway," I tell her, digging under all the junk in the box until I spot my doll, Blabby. I feel bad because I forgot all about her. I used to tuck her in and kiss her goodnight like she was really my kid. I couldn't sleep if I didn't do it, but now I hardly think about her any more. She looks different now...smaller. And when I sniff her, her powdery smell is gone. She used to smell good, like baby powder and plastic. I hold her like a real baby and tell her, "I'm sorry for forgetting about you." Then I fix her spiky black hair and promise that I'll never forget about her again.

When I'm done picking up the clothes, I put Blabby on my bed. I found my diary too, so I put that on the table next to my bed. I still haven't written anything in it. Most girls write about boys in their diaries. I could write about Dewey and some of the stuff we talk about but I like keeping that kind of stuff inside of me.

Thinking about Dewey makes me miss him. I didn't get to go on his paper route with him this Friday, because his stupid brother Jerry wanted to help him with it, but Dewey says that I can definitely help him next Friday.

I dig into the box some more and on the bottom of the box is Mr. Robard's paper Halloween witch that he gave me before he moved. She has a huge hairy wart on her nose. I pull her out, but her hat snags on a fold in the box and rips in half. Crap. I can't get another one of these because only Mr. Robard knows where to buy them. I wonder what he's doing now and if he still hangs decorations in his new windows for his new neighborhood kids. I tape her hat as best I can. It doesn't look perfect but at least she's back in one piece. Then I tape her to the closet door, even though it's not Halloween, and stand back to look at her. She doesn't scare me any more, and looks kind of cartoony. I can remember when she used to scare the crap out of me.

I'm feeling hungry, so I head to the kitchen to see what Ma's cooking for supper. It's sort of late and I'm hoping that we can get some pizza or something so I won't have to do dishes. There's nobody in the kitchen so I check the parlor and find Diana sitting there on the end of the couch watching TV.

"Where's Ma?"

"She went with Ken to get hamburgers for supper," Diana says, digging in her pack for a cigarette. Diana looks normal smoking now, like Ma, and I can't remember when she didn't smoke.

I did have to do some dishes tonight but I got them done fast. When we finished our chores, us girls went out to sit on the porch with Kelly. Kelly looked awful. Her face was puffy and red, and her eyes looked like slits with lashes.

"What happened to you?" I asked, but I could tell by the look that Diana gave me that I shouldn't have come right out and asked her like that.

"Nothing, I'm just tired," Kelly said, turning her face away and tapping her bare foot on the step like a drum.

I sat down and shut my mouth. I didn't want to get kicked off the steps by Diana. It was really quiet, no radio or yapping, but I kept sitting there waiting for something fun to happen. Finally Janice gave me the elbow and said, "Look."

I looked up and saw Alex bouncing up the street with a little brown bag in his hand. Kelly said, "Oh shit!" and jumped up, almost falling off the side of the steps. Then she ran upstairs to her apartment, but my sisters and me stayed right where we were.

Diana sat up tall and flicked her cigarette off the side of the steps. I could tell she was trying to look older. Alex spotted us sitting there and waved. He was grinning like he found a hundred dollar bill or something, and shouted over to us, "Hey ladies."

"Hi," we all said at the same time, like we were the church choir. Alex kept coming toward us, all happy and grinning. He doesn't know that Ken hates his guts because he's a hippie, and that we'll probably all get in trouble for talking to him. I'm thinking of leaving but I don't because I can't get my feet to move.

Alex started blabbing about the weather and how we should be doing something more fun, instead of sitting on the stairs like we were, but I'm not paying attention to what he's saying because I can't take my eyes off of his face. I like his sparkly eyes and how his whole face looks happy when he talks. He doesn't use a lot of hippie words, like the hippies on TV. He talks mostly normal, and his voice is soft like the Disney guy who reads all the stories like *Old Yeller*.

I breathe his cologne in through my nose and feel it filling me up inside. It makes me feel different, like I don't live in a crappy neighborhood with a creepy step-dad, but like I'm in the enchanted forest or something. He's too young to be my dad, but he could be my brother, or maybe even my boyfriend someday, but not until I'm way grown up.

"Cosette!"

"Huh?"

Diana pushes on my shoulder, almost knocking me off the side of the stairs, and says, "Alex is talking to you."

"Oh. Sorry."

"Do you want a Ring Ding?"

"Huh?"

"A RING DING, DING DONG!" Janice shouts, for the whole neighborhood to hear.

Alex is handing out chocolate Ring Dings, and Janice is already half done with hers.

"No thanks," I say, but I'm really dying for one. I just don't want to eat in front of him like Janice is. It makes her look like a little kid. Diana didn't take one either.

Alex takes the other Ring Ding out of the cellophane package and stuffs the whole thing into his mouth at once. He must have seen my eyes get big because he started laughing really hard and I could see all that chocolate cake mushing around inside his mouth like mud in a washing machine. I started laughing with him and pretty soon we were all holding our bellies laughing like a bunch of goof balls.

"What the hell's going on out there?"

"Oh God! Ken's coming!" Diana says, and then she grabbed her cigs and headed inside. Janice took off running around to the side of the house, but I'm still stuck to the steps and Alex is standing there with his mouth shut around all that chocolate looking like he doesn't know what to do next.

I can feel the stairs shaking with Ken's footsteps behind me, and I'm trying to look normal so Alex doesn't get his feelings hurt.

"I said, what's going on out here?"

At least Ken wasn't yelling, but I could tell that he was pissed off.

"Dad...Ken, this is Alex. He's an art teacher at the museum."

I looked up at Alex, and he winked, a tiny little wink at me, like he knew that Ken was a jerk, and he said, "Nice meeting you Ken."

Ken didn't even look at Alex; he just stuck his foot into my back and said, "Get your ass inside. Now!"

I got up to leave and Ken followed me inside. I was waiting for him to hit me in the head so I scrunched my shoulders up so it wouldn't hurt so badly, but he didn't hit me, instead he went right into Ma's room and started a fight with her.

"Now you're sticking up for that fucken hippie!"

"No I'm not, Ken. I'm just saying that he seems like a nice guy."

"He's a draft dodging coward!"

I flopped on my bed and turned on my radio. *End Of The World* was playing. It's my favorite old song, but it always makes me cry. I feel like the girl singing the song, and I don't care if I live or die sometimes because everything good is dead and gone now. I stick the earpieces into my ears, so that nobody else can hear it, and get under the covers. I pull Blabby under there with me and try to pretend that I'm at my old house, and that things are like they were before I brought Ken around.

After a while my thinking starts to slow down and I doze off. I dream that Alex and me are riding around in his van at night. He's got tons of Ring Dings in a big paper bag and we're laughing and eating Ring Dings while he drives around the city with the top down. I can't believe that he has a van with a top that comes down. I keep saying, "This is groovy!" and I can see the stars shining like headlights in the sky. I feel free, like a bird being let out of its cage. Beautiful music is playing, but it's coming out of the sky, and I can't tell what song it is, but I tell Alex that it's my favorite song. Alex keeps driving around in a circle faster and faster and we're laughing harder and harder, but my song starts turning into yelling, like a fight, and I put my fingers in my ears and tell Alex to shut off the radio, but he can't because it's coming from the sky. I see a big hand coming out of the sky and grabbing me right out of the van. Alex is pulling on my legs but he can't hold onto me, and I feel myself being lifted up and then thrown out onto the dark road. I wake up on the floor with Ken standing over me yelling, and Ma screaming, "Leave her alone!"

Ken picked me up by my arms and held me in front of his face. My feet were off the floor and I was hanging there like socks on the line. I tried to wiggle free, but Ken held me tighter and screamed into my face, "If you go near that fucken hippie again I'll shoot him!" Then he dropped me on the floor and walked out of my room.

Ma followed behind him, yelling at his back, but I couldn't hear her any more because my ears were ringing from my heart beating so hard. Janice scooted down on the floor with me and hugged me, but I didn't hug her back. I just sat there waiting for my breath to start up again.

"Did he hurt you?" She asked, pulling my hair out of my face, like Ma does sometimes.

"No," is all I have the breath to say.

"Come sleep in my bed with me," Janice says, pulling on my arm until I follow her.

"I feel bad that only you got into trouble, Cozy. All three of us were with Alex."

"It's okay, Janice," I tell her, and part of me is kind of proud that I got in trouble for Alex.

We got under the covers and listened to hear if the fight was over. I couldn't help thinking about us all being out on the steps and how cute Alex was. I was glad Kelly ran upstairs because she would have hogged him.

"Janice?"

"Yeah?"

"What was wrong with Kelly's face?"

"Don't say that I told you, but she popped a pimple on her cheek and her whole face blew up like a balloon."

"Nuh uh!"

"Yup," Janice said, and then she flipped over on her side like she always does when she's ready to fall asleep.

"Janice?"

"Hmm?"

"Do you think Ken would really shoot Alex?"

"He might. He has about four guns in his room and he's always bragging about how great a shooter he is." I swallowed hard just thinking about it.

Collecting

"Let Ma know that I'm going collecting with Dewey!" I told Janice, but Janice pretended that she didn't hear me, and kept watching TV. I knew that she heard me so I headed out the door.

"Hi Cozy!" Dewey says, pulling up his red T-shirt and wiping his sweaty face with it. His stomach looked soft and white, and his belly button looked dark and as deep as a cave. He caught me staring at him and dropped his shirt back down over his stomach. "Hey, I'm ready!" I said, looking away.

We started off down the street, Dewey's newspaper bag was hanging off his shoulder stuffed full of rolled up papers.

"Where's your wagon today, Dewey?" I asked, while I skipped a little to keep up with his big steps.

"I left it at home. Today's paper is skinny so I figured I'd just carry them."

"Want me to take some for you?"

"Nope."

Dewey likes to show off how strong he is so I don't say anything more about it.

First we do a big apartment building. It's full of old people and has an elevator in it so they don't have to climb all the stairs. We always get into laughing fits when we go here because it's so quiet, like church.

We start at the first floor, and then drop off newspapers all the way up to the top floor.

"This is the last one in this building," Dewey said, and then he knocked on a door and stood there waiting. Dewey looks so serious that it tickles me but I try to hold my laughing in. Pretty soon an old man opened the door a crack, and Dewey said,

"Collecting."

"Just a minute," The old guy said, leaving Dewey standing there waiting again. I stared up at Dewey, and he was staring straight ahead at the closed door.

"What's taking him so long?" I asked, just trying to get Dewey to pay attention to me.

"He's a nice old guy," Dewey says, but he doesn't even look at me when he says it.

I looked down the long skinny hallway; it was pretty dark except for the light down at this end. It smelled stuffy, like a coffin that's been shut for a hundred years, and it was so quiet that all I could hear was me and Dewey breathing.

"Do you think there are any ghosts in here?" I asked, raising my eyebrows like I might have seen a ghost. Dewey looked over at me like I was a screwball.

"No, really Dewey, look at this hallway, it looks like a ghost should be walking down it."

Dewey looked down the dark end of the hall and then back at me with his eyes wide open.

"What?" I whispered. Dewey stayed quiet but started walking away from me down the dark hallway with his arms and legs all stretched out like a mummy's.

"Oooooh, Ooooooh," he howled, and then he turned around and started walking at me like a man eating zombie.

"Stop!" I giggled, but he kept coming at me until he had me pinned up against the wall.

"Stop!"

But Dewey didn't stop; he kept pushing against me with his belly and then tickled me under my arms.

"SSSSTOP!" I yelled, but I was laughing so hard that I had to squat down and stick my heel in my crotch to keep the pee from coming out. Dewey stood up straight and acted all innocent, and just in time too, because the old man opened his door and caught me down on the floor laughing like an idiot.

"What's wrong with her?" The old guy asked, while he counted out the money into Dewey's hand.

"Oh, she's just having one of her fits."

"Hmmm," he said, and then he looked down at me, over his glasses, like he was trying to get a good look. I gave him a little wave, and he backed up into his apartment and locked the door.

"You did it now!" Dewey said, putting his hand in front of his mouth and pointing at me.

"You made me do it!" I tell him, but I'm still laughing like a hyena. Dewey turned and ran down the dark hallway until he disappeared into the scary blackness. I knew what he was going to do. He was going to make me chase him and then jump out and scare me.

"Hey, don't leave me here!" I yelled, and then I ran after him.

It's pitch black and I can't see anything, so I listen to try to hear Dewey breathing. I hear a paper crinkle, so I step toward him. My stomach is so tight that it's cutting off my breath. I take another baby step and stick my hand out into the blackness.

"Gottcha!"

"AAAAAAAAAAAH!"

Dewey pulled me into the stairwell with him and wrapped his arms around me in an iron squeeze. We were both trying not to laugh too loud but that just made us laugh even harder. I liked his hug, it felt good; strong, but soft too.

"Let's take the stairs down, Cozy."

"Alright," I say, reaching for the railing, "but you go first. I can't see a thing."

I slid my hand down the banister so I could tell when the stairs ended. Dewey was right ahead of me saying, "More," each time a new set of stairs started. We finally made it back outside into the light, but we had to squint for a while because the sun was so bright.

"We got to make up some time," Dewey says, hoisting his bag back onto his shoulder and walking really fast up the big hill in front of us. I walked as fast as I could behind him. When he came to the top of the hill he waited for me to catch up and then we stopped so I could catch my breath.

"We still have a bunch of papers left to deliver," Dewey says, looking around like he was trying to figure something out.

"You want me to show you a good short cut?"

"Sure," I say, as long as I don't have to jump any fences.

"How about climbing a tree?" Dewey asks, grinning, because he knows how much I love to climb trees.

"For sure!"

I followed Dewey through a yard and down a little hill. There was a fence at the bottom of the hill and no other way out.

"I thought you said no fences?" I grumbled, ticked off because he lied to me.

"See that tree, Cozy?"

I looked past Dewey and spotted a short stubby tree with thick arms that stretched over the fence. But there was a problem. I had to jump out of the tree onto a garage roof and then jump off the roof to the ground.

"You're kidding me, right?" I said, folding my arms over my chest.

"What? I'll give you a boost up the tree, and then help you down off the roof."

"The roof's too high."

"It just looks too high, Cozy. I do this all the time."

"Wouldn't the street be faster?"

Dewey knew how to tick me off, so he screwed up his face and said, "Cozy, you're not turning chicken on me are you?"

"Help me up the tree!" I said, making my face hard so he couldn't tell that I was scared.

We made it through Dewey's stupid short cut. It wasn't as bad as I thought, and I felt kind of proud for doing it. There was one last hill to go down. It was all grass and ended at a stone wall. Dewey looked over at me and grinned. "Watch this!" He said, and then he tossed his paper sack down, got on the ground, and rolled all the way down the hill until he hit the stone wall.

I shouted down to him, "Are you alright?" But he didn't say anything back; he just peeked up at me, spread his arms and legs out and then stuck out his tongue like a dead dog.

"You...JERK!" I yelled, and then I laid down on the ground and crossed my arms over my chest and rolled. I could see the sky and the ground, the sky and the ground, and then I ran into Dewey and that soft donut belly.

"You got to play dead!" He said, pushing me back down when I tried to get up.

"Play dead?"

"Yeah, let's see if you can play dead."

"I can play dead," I told him. But I didn't tell him that I used to practice playing dead all the time. Ma used to put on classical records, and tell us to act out the music. The death scenes were my favorite.

"I have to start from standing up," I said, brushing off the grass and trying to clear my mind.

"Okay," Dewey said, waiting for my act to start.

I dropped to the ground, kind of slow, like a leaf falling from a tree. Then I made sure my arm fell across my face so he couldn't see my eyes blinking. I stayed on the ground trying not to breathe, or move, for a really long time. Finally I got bored and when I opened my eyes, Dewey was leaning over me staring.

"Man, that was great! Pretty clever the way you fell really slowly like a feather." I sat up and brushed some of the grass off of me. I could feel my face getting hot because he said I did well. Dewey plucked a little stick out of my hair and twisted it around his fingers. I could tell that he chewed his nails too, because he had little red spots where he bit them too short and they bled.

"So you want to get going?" I asked, thinking we should finish the route and get home. Dewey just sat there fiddling with that stick like he didn't hear me talking to him, then without looking at me he asked,

"Cozy, what do you think happens when we die?"

I tried to think up something good. I didn't want to screw up my clever streak, but nothing was coming so I just blurted out what Ma, and everyone else, always said about it.

"I don't know, I think maybe we go to heaven, like the priest says."

Dewey didn't say anything, and I felt kind of bad for giving him such a lame answer.

"Let's get out of here," he said, grabbing his bag. I ran behind him while we finished the route.

"We made $5.85 in tips," Dewey said, and then he handed me two bucks for helping him, but I didn't want to take that much so I said, "No way, just give me a dollar for cigs and candy. I really didn't do anything." But Dewey's eyes got small and his mouth pulled tight.

"You better take it or I won't let you help me no more."

I held out my hand for the money.

"Thanks Dewey."

"I got to get home," Dewey said, looking at the sun like it was a clock.

"Me too. Ken will have a cow if I'm late for supper."

Dewey walked me home without saying much more.

"Don't forget school starts Monday," I said, trying to make him talk to me. Dewey doesn't go to my school any more. He's in Jr. High now, but I reminded him anyway.

"Yeah, I know," he said, and then that was that. No more talking.

We got to my house and Dewey grabbed my hand and squeezed it.

"See ya later chicken shit."

"Wha? .....I jumped off the roof."

Dewey just laughed and ran away.

Ring Dings

School stunk today. Rosemarie was gone and so was Warren. And now that Dewey is in Jr. High, I don't get to hang around with him at recess either. Jimmy Elliot hung around with his new friends and didn't even look my way. Our new teacher, Mr. Cross, seems nice, but I think he's just trying to get on our good side. He looks like he has a mean streak with those shifty eyes, and skinny lips, like Ken's.

Phyllis Garrett was wearing a short dress with fishnet stockings. She looked so cute that Steven Swenson couldn't keep his eyes off of her. I don't care about him anymore. I like Dewey more than him anyways. Lots of girls had on fishnets or nylons. I got stuck wearing crappy ankle socks like a baby, and an old fashioned dress that used to be Diana's when she was little. Ma put some lace on the bottom of it, to make it longer, but it just looked dumb dumb dumb!

I sat by myself on the school steps at recess thinking about all kinds of stuff. I didn't want to hang around with anybody but Rosemarie, but fat chance of that because she moved and I didn't even get to say goodbye to her. She always knew what to say to me to make me feel better. Mr. Cross came by and asked why I wasn't playing with the other kids, so I told him I had a stomach ache and he left me alone.

At lunchtime I walked Tommy home. We have an hour to get home, eat, and walk back to school, but the new house is way closer to the school so it only took us a few minutes to get home. Ma and Ken were working so the house was really quiet, but Crumbs came running up to us, and even our cat Ranger seemed happy to see me because he kept mushing up against my legs.

There wasn't much in the fridge, so I made us each a ketchup sandwich. Tommy said he wasn't eating no ketchup sandwich and that he wanted some real food, so I left his on the counter and sat in front of the TV and ate mine. Pretty soon Tommy was sitting beside me munching down his ketchup sandwich. I could tell he liked it because he asked me to make him another one.

After lunch I went to lie down on my bed and smoke a butt. I tried blowing smoke rings like Diana, but all that came out were puffs of smoke like smoke signals. I picked up my doll Blabby and squeezed her stomach, to make her mouth open up, and then I stuck my cigarette in her mouth and then let go of her belly so her mouth shut down on the cigarette. She looked like a little wise guy with a butt in her mouth and I laughed out loud. It felt funny to laugh all by myself in an empty house and I wished that my sisters were home so I could show them how silly Blabby looked.

It was getting late but I didn't want to go back to school yet, so I sat on the steps for a while to kill time until I had to go back to school. Tommy sat with me for a while but then he saw Jimmy walking with some other big boys so he took off with them. I didn't care. Ever since Jimmy made friends with those new kids he acts like he doesn't even know me anymore.

The sun felt good on my face, so I closed my eyes and tried to pretend that I was back sitting on the curb in front of my old house. It was easy to pretend because the birds sounded the same as my old neighborhood, and so did the car noises. I kept wanting to peek, because I felt like somebody might be watching me, but I made myself keep my eyes shut. I pictured Rosemarie coming down the street, with her twinkly eyes smiling at me, and then sitting next to me and not saying anything at all. I really felt her there, and I wondered if she was thinking about me at that same moment.

I think I would have fallen asleep if it hadn't been for somebody tapping me on the shoulder. It scared the crap out of me and I almost jumped off the steps. I looked up and all I could see was a big head shadow because of the sun in my eyes and all, but then when I heard that Disney voice say, "What's up little chick?" I could tell that it was Alex, but stupid me couldn't find my words and my stomach turned to jelly.

He acted like everything was normal and planted his butt right next to mine on the steps for everyone in the world to see. I was so glad that Ken wasn't home but I was still afraid that he might come back and catch me talking to him.

"Well?" he said.

I told him nothing was up and that I had to go to school or I'd be late. I didn't really want to leave, but I didn't tell him that. I wanted to sit with him all day and tell him about my dream and about Ken saying he was going to shoot him.

Alex's voice got small, like he was afraid he might scare me away, and he looked at me, like he could see into my head and already knew all about that stuff.

"Did you get into trouble for talking to me the other day?"

I didn't know what to tell him. I didn't want to hurt his feelings by saying that Ken hated his guts, so I lied and told him that I only got into a little trouble; but I didn't look at him when I said it.

"Ah." He said, and then we both just sat there saying nothing, like Rosemarie and me used to do.

I wanted to be his friend, even if Ken hated him, so I forced myself to say, "I still want to talk to you though." My voice sounded like it wasn't mine, too high and squeaky, like a scared mouse or something.

But he didn't seem to care because he said, "Me too," and then he told me that I better get going before I was late for school.

That was the best part of my day. I went back to school and while I was there I told Mr. Cross that I needed to use the girl's room. He figured I was still having a stomach ache so he let me go, but I didn't have to go at all. Instead, I sat in the stall and smoked a cigarette, and then I went back to class. Nobody knew what I was up to. I like being by myself, doing what I want. The kids at school act like little kids; they don't know anything about cool stuff.

I'm glad that school's over today, plus I have vacuuming this week instead of dishes. I'm going do my vacuuming now and then head out the door after supper. Vacuuming isn't too hard because you don't have to do anything but push it around the rug. Most of our floors are wood except for the parlor and Tommy's room. The kitchen has linoleum, and whoever sets the table has to sweep that floor.

I lugged out the big clunky vacuum cleaner, and the hose kept getting tangled on stuff, so I hung it around my neck like a boa constrictor and carried it into the parlor.

"Not now!" Diana yelled, when she saw me coming. "We're watching TV in here!"

Grrrr....stupid Diana wasn't gonna let me vacuum. I didn't bother arguing with her because she always wins. Tommy was in there with her but he didn't dare say anything about it because he's just a squirt. He's lucky he has Diana in there with him or I'd be vacuuming right now. I piled the cleaner into the corner and stomped out the door, walking toward the wall to get away from everyone.

Ma will be coming home soon so I figured I'd sit on the wall and wait for her to come walking down the hill. I don't like Ma working. She's gone all the time and is always tired when she gets home; plus I don't see her that much because she goes into the bedroom to watch TV with Ken right after supper.

I wonder if Ma misses me like I miss her. Sometimes I stare at her and concentrate on how crappy I feel about her marrying Ken, thinking maybe she might be able to read my mind, and feel what I feel. But she doesn't ever get it. She just sits there in her own little world.

One time I was thinking, "Leave Ken" as hard as I could, but instead of leaving Ken she planted a big kiss on him when he came into the room, and then Ken looked over at me and winked, like he knew what I was up to. I wonder if he's using some kind of mind control on Ma because she never used to let anyone hurt us, not even a little. She would get really mad if any of her adult friends even yelled at us, but now she doesn't notice us at all, not unless we're bleeding or something bad like that.

I spotted Ma coming down the hill and ran to catch up with her. She had her arms full of stuff, so I grabbed one of the bags out her hands.

"Thanks, Cozy."

"How was work, Ma?"

"Work was work. Is the house clean?"

I swallowed hard because I didn't figure she'd ask me that.

"Mostly, I just have to vacuum. Diana wouldn't let me because she was watching TV."

Ma made a little noise, like a hum, but not a happy hum, and then her smile shrunk and her face got flat looking. I was trying to think of something to say to cheer her up, and maybe get her smile to come back, but all I could come up with was that I'd help her cook supper, so I gave it a try.

"I can help with supper!"

"Don't bother," she said, with the same flat face, "You'd be more of a hindrance than a help."

"No sir, I can peel potatoes."

Ma sucked her front teeth and her eyes opened wide. I knew she was about to blast me.

"No! You can vacuum like you were supposed to do."

"But Diana...."

"Who's your mother, Diana or me?"

"You, but Diana likes to act like she's my mother because you're never around."

Ma stopped right in the middle of the road and stared at me. Her face turned red and twisted, and I was glad that her hands were full of bags, because I could tell that she wanted to smack me good.

"You smart-mouthed little shit!"

"Wha?"

"Shut your mouth!"

I could feel my eyes filling up. I really did it now. I ran ahead to the house, dropped her bag on the kitchen table, and then headed for my room so I could cry alone. I plopped down on my bed, but my stupid doll was there, under the covers, and she jabbed into my side.

"Stupid doll! Stupid, stupid, doll!"

I grabbed Blabby by the leg, and looked at her. She looked the same, all innocent and cute, but I didn't care, so I threw her across the room and yelled, "I HATE YOU!"

I watched her fly through the air, hit the dresser and land on the floor face down. Something inside of me shrunk up seeing her lying face down on the floor like that. It was like she was really my baby and part of me wanted to pick her up and make her feel better, but the other part of me that was mad at Ma yelled, "I HOPE I BROKE YOU!" and then I climbed under the covers.

I was crying hard and I could see my face in my head, like I was watching myself in the mirror. My lips looked blubbery and stretched out, and drool was stringing down my chin. My eyes were squinted shut so tight that I had old lady wrinkles around them. I kept crying but it didn't feel real anymore. It felt fake because I could see it all in my head. I felt stupid and mad, so I stopped crying and just laid there under the covers trying to think of places I could go if I ran away.

I figured I could forget Uncle Richie. He doesn't give a crap about me anymore. Meme would just hand me back over to Ma and Ken. Dewey could hide me in his shed for a while, but it would be too cold in the winter, plus his shed stinks like moldy dirt. I couldn't think of anyone else who would want me.

Maybe Alex would if he knew me better. I could hide in his apartment, like that girl who hid in the attic from the Nazis, Anne Frank. But people brought her food all the time and she read books and stuff. I bet he has plenty of room for me. I could eat Ring Dings and he could teach me how to paint. I bet he would understand if I told him about everything...Ken and all the stuff he does to me at night, and Ma not sticking up for me. But Ken would shoot him for sure and maybe me too. There's no safe place anywhere and nothing I can do about anything.

I wished that I could tell Ma about Ken but it was way too late for that. She would die if I told her now. And what would happen to Janice and Diana if I ran away? What if Ken started in on them because I wasn't around any more for him mess with? It would be all my fault. So I can't run away. I'm stuck living here forever.

I stayed under the covers because I was all worn out. No more tears, just me feeling bad for Blabby and myself. I want Ma to be sorry for what she did to me, so I figure if I stay in my room, and don't eat supper, maybe she'll feel bad and say that she's sorry for being so mean to me.

I picked up a comic book and Richie Rich was staring back at me. He was sitting in a huge golden car with dollar sign headlights. He has so much money, that I bet he could buy the Empire State Building if he wanted to. I flipped through the pages, but I wasn't reading much because my brain was still filled up with Ma yelling at me. I heard someone coming so I ducked under the covers, but it was only Janice. She stuck her head under the covers with me and said, "Ma said to get your butt out there and vacuum the floors."

Having to go back out there and vacuum was not part of my plan, but I knew better than to ignore Ma. I pulled the vacuum cleaner around the parlor rug, sucking up all the dirt, and Ma walked in, but I kept my head down so I wouldn't have to look at her. If I looked at her eyes I knew I'd smile because I can't stay mad at her. She snapped, "Don't forget to do under the couch!" I growled to myself but kept working. Pulling the couch away from the wall I cringed. Socks, cups, candy wrappers, tipped over ashtrays, EVERYTHING was under there, and it was all wrapped up in dog hair. I sorted through all the trash and threw everything away except for the ashtrays and cups. I didn't care whose socks they were because they were all crusty anyways.

I finished my chores and headed out the door. I didn't want to go back to my room because it was too easy for Ma to find me there and give me extra stuff to do, so I walked down toward High Street where all the hippies hung out. Ma doesn't allow us to go there, but I don't give a crap what Ma allows right now. I've seen the hippies and they don't seem so bad. They dress weird but they seem nice, smiling and saying peace and stuff.

I turned the corner onto High Street and spotted a group of hippies hanging around on the steps of a red apartment building. I was thinking of going the other way, but that would lead to downtown, and it has way too many hills, so I kept walking right past all the hippies. They all looked up at me, like I was their own little parade, and one guy with long wavy hair and sunglasses smiled at me and said, "Hey man... what's happening?" I smiled, but I didn't look at him, and I walked as fast as I could past them.

I got to the store but I didn't know where to go next. It was late and supper would be ready soon, so I figured I'd hang around outside the High Street Spa for a while.

I saw a bus coming and I looked away so the driver wouldn't try to pick me up. The bus stopped anyways to let an old lady off, but I kept standing there looking down at the ground until the bus doors closed and it drove away.

"Whatcha up to Cozy?"

I jumped and looked up. Alex was standing there smiling at me. He had a small bag in one hand and a cigarette in the other. I was so glad to see him, because I felt like I was kind of stuck in front of the store, so I smiled and said, "Nothing, just taking a walk."

Alex looked over at the hippies and then at me. I could tell he was trying to figure something out.

"You mind if I walk home with you?"

I wanted him to walk home with me but I was kind of scared that Ken might spot us together, so I figured if we went home the back way Ken wouldn't catch us. I looked up at Alex and said,

"Sure, but I'm going home the long way. I need some fresh air."

Alex's eyebrows squished together, like what I said was silly, and he said, "The long way?" I could tell that he didn't know which way the long way was so I told him that we had to go up Reed Street, to Ralph's store, and then down Kelly to our street.

"Ah!" Alex said, "The long way."

"Yeah, that's the way I'm going."

"Okay, you lead the way."

I walked as fast as I could so I could get us off High Street. There were too many cars driving by and Ken's car could be one of them, but once we hit Reed Street I slowed down my walking. I could hear Alex digging into his little bag so I looked over to see what he had. It was another pack of Ring Dings.

"So, you want a Ring Ding?" he asked when he caught me peeking at him.

"Is that all you eat?"

"Do you want one? I'm having one."

He tore open the package and handed one over to me.

"Thanks," I said. The hard chocolate shell was smooth, like a blackboard, and I could see a little dot of white on the side. I gave the white spot a lick and then bit into it.

Alex gave me a shove and said, "That's not how you eat a Ring Ding! This is how you do it." He bent his head back, as far as it could go, and then he opened his mouth wide and slowly pushed the Ring Ding into his mouth. His mouth wasn't big enough and the chocolate shell broke apart, like ice on a puddle, and dropped onto his face and shirt, but he didn't seem to care much because he kept cramming it into his mouth. He got it all in there too, and now he was plucking all the little pieces of chocolate off of his shirt and face and shoving them into his mouth.

He looked over and started poking and pointing for me to try it too. He couldn't talk because of all that chocolate in his mouth so he kept poking and pointing until I said, "OKAY ALREADY!"

I tipped my head back and opened up wide; my hand looked like a giant claw above my face, and reminded me of one of those cranes they use to tear down buildings. Slowly, I dropped my hand, stuffing the Ring Ding into my mouth while it squished all over my face. Alex was standing over me saying, "Keep going, keep going," until the whole thing was gone. I couldn't talk around all that chocolate cake either, but Alex was laughing his butt off.

"You should see your face!"

I touched my face and it was gooey with chocolate. I even had Ring Ding up my nose. I started giggling harder and harder, and then I snorted, like a pig, and little pieces of Ring Ding flew everywhere. I tried to swallow and laugh but laughing took over, and I was still holding all that Ring Ding in my mouth, and then "oh no!" I squatted down and stuck my heel in my crotch; I could feel the pee right at the door. Alex was staring at me; he could tell what I was up to, so he tried to tickle me. I couldn't do anything to stop him because I was weak from laughing and still crouched down trying not to pee. We were laughing like fools, but we didn't care because laughing was more important to us than what anyone who lived on Reed Street thought of us.

Alex grabbed my hands and pulled me back up onto my feet. I knew if I looked at him I would start laughing again so I walked for a while without saying too much. I kept thinking about Alex's goofy Ring Ding face, and me snorting in front of him, and how much fun it was to laugh so hard. I forgot all about Ma's sour mood because laughing with Alex erased it, and when I get home I'm going to make up with her. I don't even notice Alex's long hair anymore, or his stupid scarf. I think Ma would love him, and Ken would like Alex too if he gave him a chance.

We got to the corner of Kelly and Reed streets and I knew it was almost time to make a cut from Alex. I could see my house way down the road but I didn't feel like going home yet, so I started walking slower. Alex must have noticed me stalling because he gave me a little push and asked, "You okay?"

I didn't answer Alex right away because I felt like if I started talking I might never stop. I wanted to tell him everything...even the Ken stuff, but I knew if I did I'd start bawling like a baby, so I just said, "Yeah, I'm fine," and kept walking. Alex put his hand behind my neck and squished it a little but he didn't say anything back.

I figured Ken might be pulling up soon so I told Alex that I didn't want to be late for supper and that I'd see him later. Alex winked at me and said, "Get going," He let me get way ahead of him before he started walking again. I ran as fast as I could all the way home, just so it wouldn't look like me and Alex were together.

> *Dear Diary,*
> *Sorry it took me so long to write in you but now I'm ready. I had a blast with "A" today. He's a lot of fun and I feel like I can say anything to him. Some day I'm going to see what his apartment looks like. I bet it's full of paintings and art stuff. Besides Dewey, A's my next best friend. "A" is cute once you get to know him. Dewey and A are definitely in my tribe.*
> *Okay, I'm bored now so goodbye for today.*

I locked my diary and stuffed it under my mattress. Janice came in and stood in front of the mirror to brush her hair. She could see me watching her and made a goofy face at me, so I made one back at her and we both started laughing.

She's starting to get boobs but I don't tell her that because she's always looking at herself in the mirror sideways, trying to see if they poke out yet. They don't really poke out that much, but when she wears her triple A padded bra they look bigger. I'm jealous because she got a head start on me. Being the baby stinks.

Today Tommy is eating lunch at Grammy Green's and she's making his favorite, tomato soup with macaroni in it. She didn't invite me so I'm heading home to eat whatever I can scrounge up. I don't think Grammy Green likes me anymore. She's been acting weird ever since Ma married her son, Ken, and now she only talks to me when she wants me to run to the store for her. The old bird can go crap in a hat for all I care.

I turned the corner and spotted Ken's Cadillac parked in front of the house. "Nuts." I forgot that he was working nights this week. I stood there like a scarecrow. I didn't want to be home alone with Ken so I pushed myself toward the wall, to stall, so I could make another plan. I was thinking of sitting on the wall for my whole lunch break, but I'm really hungry, so I'll just run in, grab some food, and run out. By the time Ken hears me I'll be long gone.

I snuck around to the back porch to look in the window, just to make sure Ken wasn't in the kitchen. I couldn't see him in there, but Crumbs saw me peeking in at her, and started barking and making a racket. Crap. I walked into the house normal, because the stupid dog gave me away. Ken was in the pantry rinsing out his lunch dishes.

"You're late," he said, without looking up from the sink. I pulled on the fridge door, and started digging for something to eat. There was no more milk so I couldn't have a bowl of cereal, which I was dying for.

"There's no bread or milk, Cozy."

I cringe every time he calls me Cozy because I never gave him permission to call me that.

"What am I supposed to eat then?" I mumbled, slamming the refrigerator door shut.

"Eat some crackers and peanut butter."

He was trying to be nice; I could tell because he didn't get mad at me for slamming the fridge door. He walked toward me jingling the change in his pockets, and said, "How about I give you some money so you can go to Franks and get something there?"

I was stuck between him and the refrigerator. I could feel him twitching, like he does when he touches me, and I knew what was going to happen next. I tried to squeeze past him, and laughed, like it was a joke so I wouldn't tick him off, but he held me there with his chest, and his fingers started crawling all over me like spiders.

I sat on the school steps chewing on the Slim Jim I bought at Franks. I was trying hard not to think about Ken and me so I was counting the kids in the schoolyard to make the time go by faster until the bell rang. I didn't like talking to any of them anymore, and I hoped they wouldn't bug me. I bet they all had regular lunches in houses with no one pawing at them.

I felt like I had stains all over my soul. It was probably black by now, and I wondered if people could see how dirty my soul was by looking into my eyes. Ma says that the eyes are like a window to your soul. If Ma looked into my soul window she would fall apart and probably hate me forever.

Phyllis Garrett bounced over looking all chipper and cute. The wind kept blowing her hair into the Tootsie Roll pop that she was sucking on, and I was glad. She looked down at me and said, "We're having a math test this afternoon," like it was a big news flash or something. "So what," I said, and then I turned my head away, like I just spotted something more important to look at. Phyllis got the hint and walked away mumbling something about me being too touchy.

The rest of the day went by way too slow. I couldn't stop thinking about all the stuff that goes on at my house, and I was trying to figure out how to get away from it someday.   Mr. Cross caught me with my head down on my desk and yelled at me to pick it up. I told him that I had another stomach-ache, but he didn't buy it this time, and he made me sit up and pay attention to the math test. I heard Phyllis Garrett snicker when I got yelled at and it made me want to hide under my desk...and punch her in the face. I asked if I could go to the girl's room but he told me to wait until after school. I don't like Mr. Cross anymore.

Bad Habit

I should have worn a coat because the wind is whipping through my sweater and I'm freezing. Dewey isn't even wearing a sweater, but he said that he doesn't get cold until December. He had to bring his little sister Tina collecting with us today because his mom and dad went grocery shopping and they didn't want any kids tagging along.

Anyway, I like Tina; she's so cute with all those blond curls around her face. She was sitting in the wagon, on top of the newspapers, and Dewey was doing all the pulling. I asked to pull her too but he wouldn't let me.

"You can stay here with Tina while I deliver the papers."

I nodded okay, and looked down at Tina. She was watching Dewey walk away and her happy mouth melted into a pitiful pout, and tears started bubbling up on her eyelashes. I didn't want her to cry, because then Dewey would think that I didn't know how to take care of kids, so I stooped down to talk to her.

Her nose was running a little and her cheeks were all rosy from the cold. She had a coat on, but it was kind of small for her.

I felt bad for her being the baby and having to wear all those crappy hand-me-downs. I put my face a little closer to hers but she pulled back and stared at me like she was trying to decided if she liked me or not. I figured I'd play peek-a-boo with her, because that's what Ma used to do with us when we were little.

Tina watched me doing peek-a-boo but she wasn't saying anything. I kept on peek-a-booing, because I didn't know what else to do, and finally her eyes crinkled and she grinned at me. Tina said "peek-a-boo" right back, and then she smiled showing her tiny Chiclet teeth. Me and Tina played peek-a-boo for a while and then we switched to pat-a-cake. After a while she got bored with those games so I hiked her up on my back and gave her a piggyback ride. We were both cracking up, and I felt proud because I got her to like me. Dewey came out and spotted us goofing off so he plopped Tina in the wagon, and then he tried giving me a piggyback ride.

I was hanging lopsided off his back, dragging my foot on the ground. My shoe popped off but Dewey kept going around and around.

"My shoe! My shoe!" I yelled, and Tina ran and grabbed it, and then she started hitting Dewey on the leg with it saying, "Leave her alone!" He let me down and I stuck my shoe back on. Then Dewey picked Tina up and planted a big one on her cheek. She wrapped her arms around his neck and put her head on his shoulder like he was her dad. Dewey carried Tina, and I finally got to pull the wagon. It was heavy with papers, but I didn't care because I wanted to prove to Dewey that I could do it too.

We finished up with collecting and Dewey paid me my two bucks and said, "Let's go to High Street Spa for a hot chocolate." It sounded good to me. I'd buy some cigs too. Dewey told me to get in the wagon with Tina so I squished in and put Tina between my legs and then Dewey pulled us all the way to High Street without resting once.

There were no hippies on the steps today; I guess it was too cold for them. When we got inside the store the heat felt extra good, like a warm snuggly blanket. We sat on the shiny round stools and put Tina on the one between us. She kept saying "spin me, spin me," so Dewey and me took turns spinning her like a top.

The hot chocolate finally came, piled high with extra whipped cream, and I slid my spoon in on the side so I wouldn't mess up the whipped cream mountain. Filling my spoon, I sipped off it, trying to make it last as long as I could.

Tina had to sit up on her knees to drink hers while Dewey held her stool still so she wouldn't spin around. He told her to blow on her spoonful of hot chocolate before she sipped it, and then he leaned over to show her how. Seeing Dewey being so sweet to Tina made me like him more than ever.

I knew that Dewey and Tina were going to go home a different way than me because I live up this end of High Street and they live down the other end of it. I wouldn't want to live at their house because it's too crowded, and dirty, but at least they don't fight all the time like we do. I don't want to live at my house either though, so maybe some day Dewey and me will get our own house, and Tina can even live with us if she wants to.

On my way home I walked in the gutter kicking through the dead leaves. I liked the sound they made when I crunched through them, and all their different colors reminded me of candy apples and pumpkin pie. The trees still had tons of leaves on them, and I couldn't wait for them to fall so I could make a huge pile and jump into them. We used to do that all the time. Diana might think she's too big for jumping into leaves now, but I bet Janice and Tommy will still do it with me.

I spotted my house at the top of the hill, watching it get bigger and bigger as I walked toward it. I didn't feel like going home. I would stay away forever if I had somewhere else to go, and I could take Ma and my sisters with me. I ducked between two houses to smoke a cig and plopped my butt down on the cold cement walkway. Lighting up, I daydreamed about running away, but no matter how hard I tried I couldn't figure out where I could go.

I always ended up with a rock in my stomach because I'd miss Ma and my sisters too much.

I flicked my ashes and stared into the red-hot cigarette head. I could see a smiling devil's face looking back at me. I flicked the face away and took another long drag; it went down deep into my lungs and came out light, like half the smoke stayed in there, filling up all the empty spaces inside of me.

"It's a bad habit." I said out loud, to nobody but me.

I'm a Bum

"I forgot to buy the pumpkin," Ken said, "But you kids are too big for that kind of stuff anyway."

He's always making excuses for ruining our fun. All he had to do was remember to get one stupid pumpkin and he couldn't even do that. Nobody seemed to care but me because they were all busy fixing up their costumes for trick-or-treat tonight. We always carved a pumpkin, stuck a candle in it, and then put it out on the front stoop after dark. Ma dries out the seeds in the oven, and put lots of salt on them, and then she makes us hot chocolate to wash them down with. My mouth started watering just thinking about it, but so did my eyes. Crap.

I headed to my room to find a Halloween costume. We're all going out together. Janice is going to be a flesh-eating zombie, Diana said that she wasn't dressing up but she'll wear a cowboy hat and go with us for a little while. Tommy is Superman. He got to wear his costume to school today for his class party, and now he has chocolate stains all down the front of his big red "S". He's been flying around the house since he got home from school and if he jumps on my bed one more time I'm going to break his little neck.

"How do I look?"

I stared at Janice and forced myself to look amazed. Her face was dead man white, and she used Ma's red lipstick for blood, but it didn't look much like blood; it looked like messy clown make-up. Big red lips, red cheeks...jeesh. I lie. "You look good...scary."

"Oh goody, I want to scare the crap out of the little kids tonight. What are you going to be, Cozy?"

"You'll see," I tell her, like it's a big secret, but I really don't know what I'm going to be. Ma used to always make our costumes. One year I was the scarecrow from the Wizard of Oz, and I looked just like him. Ma's not even home from work yet, and when she does come home she's going to be too tired to care about Halloween.

I stood in the closet looking at all the clothes. Some were hanging but most of them were in piles on the floor. What a mess. I headed back to my bed and turned on my radio, but nothing happened. I felt my breath cut off…my radio is broken! I turned it off and on again and still nothing. Shit! I stomped over to Diana's room with my radio in my hand. She was in front of the mirror fixing her cowboy hat so that it sat perfectly on top of her head. "What?" She asked, without bothering to look at me. I don't know how she does that…knows who's standing there without looking. Ma does it too. "My radio won't work," I tell her, and then I stand there, like a dummy, waiting for the Queen of Sheba to fix everything. Diana sucked her teeth at me and stuck her hand out: "Let me see it." I handed it over and waited. She popped the back off and unplugged my battery, then opened her dresser draw, pulled out her radio and switched batteries. Click…."You're listening to WKAF where you hear all of the hits all of the time!" …Click.

"Dead battery. You can use mine but you got to buy me a new one."

"Thanks! I love you!" I went to give her a hug but she backed up because she was worried about me messing up her hat, so I made myself disappear before I ticked her off and she asked for her battery back.

Ma came home smiling and joking with us like she used to do. Her hair is short now. She says she cut it because it was too hard to manage, what with work and all, but she looks different to me, kind of old and faded. Everyone was showing off their costumes to her and laughing.

Ma fixed Janice's bloody face to look better and then rubbed the spots off of Tommy's "S" with a wet dishtowel. "There that's better," she said, and then she turned him around and gave him a little "go away" push. I noticed her looking at me. I took a deep breath because I could tell that it was my turn to get fixed up.

"What are you going as, Cozy?"

"I don't know yet."

Ma stared at me, not mean staring, just thinking staring. Finally she smiled and said, "I've got it. You can be a bum!"

"A bum?"

"Yeah, you know, too lazy to work, dirty, holey clothes. A bum." Ma was smiling like she just invented the yoyo. I didn't want to hurt her feelings so I smiled along with her.

"I'll be right back," she said. "I'm going to go grab some of Ken's old clothes."

For crying out loud, why do I have to be a stinky ole bum? The kids are going to tease the crap out of me. Ma was back in a minute with a plaid flannel shirt and some gray pants.

"Here put these on," she said, tossing them at me without asking if I even liked them. I put them right over my own clothes and she buttoned and zipped me into them. My pants kept falling down so Ma said, "I need a rope, Janice." Janice looked my way, and I could tell that she felt sorry for me. She gave me a big shaky smile and said, "That looks great Cozy. I'll go get you a rope belt out of the shed."

Ma rubbed some black make-up on my face, for dirt, and then half tucked my shirt in. Janice handed her a filthy piece of old clothesline rope and Ma tied it around my waist.

"There, all done! Go look in my big mirror." I headed into Ma's room with her right on my tail. Ken was lying on the bed reading the newspaper so Ma cleared her throat and said, "Honey, look at Cozy. Doesn't she look cute?"

He dropped the paper a little, so he could see over it. I could tell that he wanted to laugh at me, so I just stood there waiting.

Finally he went back to looking at his paper and asked, "What is she, a slob?"

"No silly, she's a bum."

"What's the difference?"

Ma didn't say anything back to him and steered me over to the big mirror so I could get a look at myself. I looked stupid... dirty and stupid. Ma was waiting for me to say something nice but I couldn't talk because of the big lump in my throat.

"Don't you like it Cozy?"

I swallowed the lump and said, "Yeah, its great Ma. I love it." I was praying that she believed me because I didn't want her good mood to go sour. Ma squished me into her, giving me an extra long hug, then pushed me off and said, "Good! Then all done!"

"C'MON YOU GUYS LET'S HIT KELLY STREET FIRST!" Janice's loud mouth made me jump. She took off ahead of us running with her empty pillowcase flopping around behind her like a baby ghost. Tommy yelled out to Janice, "Ma said to stay together." But Janice kept on running and hollered back, "Well hurry up then, you nitwit!"

"I'm not running," Diana said, dragging on her cigarette then handing it over to me. I could tell that she wanted me to stay with her because she was sharing her cigarette, and didn't even tell me not to get it wet. I wanted to stay with her, but I wanted to get more candy than Janice. I hung back with Diana while Tommy ran to catch up with Janice, and then I watched them until they disappeared into a three-decker.

Diana flicked her cigarette up into the air. I watched it, like a little rocket in the black sky, going up up up and then falling back down, exploding on the street with orange sparks spraying everywhere. There were lots of little kids out running from house to house. It was hard to tell what they were in the dark, but I did recognize Casper, and Sylvester the cat.

Tommy and Janice came running out of the three-decker giggling like monkeys. Tommy hollered over to us, "Hippies live in there! Honest to God hippies! We saw them!"

Diana shushed him and said, "For crying out loud, shut up or they'll hear you."

"So what," Tommy said, digging in his bag for a piece of candy.

"So, they're people too, Stupid," Diana spat, and then she put her hands on her hips like she was daring him to say something else. I was hoping that Tommy would keep his trap shut, but I guess he was feeling brave all dressed up like Superman, and he answered Diana back.

"Nu-uh. Dad said that they're all draft dodging cowards."

Pushing her hat up, so that Tommy could see her evil eyes, she hissed, "Well, Your dad is an ASSHOLE!"

Tommy stopped chomping on whatever it was he had shoved into his mouth and looked up at Diana with big round eyes. I could tell that he didn't know what to say to that one. Diana was standing there just waiting for him to mouth off again. But Tommy didn't dare say another word about it. Janice pulled on his Superman cape and said, "Let's go to the brown house, Tommy." He followed her, shuffling his feet through the dead leaves. I could tell that he was still carrying Diana's words around inside of him.

Me and Diana started walking again. Lighting up another cigarette, she said: "It's a good thing he's gone, or I might have smacked the shit out of him." I didn't say a word but I knew that Diana was really mad at Ken for all the trouble he's been causing her, and not Tommy.

Diana quit trick or treating early, saying that it was just for ninnies. Janice and me brought Tommy around to a bunch of houses before we dropped him off at home, and then Ma let us go back out without him. I could see the light on in Alex's apartment and wondered if we should try trick or treating there. Maybe I would get to see his apartment.

"Hey Janice," I said, trying to sound bored so she wouldn't think that something was up, "did you do that house yet?"

"That's Alex's house."

"Duh, so what. It's a house with C A N D Y." I said, hoping she would take my bait.

Janice stood there thinking, like it was a matter of life or death, so I ran ahead and climbed the stairs onto the porch. The door was cracked open, but I rang the bell anyways and a few seconds later Old Lady Harris showed up. She lives on the first floor and looks kind of like a penguin with that pointy honker of hers, and her big wide chest. She came over to our house one day and told on Diana for smoking. Ma was fuming, and told her that Diana had permission to smoke. After Mrs. Harris left, Ma said that she was nothing but a nosey old bird who spent all of her time sticking her big pointy nose into everyone else's business. I bet she watches Alex like a hawk because of him being a hippie and all.

Mrs. Harris had a little table set up in the hall with a bowl of apples on it, but there was no candy in sight. Janice pushed in beside me and said: "Trick or treat!" so I just held up my bag with hers while Old Lady Harris dropped an apple bomb on top of all my candy bars—CARUNCH! I hate getting apples.

I tried scooting around Mrs. Harris, but she blocked me with her barrel belly and said:

"There's nobody home on the second floor." Then she stood there staring at me without blinking. She had a look in her eyes like she was guarding Fort Knox, but she wasn't getting rid of me that easy.

"So what," I said, standing up tall like I meant it, "We're going to the top floor... not the second floor." Mrs. Harris still didn't blink, but her lips started moving: "No you're not. He doesn't give out candy."

Grrrrrrrrr.... Who made her the boss of Alex? I wanted to pop the old bird in the head with her cruddy apple for butting in. I've been dying to see Alex's apartment, and there was no way I was going to let this nosey old biddy stop me. So, I stirred up a big fat lie, and let her have it.

"Alex told us we could trick or treat at his house. He's waiting for us." Ha ha, she didn't see that one coming. Old Lady Harris's face got scrambled, like she dropped a bucket of marbles on the ground and couldn't decide which one to pick up first. I grabbed Janice's hand and flew past her, running all the way up to the third floor.

When we got to Alex's apartment my heart was dancing in my chest.

"Well big shot," Janice said, hiding behind me, all ready to run, "knock on the stupid door."

"Alright already, I was just catching my breath."

I tapped on the tall white door with the tip of my finger and waited, but nothing happened. I could hear Janice sucking her teeth at me, and I was about to tap on it again but Janice pushed me aside and rapped on the door with her big clunky fist. It sounded too loud, like we were the cops or something.

"Oh shit!" I turned to run down the stairs. Janice was already out of sight, but then I heard Mr. Disney voice say, "Trick or treating?"

I felt prickles on the back of my neck heading down my arms. I told myself to act normal, wiped the fear off my face, and then I turned to look up at him. He looked ten feet tall at the top of the stairs, and he was smirking at me; like he caught me doing something rotten.

"Hmm?"

"Yeah, we're trick or treating."

"We?"

I was going to ring Janice's chicken neck for this one.

"I guess my sister changed her mind."

"Well, I don't have any candy but I do have some Ring Dings." Alex smiled big, showing all his pretty teeth, and I could smell something good in his house. Not cooking or anything like that, more like paint, and that spicy stuff he wears on his face.

"C'mon in."

He held the door open for me so I slipped past him. I was in his kitchen... sort of. There was stuff all over the counters in neat little piles. But not regular kitchen stuff, like we have at our house; there were books, paints, pencils, and bottles with candles sticking out of them. There was neat stuff everywhere. Alex opened the oven and pulled out a package of Ring Dings. I could see other stuff in the oven too: bread, peanut butter, and those powdery white donuts in a box. I couldn't believe it! Ha!

Alex dangled a package of Ring Dings over my pillowcase and said, "Well?" I opened it up so he could drop it in there, but he didn't, he just stood there looking at me, like he was waiting for something.

"Aren't you going to say it?" he asked.

"Thank you?"

Alex laughed at me and dropped the package in.

"No silly. Trick or treat!"

"Oh. Sorry."

I could feel my face burning again; duh...I'm so slow sometimes.

"Trick or treat."

Alex rubbed the top of my head and said: "So what are you supposed to be? No... wait a sec, don't tell me." He stood back and studied me, squinting like he was stuck on a test. I hated my stupid costume and wished that I hadn't come up to see him. Finally his face got soft and he said: "Ah, I got it.... You're some kind of a tramp, or a bum."

"I can't believe you got it! Everyone else was calling me a slob."

Alex tapped the side of his head and winked at me, and there went my stupid face turning all red again. He headed for another room and said: "You want to crash for a while?"

"Huh?"

"Sit down, hang out, you know...visit?"

I do, I do, I do, but my mouth had to say: "I can't. Janice is waiting for me."

"Oh, okay then, maybe some other time."

I nodded and turned to leave. He opened the door and out I went.

"Thanks for the Ring Dings."

"Do you remember how to eat them?"

"Yup...whole."

"You got it!"

I walked down the stairs without looking back. I knew Alex was still standing there because I didn't hear the door shut yet, and I could feel him smiling at me. I was in heaven. He has the best apartment ever, and he invited me to come back and see him. I'm not telling Janice anything about it, though, because I don't want her trying to hang out with Alex. I want him all for myself.

Janice was waiting by the front steps for me and she looked like she was about to pop with questions.

"What took you so long?"

"Nothing."

"Did he let you in?"

"Yeah."

"What's his apartment look like?"

"It's okay."

"What'd he say?"

"Nothing much, he just gave me a pack of Ring Dings."

"Lucky duck, I should have stayed with you. I love Ring Dings."

We got back to the house with tons of candy. Old Lady Harris's apple bomb crushed a Nestles Crunch, and Hershey bar, but that was all. I chucked the apple out my bedroom window and then counted my candy.

Diana came into our room, all smiley and happy, but I knew she was only prowling around looking for handouts. She sat on my bed and picked up a Peanut Butter Cup.

"Oh, these are my favorite," she said, but this was her way of asking for it, without asking for it. I told her she could have it and then I handed her a Milky Way too. Next she was at Janice's bed pulling the same sneaky crap. She should have gone Trick or Treating herself so she could have her own candy. Janice gave her a few candy bars and then she finally left.

Janice and me traded off a few things until we each had our favorites. She tried hard to get my Ring Dings but I held onto them.

The door opened again but this time it was Ken. His eyes got stuck on my candy so I knew he was going to want some.

"You going to share some of that with your old man?"

"Sure," I said, "what do you want?"

He didn't say what he wanted, instead he started taking stuff. First he grabbed a Baby Ruth, one of my favorites, and then he snagged my Ring Dings. My hand wanted to snatch them back, but Ken stopped and looked at me. He was waiting for me to say something, but I didn't. I just let him take whatever he wanted so he would leave.

"Thanks, Kiddo," he said, and then he rolled his eyes around like an idiot and said, "Now go wash that crap off your faces and get to bed."

I put the rest of my candy back in my pillowcase and stuffed it under my bed. Then I went to wash all the make-up off of my face. When I got back Janice was still munching away at her candy, so I clicked off my lamp and climbed into bed.

Lucky Cat

I'm eleven, but it's no big deal. Nobody came to my birthday tonight except my regular family, and it wasn't even a real party because I didn't even get to finish my birthday cake. Last year was better, with Uncle Richie, and Meme; plus Ken wasn't there to ruin it.

Ken started fuming about us kids not shutting the lights off and how high the light bill was. Ma gave us a little lecture, to make him happy, but he could tell that she was only saying it because he was mad. The next thing we knew he was yelling at Ma for sticking up for us kids. Ma got tired of arguing and said: "What do you want me to do, Ken?" Ken didn't say anything, but I could tell that he was ticked because he stuck his bottom teeth out. He's got fangs on his bottom teeth like a vampire and sometimes he fools around and pretends he's going to bite us. But he was showing his fangs for real this time, and his plain white face was turning purpley-red.

Nobody said a peep. I tried pretending that the argument was over, and started eating my birthday cake, and pretty soon all us kids were eating cake again like nothing had happened.

Ma even started clearing away dishes so I was thinking phew, that was a close call, but then I heard Ken clearing his throat, like he was about to give a birthday toast or something and... WHAM! He flipped the kitchen table over so it landed upside down on top of my birthday party and then he started screaming like a crazy man.

His top teeth are false, and they kept popping out, which made him even madder, so he looked like an angry gorilla on the rampage. We all ran away screaming, but poor Crumbs didn't run fast enough and got hit by a coffee cup that he threw. It tore a hole in her side that looked like a little red triangle stuck to her fur. She kept licking at it and looking up at us, like she wanted us to fix her, but all we could do was clean it with some peroxide.

We all cried harder about Crumbs than we did about the fight, and even though Ma said that Crumbs cut wasn't that bad, I think it was horrible and I'm never forgiving Ken for hurting my dog.

We had to hide in Diana's room for a long time and put a chair under the doorknob so Ken couldn't get in. Janice and me kept crying, but not Diana and Tommy. Diana looked pissed off, and Tommy kept jumping every time Ken yelled.

Ken was going nuts saying all kinds of mean stuff, like us kids were worthless, and that Ma was nothing but a traitor for sticking up for us. I was tempted to tell everyone about all the nasty stuff he does to me, but I was too scared and chickened out.

Then we heard him say that he was going to shoot us all like rats. We got quiet then, but Ma yelled right back at him: "Oh go ahead Ken, kill a bunch of kids, you're such a brave man." I wanted to tell Ma to shut up because I knew he would kill us if he really wanted to, but she kept on yelling like she wasn't afraid of anything. Pretty soon things got quiet except for the sound of Ma sweeping up all that glass. Diana told us to stay put and went out there to help her. I wanted to help too but I went to my room instead and tried to figure out my escape plan in case Ken came around shooting. I squeezed myself under my bed figuring if Ken was going to shoot me he'd have to find me first.

Ken likes to ruin special days. He ruined Thanksgiving too. We went to Meme's, like we always do, and he acted normal at first, like he was having fun. We all sat around the table with our little glasses of wine, and tiny pilgrim candles, gabbing and eating. He even carved the turkey with Meme's electric knife. He did make kind of a mess of it, but nobody said anything, and Meme pretended that it was the best carving job ever.

After dinner us girls did the dishes while Meme and Ma drank coffee in the kitchen. Ken went into the other room to watch TV with Joe, Meme's boyfriend, and Tommy. I thought everything was peachy, but on the ride home Ken started in. He said, "I'm sick of being the odd man out. I sat on that couch all afternoon and nobody said one word to me." Stupid me piped up and said, "I talked to you, and so did Joe." I shouldn't have said a word because Ken just wanted to be mad. I watched the red climb Ken's neck straight up to his ears, like a cartoon thermometer, and then he exploded. "Oh screw Joe! He thinks that his shit doesn't stink. And who the hell asked for your opinion anyway, little miss know-it-all?" Ma turned and gave me the eye, so I slunk down in the back seat and kept my mouth shut.

By the time we got home they were both screaming so loud the whole neighborhood could hear them. We hid in Diana's room with the window open so we could escape, but it was freezing so we had to take the blankets off her bed and bundle up with them. That was the day that Ken threw the refrigerator across the kitchen. When we tried to come out of Diana's room we couldn't open the door because the fridge was lying in front of it. We had to jump out the window and come in the front door.

Ken took off in his car for a while, so we helped Ma put the refrigerator back where it belonged, and then we cleaned all the food off of the floor. Crumbs made out good during that fight because there was some left over turkey from Meme's house in there. I tried to give our cat, Ranger, some turkey too, but he wouldn't come out from under the bed. We haven't seen him since last week. Ma says he probably went to find another home that isn't so crazy. Lucky cat.

I feel just like my cat Ranger right now, hiding under my bed from Ken. I still wish that Ranger would come back, just so I could say goodbye to him. Then I'd let him leave again and go live in a house where he doesn't have to hide under the bed all the time.

It's pretty stuffy under here, and the wood floor is cold like an empty bathtub, but I can take it. I can't even lift my head without hitting it on the springs. Janice was under her bed too, but she climbed back into bed a while ago. She said that Ken and Ma were finished fighting and that she wasn't afraid anymore.

It's quiet, and so dark that it looks the same when my eyes are open and closed. I was going to try to stay awake all night, just to be safe, but my eyes feel heavier than bricks and I keep going on little trips in my mind.

I felt something grabbing at my side, but I couldn't tell if it was a dream or real, so I held my breath and waited. Then I felt a tug on my shirt, but this time I got my eyes wide open, so I know it's not a dream. My heart is jumping around inside my chest, but I can't move...or even scream. "Cozy?" A voice whispers … and then the hand grabs at me again. It's Ken. He pulled on my top until I popped out from under the bed sideways, like a piece of toast. I don't say anything because there is nothing to say. He found me and now he's going to do whatever he wants to do to me.

His mouth is up close to my nose and he's panting like a dog right into my face. His breath smells like poop. My stomach rumbles and warm spit fills my mouth. I turn my head away while he lifts my shirt and pulls off my pants. He tells me that he loves me and that I'm his favorite girl, and I say it back to him because he gets mad if I don't. I shut my eyes and erase my body so it's just my brain looking for something else to do until Ken finishes. I pretend that I'm over Alex's house and he's painting a picture of me. I'm all grown up and lying on a green velvet couch with a long cigarette holder in my hand and I'm wearing a red feather hat with a big green jewel in it to match the couch. My dress is red, with black lace everywhere, and as tight as a mermaid's tail. Alex looks back at me and then turns to his canvas to add some pink to my cheeks. I smile because I'm beautiful.

Ken finished his messy business and left without saying a word. I pulled on my pants and lay back down on my bed. I'm imagining how great it would be to shoot Ken with one of his own guns. I pick the biggest one, and can hardly lift it because it's so heavy. He's coming into my room to mess with me, and I smile and tell him that I have a big surprise for him, but he has to lie on the bed first, and close his eyes. I drag the gun out of my closet and yell, "Surprise!" When he sees me standing there, with the gun aimed at him, he starts boo-hooing and gets on his knees begging for me not to shoot him, but I tell him that it's too late for begging and to stop all his blubbering. Then I shoot him in the gut and he flops backwards dead.

The cops come but they don't care if I killed him because I tell them everything he ever did to me. Ma doesn't care either, because now she knows the truth, and she's glad that he's dead. We all move away from here to a better house and Ranger even comes home, and....

"Cozy?" Damn. Janice is awake. I pull the covers up and pretend that I'm asleep, but she calls again, a little louder this time.

"Cozy?"

"Huh?"

"You awake?"

"A little, what's the matter?"

"I had the weirdest dream," Janice says. "I dreamt that Ken was in here making disgusting noises like a pig, grunting or something."

I laughed, trying to brush her dream off, but my laugh was too loud and high so it didn't even sound like my voice, and I knew... that Janice knew about Ken and me.

A long time passed, and I was waiting for Janice to say something to me, but she didn't, so I figured maybe she fell back asleep and tomorrow she wouldn't remember anything. But she wasn't sleeping. She floated over to my bed and sat on the edge of it. I had a feeling she wanted to talk, and I was waiting to hear it, so I could call her a liar, but she didn't say anything. She just climbed into bed with me. I got on my side, to give her more room, and she snuggled behind me and put her arm around my waist. Big tears ran down my face, soaking my pillow. Janice reached up and pulled my hair back off my forehead, like Ma used to do, but she didn't say a word about anything.

"Cozy, you coming or what?"

Tommy was standing in front of me with his hands on his hips, like he was Captain Big Shit. I didn't give him a hard time though because he never gets to boss anybody around. I thought that Ken would treat Tommy special, because he's his real kid and all, but he hits and yells at him about the same as the rest of us, and Ma's got no patience for Tommy, so she's always picking at every little thing that he does. That's why I'm giving him a break and letting him think he has some power.

"Yeah, yeah," I say. "Cripes, give me a minute will ya?"

I told him that I'd go to the store with him; he's got a quarter that's burning a hole in his pocket, and I have just enough change to buy some butts, so we're walking down to Frank's store before Ma gets home.

I stuffed my feet into my boots and pulled on my coat. Tommy was already standing at the front door with his hand on the knob wiggling it around, making Crumbs go crazy.

"Can Crumbs come too?" Tommy asked, but before I could answer, Tommy and Crumbs were out the front door and running.

It snowed last night, just enough white stuff to make everything look like Christmas, but we still had school today. There's only two more weeks until Christmas, but it doesn't feel like it. We usually make decorations and then hang them all over the house.

Ma's real smart, and one year she made a fake fireplace with a light up log in it. She hung our stockings from it and Ranger, our cat, curled up into a furry little donut and slept in front of the fake fire like it was real. It looked so cute, like a Christmas card. Ranger moved in with Peggy, the girl who sold Ma a candy bar. She lives up the street. Peggy says her mother loves Ranger and hand feeds him steak and tuna fish. Well la-te-dah to Ranger. I could tell that Peggy liked him too, and she was afraid that we might ask for him back, because she was making it sound like her mother would die without him, but Ma said that Ranger made his choice and could stay up at Peggy's if he wanted to.

Sometimes I see him sitting on the front porch, with his new blue collar on, trying to decide where to go for the day, and I wonder if he even remembers how I used to pet him and let him sleep with me. I guess he forgot all about us kids down here at the crazy house.

"Hey Cozy, there's Dewey, your BOYFRIEND!"

Grrrrrr! Tommy better be glad he's too far away for me to smack. Dewey spots me and heads my way. He looks like a grown man walking with his head down and hands in his pockets. I couldn't find my mittens, and had to wear old socks on my hands instead, so I whipped them off and stuffed them into my pockets. Dewey looked up and grinned.

"Hiya Cozy."

"Hi Dewey."

He tugged his black and yellow striped cap out of his sleeve, pulled his hair back, and stuck it on his head. I always think of a bumble bee when I see that hat.

"You coming collecting with me tomorrow?"

Dewey's eyes were on mine and we both smiled at the same time. I nodded yes and smiled some more.

"AWWWWWW ... she's smiling, that means she likes him!"

Tommy was in my face with his finger wagging and I was about to break it off.

"Get out of here you nitwit!" I said. Tommy's smile dropped off his face, because he could tell by my evil eyes what I was planning, so he moved away to wait while I finished talking to Dewey.

Usually me and Dewey stand around and say a little bit about little things, like the weather and stuff, but lately it's like I have jumping beans in my stomach that get all peppy whenever I'm around Dewey, so I try to think up more things to say so he'll stick around longer. But I had squeezed all the talk I was gonna out of Dewey, so we said our goodbyes and then headed in different directions. I could still feel Dewey near me, even though he was getting further away. It was like we were connected with an electric cord, but it's an invisible one that won't get tangled up no matter how far away we get. And it felt like it was keeping me warm inside, even though it was freezing outside. Dewey is definitely in my tribe, and just thinking about it was making me smile.

Tommy started brown nosing me big time because he was scared that I was going to get him back for teasing me, but I felt too good to bother with him, so I let him shine up to me all he wanted.

When we got back to the house Ma already had some potatoes on the boil, and asked me to open up two cans of green beans. Tommy made himself scarce because he was worried that Ma would have him doing chores too. Ken's working nights this week, so it's kind of like a holiday around here.

Diana came in and plopped down in a kitchen chair. She makes herself invisible when Ken's home, mostly staying in her room, but sometimes she hangs out with her new best friend, Gina Castrati. Gina's shorter than me and she's sixteen. Everyone in her family calls her half-pint, but she hates it, so we just call her Gina.

I dumped the green beans into a pan and set it on the burner for Ma to heat up later.

"So, how was school today, Cozy?" Ma's voice sounded friendly, like the doorbell ringing on Christmas Eve. She used to sound like that most of the time but I forgot all about that voice. She dropped a pork chop into the hot frying pan, and I watched it spit and hiss, like an angry cat.

"Well?" Ma said.

"Great. School was great," I said, grinning up at her because I was feeling so good about supper, and Dewey, and Ken being at work. Diana rolled her eyes at me, and I knew she was thinking that I was kissing up, but I didn't care as long as Ma stayed in a good mood.

Then Ma asked, "How about you Diana, how was your day?" in the same jingly voice. I stared at Diana thinking she better not screw up Ma's good mood, but Diana didn't look at me because she knew it was her turn to be a kiss up and she was embarrassed. "Mine was great too," she said, while her cheeks turned red.

"What's so great?" Janice asked, bouncing up to the kitchen table like she missed out on some big news. Diana and me both said "School" at the same time and gave Janice the biggest eyes we had. Janice looked confused for a second, because she knew we hated school, but then she caught our clue and said, "Yeah, school was great for me too, Ma."

We didn't have one argument during supper tonight and there was no fighting during clean up either. Ma didn't run into her room right after supper, like she'd been doing since she married Ken. Instead, she hung around with us in the parlor and we played some of her old records on the hi-fi.

Ma loves to dance, and when we were little she used to dance around with us standing on her feet like puppets. We're way too big for that now so tonight she taught us how to dance for real. We moved the furniture out of the way and rolled up the big braided rug so that we could dance on the wood floor in the parlor. That girl Peggy, the one who our cat Ranger moved in with, came by to see if Janice was home and Ma invited her in. She was shy at first but after a while she loosened up and had a blast too. I like Peggy; she isn't a snob like I thought she was. Even Tommy learned how to dance, something Ma says will help him with the girls someday. But he still has a lot of learning to do; we nicknamed him "The Toe Stomper."

Ma turned the music up so loud that you could feel it vibrating through the floor. Crumbs' ears were lying down flat on her head, and twitching like nervous kittens, so Ma made me put her in my room and shut the door.

Most of the songs we played were slow floaty songs that grown-ups in love like to dance to. Ma said that dancing is easy if you have a good leader. She made me stand in front of her and put my arm around her waist, and then she held my other hand. It felt silly at first because my face was right up next to hers, and I wanted to laugh, but I knew if I did she would get embarrassed and tell me to forget it, so I let her lead me around the parlor with everyone watching.

Ma closed her eyes most of the time, and her face got soft, like she was sleeping, except for a little smile that she kept going the whole time. It wasn't a big cheesy smile, like you give the camera; this one was more like a dreamy smile, the kind you get when you're thinking about something that you're wishing for. After a while we all got used to dancing in front of each other and when my turn came up again I put my head between Ma's neck and shoulder, closed my eyes, and let her lead me around. I wasn't thinking about the steps any more. I was just moving along, like there was no ground under my feet, and sniffing into Ma's hair, catching memories.

I watched Ma dance with Diana; she's the best dancer out of all of us kids, and Ma picked her the most to dance with, but we didn't care because we could see that Ma was happier than we'd seen her in a long time. They danced to a song called *That's All*. I know the name is *That's All* because it's Ma's favorite song. Anyways, it's a sad little song about a man who had nothing much to give his girlfriend but country walks and his love. Ma's happy little smile melted away when it came on. She kept on dancing, but I knew she was thinking about all the things that she wanted, but didn't get, and how she's stuck with Ken who doesn't give a crap about what she wants.

I could feel my nose tingling the way it does when I'm about to cry, so I pushed back the waterworks long enough to get to my room and stick my pillow over my head. Then I cried the way I would if somebody I love died; not Ma because I would still be crying, but maybe Meme or someone like that. I wanted to tell Ma that us kids could give her what she wanted, and make her happy, because we're older now, and could do more things for her. I wanted to tell her that I was sorry for dragging Ken to her door, and pushing him on her, like I knew what was good for her, and that I wished I could erase that day forever. But I knew it was way too late for that, and that Ma would never be happy again like she used to be. And that I probably deserve everything I get, and I mean everything, because I'm the one that brought all this trouble into our house.

But I never did say anything to Ma about being sorry. Instead, I went right back into the parlor and pretended that everything was great. I helped Janice and Diana clean up the house and we did such a good job that Ken couldn't even tell that we had a little party while he was working. He would have been pissed at Ma if he found out.

I'm trying to make myself go to sleep because I have school tomorrow, but I can't stop thinking about everything that we did tonight. I don't give a crap about school anymore. I already know how to read and write and that's good enough for me. It's not like I'm trying to be a doctor or something. Ma quit school when she was sixteen and she says it was the best decision she ever made. She says that school is more about being popular than it is about learning anything. Diana says she's going to quit when she turns sixteen and work at Kresge's. I have a lot of years left before I can quit and it feels like I'm in school jail because I don't have any choice about it. Janice will stick with school because she's so good at it and she has tons of friends there.

I'm sick of watching all those shiny haired girls at school make a fuss over stupid crap; like the new clothes they got, or what boy likes them. The boys at school are okay, but I don't really hang around with any of them. Dewey is my best friend now, seeing everyone else moved away, but I only see him on Fridays when we go collecting. I think I'm going to ask him if he wants me to help him more, that way I'll get to spend more time with him... and get away from this house.

School was boring today. I kept dozing off at my desk because it took me forever to fall asleep last night. The best part of my day was when Mr. Cross caught Phyllis Garrett passing a juicy note to Stephen Swenson and read it to the whole class. Phyllis's face got all blotchy, and Stephen stood up and shouted out, "I don't even like her." I felt kind of bad for Phyllis when Stephen told everyone that he didn't even like her. She stayed red for a long time and at recess she went off by herself. Stephen stuck around with his buddies and hid his face behind all that hair of his. The note wasn't too bad except for the part where she said that she was going to give him a kiss for his birthday. That's why I don't write juicy stuff in my diary. Someone's bound to find it and stick their nose where it doesn't belong. Anyway, the rest of the day took too long to go by, but now I'm heading home to get ready to go collecting with Dewey. I'm going to ask Janice to brush the rats nest out of my hair so Ma doesn't chop it off this weekend.

I found Janice lying on the couch watching TV and smoking like she had permission. It's too cold to sneak outside to smoke and Ma and Ken weren't home yet, so she figured she'd stay right where she was and have a cigarette. She looked funny because her face caved in every time she took a drag. It looked like she was trying to play grown-up but didn't have the cheeks for it, and I wondered if that's what I looked like when I smoked too.

"Hey Janice, will you do me a big favor?"

"No."

"You don't even know what I want yet. It's nothing big; I just need you to help me brush the rat's nest of out my hair. I can't do it myself because my arm gets too tired."

"Well if you brushed your hair every day, like normal people do, you wouldn't need me to brush it out for you."

I could tell this wasn't going to be easy. Janice likes to give lectures and if I don't go along with her she'll get mad and tell me to do it myself.

"I know," I said. "Please? If you help me I'll buy you a pack of butts." Janice looked at me and said, "come here." Sitting up taller, she grabbed a clump of my hair and pulled me down on the floor.

"Sit down; I can't reach it with you standing up."

I dropped to the floor in front of her and she started brushing like she was raking a lawn.

"Ouch! You're killing me!" I said, grabbing the back of my head, but Janice rapped me on the knuckles with the brush and told me to shut up and sit still or she'd leave it half done. My eyes were watering from the pain, and I wanted to smack her good for hitting me with the brush, but instead I clenched my teeth and waited for it to be over with.

"Done," she said, pushing me away from her. I ran into the bathroom and jumped up onto the sink to get a good look in the mirror. My hair looked longer, and shiny, and I could stick my fingers through the back of it without bumping into a single snarl. Janice came into the bathroom holding up the brush, and said,

"Look at the size of the rat I found in your hair!" The brush was fluffy with brown hairs and it did kind of look like a rat.

"Thanks Janice."

"Winstons."

"Huh?"

"Buy me some Winstons."

"Okay."

I dropped the brush in the sink, snagged Tommy's mittens off his bed, and then I headed out to meet Dewey.

First Kiss

The sky was white, like it was one big cloud, and I could see tiny snowflakes blowing around, like bugs with no where to land. I headed up the hill to meet Dewey on the corner of Kelly and Manchester Streets. Manchester is a busy street with two lanes going in the same direction.

I sat on the metal guardrail to wait for Dewey. It was close to the traffic and every time a car drove by, it blew the sand in the gutter into my face. Dewey finally showed up with a full bag of papers and a mouthful of bubble gum. I could smell it, original flavored Bazooka, the best kind for blowing bubbles.

"Hiya Cozy!"

"Hey Dewey!"

Dewey tried showing off by blowing a big bubble, but it popped while it was still small.

"This stupid cold weather is killing my bubbles," he said, chomping at his gum to get it soft again. Grabbing my arm, Dewey pulled me up onto my feet and we headed out. I walked extra fast, to keep up with him.

"You want me to carry the bag for a while?" I asked, hoping he'd say no because it was really heavy, and this hill was already killing me. I could see a slip of a grin on Dewey's face, like he was up to no good, and then suddenly he flung the bag over my shoulder and said, "Thanks Cozy!"

I watched him run up the hill ahead of me while I struggled to stay on my feet because the bag was pulling me sideways. I let it go and it slid off of my shoulder and landed on the ground. His newspapers spilled out onto the sidewalk but I caught them before they blew away. Dewey was nowhere in sight, but I knew he was probably hiding somewhere waiting to jump out at me.

I lugged the bag up to the top of the hill, but still no Dewey. I crossed another busy street and then headed down the hill toward that big apartment building where all the old people live.

I figured that Dewey was hiding in that old people building, even though he knows how much I hate the dark halls in there. The apartment building was made of orangey bricks and had a ton of windows in it, and most of the curtains looked raggedy and old, like the people living inside the building.

I stopped at the side door to catch my breath but there was still no sign of Dewey. I didn't know which apartments to collect from so Dewey needed to show up soon. I pulled the door open and slipped through it. It was warm, but really dark inside, with just one window at the end of the long hallway. There was usually a light on, but the light bulb must have blown. I leaned against the wall waiting for Dewey to show up. I couldn't figure out why he was playing this trick on me. He never did anything like this before.

I'd been waiting a long time in the hallway and I was getting pretty sick of it. I would have been better off outside, in the cold, where I could at least see what I was doing. I tugged on the door to leave but it wouldn't open. I pulled harder and could feel it moving a little, but it still wouldn't open up. My arm hurt from holding the stupid paper sack, so I put it down and tried the door again with both hands this time. The door opened enough for me to see light coming through the crack but then it pulled shut. I knew it had to be Dewey hanging onto the other side of the door.

"Let go of the door Dewey!" I screamed, waiting for an answer. "Dewey? DEWEY! Grrrrr! I'm going to kill you. Open the friggen door!" He still wasn't answering me. "I'm going to leave all your papers in this hallway and go home if you don't open the door." I didn't want to go home, and just saying that to him pinched me inside. I tried the door one last time and it didn't budge. "Fine, then! Be that way!"

I left his bag on the floor and hid behind the door to wait for Dewey to come through it. I was going to jump out and scare

the crap out of him when he came in. Finally the door opened…
really slowly. My heart was thumping so loud that I could hear it
in my head; this was going to be a good prank. I waited one more
second and then I jumped out yelling…"RARRRRRRR!" Dewey
charged at me like he meant business. Oh crap! He kept coming,
and I kept backing up until I hit the wall behind me. He was up
against me pressing in and scrunching down so his face was right
in mine. The tip of his icy nose touched my forehead. His breath
was cold bazooka breath…yum. I wasn't sure what he was doing,
but I liked it so far, so I stood and waited to see what was coming
next. He put his cold hands on both of my cheeks, pulling my
face up a smidge, and then Dewey Sloan put his mushy lips on
mine and kissed me. My heart took a high dive into my stomach,
making my toes curl! Then Dewey took off running. I didn't even
care that he was gone, because I just got kissed and I needed a
minute to figure things out. I slumped down to the dusty floor
and licked at the bubble gum taste on my lips.

I figured Dewey wanted me to hunt him down. He could be
hoping for another kiss, but I wished he took his stupid bag with
him because all this paper hauling was killing my shoulders. Just
thinking about Dewey's kiss made my stomach jump. I could
still feel it if I thought about it hard enough, and I wouldn't mind
another one.

I dragged the paper sack down the long hallway until I got to
the stairs. The stairwell was pitch black, and when the door shut
behind me, my ears felt blocked. It was like being in an Egyptian
tomb. I moved my foot forward until it bumped into the first step.
Once I got on the first step I'd be all right because I knew that all
together there are sixteen steps to get to the second floor; eight,
to the first little landing and then eight more to the second floor
hallway.

I was three steps up when I heard something breathing…
definitely breathing, and it wasn't me. I held still trying to decide
if I should be scared. It was probably Dewey waiting for me, but
what if it wasn't? What if it's a crazy killer waiting to murder

me, or a bum sleeping on the steps? I turned to leave, figuring it wasn't worth risking my neck for another kiss, no matter how good it was, and I took a step down. But my foot got tangled up in the newspaper sack and I fell forward, through the darkness, and slammed onto the floor.

"SHIT! Cozy, are you okay?"

My ears were ringing and I was seeing little silvery tadpole lights swirling around like pin wheels.

"I think so."

Dewey's hands found me on the floor, but it was too dark to see, so he opened the hall door and jammed his paper sack against it to hold it open. The light from the hall window spread across my face. Dewey was kneeling down in front of me moving my hair aside and tilting my head up so he could see me better.

"Damn!" Dewey whispered.

"What?" I whispered back.

"Your head's bleeding."

"How bad is it?" I asked, trying to whisper and swallow the lump in my throat at the same time.

"I can't tell for sure but there's lots of blood. Can you walk?"

"Yeah, I can walk." I said, "My head's bleeding not my feet." I tried getting up but my legs felt wobbly, so I flopped back down on my butt. "Just give me a sec will ya?"

"I'm sorry Cozy, it's my fault. Stay right here. I'll be back in a minute."

Before I could say a word Dewey disappeared again. I swiped at my face and my hand slid across my skin and came up wet. I didn't know what to do with the blood, so I laid my hand on my legs and waited for Dewey to get back.

"I got some tissues from Mrs. Hallburg." Dewey said, stooping down and wiping at my face. He was breathing heavy from all the running he'd been doing, and I could still smell Bazooka. He lifted my hair off my face, being as gentle as a nurse, and said,

"It's not as bad as I thought, just a shit load of blood coming out of a little cut, but you have a good size bump starting too."

I didn't say a word because I was enjoying all this Dewey attention and I felt almost normal again.

"Here." Dewey took his knit cap off and pulled it over my head so it covered my cut like a bandage. "This will keep the blood off of your face." The cap was still warm from being on his head. I reached up and touched the bumpy knit; it was really soft, and fit just right.

"I don't want to get blood all over your favorite hat."

Dewey pulled me back up onto my feet and ignored what I said.

"How you feeling now?" he asked, looking me over to see if anything else was bleeding.

"I'm fine, really, but I can't take your hat."

"Shut up. You're wearing it."

I was glad that I got his hat, but I had to put up a little fight so he wouldn't know how much I wanted it.

"Thanks Dewey."

"Do you want me to take you home now?"

"No way!"

"You sure?"

"Yeah, I'm fine now. Honest to God; I just needed a little time to catch my breath, that's all."

"Okay then," Dewey said, hanging his paper sack over his shoulder. "If you say so."

Dewey grabbed my hand and pulled me along with him, saying, "C'mon then, let's get this thing done."

It took us longer than usual to finish collecting because of all our horsing around and my accident on the stairwell. When we finished we decided to go have a hot chocolate.

I spotted two empty stools at the other end of the counter and raced to claim them before anybody else could. Dewey laughed at me the same way my Uncle Richie does when he gets a kick out of me.

"What?"

"Huh?"

"What's so funny?"

"You are Cozy."

"Me. Why?"

"Go look in the mirror."

I headed to the rest room and flicked the light on. ARG! I looked disgusting. Dry blood was smeared down the side of my face, like brown mud, and Dewey's hat was soaked through on the forehead band so I looked like one of those guys who got wounded in the *Civil War*. I snagged some paper towels from the top of the toilet tank and ran water over them. I still hadn't seen my cut up close so I leaned in to get a better look.

It looked like a little sideways mouth, open...with no teeth. Yuck. It definitely needed a butterfly stitch...maybe two, but it was hidden under my bangs so it didn't show too much. I rubbed the blood off of my face, put Dewey's hat on backwards, so the blood stain wouldn't show, and then headed back to my stool. My hot chocolate was already waiting for me, piled high with extra whipped cream, so I grabbed my spoon and dug in.

"Why didn't you tell me that I looked like crap?" I asked, in between slurps.

"Why bother," he said. "It wasn't like you could have fixed it."

He was right. Sometimes I think Dewey is smarter than most of the adults I know.

"I'll have my mother wash your hat and get it back to you. She can get stains of out anything."

Dewey stared into his hot chocolate, and said, "Don't worry about it Cozy. It was my fault in the first place."

"Nuh uh."

"Yah huh."

"Dewey?"

"Yeah?"

"I was thinking that maybe I could help you with your paper route more, and not just on Fridays."

"After what happened today you still want to help me with my route?"

"What do ya mean? Of course I want to help you. Duh, it was my fault too for jumping out at you like I did."

"No it wasn't, besides I'm supposed to keep you safe."

"Who says?"

"Everyone knows that the man keeps the women and children safe."

"Not in my world."

"Yeah, in your world too."

I wasn't about to tell Dewey about Ken and how safe he keeps me. Just thinking about it with Dewey sitting beside me made me feel dirty. "So, can I?" I asked, waiting for the answer. He reached over sideways, without looking my way, and squished the top of my shoulder.

"I wouldn't mind if you helped me more."

"So, that's a yes?" I asked. But he never did answer me. Instead he paid for our hot chocolates and said, "Let's get out of here."

We stood out in front of the store stomping in the cold. I knew that I had to walk home a different way than him, because we lived on different ends of our neighborhood, and that it was time to say goodbye.

"So," I said, trying to get some talk going, but I couldn't find any interesting words to say, so I kept quiet.

Dewey took my hand and squeezed it a little then said, "So... you want to meet me Monday, same place same time? It won't take us as long because I don't have to collect, and I promise not to run off on you like I did today."

"That's okay. I had fun, and it's just a scratch anyway." I wanted to tell him that his kiss was divine and that it was my first real one, and that I was hoping for lots more, but with him being so shy and all I didn't dare say a word. I wonder if it was his first kiss too and if he liked it like I did.

"See you then Cozy."

"Monday, same place and time." I said, to his back, because he was already walking away.

Happy little butterflies, that's what's in my stomach. I think I love Dewey for real and maybe I really will marry him some day. He's funny, but quiet too. I wouldn't have to worry about him yelling and fighting all the time like Ken does, and he would be a great father because he treats his little sister Tina like a princess. My head was full of ideas, and it was nice and toasty warm because Dewey's hat was hugging it. "Oh crap!" I forgot Janice's Winstons.

I was already half way home, but I turned around anyways because Janice would have a conniption if I showed up at home without her butts. By the time I got home, supper was long gone and everyone was in the parlor watching TV.

Ma turned the corner into the kitchen and spotted me trying to be invisible.

"It's about time!" she said, with her mad face aimed right at me. But then she stopped, tilted her head, and looked at me like she was trying to figure something out. I stood still waiting for the inspection to be over with.

"Where did you get that hat?"

"It's Dewey's."

"But, why are you wearing it?"

"He let me use it because.." Oh crap crap crap..."I cut my head a little falling down some stairs when I was helping Dewey with his paper route." Now Ma was up close squinting into my face. She lifted the cap off of my head and moved my hair aside.

"Ouch!" I said, pulling away, not because she hurt my head, but because she gave me a shock. Ma laughed because she got one too, but then she pulled me closer and said, "Let me see it Cozy." I tipped my head back so that she could see it better.

"That's no little cut! You need stitches." Ma didn't seem too upset. She had that face on, the one she gets when she's busy sewing, and she almost seemed excited, like she was glad to have an interesting project to work on.

"I'll go get my stuff while you take off your coat and wash up."

Everyone followed me into the bathroom and was asking to see my cut.

"It's just a little cut," I said, acting all brave, but every time I looked at it my stomach flip flopped like a fish in a bucket. Janice was hanging over me like a vulture. I could tell that she wanted her cigs but didn't want to ask because I was hurt. I slipped my hand into my coat pocket and passed the pack of Winston's to her. Janice's eyes smiled, then she stuffed the pack under her shirt, and left.

Ma came in and cleared everyone else out of the bathroom. She looked at my cut again in the good light.

"Two stitches," she said, then she dragged me into the parlor where she had everything set up on the end table.

I laid there letting Ma play doctor. Every time she touched me it felt good. Even when it hurt it felt good because it was her touching me. After she was all done she let me lay on her lap for a while. I asked her if she could get the blood out of Dewey's hat and she said she'd soak it overnight in cold soapy water. I closed my eyes and floated away. I was thinking about Dewey's kiss when Ma gave me a little push and said: "Let me up."

"Huh?"

It took me a minute to figure out what was going on. Everyone was busy doing something. Ma and Diana started moving furniture around, and Janice and Tommy were pulling a big Christmas tree into the parlor by its trunk.

"We're setting up our tree?" I asked, but nobody was listening to me because they were too busy helping out. Crumbs climbed up on the couch with me to get away from all the commotion.

"Can I help?"

Ma was lifting a table with the lamp still on it. I held my breath because if she dropped the lamp she was going to get ticked at me for asking her questions while she was busy. She set the table down, with the lamp safe and sound, and then plopped down in the stuffed chair and said, "No, not right now. Wait until we get it all set up then you can help decorate it." That sounded good to me because I felt kind of tired and my stomach was talking to me about finding it some food.

I headed into the kitchen and opened the fridge when Ma yelled out to me: "There's a plate for you in the oven. It's hot though, so use the mitts." I opened the oven and spotted my plate covered up in aluminum foil. I set the hot plate on the table, peeled back the foil, and a delicious cloud of steam puffed up into my face. There was fried chicken, mashed potatoes and corn. Mmmmm! This was my second favorite. My first favorite is stuffed turkey with cranberry sauce.

Ma strung the lights and then I helped hang the ornaments and tinsel. We shut off the TV, and the house lights, so that we could see the tree lights better. I kept squinting my eyes until they were nearly shut, making the colored lights run into each other so it looked like downtown on a rainy night. We all asked if we could sleep in the parlor with the tree lit up but Ma said no. Ken came home and walked right past the tree without saying a word about it. "Go to bed" was all he said, so we did.

All weekend I kept thinking about kissing Dewey. I even bought some original flavored Bazooka bubble gum so I could taste the kiss again. I told Janice and Diana about it and they said I had puppy love, because I'm only eleven, and that it was cute. That ticked me off because they made me feel like a little kid and that our kiss didn't really count. I'll never tell them anything like that again; but at least they promised to keep it a secret.

I love having the Christmas tree up. It makes the parlor seem comfy and special. We hung our homemade paper chains on the walls and Ma even dug out that fireplace that she made and lit it up. I felt sad because Ranger wasn't around to curl up in front of it, but I couldn't get mad at him for wanting to leave because I hated this house too. I don't hate Ma and my sisters, or even Tommy. I hate Mr. You Know Who for ruining everything.

Monday I'll get to help Dewey with his paper route again. Ma said I couldn't go if my room wasn't clean so I already cleaned it up today and then I told Janice that she better not mess it up. Janice usually cleans the most, and even makes my bed for me sometimes, so I felt kind of bad for saying that to her.

I'm glad that, starting tomorrow, my chore is dishes because I don't have to do them until after supper. That means I won't have any chores to do when I first get home from school and it will leave me plenty of time to get ready to go with Dewey. I've been brushing my hair out every day to keep the rat's nest away. I'm too old to have a rat's nest anyway.

Sundays we usually go over Meme's for dinner and then we watch Walt Disney on her color TV, but we didn't go today because Ma and Ken got into it again. That's why I had so much time to clean my room today, but now I have to watch good old Walt in black and white tonight.

Ma and Ken quit fighting before lunch, thank God, and Ken's been in a good mood ever since. He even played his harmonica for us after supper. Crumbs howled like a coyote through all of *Oh Susannah*, and Pretty Boy, our parakeet, chirped up a happy storm too. Ma ended up throwing Crumbs out so Ken could play a song without her barking. Ken kept raising his eyebrows and rolling his eyes while he played like he was proud of himself because he was good at something. Sometimes, when Ken's nice, it's hard to keep on hating him.

"Hey squirt, time for bed."

"Huh?" The TV was all snowy, making a sound like the ocean in a shell, and Ken was carrying me, like a baby, to bed. I must have fallen asleep after Disney and nobody woke me up. I faked falling back to sleep, laying my head on his shoulder, hoping that he would just plop me in my bed and leave me alone. Ken leaned over and set me on my bed really gentle, like he was putting an egg in a basket, then he started pulling my socks off. I knew that my pants were coming off next, and there was no way I wanted Ken undressing me like a Barbie doll, so I opened my eyes and told him that I could do the rest myself. Ken stood there, like he was waiting for a striptease show, so I told him that I had to pee and headed for the bathroom.

I don't get why he needs to mess with me. It's not like he doesn't have a wife in his bed. Besides, he must be able to tell I don't like him messing with me because I always try to dodge him, and I never smile when he's doing it to me. I turned on the little light over the medicine cabinet and squatted on the cold toilet seat. I got a creepy feeling, like Ken was standing outside the door listening to me pee, so I leaned forward and turned on the cold water so he couldn't hear me. I stayed sitting on the toilet, and begging God to please make him go away, for a long time. When I cracked open the bathroom door, Crumbs was there, but Ken was nowhere around, so I hauled my butt back to my room, shut the door, and crawled under the covers with all my clothes on.

Crumbs curled up at the foot of my bed and let out a noisy sigh, like Ma does when she's had a long day.

"I know how you feel," I whispered back to Crumbs, and then I rolled over onto my right side so I could watch my bedroom door in case Ken opened it again. I stared at my door knob for a long time, with my stomach full of squirming night crawlers, waiting for the door to open, but it never did.

Painting Lessons

"School's cancelled!" Janice was shaking me so hard that my teeth were clacking together like skeleton bones. I grabbed her hand and twisted it away, shouting, "Quit with the shaking!" Janice was sitting on my bed with my transistor radio on her lap and the ear plugs hanging around her neck like a stethoscope.

"Aren't you glad that we got the day off?" Janice asked, looking all let down because I wasn't bouncing off the ceiling with her. But I was still feeling all mixed up inside because I could remember Ken carrying me to bed last night and then I remembered watching the door knob, waiting for it turn, but I couldn't remember him ever coming back. I guess he got tired, and I better thank God for that one because I don't think I could have stood having him pawing at me last night; especially after Dewey giving me my first kiss the other day.

Dewey. Oh yeah! I get to help Dewey today and I don't have school. I could feel the happy butterflies waking up in my stomach tickling my insides. Janice was still sitting on my bed staring at me like I had two heads.

"HELLO......EARTH TO WEIRDO!"

"Hello. I mean WHAT?" I said, trying to remember what she just said to me. Janice jammed her long fingers into my ribs and started tickling me. I pushed her hands away, trying not to laugh, because if I did she'd never stop. But my mouth was stretching out like a rubber band and the laughing started anyways. I was too weak to get her off of me because I was laughing so hard. Even though it hurt more than it tickled, I was having a tough time breathing. Finally I sucked in a big gulp of air and screamed: "STOP!" Janice's face went flat, and she rolled off of me and lay on her back on my bed. I was still ticked so I pushed my feet into her side and knocked her onto the floor.

"I couldn't breathe, you idiot!"

"You always say that just to get out of being tickled."

"Nuh uh."

"Yes sir."

"Shut up. How much snow did we get?"

"The guy on the radio said eleven inches."

"Man."

Janice disappeared out the door, but I stayed in bed listening to my radio. I figured Janice would probably want to go shoveling but I didn't feel like it. I already had some money from collecting with Dewey, besides I needed to save my energy for later when I helped him with his route. It was going to be tough walking through all that deep snow carrying a heavy paper sack and he might need me to lug it for him if he gets tired.

Janice popped back into the room crunching on a piece of toast with peanut butter on it. Swallowing a mouthful she said,"You want to go shoveling?"

"Oh man, I knew you were going to ask me that."

"What? Don't you want to go?" Janice asked, sitting in front of me with her heavenly blue eyes digging holes into me. I wiggled around, and coughed a bit, trying to give myself more time to answer.

"Well?"

"Well what?"

"Don't you want to go with me?"

"Grrrrrrrr."

"Cozy don't growl at me like a dog, it's stupid. Do you want to go with me or not? Because if you don't, I know someone else who will."

I'm wondering who the heck she could take shoveling with her besides me.

"Who?"

"Peggy said that she would go with me because she wanted to earn some Christmas money too."

This changed things. Now I kind of wanted to go because it might be fun hanging around with Peggy. "I'll go if Peggy goes."

Janice jumped up and started getting dressed but she wouldn't answer me.

"Did you hear me?" I asked, waiting for her to say something.

"Yes I heard you but you're not invited anymore. Me and Peggy will go ourselves and you can stay home and play with Tommy."

Janice had a tight grin on her face, like she got the best of me. I stuck my earplugs in my ears and turned up my radio, pretending that it didn't matter, and then I shouted out to her: "Fine...I didn't want to go anyway!"

"FFFINE!" Janice shouted back, and then she scooped up the rest of her clothes and left, slamming the door so hard that the windows rattled.

Ma told me that Ken didn't have to go to work until three o'clock today so that meant it would be just me and Ken...all day long, because everybody else was doing other stuff. I could see the happy little butterflies in my stomach flying away and a big black snake curling up and making himself at home in the middle of my gut. I knew what Ken was going to want to do. I should have gone with Janice and Peggy when I had the chance, but how was I supposed to know that I was going to get stuck home alone with Ken. I only had about an hour to find some place else to go before Ken got up.

I crouched on my knees with my chin on the parlor windowsill staring out at all the snow. Everything looked too white, like someone forgot to color in the picture. There were a couple of people shoveling their cars out, but it was mostly quiet outside. I was all dressed, and I even had my coat and stuff waiting by the kitchen door just in case I had to leave in a hurry, but I had no where to go... yet. I thought about going upstairs and playing with Pam, but that's way too boring and I couldn't even smoke if I wanted to. I'd only go there if nothing better popped up.

The front door to Alex's house pushed open and out popped skinny old Alex with his hair bouncing and that long scarf blowing around like it was trying to escape. I forgot all about Alex being my friend because I'd been so busy with Dewey and all, so I ran for my coat and snuck out the door; making sure I didn't wake up Ken.

Alex was walking pretty fast down the street so I ran to catch up. I didn't dare yell out to him because Ken might hear me. Alex couldn't hear me coming, because the snow was sucking up all the noise my footsteps were making, so I got right up behind him and said "Hey."

"Hey little chick! I didn't even hear you coming."

"It's the snow." I said, sticking my arm out and scooping some of it off of the top of a shrub. It was the sticky kind of snow, so I scrunched it into a ball patting it on all sides so it would get nice and round. Alex looked over at the snowball and then at me and said, "Don't do it."

"What?" I had no clue what he meant. But then I saw he was still staring at the snowball like he was scared of it. Duh, he thinks that I'm going to throw it at him. I wasn't even thinking of that but now I couldn't help it. I took a step back and heaved it at him so that it broke apart on his shoulder, leaving a white stain on his dark blue coat. Alex looked at me with his mouth wide open then he squatted down and scooped up some snow of his own, working his slick black gloves around it until he made a perfect snowball. It was a beaut… big and solid like a rock. He tossed it up and caught it like a baseball then he looked over at me and said, "This one's going to sting so you better start running."

"Huh?" Crap! He's going to throw that at me! "That's not fair, mine wasn't even big." I whined, but he ignored me and started counting.

"One…Two…Three…." Alex was doing the count off, and I wasn't waiting around to see what happened at ten, so I shot off down the street, slipping and skidding through the snow like a car with no snow tires.

"Ten!"

I was still running, as best I could, and then WHACK! I got hit in the middle of my back. I fell forward, just to make it look good, but it didn't really hurt that bad. I stayed on the ground, with my face in the snow, fake crying, trying to make Alex feel bad about bonking me with his snow bomb. Finally Alex walked over to me, but instead of stopping, he walked right past me without even asking if I was okay.

"Hey!" I shouted after him, but he kept on going, so I jumped up and ran after him.

"I thought you were dying." he said, while he made another monster snowball.

"Nah, it didn't even hurt," I said, eyeing the snowball while he patted it into a hard ball. "Well," he said, "this one's going to be a killer. One…Two…Three."

"ALEX!"

"Four…."

"Damn!" I took off again, but the numbers were going by too fast, so I hid behind a big tree hoping for the best.

"Ten."

Nothing happened. No snowball, no Alex… nothing. I started tracing my finger through the deep lines in the tree trunk, forgetting all about the snowball danger, when I felt a tap on my shoulder. I turned and there was Alex holding his arm back like a giant slingshot loaded with his snow bomb.

"DON'T!" I yelled, crouching down to the ground; hiding my head under my arms, just waiting for the pain to come. Alex bent down, pulled me up by my elbows, and said: "I'm just kidding. I wouldn't hit you with it, Cozy."

"Well it sure looked like you were going to."

"I was just horsing around. I wouldn't hurt you."

"What did you do with the snowball?" I asked, just to make sure he had no surprises waiting for me. Alex pulled the snowball out of his coat pocket and chucked it at the tree.

"That was a good one," I said, happy to see it gone.

"Don't you have to teach art today?" I asked, walking fast to keep up with his long legs. Alex jumped up and slapped a branch above us making it snow all over again.

"Nope, school's been cancelled for me too."

"What are you gonna do all day?"

"Buy some Ring Dings and cigarettes and then go home and paint for a while."

"But it's your day off. Don't you want to do something fun instead?"

"I like painting more than anything else in the world," he said, smiling and staring up at the sky like he was talking to God. "That's why I'm becoming an art teacher. So I can do what I love and get paid for it." Now he sounded just like a real teacher and not some hippie draft dodger like Ken said he was. We walked for a while without saying much more. I was hoping I could weasel my way into his house today.

We got to the store and Alex held the door open for me. I ducked under his arm and went in. It smelled like coffee and bacon inside, and there were tons of people sitting down eating, reading newspapers, and talking about the snow while they waited in line to pay. I spotted Pam's father standing at the register, paying for some Old Golds. He looked handsome with his shiny black hair combed back; all those comb lines in neat rows like fork marks through chocolate frosting. Pam's father! I couldn't let him see me in here because he'd tell Ken that I was with Alex. He doesn't like hippies either and when he's with Ken they like to get all worked up over how the G-D hippies were ruining our country.

I slipped past Pam's dad, ducked into the restroom, and locked the door. I don't think that he saw me. I didn't tell Alex what I was up to and I was hoping he wouldn't take off without me. Over in the corner there was a silver bucket with a wooden

172

mop handle sticking out of it, so I took a closer look. Yuck! It was filled with disgusting black water with little hairs floating all over the top of it like a witch's brew. BLAH! I went back to the door, and counted to sixty a few times, and then I left.

Pam's dad was gone alright; but so was Alex. Crap! I gave the place another look over and still couldn't see him anywhere, so I headed outside to find him. Coming out of the warm store made the cold feel colder so I zipped my coat up and stuffed my hands into my pockets. I walked as fast as I could, without running, and when I turned the corner I spotted Alex bouncing up the street without me. "Hey!" I shouted as loud as I could. Alex stopped, without turning to see who was "heying" him, and waited for me to catch up.

"Why'd you take off without me?"

"I didn't take off without you. I saw that guy who lives on the third floor at your house and figured it would be better if he didn't know we were together." I felt my stomach do a little flip when he said, "we were together." It was like he was claiming me as a part of his tribe. Sometimes, I feel like I'm more like Alex than I am my own family, and if I could, I would start my tribe and invite him, only we would live in regular houses and not mud huts, and we'd wear normal clothes. Dewey would definitely be in my tribe too; but not Ken, that's for sure. I would have him banished to the forest or something.

We kept walking, getting closer and closer to home, and my stomach started filling with rocks because I had the whole day stretched out ahead of me and didn't know what to do with it.

"Who was that guy at the store anyway?" Alex asked, looking over at me with his forehead all wrinkled.

"That was Ken's brother, Steve. He tells Ken everything. My mother says that those two are worse than two old ladies the way they gossip."

Alex rolled his eyes and said, "Small people have small minds." I wasn't sure what he meant, so I laughed a little and said, "Thanks for covering for me." Alex put his hand on the back of my neck and gave it a little squeeze, and I knew that was his way of saying that he wasn't worried about Ken or his brother Steve.

We were almost home when Alex said, "So...what do you have planned for your snow day?" I looked down at my boots and said, "I don't know. Ken's the only one at home so I don't want to go there." My voice squeaked a little when I said it, making me sound like I was about to cry. Then it got quiet again. I was trying to work up the nerve to invite myself over to Alex's house, and I was just about ready to say something too, when Alex said: "You want to watch me paint for a while?"

Eureka! "That would be cool!" I said, stepping in front of him and walking backwards so I could look at his face while we walked. Alex laughed and the wind blew a patch of his long curly hair over his face so all I could see was one smiling eye. My stomach was doing the happy dance until I remembered that Ken was home and he might catch me going into Alex's house. "But" I turned and walked beside him again because all the fun was leaking out of me like a tired balloon.

"But what, Cozy?"

"But how am I gonna get into your house without anybody seeing me?"

"Oh that's easy," Alex said. "Let me go in first and then ten minutes later you can sneak around and come up the back way."

"I can do that. I'm used to sneaking around all the time to smoke, so this will be a snap."

"So it's a plan?"

"It's a plan."

We walked a little bit further till we reached the beginning of the hill. Alex looked at me and then he looked up the street, like he was pushing me with his eyes. I knew that he wanted me to go on ahead, so I ran up the hill leaving Alex far behind.

I was out of breath when I reached the wall. It was piled with snow, like the meringue on Ma's lemon pie, so I wiped off a spot and sat down to wait.

I looked across the field through the trees and saw a bright white spot in the sky. It was the sun trying to burn a hole through the clouds. The spot got brighter and brighter until the cloud melted away and a sunbeam poked through, like God's finger was pointing right at me.

I closed my eyes and let it shine on my face. A noisy bird started singing in the tree above me. He kept on getting louder and louder, like he was trying to tell me something important, so I took a little peek. The snow was sparkling now, like somebody sprinkled diamond dust all over the top of it. It was the most beautiful thing I'd ever seen in my life! I had to squint because it was so bright; and the sunbeam was still pointing at me; like I was in one of those big spotlights they have at the circus.

I was thinking that God might want me to say something, seeing that he's got his spotlight on me, and I knew what I wanted to say, because I was filled up with it, so I closed my eyes and whispered: "Thank you God for letting Alex invite me over today." I waited for a few seconds, in case he wanted to say something back to me, but nothing happened. After a while the spot light went out and the cold started biting at my face again, so I figured it was time to head over to Alex's house.

Nobody had shoveled the back path to Alex's house so I had to push through the deep snow like a plow. Climbing the steps my chest felt tingly, like it had electric needles poking into it, and my breath felt as thin as a ribbon. I thought of Ma at work, cutting and sewing, thinking that I was at home watching cartoons while Ken snored into his big white pillow. If she knew what I was up to she would wring my neck. But she doesn't know, and she doesn't know what Ken is up to either when she's not around, so I don't feel a bit bad about sneaking up here to see Alex.

I reached Alex's porch and tapped on the little window in his back door. Then I waited, with my boots full of snow, and my heart climbing up my throat like a monkey in a tree. Alex finally pushed the door open a bit, but it got stuck in the snow.

I had to kick away at the drift so he could open the door enough for me to squeeze through.

"Hey little chick," Alex said, smiling like he'd been waiting for me. I could feel my face turning red, so I bent over and started pulling off my boots. Alex put a yellow towel on the floor and said, "Just put your boots on the towel when you're done. I'll be in the other room getting things set up."

I was in the kitchen and I could see part of the parlor from here. There was no real furniture in it; just fancy pillows on the floor and little colorful rugs here and there. My heart was still thumping hard, but I think the red had gone out of my face. I banged the snow out of my boots onto the towel and stuffed my wet socks into them. The linoleum floor felt warm on my bare feet.

"C'mon in here," Alex shouted from the other room, so I walked on my toes till I got there.

Alex was sitting on the only chair in the room fussing with a big white canvas. "Grab a pillow," he said, shoving one toward me. There were no curtains in his windows, and even though it was still cloudy outside, the light was shining in, making everything look too bright. I picked a big green pillow with swirly designs and sat down on it.

"Come closer so you can see what I'm doing," Alex said, looking over his shoulder at me. I drug the pillow over, accidentally pulling the rug with me. "Sorry," I said, while I tried to straighten out the rug and hold the huge pillow at the same time. Alex took the pillow and plopped it down beside his wooden chair while I fixed the rug. Then he told me to sit down. It felt sort of like I was sitting in the front row at school and I was hoping that this wasn't going to be boring.

"First you have to prepare your canvas for the paint," Alex said, shaking a little can as hard as he could. "This is gesso. I always paint my canvas with it first so the paint will stick better." He set the can down on a piece of newspaper and lifted the lid with a screwdriver. It smelled a little like lemons and glue, and was the same color white as the canvas. Alex stirred it for a while with a butter knife, and then scraped the knife off against the can.

"Now we're ready," he said, looking over to make sure I was paying attention. "All we're going to do is put one coat on with a brush and then wait for it to dry."

We're? I'm hoping he doesn't mean I was going to be doing it because I was just planning on watching while he did it all. Alex looked over at me and frowned a little, like he was wondering what I was waiting for.

"Stand up."

"Oh. Sorry. It's just that I didn't know you wanted me to do it too. I thought I was just going to watch."

"Well...you thought wrong, Little Chick."

I let out a loud sigh, like I was trying to blow out a hundred birthday candles. Alex stopped what he was doing and asked,

"Don't you want to try it?"

"Yeah, it's just... what happens if I mess it up?"

"You can't mess this up, Cozy. It's just white on white."

He dipped a big paintbrush, the kind Ma used on the woodwork at our new house, into the can then wiped some off against the rim. I thought he would be using a little skinny brush like the artists on TV use. Then he started teaching me again.

"Start at the top and bring the brush straight down to the bottom of the canvas without stopping."

I watched him, feeling jumpy inside because it was my turn next. I couldn't even tell where the gesso was except for the shiny little road it left behind the brush. Alex's tongue came out of his mouth, hanging low like a turtle's head searching around for food on its chin. It reminded me of how Janice looked when she concentrated hard on something. Part of me wished that I went shoveling with her today because this was putting my nerves on edge.

"Your turn."

Alex handed the brush over to me. I wasn't sure what to do with it so I reached for the canvas to start painting. Then out of nowhere he shouted: "ERT!"

I jumped back, "WHAT?"

"Aren't you forgetting something?" Alex asked, eyeballing the can of paint on the floor.

"Oh yeah... duh! Sorry."

I dipped the brush into the milky paint, and then wiped it off against the side of the can like he did. Then I lifted my hand up and set the brush against the canvas. I hated my hand because it was shaking like I was a 3-year-old trying to color inside the lines. Alex put his hand over mine and pulled the brush down the canvas in a straight line. His hand was warm and he smelled spicy good. I tried again, by myself this time, but I was still a little shaky, so he helped me finish that row too. The next try I did by myself, and Alex told me that I was doing fine. I wanted him to take the brush back, but he didn't. Instead, he made me finish the whole thing by myself; then he took the brush back.

"You did great!"

"No sir. You had to help me."

"Just the first two rows, but you did the rest all by yourself."

I didn't know what to say so I smiled, but if he could have seen what a mess I was on the inside of me he wouldn't be saying that I did so great.

We couldn't do any more painting, because we had to let the canvas dry, so we headed into the kitchen for a while. I sat on a folding chair at the kitchen table, only the kitchen table wasn't a real kitchen table. It was a big wooden spool with a hole in the middle of it like a 45 record. Alex plopped down in the other chair and lit up a cigarette.

"You want one?"

"Sure," I said, pulling one out while he held the pack.

"Here, let me." Alex flicked his silver lighter and I leaned forward, putting my head sideways and puffing in, so it would catch. I felt like a grown woman sitting there smoking with Alex, like it was no big deal and I did it every day. He snapped the lighter shut, leaned back, and lifted his leg up onto the chair so his knee was under his chin. He was so skinny and wiry, just like Janice; only a boy.

"So," Alex said, dragging on his cigarette, "What's the deal with you and Ken?" He blew out his smoke in a ropey line at the ceiling and waited. He was looking at me like he knew everything that Ken and me had been up to. "What do you mean?" I asked, flicking my cigarette over and over until the head nearly fell off.

"Well, I get the impression that you don't like him and I was just wondering what the story was."

I don't know why, but I started singing like that little bird that I saw in the tree today. I told him how I brought Ken home, because I thought he was a nice man and would make a good dad, but then he turned nasty and has been messing with me ever since I was nine. I told him how I didn't dare tell my mother, because it was my fault in the first place for bringing him home, and that it would kill her if she ever new. Alex's jaw was hanging open like the hinge was broken. I put my head down but kept on talking. I felt split open, and all the words were spilling out of me.

When I finally stopped talking I was crying. Not like I usually cry—all hard and forceful. These were polite little tears dripping, one at a time, down my face like they were taking turns. Alex came over and hugged my head against his stomach, saying that it wasn't my fault because Ken should know better, and that he was nothing but a pervert. I wanted to believe him, and I did a little, but some of the blame was still stuck way inside of me and I don't know if I'll ever get it out.

I got Alex's nice blue shirt all wet, but he didn't seem to care. He didn't ask me any more questions either, except if I wanted some soda and a Ring Ding. I felt better after all my talking, even though I knew that Alex couldn't do anything about it. And maybe that's why I picked him to tell. I knew he wouldn't go blabbing it around and stirring things up.

We ate our Ring Dings whole, like they should be eaten, and then guzzled our sodas down until the bottles were empty. Alex burped so loud it echoed off the walls. I started laughing, and then right in the middle of my laughing spell, I let a little hollow burp slip out because of drinking that soda so fast. Now Alex and I were both laughing at each other for burping and the more we tried to stop the harder we laughed. It seems like I always end up having laughing fits with Alex.

After a while Alex got up and started clearing away the soda bottles. I asked him if anybody ever messed with him when he was little. He stood still for a minute, so he could think, and then said, "No, but one time in high school I caught a kid jerking off in the bleachers so I took off the other way."

Part of me was kind of hoping that he had it done to him too, so we could be alike in that way and I wouldn't feel so different from everybody else. But I'm glad that it never happened to him and that he doesn't have to feel like I feel. Sometimes when I look at the other girls in my class I try to imagine what it would be like to be them. To not know what a man's thing looks, and feels like, and to be so happy that I skip around without even noticing it. I'd like to have a dad that loves me, and thinks I'm pretty; but doesn't want to sit me on his lap so he can move me around until his thing gets hard. Having a creepy step dad is worse than not having a dad at all.

Doing all that crying, and laughing, must have made me tired because I couldn't keep my eyes open and the folding chair I was sitting in was killing my back. Alex must have noticed me fidgeting because the next think I knew he was shouting, "Nap time!"

"Huh?"

"It's time for a nap," Alex said, pulling my chair out and leading me down the hall.

"Where?" I asked, ducking through a curtain made of beads into his dark bedroom.

"Here."

Alex set me down on a little red couch. Then tossed me a pillow from off of his bed and dropped a blanket over my head so I couldn't see anything. The blanket was purple, soft as a pussy willow, and smelled just like him.

"Are you taking a nap too?" I asked, because I didn't want to miss out on anything.

"Yup. So no talking until I say so."

I curled up with the blanket, looking around at the different stuff in his room. He had boards sitting on cinder blocks for a bookcase, with a bunch of albums stacked on one side of it next to a fancy record player on the other side. There was a small table in front of the couch with a glass top; it was shaped just like a kidney bean, and a white tree trunk was holding it up. It was neat. Everything was neat in here and I wished that I could stay forever.

I woke up to Alex kneeling down beside me shaking my shoulder. "What time do you have to be home?" he asked, but I couldn't remember where I was, so I sat up fast, squinting and blinking like a baby chick fresh out of its shell.

"Uh."

Alex stood up and chuckled at me. "It's almost two o'clock. I wasn't sure what time you needed to be home."

"Ummm. After Ken leaves."

"What time does he usually leave?"

"About two thirty."

"Oh good, then we still have time for some tea before you go."

"Okay." I said, glad that he wasn't going to kick me out.

Alex brought in two cups of tea, set them down on the glass table, and told me to scoot over. The tea didn't have any milk in it, like I was used to, but I wasn't going to say anything because he might not have any milk, being a bachelor and all. I lifted the cup and noticed that it was warped, like somebody who was just learning how to make cups made it. I tried a sip, but it was too hot, so I sniffed at it instead. It smelled good; like Ma's spice cabinet.

"This smells good. What kind of tea is it?"

"It's herbal tea. They say it's supposed to calm your nerves," Alex said, blowing down into his cup and taking a tiny sip. "Still too hot," he said, and then he got up and pulled an album off the shelf. I couldn't tell who it was from here so I waited and listened.

Music from another country...that's what it sounds like. At first it sounded funny, and I had to fight to keep a straight face because Alex was all into it, closing his eyes and nodding his head. But after a while I noticed that the music matched the tea, and the beaded curtains, and I liked it.

The tea was sweet, in a flowery sort of way, but really good. We sat side by side on the couch sipping, and listening, and it was like I was far away from my other life, even though I was only across the street from it. I think the tea was working on my nerves because I'd been sitting there for a while without thinking about anything bad. I usually think too much. That's what makes me stay up so late sometimes.

I knew I had to go home pretty soon, but I didn't mind too much because Ken would be gone, and I was still looking forward to seeing Dewey later on. I finished my tea and the music ended at the same time. Alex got up to take the record off and asked, "Did you like that music?"

"I did," I told him, putting my cup on the table. "It made me feel good, or maybe it was the tea making me feel good, I don't know. I did like it though."

"Do you want to check to see if Ken's left yet?"

"Yeah, I guess I better so he doesn't catch me coming out of here."

Alex told me to go look out the window over his bed. I lied on my stomach across Alex's bed and looked out the window. There was a brown spot in the snow where Ken's car used to be. "Yup, he's gone alright! Thanks for the tea and everything," I said, as I crawled off his bed and headed to the kitchen to put my boots back on. I was a little sad that it was time to go, and even though

I turned myself inside out and Alex saw everything, I was glad I came over here and talked to him.

I decided to go out the back way, just to be sure nobody saw me. Alex gave me a little hug, and told me that I could come back any time that I wanted to. His hug filled me up with electricity, like I was plugged into him, like I was with Dewey, making me smile as I headed out the door.

Nobody was at my house when I got there. I was glad because I wouldn't have to say where I was today. I'm not telling anybody about visiting Alex because I don't want my sisters asking to come with me and trying to be his friend too. That would ruin everything. If anyone asks where I was today I'll just say that I bumped into Phyllis Garrett down at the store and went over to her house.

My house looked different to me: boring...and kind of cruddy. The furniture was old-fashioned and worn out, like it was there because it had to be there and not because it wanted to be there. Alex's house was different. Everything looked happy to be there. The music, herb tea, pillows...all his stuff looked like it was glad to be there, and he didn't even have any real furniture, except in his bedroom.

I went to my room to lie down for a while and think about my visit with Alex. I really did spill my guts. I'm glad he's on my side because now I have somewhere to go to get away from Ken. Its funny how sometimes the people who look nice end up being bad, but the people who look weird end up being the good ones. I thought Ken was the greatest, with his important uniform and smiling daddy face, and Alex was the flaky one, with all that hair, and his scarf flying behind him like a kite tail. But that's all different now because Ken ended up being the creep and Alex is the nice one.

I think telling Alex about Ken made me feel better, or maybe it's just the tea still working on me. But I feel wide open inside, like I got more room in my chest. When I take a deep breath now it goes all the way in and doesn't get stuck halfway like it used to do.

I looked over at my Halloween witch and thought about how things seemed so happy when I was little. Ma used to listen to me like everything I said was written in gold. Now she shushes me, and keeps her eyes off mine. I think it's because she doesn't want to know about what's going on in her own house.

The front door slammed so I sat up and tried to look normal so they wouldn't go asking me questions about my day. Janice bopped into the room fanning her face with a bunch of dollar bills.

"I made fifteen bucks today! We did three houses on Cherry Street and that Peggy can shovel better than a man." Janice tossed her money into the air and the dollars floated down like leaves falling from a tree.

"You should have come with me instead of sitting around this boring house all day doing nothing." I wanted to tell her that I had a way better time than her but I didn't. Instead I pretended that I was mad that I didn't go with her.

"Damn!" I said, frowning and folding my arms over my stomach, "I should have gone with you." Janice scooped the money up and counted it again; then she folded it in half and shoved it into her pocket.

"I'm going to the store to get some butts and candy. You want to come with me?"

"I can't. I have to meet Dewey pretty soon to help him with his route."

"Dewey, Dewey, Dewey, all you talk about is Dewey. I bet you two do a lot of smooching when you're out there on his route."

Janice mushed her wormy lips into a circle and smacked them so she looked like a kissy fish. I grabbed a pillow off of my bed and whipped it at her, just missing her head, and screamed, "SHUT UP!" She ran out of the room, so I lied back down on my back looking up at the cracked ceiling. Just thinking about Dewey's kiss set the butterflies loose in my stomach again. I don't know why God invented kissing, but it was a good idea, and I'm glad that he did. I'm dying for Dewey to kiss me again.

Dewey's Girl

When I got to the spot to meet Dewey, he was already standing there waiting for me.

"Hey Cozy!"

"Dewey!" I could feel my face getting hot and I was glad it was cold out because he wouldn't be able to tell that I was blushing. Bazooka! I could smell it already. His jaw was dancing around a big glob of it and I knew he was working on a bubble to try and show off for me. "Watch this!" He said, blowing out really slowly, until a humongous bubble was sitting on his face. I laughed out loud and reached over to pop it, but he jumped back holding his head high, so I couldn't reach it. He did some more blowing until it got so big that it popped and hung down his chin like a pink beard. Now we were both laughing. "That was a good one!" I said. Dewey grinned and then he picked up his paper sack, grabbed the cuff of my coat, and pulled me along with him like I was on a leash.

We hit the old people's building and dropped all the papers off as fast as we could. Coming down the dark stairwell I thought about the last time we were in here and me falling on my face... and the hallway kiss. I walked extra slowly, giving Dewey enough time to get up the nerve to kiss me again. He was holding my hand now, and squeezing it a little, like he wanted to make sure that I knew that he was there.

When we hit the landing Dewey got right in front of me, with his back against the door, so I couldn't get out. I didn't want to get out though. I wanted Dewey to kiss me more than anything. My body was shaking inside; tickly little shakes in my belly that made me feel like I was starving for him to kiss me. Dewey grabbed both my hands and moved them behind my back like I was under arrest. I could feel his sneaky breath on me, sweet from all that bubble gum. I closed my eyes and waited, with my face up like a baby bird waiting to be fed. Dewey's lips were on my cheek creeping over to my mouth. I turned my face a little so his lips could reach mine and.... holy crap! It was like the kiss was in my belly, and not just my lips, and it was heading down to my you know what! Dewey pulled his head back and said, "Yeah," in a whispery voice. I knew he must have been feeling it too because he was coming in for another kiss.

I was feeling too many feelings at once and it was starting to scare me because some of it reminded me of how I felt when I was with Ken. Sometimes, when Ken touches me, it feels good and I feel evil because of it. I try really hard for it not to feel good, but I can't help it, and then I feel really rotten afterwards.

I yanked away, sending Dewey the signal to knock it off. Thinking of Ken spoiled the whole kissing thing and I wished that I could erase Ken out of my head forever. I gave Dewey's hand another squeeze, so he wouldn't get mad at me for stopping him. He squeezed back and then opened the door for us to leave.

He decided to take us on a shortcut behind the big brick building. It was the shortcut I hated because I had to climb a fence. But I didn't complain about it. I just kept taking long hard steps, and I was keeping up with him, pretty much, even though the snow was way over my knees. We finally got to the fence and I was waiting for Dewey to give me a boost up, but instead he grabbed my hands and looked down at me. I was staring back at him, watching his white face turn blotchy red, and I was worrying that he was mad at me for busting up our kiss. He looked up at the sky and swallowed hard, so his Adams apple rolled up and down his neck, and then he looked down at me and said; "Cozy, will you be my girlfriend?"

"YES!" I blurted out, like he just asked me if I wanted a million bucks. A big smile took over Dewey's face. Then he pinched the end of my nose and started laughing.

"What?" I said, pushing his hand away, feeling like I said something wrong.

"Nothing," he said, still smiling. "It's just…didn't your mother ever teach you how to play hard to get?"

"Huh?"

"Never mind, I'm just teasing you."

I tried to tackle him but he grabbed my arms and we both fell in the snow. We wrestled like puppies for a while, and the snow was probably really cold, but I couldn't feel it. I was too filled up with being Dewey's girlfriend.

Back at the house I couldn't stop thinking about Ken butting in on my kisses with Dewey. If Ken had never messed with me I bet I would be a regular girl who could kiss a boy without getting so many feelings down there. It was a strong feeling too, and hard to stop. It was kind of like being hungry, but for a touch and not food. But I'm still glad that I got the most fantabulous kisses from Dewey and that I'm his official girlfriend now; plus I got to hang out with Alex all day too. That was the coolest.

I feel like my luck is changing and lots of good stuff is starting to happen to me. I just wish I could forget all the Ken stuff. I'll never tell Dewey about Ken and me. That way when we get married he'll think that he's the only one. My stomach does a little spin; like it doesn't like what I'm thinking about. It always does that when I think of the Ken stuff. I try switching my thoughts to something else, but I can't. My thinking keeps taking me back to Ken messing with me, and the black hole it dug in my soul. Maybe I should work up the nerve to go to confession. The priest says that God forgets about sins, once you go to confession, so if God can forget about it maybe I can too. I don't know if I can tell a priest though. They're so ......holy and good.

Hippie Christmas

It's Christmas Eve and no one can sleep. Me and Janice put our mattresses on the floor so we could sleep together and have lots of room. Tommy keeps showing up, and begging to sleep in here too, but we said no because then we can't talk about girl stuff. I feel bad for him though, and I think Janice does too, because the last time he asked, Janice said it was up to me. I said no, but I couldn't look at him when I said it.

Tommy comes in our room again; only this time he's walking on his knees like he's praying. "Please! Please! Please!" He says, like a pitiful little beggar.

Janice looked over at me with her long face and I knew she wanted to say yes. She's such a schmuck. I sigh and say, "It's up to Janice." So Tommy kneels in front her, like he's waiting for communion and Janice touches the top of his head and says, "Yes you may!" I could tell that Janice was glad that she got to be the good guy until Tommy tried hugging her and bonked her in the mouth with his fat head. They both toppled over, and then Crumbs joined in, whining and poking her pointy nose in between them, because she was afraid that they were fighting like Ma and Ken do all the time.

"Get the hell off of me you friggen idiot. My mouth is bleeding!" Janice shouts, holding her mouth with one hand and pushing Tommy away with the other. I couldn't help but laugh because Saint Janice was swearing up a storm. Poor Tommy was trying to wipe her mouth with his pajama top but that was just making Janice madder.

I couldn't stand watching him squirm so I said, "Come here Tommy. You can sit with me." He rolled over to my side of the mattress and Janice got up to investigate her bloody mouth.

"I didn't mean to hurt her."

"I know." I told him, and then I gave him a little one arm hug to make him feel better.

Janice came back holding a washcloth on her lip. She seemed okay, so I shut the big light off and turned on the table lamp so we could read. I let Tommy look at one of my Richie Rich comics, but me and Janice dug into the *True Story* magazines. Tommy knocked out pretty fast, but me and Janice weren't ready to sleep yet so we kept on reading. After a while Diana came in swearing. She was mad because Ken kicked her off the telephone, and now she was bored. She sat on Janice's mattress, lit a butt, and then opened a magazine.

This is the weirdest Christmas Eve ever with all of us smoking on the floor and an extra kid sleeping on the mattress. Ma used to watch Christmas specials with us but tonight she was locked up in her room with Ken. I asked Diana if she missed watching the Christmas Eve specials with Ma, but she kept her head in her magazine and didn't answer me. Janice frowned at me and I knew that she was mad at me for bringing up the olden days.

After a little more reading Diana said that she was going to bed. She got up, put a fake smile on her face, and said,

"Merry Fucken Christmas," and then she left. Janice and me just looked at each other and let Diana's words find their way inside us.

I woke up to a dark room with somebody pulling on my arm. I though it was Janice trying to get me to sneak a peak at what was under the tree until I felt Ken's pointy whiskers rub against my hand. I tried to pretend that I was sleeping, but it didn't work, because Ken pulled me up onto my feet and then led me through the dark house into Tommy's empty bedroom. I smacked my face against the door jam going in, but I didn't dare yell, because I didn't want to wake everyone up. And I could see myself... just like it was a movie in my head, getting dragged away by a caveman into his dark cave.

Ken was all sappy this morning, playing good daddy, and handing out presents like Santa Claus. Ma had her movie camera rolling and kept telling us to smile and hold up our presents. She kept pointing the stupid thing at me and telling me to do something funny. I got soap on a rope in my stocking so I pretended to wash my armpits with it for the camera. I was only doing it for Ma, so that Ken stayed in a good mood, because if I acted sour he'd get sour too.

Meme is supposed to come this afternoon with Uncle Richie and Carla. Once they leave I'm heading out too. I don't know where I'm going but I'm not sitting around here and looking at Ken's ugly mug all day. Dewey said that he would try to meet me at three o'clock if his mother lets him out. I hope he shows.

"What's that scrape on the side of your face, Cozy?" Ma pulled my hair back to get a better look at it. I pulled away and told her that it was just a little scratch from me and Janice horsing around on the mattresses last night. I could have told her that Ken did it when he was dragging me into Tommy's room so he could fiddle around with me, but I doubt that that's something she would want floating into her ears on Christmas morning.

Ma told me to keep the scratch clean and then moved on with her movie camera.

Diana looked like she couldn't wait to ditch the house, sitting there with her arms folded tight and her foot tapping to no music. Janice was hamming it up with Tommy in front of the camera. She got a new coat with fake pink fur on the hood so she was acting like Greta Garbo, looking sideways through the fur and kissing at the camera. Tommy was making two action figures fight above her head and she kept swatting at him like a fly because she didn't want him to screw up her little movie.

I hauled my load of presents into my room and stacked them on the floor next to my bed. I got mostly clothes, a new Parcheesi game, and a Paul McCartney Beatles doll. He didn't look too cute as a doll, but I liked him anyways. I set him on the windowsill next to Mr. Blue, my Wishnik, and then I headed for Diana's room so I could have a smoke.

Diana's door was shut, so I tapped on her door and held my breath, hoping that she'd let me in.

"What?" She said through the door so she wouldn't have to get up and open it.

"It's me...Cozy. Can I come in?"

"I suppose."

I could tell that Diana wasn't in a talking mood so I sat on the floor next to her feet and kept my trap shut. I was dying for a cig but I'd have to wait until she lit one up and then I'd light up one of my own. Diana must have heard me thinking because she pulled a butt out of her pack and lit it up. So I did too.

We sat smoking and sighing because we had no words and Christmas stunk. I wanted to ask her about all the feelings I had when Dewey kissed me, but then I would have to tell her about Ken, and I didn't think that would be too smart because she would tell Ma about it for sure. So we sat and puffed away until the room was foggy with smoke.

I was just scrunching my cigarette out in the ashtray when the door popped open and Ken waved his hand in front of his face, trying to clear the smoke, so he could see in.

"What the hell is all this friggen smoke in here?" he said, looking at me like he knew what I was up too. I kept a straight face and ignored him, but Diana popped off at the mouth saying that it was her room, and that she could smoke if she wanted to, and that he should knock before he comes barging into her room because she could have been naked. I could see the muscles in Ken's face working his jaw, like he was chewing on something. This usually means he's pissed but doesn't know what to say yet. I stared at the floor and waited for the fight to start. Diana was braver than anyone I knew, talking to him the way she did. But he didn't fight with her; instead he left, slamming the door so it bounced open again, making the smoke swirl around and float out through the door like a ghost leaving.

"Aren't you afraid of him?" I asked, picking dog hairs off my socks. Diana laughed one little "ha," and then she got up and pushed her door closed. Her face was winter white, and her eyes kept jumping back to the door like she was waiting for Ken to come back.

"I'm afraid of him," I said. Saying it out loud was like making a promise that he scared me, like I quit fighting, and it made me so mad that I wanted to spit.

"I'm not scared of that jackass!" Diana said, way too loudly, and she knew it too, because she hurried over to her record player and put a Herman's Hermits record on, thinking that maybe *Mrs. Brown's Lovely Daughter* would erase her words from the air. But Ken didn't come snarling back like an angry dog, like I thought he would. So I scooted back to my room and left Diana sitting on her bed, tapping her pretty nails on her dresser like they were feet running away.

Meme swept into the house carrying shiny bags full of wrapped gifts, followed by Uncle Richie, carrying more bags, and then Carla rolled in, all dolled up and carrying nothing.

They looked like rich people. Meme and Carla were wearing fur coats, and sparkly Christmas jewelry, and Uncle Richie had a black suit on with a red tie. They sure didn't look like they belonged at our crappy house. Meme gave us cheek kisses and Uncle Richie gave us his lame half hugs. Carla just stood behind him smiling and nodding. I guess she was afraid that she'd get cooties if she touched us. Ma took their coats, like she was running a fancy restaurant, and told me to go lay them on her bed.

The bed was all rumpled, with hills of blankets and sheets, surrounded by stained pillows. It seemed funny laying these fancy coats on such a messy bed. But I tossed them on there anyways, and then joined everyone back in the parlor. Ken was standing up against the parlor heater, with no shirt on, smiling like he had stage fright. Ma seemed like she wanted to be two people at once. One person was making sure that our company was happy and the other one was trying to make Ken fit in with family. I didn't even feel like I fit in any more and if I was making my tribe right now I wouldn't invite any of these grownups to join it.

It was pretty quiet in the parlor with nothing much going on, so Meme opened a red gift bag and starting dealing out our presents. I got an ugly brown skirt, lilac powder that shakes out of a cardboard tube like salt, and some stationary with little yellow ducks on it. Things got too quiet after all our presents were opened. Ken didn't know what to do and was fidgeting around like he had to pee, then he disappeared into his bedroom. Uncle Richie rolled his eyes, and I knew on the inside he was saying, "what an idiot." Ma must have known what Uncle Richie was thinking because she made an excuse for Ken, saying that he didn't get much sleep last night. I was wondering if she knew why he didn't get much sleep last night. I pictured myself getting up on stage, in front of the parlor heater where Ken was standing, and giving a little speech of my own about why Ken didn't get enough sleep last night. Would Uncle Richie knock Ken's false teeth down his throat because of what he did to me, or would he melt down into an

Uncle Richie puddle and slide out the front door and never come back again?

I kept trying to get Uncle Richie to look at me. I wanted to check and see if his eyes still smiled when he saw me. But he didn't look my way very much, and when he did he was already smiling; so it didn't count.

Things got better after Ken went into his room. Everyone was laughing, and remembering stuff from when us kids were little. I felt kind of bad for Tommy because we didn't have any memories for him because he just got into the family. He kept wiggling around, and picking his nose and stuff. Meme gave him a dirty look and said: "Hasn't this kid ever heard of a tissue?" Tommy put his head down and folded over like an empty sock because he was embarrassed. Ma didn't say anything to stick up for Tommy, because Meme is her mother, and even though she's a grown up now, Ma still never talks back to her.

I caught up with Uncle Richie while he was in the kitchen pouring himself some more coffee. I went right up to him and gave him a real hug. He put his cup down and hugged me right off my feet, and then he twirled me around like he used to do. (I might let Uncle Richie join my tribe, but definitely not Carla.) It felt so good to be twirled again. Like I was still me and he was still him. But then he set me down and headed back to the couch to cuddle up with lover lumps, Carla.

After dinner it was getting near time to meet Dewey at three o'clock. I helped with the dishes and then I planned my escape. I was praying that Dewey could get away because I was dying to see him. I had to be kind of sneaky about leaving because I never tried going out on Christmas day before. We always stayed together, as a family, but back then Mr. Creepy Fingers wasn't living with us, and I liked staying home.

I slipped out through the back door onto the street and then I walked as fast as I could past all the cars that were parked along the road. I made it to our corner, but Dewey wasn't there yet. I felt my stomach filling up with rocks because I didn't have anywhere else to go if he didn't show up.

I sat on the steel guard rail and tucked my feet behind me so I wouldn't fall off. I started counting blue cars, to make time go by faster, but after a while that got boring so I sang all my favorite songs, but that got boring too.

The sun was turning white and hanging low in the sky. I got up, because my feet were cold, and walked back and forth to warm them up. Over and over I walked until it seemed like I'd been walking for a year. Finally, I sat back down and closed my eyes, trying to make myself believe that Dewey was coming. I pictured him running all the way to meet me, but I couldn't see his face, and the rocks in my stomach were piling up, telling me that he wasn't going to show.

I felt like an idiot for sitting in the dark by myself. I knew I should go home but I couldn't make my feet move because they were sleeping. I was ticked at Dewey for not showing up, but I figured his dad was making him stay home because of it being Christmas and all.

I pushed myself up off the rail to leave and fell forward, landing in the gutter on my hands and knees. Looking up, I saw some headlights aiming right at me. I couldn't move fast enough so I ducked my head under my arms and waited for the car to hit me. Its horn blasted, long and loud, like a train whistle blowing, but the car didn't hit me. It went right by, blowing me with its car breeze. I jumped up before another car came by, and ran down the hill toward my house.

My tears felt hot, like wax dripping down my face, but I was more scared than sad. I passed my house, without looking, and kept on going. I didn't know where I was running to but I knew I couldn't go home yet. After a while I stopped to catch my breath and take time to figure out what I was going to do. Christmas lights were glowing from people's windows, bushes, and doors, making night time look friendly, so I wasn't even afraid of being out after dark by myself. The neighborhood looked like a Christmas present all wrapped up in lights. Christmas was pretty much over though, because tomorrow people would start unplugging all those lights and yanking them out of their trees. I lit a butt and started walking again. If I could freeze time so that Christmas would never go away I would. But I would freeze it to last year's Christmas because that was before Ma married Ken.

Loud music was coming from somewhere but I couldn't tell where, so I let the music lead me to a little brick house squished between two three-deckers. The front door was open, like it was summertime, and people were hanging around the front porch laughing and gabbing, and passing a big bottle of something back and forth. I looked past them into the house, and saw clumps of hippies moving to the music.

I crossed the street to get a better look, and hid behind a big tree that was growing out of the sidewalk. My stomach got tingly worrying about getting caught spying on them, and I was freezing. So I lit another cigarette, hoping it would make me feel warmer, and stood behind the tree to take a break from my spy work. I could see my house up the road, and the TV light dancing against the shade to Ma and Ken's bedroom window.

"Hey man, can I cop a smoke?"

"HUH?" I flinched, like I was about to get smacked, and spotted a boozy smelling hippie leaning against my tree with me. I swear he popped out of thin air just like a leprechaun.

"Be cool. It's just me."

Just me? I tried to recognize "Just Me," but it was dark, and the harder I stared the weirder he looked. He had long stringy hair, parted down the middle like Ma's kitchen curtains. His nose was too long, and he had a black billy goat beard growing out of his pointy chin. I tried to act "cool," even though he looked kind of witchy, and handed him a cigarette. He snatched the butt and flipped it into his mouth, and then he started digging in his pockets for a match. I passed my matches to him and watched him light up. He looked cuter in the match light.

"Merry Christmas man. I'm Wayne." Wayne leaned over and gave me a full hug, like he was my long lost brother or something. He smelled like cinnamon buns and booze. I didn't hug him back at first, because I didn't know him, but then I started to feel bad for acting snooty so I patted his back like I was burping a baby. "Man. It's not cool being out here in the dark all by yourself on Christmas. We got plenty of wine and shit inside."

Wayne wrapped his arm around me and walked me into the house. It was crowded with hippies moving around, smoking, dancing, and smiling. I stayed close to Wayne while he steered me over to a couch. It had three people sitting on it already, but Wayne squished us in on the end, so we just fit. There was a skinny wooden coffee table covered with beer bottles, plates filled with cigarette butts, and a candle in a bottle melting into itself, forming a volcano of wax.

Wayne stuck his hand in front of my face with a tiny cigarette in it. It was skinnier than a cigarette and smelled strong.

"No thanks," I said, because I already had my own cigs, but Wayne kept shoving it at me telling me to try it. So I did. It tasted like dried leaves, and burnt my throat when it went down. I coughed it out; choking like it was my first cigarette. Wayne laughed, took back the tiny butt, and said, "No bogarting man. One toke is all it takes."

All those little cigarettes got to my head, and after a while I lost track of Wayne, but nobody kicked me out for being too young, so I stayed. I was feeling smiley and wandered around the house until I finally ended up at the kitchen table, where I smoked some more funny cigarettes with a bunch of other people.

I met Bimini and Frank, who live there with their little baby girl named Summer. She has a funny top lip, like God went out of the lines when he was drawing it, so it kind of twists up toward her nose, and when she smiles it looks like it's split in two. I held her for a long time while she chewed on a long strip of leather, but I had to put her down because I started with one of my laughing fits and couldn't stop. I don't even remember what was so funny. I kept on laughing with my cheeks bouncing up and down, making my eyes open and close, like I was behind a Venetian blind. It scared the crap out of me because I couldn't stop, and I didn't want to drop the baby. Frank told me that I smoked too much pot for my first time and that I should go nod off for a while. I can't believe that I smoked pot with a bunch of hippies. Ma would croak if she knew.

Anyway, I sat on the floor, like an Indian, trying to make myself feel normal again, but my head kept sagging down on my chest and I couldn't lift it up no matter how hard I tried. I could hear people talking, and the music playing, but my head wouldn't lift up, and I ended up falling asleep sitting right in the middle of the Hippie's Christmas party.

The next thing I knew, somebody was tapping me on the shoulder, asking me if I wanted some pancakes…like it was a normal house. I could smell them cooking, and I felt like I could eat a whole batch by myself, so I got up and had some. Just like that. Those were the best pancakes I ever had too; even though I had to share them with a frizzy haired girl named Windy who kept crying and telling me that she loved me.

It was two o'clock in the morning before I snuck back home. I had to climb in my bedroom window, because the door was locked, but Janice didn't stir a bit, even with the cold air blowing in on her.

Ma asked me where I was last night and I told her that I went over to Dewey's house and that we were playing games and stuff, and that I lost track of time, so Dewey's dad had to drive me home. I didn't say anything to her about climbing in my window. But she bought it! The only thing she said was, "Next time call if you're going to be late." That's it. I could probably go to friggen California if I wanted to. All I'd have to do is make up a good story. Ma never used to let me run like I do. I don't get her anymore.

Dewey showed up at my house today to tell me that he was really sorry for not meeting me like he said he would. He said he ate some bad fish that his dad had in the back of the freezer and spent all Christmas day puking his guts out. I didn't tell Dewey about the party I went to, or the little pot cigarettes that I smoked. Some things need to be kept secret.

Dewey gave me a pretty silver ring with an angel on it for Christmas. He told me that it wasn't really a Christmas present, because he was going to give it to me anyways to prove that I was his girl, but I think he was just saying that so I wouldn't feel bad about not getting him anything. He said that the angel could watch over me when he wasn't around to do it. I like how Dewey tries to take care of me, so I gave him a little kiss on the mouth and watched his cheeks turn blotchy all the way back to his ears. Kissing Dewey Sloan gets easier the more I do it.

I see Dewey all the time, now that I help him with his route nearly every day, plus I've been sneaking out at night to meet him at the fort that we built in the field. It's right up the road from my house. We built it with some dirty plywood that Dewey's dad had lying around in his back yard. Dewey hauled the wood up in his wagon and we built it together. Well... Dewey did most of the building while I held the plywood up so he could do the nailing. It didn't have a door so I hung an old brown towel up there instead. The floor is cardboard, but I painted it green, brown, and red, so it looks like a rug, then I put an old orange sleeping bag in there and a little wooden box for a table.

Dewey says that it looks cool. He made the roof so it slides off. He calls it a moon-roof because we like to look at the moon and stars at night when we're in there. We make sure to sneak back to our houses way before breakfast so we don't get caught. Diana knows what I'm up to because she caught me slipping out the door one night, but she was on her way out too, so she said she wouldn't tell if I didn't. She goes off with Gina sometimes at night but I don't know where they go.

Sometimes I go to the fort in the daytime, when I don't have anywhere else to go. At least I get away from Ken because he's always trying to mess with me. It gets super hot in the fort when the sun's out, so I have to take the towel off the door to let the air in, but it's still better than staying at the house and dodging Mr. Horny Toad all day.

There's a big pear tree behind the fort that I like to climb. I can go all the way up to the top, because there are so many branches that it's like a ladder, and I can see way down the street to my old school. I call it my old school because in September I start Jr. High with Janice and Dewey. Janice told me not to expect her to hang around with me because she's in the ninth grade and already has all the friends she needs, but who gives a crap anyways because I'll have Dewey to hang out with. Diana is in high school and Tommy's still at our old school.

Sometimes when I'm up in the top of the tree I watch people. One time I saw Janice and Peggy hanging out at the wall smoking. It seemed like Janice did most of the talking while Peggy kept nodding her head, just to make it look like she was listening, and taking lots of drags off of her cigarette.

Part of me wants to hang out with them but the other part likes to be by myself at the fort listening to my radio. Janice doesn't really want me hanging around with her anyways. The last time I tried to hang out with her and Peggy, she said, "Get lost, Twerp," and ran off ahead of me so I couldn't catch up with her. Janice has long legs that get her places fast. She's the best runner around. Sometimes Janice is such a jerk.

I can't wait for the pears to get ripe. They're the fat yellow kind that get real juicy and sweet. Dewey can't come to the fort in the daytime because he's helping his uncle Laddie paint houses all summer. He gets paid eighty-five cents an hour; plus he has all that money from his paper route. Dewey saves most of his money in the real bank, not a jar or piggy bank, and says that he's saving it so he can go to college some day and learn how to build buildings and stuff. I bet he does it too.

I've been hanging around Alex's house when he doesn't have friends over. Alex is teaching me about art and music. He makes me listen to the words in songs and then asks me to tell him what they mean. Some of the words are screwy and make no sense, but I try to look like I'm deep thinking, and then I guess what they're about so he doesn't get ticked at me for not trying. I like most of the songs though, and I know the names of lots of bands.

Alex is my next best friend after Dewey. When I first told Dewey about Alex he said that he didn't want me talking to him, but then he met Alex at the spa one day when we were having a Coke, and now he says it's okay, because Alex is a teacher at the art museum and not a dopehead like some of the other hippies. I let Dewey think that he had a say in what I did but I always do what I want to anyway.

I never did tell Dewey about me smoking pot at Frank and Bimini's house. He hates dopeheads almost as much as he hates murderers. That's another secret I will never let him in on. The first secret is what Ken's been doing to me all these years.

I still go over to Frank and Bimini's house to baby-sit for Summer whenever I can. I told Ma how sometimes when I feed Summer, the milk is so sour that it stays stuck in the bottom of the bottle like cottage cheese. Ma said that babies shouldn't drink cow's milk and gave me ten dollars to get Summer some baby formula. She drank that down like she was dying of thirst. I thought Ma was going to forbid me to go over to their house because of them being hippies, but she didn't.

I like Bimini but I don't think that she's a very good mother. It seems like she cares more about her friends, and getting high, than her own baby. I go over whenever I can to make sure that little Summer is being fed and changed like she should be. Sometimes, when I go over in the morning, I can hear Summer crying so hard that she sounds like a mad cat screeching until her voice disappears. I knock really hard, but nobody answers, so I wait on the front porch and knock every five minutes until Bimini lets me in. Bimini usually goes right back to bed and leaves me to take care of the baby by myself. One time she answered the door stark naked and didn't even try to cover herself up. I watched her bum bounce all the way back to the bedroom.

Summer's little eyes push open wide when she sees me and her arms and legs swat through the air like she's trying to swim to me.

All I have to do is say, "Suuummer!" and she smiles real big at me, with her mixed up mouth.

I still smoke pot when I can get it. It makes things seem fuzzy and fun. Frank taught me how to roll a joint. It's easy. I just take a cigarette paper, put some pot in a line on it, and then pinch, roll, and lick. I have to pick all of the seeds out first though because they pop and burn holes in my clothes. Sometimes Frank gives me a joint for babysitting, because he never has any real money, and I smoke off of that for a while. I can make a joint last a long time because it only takes me a puff or two to get stoned. I hide it in my doll, Blabby's, diaper and put her right there on my bed in plain sight.

A harelip and a cleft palate. That's what Summer has. Her grandma came to visit when I was babysitting one day, and she told me all about it. I knew something was wrong with Summer because of her mouth being so crooked, and sometimes when I'm feeding her, the baby food comes out of her nose, like a long noodle, and I have to wipe off her face and try again.

Her grandma looked really sad when she held Summer. She was asking me all kinds of questions about how Frank and Bimini live. Only she called Bimini, Nora, because that's what her real name is. She looks more like a Nora too with her flat brown hair and teacher's glasses. I didn't tell her much, because I didn't want to get them in trouble, but I did tell her that sometimes Nora runs out of formula and stuff. I don't think that was ratting on them or anything. I only said it because Summer was too little to tell her grandma for herself.

Janice has a babysitting job too, only the little girl she watches is two, and Janice gets paid real money for doing it. The lady she baby-sits for talks with a French accent and says motherfucker all the time; even when she's not mad. Her name is Marcia and she likes to go to protests and marches with the hippies, trying to get them to stop the war in Vietnam, and one time she got arrested for it and Janice had to keep Jessica, that's the little girl's name, overnight until Marcia's boyfriend Kevin got her out of jail. Kevin's not a hippie like Marcia. He wears a suit and tie most of the time and he's black. That's what he says colored people like to be called now, and he told me that Jessica is mulatto because she's half and half. Her skin looks like Ma's coffee with just the right amount of milk in it.

I baby-sit with Janice sometimes when I ain't got anything else to do. They have a little basement apartment with green tiles on the floors, like a hospital, and no pictures on the walls; except for a poster with a big black fist on it. When I talk loud in their house it echoes, like I was talking into a big barrel.

Once in a while Marcia lets me baby-sit when Janice isn't around. Her apartment is right on the corner of Kelly and Manchester streets, across from where I always meet Dewey when we do his paper route. I like baby-sitting for Jessica because she can talk and likes to watch TV with me, plus I like the money. But I'd rather spend most of my time taking care of Summer because she needs me more. I found some cigarette papers in a basket on top of the fridge at Marcia's house so I bet she smokes pot too.

Me and Dewey are looking up through the moon roof at the stars. The sky is showing off tonight, like a rich lady putting on all her diamonds, just because she has them. Ma always says that, "less is more." But tonight I'm glad that the sky wore more. Dewey told me that the stars were extra bright tonight because there was no moon out yet. Laying here, flat on our backs, side by side, looking up through our moon roof is my favorite thing to do.

I asked Ma if I could stay over Phyllis Garrett's house tonight, she's a good one to use cause Ma doesn't ever talk to her, and Dewey told his mom and dad that he was camping out with some buddies in their back yard. Now we get to spend the whole night out here without even having to sneak out.

I made some peanut butter crackers and red Kool-Aid that I mixed up in a glass milk jug. Dewey already gobbled up half the crackers and he's working on the Kool-Aid. It's pretty quiet outside, except for the crickets strumming, so it's easy to pretend that we're way out in the woods. Sometimes a car's headlights will erase the stars for a minute but then they always pop right back out again.

I could hear Peggy's mom calling her from the front porch, "Peggy Ann!" making me think of Ma at home watching TV behind her locked door, all relaxed and lazy, thinking that I'm over at Phyllis's playing records or something. Peggy's mom sounds mad all the time and if I were Peggy Ann I wouldn't want to go running home to that voice. A few minutes later I hear Peggy's feet slapping at the road, trying to get home before her mother got back out on the porch to do some more yelling.

Dewey sat up, leaning on his elbow and signaled the flashlight in my face.

"STOP!" I said, swatting at the light. He was being a pest with that flashlight of his and I wished his dad never let him borrow it. I covered my face with my arms to block the light and Dewey set the flashlight down, like a lamp, and dove into my armpits with both hands. He started tickling me, digging and wiggling, making me laugh like I belonged in the loony bin. I was trying to put my arms down and roll up into a little ball, so he couldn't find my ticklish spots, but he was too strong and he uncurled me, like a roll of wallpaper, making me lay flat on my back. Then he pinned my arms over my head, and sat on me so I couldn't move.

"Get off…. I can't breathe!" I yelled, pushing and squirming, trying to get loose. But Dewey wouldn't get off of me; instead he got up on his knees a little, so he wasn't sitting on my stomach, so I could breathe better, and then he leaned down so his face was almost touching mine. I could smell peanut butter swimming in his breath from all the crackers he chowed down.

I shouted, "Get off of me, Mr. Stinky Breath!" hoping this would get to him, because he was always blowing into his hand

and smelling it, worried that his breath didn't smell minty fresh enough.

"Who's the most handsome boyfriend in the world?" he asked, wanting me to suck up to him.

"Paul McCartney."

"Who?" Dewey plopped back down on me and moved his hand down to my knobby knees. He knew that I couldn't stand my knees being touched. I started laughing before he even found them, kicking and screaming like I was being tortured. He gave my knee a squeeze, and I let out a bloody scream that could have scared Frankenstein.

"SHHHH! You're going to get us kicked out of here."

"Then get off of me."

"Who's the most handsome boyfriend...?"

"You." I whispered, so he could hardly hear it. But he started the tickling up again.

"You." I said, a little louder, hoping that it did the trick. But it wasn't good enough so Screwy Dewey sent one irritating finger slithering up toward my armpit like a sneaky snake.

"YOU!"

The finger disappeared but he was still on top of me. "You can get off of me now." I said, trying to wiggle free.

"Hmmm... Maybe I'll just sit here a while and pick some boogers out of your nose."

"YUCK!" I turned my head sideways and started kicking again. Dewey's fingers crawled over my face like a tarantula searching for food.

"CUT! IT! OUT!" I hissed, trying to stay quiet and yell at the same time. Dewey stopped with the boogieman hand and brought his face right up to mine so that his nose was sitting on my cheek. His hands went soft, so I could move my arms, but I left them right where they were and waited. I felt a light smooch on my cheek, like a bubble popping, so I turned my head to get some more. He pushed down a little, so he was lying on top of me, and then he kissed me on my mouth.

Dewey never acted like this before. I mean he kisses me but he never laid on top of me before. I could feel my heart beating between my legs, making me want to rub up against him, but I didn't do it because I didn't want Dewey thinking that I already knew anything about S-E-X. But Dewey knew something about it because he was moving very slowly, sneaking a rub against me, and getting big down there. I was tempted to rub back, but I was scared that Dewey would want to do more than that and then I'd have another black spot on my soul and have two really bad things to tell the priest in confession.

He kept on rubbing, but I stayed still, pretending that I didn't know what he was up to. His body was trembling, and his breathing matched his shakes, casting a spell on me and making me shake too. I knew that spell. Ken puts that spell on me sometimes when he touches me, so I can't stop it from feeling good, and then I feel like I belong in hell when it's over with.

I pushed away from Dewey a little, letting him know that I wanted him to stop, but he kept going, pressing harder than ever into me. I wanted to let him keep going because it felt so good, and I almost did, but instead I moved my butt sideways, so he couldn't rub on me, and then I pulled myself out from underneath him.

Dewey didn't say anything, and rolled onto his stomach, groaning like he was having a bad dream. I flopped over onto my stomach too and shut off the flashlight. I felt bad for him because I had to say no. He never tried anything like that before so he was being pretty brave doing what he did. I stayed still and waited for Dewey to settle down. After a while he found my hand and gave it a little squeeze, letting me know that he wasn't ticked at me for stopping him. I smiled to myself and squeezed back.

I reached for the radio and found a good station. I created mini movies in my head for each song. *Wouldn't it be Nice* by the Beach Boys came on and I saw the movie of me and Dewey. I felt like the whole song was about us because I wished that we were older, like the song said, so that we could spend every day and night together.

"Can this be our song?" I asked Dewey. Dewey waited until the song ended before he answered. I was worried that he was stalling, but then he kissed my cheek and said, "Some day that will be us, Cozy." I laid my head on his chest, listening to his heart beat, and smiled, because I knew that someday that would be us.

When I woke up in the morning the sun was shining hot through the moon-roof and Dewey was gone. It seemed late. I stuck my head up through the moon roof and squinted into the morning. An old man, still in his bathrobe, was walking his little black and white dog. The old guy was clucking, and chatting, like the dog could understand what he was saying, but the dog was busy, leading them both down the hill with his nose. I didn't see Dewey anywhere and figured he must have taken off for home.

I felt kind of guilty about last night, letting Dewey rub against me like I did, but at least I didn't let him go too far. Why do things always seem worse in the morning, like the sun can see everything? I was glad that Dewey wasn't here to look at my face in the light because I might look different to him...dirty or something.

I rolled the sleeping bag up like a log, catching my angel ring on a loose thread. I bit it free, and twisted the ring around on my finger, pointing the angel's chubby face out so she could watch over me like Dewey said she would. I hoped this angel could keep Ken from trying to put his thing inside me. He keeps asking, but so far he stops when I tell him no. I don't know how long that will work. I would die if he did that to me. Maybe I should just go ahead and let Dewey do it before Ken gets to me first.

I pulled my sneakers onto my dirty feet; mashed my hair down with my hands, and headed home.

Ever since Ma married Ken we have lots more food in the pantry. No more "Old Mother Hubbard" for her. She even buys sweet cereal and soda in those big bottles for us. She's got a phone on the kitchen wall, a car in the yard, but only Ken drives it, and money for extra stuff like a color TV in her bedroom. Used to be we didn't have all that stuff but I didn't know it was missing until Ken came along. I didn't think Ma cared about things like that either, but she must, because she's always hiding away in her bedroom with Ken watching that stupid TV and munching on cookies and stuff.

They lock themselves in their room right after supper and if any of us come knocking Ken shoos us away through flat lips and gritted teeth. Ma doesn't ever say a word and lets him talk to us any way he wants to. Sometimes Ma sticks up for him and says stuff like: "He doesn't mean anything by it." Or. "His bark is worse than his bite." She doesn't know how sharp Ken's teeth are, but I wouldn't dare say anything to her about it seeing she's so happy with him.

This summer Tommy has been spending most of his time with Jimmy at Grammy Green's house. I know he's in there eating fluff-a-nutter sandwiches, with the crusts cut off, and watching her big color TV that sits on the floor. Janice and Peggy are like Siamese twins, stuck together all the time, walking the neighborhood whispering, giggling, and gossiping about anyone who walks past them. And Diana hangs out with Gina down the road, because she likes Gina's brother, but when she's home she locks herself in her room just like Ma and Ken do. Thank God I have Dewey to hang out with. When he's working with his uncle I see if I can baby-sit for Summer, or I visit Alex, if I can catch him at home.

Alex is pretty busy with summer school and his new girlfriend Shelly. She has long red hair, straight as a road, and white skin sprinkled with orange freckles that look like goldfish food. I only met her a couple of times, and when she's there Alex pays most of his attention to her. I try to visit when she's not around so I can have him all to myself.

When there's nothing else to do I sit on the wall and watch people, or I go to the fort to think.

I try to make a plan for every day so I don't get stuck at home with Ken. It's like everyone in our house has their own little world and we only bump into each other at supper time because we have to. When I see real families on TV talking and joking around at the kitchen table, it makes me feel like we're a family of skeletons with nothing to say. All I can hear are our forks scraping across our plates, and our smacky chewing. Sometimes I feel like I'm caving in, like a condemned house, and that there's nothing much left inside of me except for some old bones, empty rooms, and dirt. That's why I need a plan every day because it keeps my mind off of stuff so I don't cave in.

I've been knocking on Bimini's door for about an hour now and so far she's ignoring me. The birds are singing, like they have a lot to talk about, making the air seem busier than the ground. Ma was in a good mood this morning, maybe because it's Friday, but she had me turn on my radio and was singing along with it like these birds out here. It's kind of hard to smile at Ma, because of how she's been ignoring me lately, but my insides where smiling because of seeing her so happy, and my face couldn't hold the smile back. I just let her stay in her chirpy little mood.

The sky was starting to fill up with clouds, and the leaves were blowing backwards showing what's under their skirts. When Ma sees the leaves blowing like that she says it's going to rain, so I needed to find some place to go before it started. I figured that Bimini wasn't going to let me in.

The fort leaks; plus its scary in there when it's storming out, so I won't be headed there. Alex is gone to school until two o'clock so I can't go there. I could sit in his hallway, I do that sometimes when I'm really desperate, but that's way too boring. The only other place to go on a rainy day was home. Ken doesn't have to be at work until three o'clock, so I really don't want to go there.

It was getting darker out, and it looked like the day was over instead of just starting. I could hear a little thunder, like the sky's stomach was grumbling for breakfast, so I hopped off of the porch and walked toward the house. I was hoping that maybe Janice would stick around today and I wouldn't have to leave.

Big fat drops of rain started splatting on the dirt, sending up little smoke signals, so I ran as fast as I could back to the house. Peggy was in the hallway, the same way I was on the porch at Bimini's, waiting for someone to let her in so she could wake up Janice.

I felt important, because I had the ticket to Peggy's day, and I was thinking that maybe I'd make her wait a little longer, or tell her that Janice said she was too busy to hang out. I needed Janice to stick around the house or it would be just Ken and me.

"Hi Cozy," Peggy said, smiling wide like she was glad to see me, but I knew she was only smiling because she thought that her wait was over.

"Hi Peggy," I said, squeezing past her and opening the door. She leaned sideways trying to see past me into the kitchen.

"Will you tell Janice that I'm here?"

I was on the other side of the door now peeking out at her, keeping the door almost closed like I was hiding what was behind door number three.

"Yeah, wait a minute," I said, shutting the door in her face and racing to my bedroom. Janice was still sleeping, rolled up in a ball with her blankets kicked off, and her stringy hair stuck with sweat to her face. Hmmm.. She looked like she needed her sleep, and the way she was sweating like a hog might mean that she's sick. I bounced back to the kitchen, put on a straight face, and opened the door. Peggy's smiley face went flat when she saw that it was still me standing there and not Janice.

"She's still sleeping, and she's sick, so I don't think she'll be going out today."

Peggy looked both ways, like she was crossing the street, but she was just trying to figure out a new plan for her day before I shut the door.

"What are you doing today?" Peggy asked, in a whisper, like she didn't want to get caught liking me. I could shove off with Peggy, but then Janice would be stuck with Ken, and I couldn't do that to her. Besides I already ruined her day by chasing off her best friend. I told Peggy that I had to stay and watch over Janice in case she needed anything, so Peggy headed down the dark hallway and out into a rainy ho hum day with no plan at all. It was like I traded days with her, without her even knowing it, and now I had a plan and she didn't.

I poured some cheerios into a coffee cup, all the bowls were dirty, and sat smack in front of the TV with my pillow and Indian blanket. I had to sit up close to the TV to hear it because Ken's room was right off the parlor and I didn't want to wake him up.

I was watching Captain Kangaroo tease Bunny Rabbit with a handful of carrots with the fuzzy greens still on them, when Ken's door opened. I was right in his way, because I was sitting up so close to the TV, but I couldn't move so I sat frozen in that spot like a snap shot on one of those Polaroid cameras. Ken was in his blue and white striped under shorts, with the fly open just enough to show some black bushy hair poking out of it.

I dropped my eyes, looking at the zig zaggy designs on my blanket, following them into the wrinkles and out again, when Ken reached down for me and pulled me up by the back of my shirt.

"WHAT?" I yelled, yanking back so he lost his grip on me. Ken's skinny lips disappeared inside his face, and his nostrils opened wide. I could tell he was about to grab me again so I piped up and said, "Sorry." And then I smiled at him. "It's just that I was concentrating on the TV and you scared me." He bought it and turned nice again. "Come on in the bedroom," he said, rubbing his potbelly and letting his hand walk down into the front of his shorts, straightening out his man stuff, like it was a present for me.

214

I could see my face in my head, my eyeballs looked like round white eggs...like a dead person's eyes, and I had a tiny slit of a mouth stitched up like a scarecrow's. Everything was pushed inside of me and there was no room for anything else. "Oh God, no," I said to myself through my sewn up lips, and then I turned and my legs ran away.

I shot out of the kitchen door, and stumbled down the stairs and onto the sidewalk, like the house was puking me out. I landed on my hands and knees, skinning them on the cement, but I ignored it and started running again. The rain was dripping off my hair and down my face like blood. But it didn't feel cold. It didn't feel like anything. I pushed, barefooted up the hill, smack stepping on the hard wet road. I could feel little rocks and stuff collecting on the bottoms of my feet, sticking into them like candles in a birthday cake. I wasn't crying though because I couldn't feel the outside of me. All my feelings were on the inside of me, sitting in my throat like a big lump that I couldn't swallow.

The further I got, the smaller Ken got, so I kept on going and going, running past the wall, and the field with me and Dewey's fort sitting there, holding all our good times in its belly. I stopped at the schoolyard to catch my breath. I'd really done it now. I never ran away from Ken before and I knew that he was going to make me wish I'd stayed put. I lifted the horseshoe bar and opened the school gate, walking through it into the schoolyard. Everything looked all blurry with rain. I headed to the side of the school building, and then walked down some cement steps to the janitor's door. It was like a little dungeon down here because it was tucked under ground and you couldn't see it from the schoolyard. The rain couldn't reach me down here either, but it was hitting the building hard and running off of it in angry little rivers, splatting and splashing back up at my feet. There was a grate in the floor, like the ones on the sewers, only smaller, and the water rolled down it just as fast as it landed.

I sat on the hard steps, bloody knees together, scraped palms up, investigating my cuts and scratches. My wet hair fell forward, clumpy, like ruined spaghetti and dripping on my hands and knees, mixing with the blood and making drippy pink roads down my legs. I scraped the bottoms of my feet against the edge of the steps; clearing off the pebbles and dirt that hitchhiked a ride, and then I turned them over for a look. Dents, and one stubborn diamond shaped stone was still hanging on. I pinched it out and watched a dot of red pop up on my foot where the rock used to be. Nothing hurt. Not the cuts, scrapes, or holes. I could probably stick a pin in me and not feel a thing.

I was thinking about lifting the lid off of that grate on the ground and dropping down into it like a plop in the toilet. I would lie on the black water under the school, with my hands behind my head, like I was relaxing on the couch, and listen to what everyone said about me being gone. "That girl Cosette disappeared into thin air" or "I heard her step father drove her to craziness and she drowned herself in just six inches of rain water."

All of the houses looked shut up and empty because of the rain, but I knew that there were people in them doing whatever they felt like. I could picture Phyllis Garrett, with her long silky hair, laying on her couch with soft blankets and cool pillows watching her favorite TV show without worrying about a sex crazy monster popping out of the bedroom and making her do all kinds of disgusting stuff.

When Ken gets done with me he acts like nothing big happened and tells me to go play. I do go play. I try to erase what we did as fast as I can, so I get busy doing something else to push it out of my head.

It stopped raining but the sky was still dark and the leftover rain kept falling off the leaves every time the wind blew. I came out from under the school and walked down the road like it was any normal day. I had to pee really bad so I decided to turn back toward the fort to pee in the field. I could see Ken's car still parked right where he left it and I knew he was in that house spinning like a tornado because of me taking off and leaving him all hard like a walking stick. I peed behind my pear tree and ducked into the fort.

It was a little wet inside from the leaks, so I wiped them up and then I pushed the moon roof open a smidge, and peeked up at the sky.

I played my morning back through my head like a movie, telling me how I ended up here. When I got to the part of telling Peggy that Janice was sick, I could see the black spot that that stupid lie left on my soul. Peggy was stuck at home with her snappy mother and poor Janice was home in her bed all alone with Ken. I should have let Peggy in and then maybe the three of us could have done something in the house because of the rain. But no, I had to go ahead and make up a huge lie, and now everyone's day was messed up.

I couldn't stand the thought of Ken prowling around the house with that stick in his pants, looking for somebody to take it out on. What if he goes after Janice and it's all my fault? My stomach twisted up just thinking about it. I had to warn Janice to get out before it was too late, so I took off running down the hill and around to the back of our house to rap on the window near her bed.

The grass was really tall close to the house, and there was a road of a puddle from all the rain falling off of the roof. I sloshed through it, smacking at the bugs, and trying not to think about the squishy stuff that was sticking between my toes. Janice's shade was down but I could still see inside our room a little through a skinny rip in the shade.

I stood on my toes peeking in trying to decide what was what. I could see the closet door with my Halloween Witch decoration taped to it. She was grinning through all those black teeth like she always did. I could only see the foot of Janice's bed so I moved sideways a little and spotted Janice sitting up on her bed with no shirt on. If I knocked on the window now Janice would freak out because she was half naked, so I stayed still, waiting for her to get dressed before I started knocking.

Janice stood up, only I was seeing that it wasn't Janice at all but Ken's blue and white shorts with his stick poking out of them! I couldn't breathe because of what I was seeing, and I knew this was all my fault. I had to do something to stop Ken from getting to Janice!

I ran around the house and barged through the door into the kitchen, making as much noise as I could so it would scare Ken away from Janice. I started talking really loudly to Crumbs who was sniffing at my legs trying to figure out where I'd been. I heard footsteps, and swallowed hard, trying to look normal, like I didn't know what was going on in my room. The bedroom door opened a little and Ken yelled, "Who's out there?"

"Me, Cozy," I said, in a little voice, like I was talking to the troll under the bridge.

Ken threw the door open and I shouted, "Janice!" and then I tried walking past him and into our room, but Ken hooked onto my arm and held me there. I yelled for Janice again, but Ken smiled a skinny sideways smile, and said, "Janice left ten minutes ago with her little girlfriend."

Dewey met me right on time but I didn't have much to say to him. I was trying to act all happy but I felt weird, like I was unplugged from my life. Ken got hold of me and kept me in his room for a long time today. He tried to get me to go all the way with him too, but I said no and then I tried rubbing him the best I could to get his mind off of it. I guess it worked because he couldn't hold it any more and made his sticky mess all over my hand. I wanted to puke when he did that.

I've got to find a way to keep Ken off of me so I decided that I'm going to go to confession tomorrow and tell the priest everything. I don't even care if I shock him to death or end up in purgatory with all those unbaptized babies, I got to get this stain off of my soul and ask the priest how to keep Ken away from me.

Dewey grabbed my hand and gave it a little squeeze, and I squeezed his back, but I couldn't look at him because if he knew where my hand was this morning he wouldn't be squeezing it.

We finished the paper route a little late, because of all that collecting, and headed to the store for a Coke. We were sitting at the counter, sipping our Cokes, and he was yapping about a cool car that he wanted to buy when he turned sixteen. I ignored most of what he was saying, because I couldn't get my head out of the confessional. I kept practicing over and over, in my mind, what I was going to say to that priest tomorrow.

"Bless me Father, for I have sinned. It has been...too long since my last confession, or if I should only say a month, so that he wouldn't think that I was a rotten Catholic. Anyways, I kept getting stuck at the other part too, where I say, "And these are my sins." That's when I have to tell him my list of sins. Do I just blurt out that I've been letting my stepfather fiddle around with me or should I say that I let a man touch me? I hate this.

Dewey sucked his soda dry, making that irritating vacuum cleaner noise in the bottom of his glass, but mine was still half full because of all the thinking I'd been doing.

"C'mon slow poke," Dewey said, jabbing me under my arm with his straw.

"I'm coming," I said, pushing the glass away, and walking toward the door.

"What's eating you?" Dewey asked, running to catch up and open the door for me. He always opens doors for me. He says it's the sign of a true gentleman.

"Huh?.... Cozy!"

I pasted a smile on my face and said, "Nothing's eating me. I'm just thinking about stuff that's all."

"What kind of stuff?"

"Regular stuff. You know, school, chores. That kind of stuff."

"Oh that stuff ain't worth thinking about," Dewey said, following behind me. "It's summer vacation! Time to have fun."

"You should talk. You're always worrying about saving money and working with your uncle all summer just to get money for cars. I hardly get to see you anymore because of it."

Dewey got quiet because he wasn't used to me picking a fight with him. I felt bad for doing it, but I couldn't help it. If he was around more I would have a plan every day and I wouldn't get stuck at home with Ken. Dewey doesn't know a thing about what goes on when he's not around.

We kept on walking, without talking, until we got to the spot where he went his way and I went mine. I wished that I was nicer to him today instead of trying to make him feel like crap. Dewey looked down at me, his lips were missing. They were all tucked inside of his face like he was trying to hold back some words. I spoke up.

"I'm sorry Dewey. I didn't mean what I said. I'm just in a lousy mood that's all."

Dewey's lips popped out looking all soft and shiny. I wanted to kiss them, but I didn't dare do it in public, so I smiled instead, and blew him a kiss goodbye. He caught my kiss and planted it on his mouth.

I decided to wear the ugly brown paisley skirt that I got for Christmas to confession today. It's a wrap-around that has a tie at the waist. Janice let me borrow her white shell and thongs to go with it. If I stood sideways in the mirror I could see little bumps where my boobs were growing. Janice said that I was developing and that I should be wearing a training bra so my nipples wouldn't poke out. I remember when I couldn't wait to get boobs but now that I'm getting them it doesn't seem to matter much any more. Boobs are part of sex, and that's what's gotten me into all this trouble, and why I have to go running to the priest to get rid of these black stains on my soul.

"Shit." I probably shouldn't be swearing, seeing that I'm on my way to church, but I don't care because I am scared SHITLESS about going to confession. Janice just had to come with me because she couldn't stand being outdone by me. I think that she thinks that I'm trying to be holier than her. I wish. I'm just going for a good soul scrubbing but she's going because that's what Janice does. I'm making her go into the confessional first so that she'll be up at the alter saying her penance while I'm spilling my guts to the priest.

We blessed ourselves with holy water and walked toward a pew at the back of the church. All the confessionals were lined up, like dressing rooms with fancy red velvet curtain doors. Janice's stupid thongs kept slapping against my feet, because they were too long for me, making everyone turn to look at me. I squished my toes tight onto them, and the slapping stopped, but I was walking like a robot with no knees.

I sat on the wooden pew but Janice knelt. She was probably praying, but I'm way too nervous to pray. So I sat with my head full of words, and a stomach full of hornets buzzing around stinging my insides. I still didn't know what I was going to say to the priest.

An old lady came out from behind one of the red velvet curtains with her chin leading the way up to the altar, to say her penance. She didn't look sorry for anything and acted like she just tried on a new dress and now she was heading for the cash register to pay for it. She was an old lady though, and probably didn't even have any sins left to tell. The more sins you have the longer your penance is.

Janice moved out of the pew and slipped behind the confessional curtain. I could hear her voice from behind there; low and hummy, like a fat bumblebee. But I couldn't make out what she was saying. I knew it was nothing compared to what I had to say.

Sure enough, Janice popped out in less than two minutes, keeping her eyes down and her prayer hands in place. She takes this very seriously, but I feel like I'm only going to get off the hook with God.

I pulled back the heavy red curtain to the confessional and knelt down on the little wooden shelf on the floor. It was as dark as a coffin until a little window slid open, just like on the ice cream truck, and a shadow waited behind the screen. I could tell that the shadow was Father Bigglio because of his high hair and big nose. Once I caught him picking his nose before church. I didn't take communion that day.

Father Bigglio cleared his throat so I began. "Bless me Father for I have sinned it has been — almost a year since my last confession and these are my sins: I lied a few times, smoked, snuck out of my

221

window at night, let my stepfather touch me down there, swore, and picked on my step brother." I put the Ken-touching-me sin near the end hoping that it would get mixed up with the other sins and he wouldn't notice it too much.

"My child, how does your stepfather touch you down there?"

Huh? I didn't think he would ask for all the juicy details. I put my head down and tried to tell him without it sounding too dirty.

"With his hands and his dinky." The word dinky turned bad in my stomach, like sour milk, because no matter what I called his dick, it sounded nasty. Cripes…. I hate this.

Father Bigglio stayed quiet some more, but I could see his shadowy head moving behind the screen, and I wondered if he was trying to look up the answers in a priest book or something. My heart was drumming like a bongo in the darkest of Africa, and I wouldn't mind being there right now instead of here spilling my guts. Even in confession I didn't want to think about it too much, so I was counting the little diamonds on the screen of his window until he answered me again. Finally the Holy Shadow started talking to me.

"Does your mother know about this?"

"No. I can't tell her."

"Have you told anyone?"

"Just you… and my friend Alex. He's a grown up but I can tell him stuff."

"Do you enjoy it when your stepfather touches you?"

I couldn't breathe because the priest had his hands down my throat, digging up all the bones that I buried in my soul, picking each one up and inspecting it and then showing it to God. I wanted to slam the little window shut in his shadow-puppet face, and run, because he had no right to ask me stuff like that. He was just being nosey. God already knew all about Ken and me, and how hard it was for me to say it out loud.

I could feel my insides dripping out of my eyes and nose, and down my throat, all prickly and hot. The tears wet my face faster than

I could wipe them off. I swallowed, trying to cut off my crying, and said, "No. I hate it when he touches me. But, sometimes it feels good, but it's only because he puts a spell on me with all that touching that he does to me, and I try to not let it feel good by thinking about Jesus or Mary, and most of the time that works. I really just want him to stop messing with me, but I don't think he's ever going to stop." I flipped the front of my wrap skirt over, wiped my nose on the underneath part, then I waited for my penance.

"My child," the priest said, in a voice softer than butter. "You have a very grown up problem and it's going to take a lot of courage for you to do what I'm about to ask you to do. You must tell your mother what her husband is doing to you. If you don't, he will never stop touching you."

I pictured myself standing in front of Ma and telling her about Ken and me. I could see her grabbing at her heart and falling to the floor screaming, "No! No!" I try hugging her but she pushes me away and calls me a liar and a tramp.

"But it will kill her. And she might blame me...or not believe me."

"I will be praying for you my daughter. Be brave and go in peace. The Lord is nigh unto them with a broken heart. Say three Hail Mary's and help your mother with the dishes. The Lord bless thee and keep thee and bla bla blee blaaa. Amen."

"Huh?"

The little window slid shut in my face, and the Great and Powerful Wizard disappeared. Tell my mother. Do the dishes? Three Hail Mary's? I sat in the dark with his words. He didn't believe that I couldn't tell my mother. He should have told me to get the broom from the wicked witch of the north because that would have been easier than telling Ma about Ken and me. I left the little room and the holy shadow behind the diamond window, who now knew all my sins. I went straight to the altar to say my penance, with my thongs clapping as loud as they pleased behind me.

Janice was outside talking to Debbie Sullivan, a girl from her catechism class. She has a pretty face but her front teeth have cavities and it ruins her prettiness every time that she smiles. I sat on the steps in front of the church to wait for Janice to finish her yapping.

The sun felt really good, after being in that cold church for so long, so I leaned back a little so it could hit my face. I'm supposed to be feeling better because I got my soul cleaned. But I don't. Well, maybe a little. I know my soul is white and clean for right now, but it's just going to get dirty all over again. I said the Hail Mary's, and I already do the dishes at home, but I can never — EVER tell Ma about Ken. That priest doesn't know a thing about Ken or Ma. If I told Ma, then Ken would probably shoot me, or Ma would hate me forever.

Janice finished her gab session with Debbie and shouted over for me to start walking home with her. She filled me in on all of Debbie's business while we headed home, but I wasn't listening. I was doing like Peggy does, nodding yes and saying uh huh, to make Janice think that I was listening. At least she wasn't asking me about confession. Thank God for Debbie Sullivan.

I've decided that I'm not going to let Ken touch me anymore no matter how mean he is to me. He can kill me if he wants to but I just can't take it any more. I've been dodging him for a week now and he keeps throwing me pitiful looks, hoping that I'll feel bad for him. I know how he works. First he begs, and then he takes. Right now he's begging but it won't be long before he starts taking. I figure if I only go around him when someone else is in the house he won't be able to do anything to me.

I still have a white soul, except for all the smoking and swearing that I've been doing, but heck, they're the same sins that Janice has, except for the pot smoking, but I only did that once all week because I ran out of the stuff. Pot helps me forget stuff, so I smoke it, but this week I didn't really need to forget anything. I feel a lot better now that I don't have any huge stains on my soul, and even though I didn't tell Ma about me and Ken, I think Father Bigglio would be proud of how brave I'm being by dodging Ken all week.

Thirteen Stitches

I'm meeting Dewey at the fort once everyone goes to bed tonight. I made some fluff-a-nutter sandwiches, no crusts, and some orange Kool-Aid to take with me. Ma and Ken are going to the drive-in to watch some horror movies but I don't have to go because they give me nightmares. Tommy doesn't have to go either but I hope I don't get stuck at home babysitting for him.

Janice and Diana are already gone. They left right after supper. Janice is babysitting for Jessica and Diana is supposed to go to some club for teenagers with Gina. She looked really pretty when she left. She had on a mini dress, with sideways black stripes, and long dangly earrings that looked like cherries on a string. Her hair goes way down past her shoulders now and she ironed it so it would lay straight like Cher's. I hope I look as good as Diana when I grow up.

It was finally dark enough for Ma and Ken to leave for the drive-in, so I sat on the porch steps, hoping to dodge any last minute rules from them. As they backed out of the driveway Ken stopped in front of the steps and rolled his window down to talk to me. "Tommy is sleeping over Jimmy's house. Be in by ten." Up went the window and so long to them. I figured I'd hang out at the fort until eleven, zip home before Ma and Ken got home, and then I'd slip back out after they went to bed.

I got the sandwiches, and Kool-Aid that I made earlier, and stuffed them in a paper bag along with my cigs, radio, and some matches. Dewey was already inside the fort waiting for me when I got there; lying back with his sneakers off and an extra sleeping bag stuffed under his head. "Comfy?" I asked, standing all bent over like Quasimodo because the ceiling was so low. Dewey just wiggled his toes inside his holey socks and grinned. I ignored him and said, "I got some fluff-a-nutters, no crusts, and some more of that Kool-Aid that you like." Then I set things up on the wooden box, like it was a real kitchen table.

I lit a butt and leaned back on my elbows, blowing my smoke upward so it went out through the open moon roof. Then I said to the sky, because that's where I was looking, "I can only stay until eleven, and then I have to head home and wait for everyone to go to sleep." Dewey sat up and reached across for my cigarette. I handed it over and watched him take a drag. He doesn't inhale like a real smoker. He sucks some smoke in, moves it around in his mouth like mouthwash, and then spits it out in fat little puffs. I wanted to tease him about it, but I didn't. Instead I opened the jug of Kool-Aid and took a swig. Dewey handed me my cig, and I gave him the jug.

It was pitch dark except for the stars, so I cuddled next to him, with his arm around my neck, and we stared out at the sky. He played with the hair near my ear, and it tickled, but not enough for me to make him quit. I started thinking about how being here right now was better than anything in the world, and pictured happy stuff in my head to the songs that were playing on my radio.

"Cozy, wake up!" Dewey pulled on me, sitting me up like a baby.

"What?" I said, ticked because I was having a neat dream about Crumbs when she was a puppy.

"We fell asleep and I don't know what time it is."

"Crap." I searched around on the floor, bumping into shoes and junk, until I felt the hard square shape of my radio. I clicked and spun through the channels until I heard a man's voice instead of music. The guy was blabbing on about a car accident out on 495 and then he said, "Tune in for more on this story at two o'clock for news on the hour, every hour." I could feel my blood turning into army ants, marching through my veins, with their prickly little feet, all the way up to my head, making it buzzy with fear. Dewey handed me my shoes and shouted, "GO!"

"But where am I going to say I've been?"

"I don't know, but you better go before they call the cops or something."

I started crying and Dewey told me that he'd wait there for me no matter what. Then he pushed me out of the little door and told me to run.

I ran hard and fast with my shoes in my hand and my heart in my throat. All the lights were on in our apartment, a very bad sign, and the shades were up so I could see Ken and Ma sitting at the kitchen table. I stopped in the hallway to catch my breath and think. I'd tell them I fell asleep in my fort but I won't say anything about Dewey.

I pushed open the kitchen door and Ma and Ken both jumped to their feet.

"WHERE THE HELL HAVE YOU BEEN AT THIS HOUR OF THE NIGHT?" Ma screamed. I'd never seen Ma this mad at me before. I could feel myself caving in, losing my words so I couldn't remember what I was going to tell them.

"Um."

Ma grabbed my hair and pulled my head back so I was looking up into her snarley face.

"I ASKED YOU A QUESTION! WHERE WERE YOU?" she shouted, and then she dragged me by my hair across the room.

"I FELL ASLEEP AT MY FORT!" I shouted, hoping it would save my life.

"WHAT FORT?"

"The one me and Dewey built in the field," I mumbled because I wasn't so sure this was going too good for me. Ma let go of my hair and I slumped to the floor. I could see Janice peeking out from behind the bedroom door and I knew that she was thinking that she was glad she wasn't me. Ma lit up a butt, took a deep drag, and then blew out her smoke hard and straight.

"Who were you with Cozy?" She wasn't yelling any more but I knew that she was going to dig until she got the whole story. I put on my honest face, and found my convincing voice.

"Nobody. I was alone."

Ken piped up and said, "BULLSHIT! You can't tell me that you were alone in those woods. I can't even get you to go to the drive-in with me because you're afraid of the scary movies."

Ken used a sissy voice when he said it, trying to make me feel stupid, but that ticked me off more than anything so I yelled back at him.

"I WAS ALONE! AND I'M NOT A SISSY!"

Ken grabbed a jar of instant coffee off of the kitchen table and screamed, "SONOFABITCH!" Then he flung it at me. It bounced off my elbow and then smashed onto the floor. A sharp pain bit at my elbow, like a big dog had a hold of it, but I didn't look at my arm because I was too mad. I stared back at him and used some of Diana's words.

"YOU'RE A COWARD FOR HITTING LITTLE GIRLS!"

Everyone was in the kitchen now; gawking — waiting to see what was going to happen next. Ma looked like she was standing in the middle of traffic and didn't know which way to cross.

Ken said, "Aw, that's fucken rich. Go ahead and let the little twerp talk to me any way she wants." Then he stomped off to his bedroom and slammed the door.

Once he was gone Ma rushed over to me to inspect my elbow. I was so mad that I didn't even care about it, but now that Ken was gone, and Ma wasn't screaming at me, it started to smart like a bad toothache. Ma touched it and I pulled away.

"Damn him," she said, soft like she meant for just us two to hear. I looked at my elbow and could see blood from where the jar cut me. I never had a cut hurt this bad before and all this blood was making me dizzy. Ma told me to stay put, like I could go anywhere feeling like this, and then she grabbed a dish towel to wrap around my arm.

Diana smiled at me, like she was proud of what I said to Ken, and then she started sweeping up the mess, until Ma yelled at her for doing it barefooted, so Janice grabbed the broom and Diana ran to get some shoes on. Crumbs was under the kitchen table shaking, and looking pathetic, but I didn't blame her for shaking because I felt pathetic too.

Once the glass was cleaned up Ma slipped Janice's thongs onto my feet and walked me into the bathroom where she sat me on the toilet. She ran some water over a dingy gray wash rag and wiped at the blood.

"OUCH!"

"Sorry, but I have to see what it looks like."

Ma dabbed and wiped, as softly as she could, but it still hurt. I looked down at it. It was like the one I got on my head with Dewey. A long open mouth with no teeth; only this one was a lot bigger and made me want to puke when I saw it.

Ma sighed and said, "We better take you to the emergency room for this one."

She left me sitting on the toilet while she went to go talk to Ken about taking me to the hospital. Diana and Janice were gawking at my cut, and fighting over who would get to go with me. I could hear Ma and Ken fighting in their bedroom behind their locked door. I was going to call Ken a FUCKEN coward, but I changed it at the last minute. Good thing I did or he might have killed me.

Ma finally came back to the bathroom and began wrapping my elbow with some gauze.

"We're not going tonight, Honey, but first thing tomorrow, I'll have Meme drive us in."

I let out a sigh, because it was killing me, and I couldn't believe that he wouldn't even drive me to the hospital. Ma looked at me and said, "You'll live. Now go to bed."

I don't know what time it is but I can't sleep with this elbow pounding every time my heart beats. I can't stop thinking about Dewey sitting up there at our fort waiting for me to come back, so I'm heading back to the fort to tell Dewey to go home. I figure everyone in the house is sleeping, so now would be the best time to go. I don't even want to think about what would happen to me if I got caught going out again.

I walked the sidewalks, close to the shrubs, so I could jump into them if a car came by, but it was cemetery quiet, with not a car in sight.

"PSST!"

I stopped flat...waiting to make sure I heard something. I already felt weak and shaky enough without getting myself spooked, thinking that I was hearing things. But then I heard it again.

"PSST. Cozy."

Whew! I'd know Dewey Sloan's voice anywhere because of how he drags his "S's". I stayed put and waited for him to get to me.

Dewey trotted up beside me breathing heavy like a race horse.

"I've been waiting down by your house," he said, reaching for me, but I pulled back because I was afraid that he was going to bump my elbow. "I saw what your stepfather did to you."

Dewey had his hands squeezed into fists, like two sledgehammers waiting to slam something.

"I ought to kill him for doing this to you."

I didn't say anything because there was nothing to say. If Dewey saw it then he already knew the whole story.

We started towards the fort, walking in a quiet bubble. Dewey kept looking at me, like he was trying to think of something to say. Finally he asked me, "Does it hurt much?"

I had to laugh to myself because I could tell how nervous Dewey was, so I smiled.

"Only when my heart beats."

He grinned and we kept walking back to the fort to have a smoke. We didn't bother with the radio or kissing. We just sat there, keeping all our words inside us.

I got thirteen stitches on my elbow. The doctor, an old guy with serious bad breath, found a chunk of glass in it. He had to dig around in there with some tweezers to pull it out. I grit my teeth and shut my eyes until it was all over with. Then he stitched it up and put it in a sling to keep me from using it too much. He told me not to worry about the scar because the cut was on the wrinkly part of my elbow so I probably wouldn't notice it.

Ma and I rode the bus to the hospital because she said that Meme was too busy to take me. I knew that Meme only had to worry about going to church today, because it was Sunday and all, so I figured that Ma was just trying to skirt telling Meme what Ken did to me. When the doctor asked me how I cut myself Ma jumped in and said that I fell, before I could open my mouth to say anything. She didn't even look at me and wink. She said it like it was her secret alone. That ticked me off because she was more worried about protecting Ken's butt than anything else.

She didn't say a word about last night to me today and has been trying to act like everything is normal. Ken was acting the same way too. I'm glad that they didn't push me for answers about who I with last night, but it's still creepy the way they can forget about stuff so fast. I figure these thirteen stitches are the price I paid for having a nice time with Dewey...seems like everything costs something these days.

Dodging Ken keeps getting tougher and tougher. It's been nearly three weeks since I started dodging him and he keeps on cornering me and saying stuff like, "Don't you love me anymore?" or, "I thought you were my special girl," or, and this is the worst one, "If you keep ignoring me I can always make Janice my favorite."

I don't know what I'd do if he started messing with Janice the way he does with me. Even though she's my older sister, and smarter than me in most stuff, I'm a lot tougher than her and I think that if Ken touches her she would land in the nut house or something.

I'm running low on ideas on how to keep Ken away.

Ma took out my stitches using her little scissors and eyebrow tweezers. She said that she's a seamstress and removing stitches was no different then taking down a hem. I let her do it because I didn't have any choice but I would have rather had a real doctor doing it, even if his breath did stink like dog crap.

My arm doesn't hurt anymore but the scar is still red and thick with little stitch dots on the sides so it looks like Frankenstein's elbow. But it's mostly just itchy now.

My plan today is to visit Bimini and Summer for the morning and then go swimming up at Keller's Pond with Janice, Diana and Tommy. It's a pond sitting on the top of a steep hill, with a sandy beach and a neat store across the street that sells grinders and stuff. It's right here in the city so we can walk there. Peggy might come with us, if her mom lets her go, and Kelly, the girl upstairs with the Jell-O boobs, says she might come too.

When I got to Bimini's I didn't even have to knock because there was a big rock holding her front door wide open. I looked inside, and the back door was open too, so I could see clear through from one end of the apartment to the other.

It was too quiet so I yelled, "Hello." And then I waited. I felt a knot tying in my gut telling me that something wasn't right. "HELLOOOO!" I shouted, this time walking into the parlor... the empty parlor! All the furniture was gone and even the big mushroom poster they had hanging over the couch was gone too. I steered into the kitchen, and it was empty, like the parlor.

Their beat-up shades were pulled all the way down, like thirsty white tongues, and there was a can of powder cleanser sitting on the dirty floor.

The stove was still there, sticky with grease and shriveled up macaroni. They moved. They moved without even telling me and I'll probably never get to see baby Summer, with her crooked smile, again. I spotted some trash somebody had swept into a pile in the corner of the room. Dirt, hair, empty cigarette packs, old mail, and the little strip of leather that Summer liked to chew on. These were the last sad pieces of them living here, waiting to get tossed.

All of a sudden I felt like a cat burglar, being in the empty house that wasn't Frank and Bimini's anymore, so I flew out the door before whoever was cleaning came back and caught me in there. I sat across the street on the curb, hoping to spot someone who could tell me where they all went.

I couldn't believe that they left without saying a word to me. It reminded me of my old neighborhood being torn down and me and Rosemarie never getting a chance to say goodbye. I still had a picture of Rosemarie in my mind but it was starting to get a little blurry, and now I'll have to keep a picture of Summer in their too.

A guy with a head full of curly brown hair pulled up to the curb in a blue car. He reached around into the back seat and pulled a can of paint and some brushes out, and then he went into Bimini's old house.

I rushed across the street and caught him before he was all the way in.

"Do you know where Bimini and Frank moved to?"

He turned and had to look down to find me.

"Who?" He said, scratching at his chin like a chimp.

"The people who used to live here. Frank and Bimini, and their baby Summer."

"Oh yeah. Frank told me they were moving back in with his wife's mother because she was threatening to have that baby of theirs taken away. Wasn't that baby sick or something?"

"Harelip."

"What?"

"Summer, that's the baby's name. She has a harelip."

"Oh. Okay. Anyway they didn't give me much notice and left the place filthy. I'll never rent to long hairs again."

"Thanks," I said, walking away, chewing on this news, trying to bite it into little pieces so I could swallow it better. I couldn't help thinking about that day when Bimini's mom asked me all those questions, and how I told her that sometimes they ran out of food and stuff for the baby. I'm thinking that it might be my fault that they had to move in with Bimini's mom, but I had to tell because Summer was too little to say it for herself.

I'm really going to miss Summer, but I'm kinda glad that Bimini's mom is going to be taking care of her from now on and I won't have to worry about her any more.

I headed back home, because my plan got trashed, but everyone was still there, except for Ma, she was at work. I went to my room to dig out my bathing suit and find a clean towel before everyone else snatched them up. Janice told me that she was going to pack an old sheet for us to lie on while we tanned. Kelly and Peggy are both coming, so this should be fun. Plus we all have enough money to buy sandwiches for lunch.

"Hurry up Tommy!" Janice shouted, marching forward like she was a general in the Army. She was way ahead of everyone. Poor Peggy was right behind Janice; her red face dripping from the heat. Kelly, Diana and I were next, and then there was Tommy. He was way behind, dragging his towel on the ground, walking like it was his last step and boo-hooing because nobody would wait until he caught up. I felt bad for him so I hung back to wait for him.

Climbing the hill was the worst part of swimming at Keller's Pond, and sometimes I stayed home just because I hated climbing it. Tommy caught up with me and I took his towel so he wouldn't have to carry anything. I would carry him, if I could, just to get him moving faster.

By the time Tommy and me got to the pond Janice already had her sheet laid out and Peggy was rubbing her down with baby oil. Tommy took off for the water. A minute ago he was dying but now he can run. He has to stay inside the crib (it's really only a white fence in the water) because he doesn't know how to swim. I hardly ever go into the water at Keller's, except to get wet, because I don't want the life guard giving me a swimming test and telling me to stay in the crib with all those little kids.

Diana and Kelly had their own blanket and Kelly brought her transistor radio and already had it tuned in to WKAF. I dropped my shorts, and peeled off my tee shirt, leaving me feeling nearly naked in my black and white polka dotted one piece. Most girls were wearing two pieces but when you ain't got nothing to show why bother. Kelly and Diana looked like bathing beauties in their bikinis. They filled them out on the tops and the bottoms. Janice and Peggy, well…er… not really.

The Searchers are blaring *Love Potion Number Nine* on Kelly's radio. I'm lying on my stomach, with my eyes shut, picturing the gypsy lady with the gold-capped tooth mixing up her love potion. She has a turban on, like Ali Baba, and a long purple dress that's tied at the waist with a glittery rope. I don't suppose there's any such thing as a real love potion but I learned in history that Ponce De Leon discovered the fountain of youth in Florida, where Flipper probably lives and that cute kid Sandy with the blond hair who's always hanging onto Flipper for a ride.

"We're gonna take a walk to the other side." Diana announced, to only me because everyone else was splashing around in the water.

"Okay." I said, watching her and Kelly walk away, flipping sand off their heels, and swinging their hips like they were about to do a hula dance. The lifeguard watched them too, turning his head all the way around like a telescope so he wouldn't miss anything.

Kids could be drowning and he wouldn't notice because he was too busy girl watching.

I sat up and looked across the pond to the other side. There were some big flat rocks that looked like ginger snaps sticking out of the dirt right above the water. The teenagers liked to jump off of them into the deep water. If you try to swim across from here the lifeguard blows his whistle at you and waves you in. But he can't stop you from walking over to the rocks, and then jumping off the rocks, because he's too far away.

I watched Kelly and Diana making their way around, disappearing every now and then behind the woods and then popping out, a little smaller each time. They're probably going to meet up with some boys, maybe Gina's brother, Vic. Diana's still trying to make him her boyfriend.

I laid on Kelly and Diana's blanket so I could watch their stuff. After a while it felt like someone turned the sun on high so I'd cook faster, because the sweat was popping up all over me like the measles, and I was feeling weak for some water. I sat up and spotted Janice and Peggy sunning themselves on their blanket so I walked over and handed them Kelly's transistor radio to watch while I went to get a drink from the bubbler.

Each step felt like I was walking in boiling oatmeal because the sand was about a million degrees. "OUCH, EEECH, OOCH!" I made it to the little gray cement building, where the boys and girls rooms are, and stood in the spilled water from the bubbler to put the fire in my feet out. "AHH."

I started gulping at the skinny rope of water squirting out of the bubbler, and I could probably have drunk a tub full of it, except I got the feeling that someone was waiting behind me for a drink too, so I cut it short and stepped away. There was something familiar about the girl standing in front of me drinking, making slurpy noises like a dog lapping at a puddle, but I couldn't figure it out, so I waited until she lifted her head up to see who she was.

She quit her slurping, wiped her mouth with her arm, and then pushed her short blond hair back from her face. I froze, because

I knew who was standing in front of me. She turned and spotted me watching her. Her beady eyes were peering into mine, like she was reading the insides of me like a book, flipping through the pages of my life until she got to the part where she was in my story and my dog was biting her ass off.

"Aren't you going to say hi?" she asked, through big white donkey teeth that used to be little rotten pegs. It was Mean Carlene! She smiled a big hee-haw smile like she was trying to show off her new choppers.

"Hi," I said, giving her a smidge of a grin, like I didn't know who she was, and turned to head back to Janice and Peggy for safety.

"Hey...wait! Where are you going?"

"Huh?"

"Wait up for me."

Wait up for her? Did she think I was crazy or something? I kept on walking but I could feel her on my heels. I only made it halfway to Janice's blanket when I felt, tap, tap, tap. She was tapping me on the shoulder like she needed to tell me something important, and I was hoping that Janice noticed that I was in a little bit of trouble here. But Janice and Peggy had their feet aimed toward me and their heads facing the water so they couldn't see what was going on right behind their backs. I stopped and turned, waiting for her to give it to me good, but she was still smiling like we were old friends.

"What's up?" she said, and then she waited for me to tell her my plan for the day. I swallowed hard, keeping my eyes on Janice's boney feet, and said,

"Nothing, what's up with you?" I really didn't want to know what was up with her...it just fell out of my mouth like old bubblegum before I could stop it.

"Nothing man, just working on my tan." She was browner than an over cooked pancake in most places except for the tops of her feet and a strip across her wrist where her watch must have been.

"Me too," I said, looking down at my legs that were whiter than a bottle of milk.

I kept walking because my feet were burning off, but she walked right beside me grinning like she was waiting for me to say something else, so I said,

"Nice teeth." Why did I have to go and say that? I cringed inside waiting for the hit for talking about her false teeth, but instead she smiled wide, showing them off real good, and said "Thanks." I was wondering if this was the real Mean Carlene or just her nice twin that I never knew about.

"Where you sitting?" she asked, looking around, trying to figure out which one was my blanket. Crap, now Chomps wants to sit with me. It was bad enough having her walk with me, but I reeeeally didn't want to spend the day with her.

"Uh, over there, with my sister and her friend." I said, pointing to Janice and Peggy's feet. Carlene smiled and said, "Groovy." Hippie words sounded fake coming out of her rough mouth, but I smiled and said it back to her like a stupid parrot.

"Well, I have to go back to my blanket now," I said, walking backwards, trying to get a start on my escape.

"Can I sit with you?"

"Huh?"

"Can I sit with you?"

I could feel my insides turning into sand and piling up in my stomach. If I said no to her she might get ticked off and smack the crap out of me, so I said, "Okay," but I headed to Diana's blanket instead of Janice's. I figured I didn't want Janice and Peggy thinking that she was my friend; plus I needed time to get rid of her before Diana got back. If Diana finds out that she's Mean Carlene she'll kick her ass for what she did to me.

Carlene must be sixteen by now and pretty hard up if she wants to sit with me, a puny eleven and a half year old. I lay on my stomach and she did the same. Her shoulder touched mine and it felt creepy; like I was all cozy with the devil. She reached behind herself and pulled out a pack of Old Golds from the back of her bikini bottom. It reminded me of the time in Woolworth's when she stuck the black stockings that I was going to buy Ma for Christmas, in the back of her pants so she wouldn't have to pay for them. She must stick everything in her pants.

"Want one?" She handed over a cig, bent in the middle from living in her bathing suit bottom for so long.

"Sure," I said, putting it in my mouth while she cupped her hand over a match and lit us up. We smoked without saying anything. All the while I was trying to think of a way to ditch her. I finished my cig, pushed it into the sand, and then laid my head down on my arms with my face looking away from her. I was going to ignore her so she'd get bored and leave. That's how I get rid of Tommy when I don't want him hanging around me.

Lying in the sun got boring so I started watching a black ant walk over the sand. Every little piece of sand was as big as a boulder to him so it was like he was walking on the moon. He ran zig-zaggy over the moon rocks until he bumped, head on, with another ant, and then I guess they passed a secret message to each other about where the best place was to find some picnic crumbs, and then he headed back out, alone, walking and looking everywhere for those crumbs. I tossed some sand over him and waited. After a while the sand started bubbling up and out he popped, looking like nothing happened at all. Ants must be the strongest bugs of all, carrying big dead bees and stuff and walking everywhere they have to go.

"I'm starving."

I looked up to see Tommy standing over me dripping and shivering, even though it was hot enough out to boil spit on the sidewalk.

"Is this your brother?" Carlene asked, sitting up and squinting into Tommy's face.

I said, "Yeah." I gave up explaining to everyone that he was my stepbrother, because that just makes people ask more nosy questions.

"He's so cute!" Carlene said, rubbing Tommy's arm like she was petting a puppy. Tommy turned to mush and plopped his wet butt down right next to her for some more lovin'. Her boobs were popping out of her bathing suit top like the golden hills of sunny California and Tommy's eyes were glued to them.

"Can we get sandwiches now?" Tommy asked, keeping his eyes on Carlene's hills.

"Yeah, I'm hungry too." I said, hoping that Carlene would be gone when we got back from the store. I pulled my shorts and thongs on and told Tommy to c'mon. He looked at Carlene, and then me, like he was choosing which team he wanted to be on, and then he said, "Can she come too?"

Carlene wasn't waiting for an answer, because she was already up and ready to haul butt. I didn't bother saying anything and headed across the street with both Tommy, and his new girlfriend, following me.

Turns out Carlene couldn't come into the store barefooted so we left her standing outside waiting. I ordered two Italian grinders, two Cokes, and two chips. Tommy was watching Carlene while she watched us through the big store window. I paid the guy and then I headed back, still ignoring you know who, hoping she'd take the hint and disappear.

I made plates out of the papers that the sandwiches were wrapped in, dumped the chips onto them, and then opened the sodas. Carlene's shifty eyes zoomed in on our sandwiches, and even though I couldn't stand her, I couldn't help but feel bad for her, so I gave her half of my grinder. Then Tommy gave her half of his too. So now, she's got a whole sandwich and I only got a half, and if I knew that he was going to do that I'd a kept my sandwich to myself.

Tommy and me finished our grinders but Carlene was just starting in on her second half. She nibbled and nipped at it, spilling flakes of lettuce between her boobs. Tommy reached over to brush them off and Carlene howled, rolling backwards so he couldn't reach her.

"You're a horny little shit!" she said, squinting and laughing, her horsy teeth filled in with clumps of bread so it looked like she had one big tooth. I rolled my eyes trying to send Tommy a signal to knock it off but he was too busy drooling all over the devil.

I can't believe I'm sitting here with Mean Carlene. All this time I've been worrying about bumping into her and now she's all buddy buddy with me. All that worrying I did was for nothing. Not that I want to be friends with her now, she's too...I don't know...rough. But seeing her sitting here so smiley and nice, makes me wonder if people really can change. And if they can, then maybe Ken can change too.

I spotted Janice coming our way and jumped up to fill her in on the Mean Carlene problem before she got to the blanket.

"Who's that?" Janice asked, while I turned her back around toward our sheet.

"Um. You remember Mean Carlene?"

"Yeah?" Janice said, still not getting it, and waiting for me to give her some more juicy info.

"Well, that's her."

Janice turned around and gawked.

"Stop looking!" I said, pinching her arm to get her attention back to me.

"Ow! That's Mean Carlene on the blanket?"

"Yup."

"No way! I thought you guys hated each other. You better get rid of her before Diana gets back or she'll kick Carlene's ass!"

"I know, I know...that's what I'm trying to do but she won't get lost."

"What's she eating?"

"Half my sub."

"You fed her?"

"Yeah."

"Great. Now you'll never get rid of her."

"Duh." Stupid me. I thought that was only true for stray cats and dogs. I looked over and Carlene was shoving the last piece of bread into her mouth, and chugging the rest of my soda to wash it down. Her stomach was poking out like a beach ball with her toasty boobs laying on it.

"Help me!" I begged, but Janice just rolled her eyes, like I was the pest of the century, and said, "Let me think about it a while. Go back to your blanket and act normal."

I laid on my back and put my shirt over my eyes to pretend that I was taking a nap. Tommy was begging Carlene to go in the water with him but she kept telling him that she couldn't because she was on the rag. She's so gross. Tommy doesn't even know what the rag is, so he's still begging, and it's getting on my nerves. I yelled for Tommy to stop begging, and it got quiet for about a second and then I heard Tommy grumbling, "Jeesh, I just wanted someone to play with for a little while."

"Go play with yourself," I snapped, but right after I said it, I wished I hadn't. "Just kidding," I said, trying to take back my words. "I'll take you to the water," I said, standing up and reaching over to pull him up onto his feet. Tommy stared at me without moving. "C'mon!" I said, grabbing his hand, and yanking on him.

I dragged him past Janice, who was sitting there with her mouth wide open wondering why I wasn't still sitting on the blanket waiting for Her Cleverness to rescue me. But I was done with waiting around for her to come up with an idea, besides I had one of my own. I figured if Carlene was on the rag then she wouldn't be coming into the water, so maybe she'd disappear seeing that she was all by herself sitting on a strange blanket. I splashed into the water, blocking my nose, and dove under. It was so cold that it took my breath away, but it felt really good at the same time. Tommy was still standing in the shallow water, creeping in a little bit at a time, holding his arms up high and sucking in his stomach.

"Just jump in!" I yelled, past a pack of little kids splashing around me. But Tommy wasn't buying it, and was only up to his knees.

I stared past all the noise, past Tommy, and the blankets, and spotted Carlene walking toward the street next to a boy with no shirt on. His muscles looked carved out like a statue's. I watched her pull her cigs from the back of her suit and light up. She was chatting at him like she'd been saving up her words for a whole year, but he was real busy paying attention to the traffic, making sure they didn't get run over crossing the street. Part of me was glad that she left, but the other part was kind of ticked that she didn't bother to stop and say goodbye. I even fed her.

Meatloaf

I haven't snuck out since Ken hit me with that jar of coffee. I'm afraid of what he'd do if he caught me. Me and Dewey still hang out at the fort, but we go home when we're supposed too. I would move out for good if I could. Even if it meant that I wouldn't get to see Ma much. Just thinking about not seeing Ma makes my stomach break open like an egg. She keeps putting up with all the mean stuff that Ken does. Sometimes at night they'll fight like banshees and then in the morning Ma acts like it never happened. Like she just started living with Ken all over again and is hoping that things will be dandy.

I got a pile of stuff that Ken's been doing to me saved up inside of me, but I can't pretend that it's not there like Ma does. She wants to be happy more than anything else in the world and that's why she keeps starting over every day with that scared smile on her face. She doesn't know that each new day I have to play dodge ball with Ken's hands, trying to stay out of his way.

Ken still comes in my room at night to make sure I don't sneak out but he hasn't climbed in with me. He's been giving me money and letting me stay up late. I figure he's trying to play nice daddy for a while because he knows it was against the law throwing that jar at me. At least that's what Marcia, the lady Janice baby-sits for, told me. I want to believe that he changed, like Carlene, because I like him acting nice, but I figure the act won't last long because he can't change himself, just like a snake can't change being a snake. He's like Ma, always forgetting about all the bad stuff he does and trying to act like nothing is wrong. Sometimes I fall for his niceness. It's like I want a father so bad that I push the bad stuff away and pretend that his niceness is all there is. But then he makes a pass at me and I remember everything that he's ever done to me.

He's working the night shift tonight so I'm going to tell Ma that I'm staying at Phyllis's house but I'm really going to stay with Dewey at the fort. Dewey's doing the same, saying he's sleeping over at a friend's house. I'm excited because it's been so long since we got to stay all night at our fort. I don't have a plan for today, but I'm keeping myself busy drawing pictures and stuff in my room. Diana is still home, which is weird because she usually cuts out first chance she gets. She's shut up in her room, but at least she's home and I'm not alone with Ken.

I'm trying to draw my favorite tree from the old neighborhood. It's hard because of all the branches and leaves. I want to do a nice job and show Alex that I can draw well. Janice is the best drawer. She makes things look real and not cartoony. My tree looks kind of flat and one of the branches is bigger than the trunk. But it's too late to erase it; besides some trees have pretty big branches.

I held up my picture, next to light, to see if it looked good enough to show to Alex, when Ken came barging into my room like a blind buffalo. My picture fell between the bed and the end table, so I went to reach for it, but Ken rushed over and grabbed me by the wrist.

"WHAT?" I yelled, trying to twist my wrist free, but he had got a good grip on it and pulled me into the kitchen. "OW! Let go! You're hurting me!" Ken dropped my wrist and I rubbed at the Indian sunburn he left on it.

"Whose dish week is it?"

"Huh?"

"WHOSE FUCKEN DISH WEEK IS IT?"

"Mine," I said, wishing that it wasn't. "Why?"

"Because there's not a clean bowl in the house that's WHY. I went to get a fucken bowl and they're all filthy and lying around the house like a bunch of slobs live here. There's bowls on the floor, the coffee table, in you kid's rooms, but there's not a single bowl where it should be."

"I'll wash them," I said, trying to keep him from going off on me.

"You bet your ass you'll wash them. You're going to wash every dish in this fucken pig sty, even the ones in the cabinets." Ken said this like he was on stage, or practiced saying it in front of the mirror. Something about the way he was saying it sounded fake. I knew he was waiting for me to get smart with him so he could start screaming at me, but I didn't. Instead I smiled and said, "Sorry. I'll clean them all up so they shine like new." This made him madder than ever. I could tell by the way he was holding his breath like a puffer fish, trying to think of something else to say to me.

Diana poked her head out of her door to see what was going on. I kept the smile on my face going because I didn't need her butting in and making things worse for me. Diana is braver than anybody I know and isn't a bit afraid to say what's on her mind. She noticed my smile and then looked over at Ken, all huffy and puffy, and then she frowned at me because she didn't get it. But I just keep smiling so she'd go the hell away. I figure Ken was just trying to make me do something bad so he could make me stay in tonight because he wasn't going to be around to keep a watch on me and make sure that I didn't sneak out. He definitely won't believe me when I say that I'm staying with Phyllis. He already calls her my phantom girlfriend because he still hasn't met her yet. I wouldn't bring any of my girlfriends around here anyways because I wouldn't want him staring at their boobs and giving them the creeps.

Ken turned to see what I was looking at and caught Diana spying on us. "What the hell are you looking at? Stop sticking your nose where it doesn't belong!"

Oh crap. Please don't say anything Diana... Please.

"Well, excuuuse me," Diana sings, and then she spat out her words like they were burning her tongue. "I was just checking to made sure you weren't throwing any COFFEE JARS AT COZY!"

SLAM!!

Ken stood still, looking at the back of Diana's door, while I stood still looking at him. I was waiting to see who he was going to be the maddest at but I guess it was a tie because he yelled; "YOU TWO ARE GROUNDED!" and then tromped off to his bedroom and slammed his door. Crap.

I'm sneaking out anyways. I haven't done it for a long time because one day Ken told me that he knew I'd been sneaking out all along. He said that when he would come into my room to see me and I wasn't there, that he knew what I was up to but he didn't tell on me because he was being nice. But now he's really ticked because of the way I've been dodging him. He's trying to wreck my life because I won't let him mess with me. What got me the maddest though, was the other day when Ken said that he knew I was sneaking out so I could go fuck that Sloan boy. It felt like he wiped dog crap on me when he said that. Me and Dewey don't do anything bad but Ken thinks that all we think about is sex... like he does.

Ken left for work half an hour ago and I made sure I was tucked in tight so that when he peeked in on me it would look like I was already sleeping. Diana was in Ma's room watching the nine o'clock movie with her, but Ma will be snoring before long and Diana will have to fill her in on how the movie ends.

Janice is staying over at Peggy's. Peggy's house looks good on the outside but inside it's just as crappy as ours, with her loud mouth mother shouting orders at everyone and her drunken step-father picking fights with her mother, so I don't get why Janice would want to sleep over there, or why our cat Ranger thought it was so wonderful.

Dewey was sitting in the doorway of the fort smoking a butt when I got there, but I think he only lit up to keep the bugs away because he still doesn't know how to smoke right.

"Hoo hoo."

He was doing his owl call, trying to give me a spook, so I Hoo-hooed him right back just so he knew that I didn't fall for it.

"Hey Cozy. You look a little scared. What's the matter?"

I ducked in, pushing past him so he nearly fell over and said, "I'm not scared because I knew it was only you making that stupid noise." I was feeling a little jumpy, even though I knew Ken was at work, because the last time I was here this late I ended up with stitches and Ken sticking his disgusting nose in all my business. Dewey came crawling over to me with his thick hair flopping down in front of his eyes, like a shaggy dog. I could tell he was in a good mood and ready to stir up some fun. I giggled just enough to let him know that I was game for some fun too and could feel the fun pushing all my Ken worries away.

"I got meatloaf."

"Meatloaf?" Dewey said, like it was cod liver oil or something.

"Don't you like meatloaf?"

"Meatloaf. Ah, not really. I like fluff-a-nutters, Cozy. My Ma makes me eat meatloaf but I hate the stuff. I'd rather eat green squash than meatloaf."

"Yeah," I said, "but my mother makes the best meatloaf in the world because she uses secret ingredients." I was trying to think of what her secret ingredients might be because I was really just making this entire story up so he'd eat the stupid sandwiches.

"What are her secret ingredients?" Dewey asked, grabbing for the bag with the sandwiches in it.

"That's for me to know." I said, sticking the bag on the other side of me where Dewey's hands couldn't reach. "Do you want to try one?"

"Okay, but if I puke you have to clean it up."

"Forget it." I said, opening the bag and pulling out a fat sandwich. I opened the foil and took half out. The bread was still soft, and sticky, because I smeared it with margarine. I bit into it and the bread got stuck to the roof of my mouth, like the host at church, so I had to jam my tongue behind it to get it loose. I started chewing it to bits, spreading the flavor around in my mouth. "Yum." I said, hoping that Dewey didn't want a sandwich so I could eat them both.

It got quiet, except for the nibbling I was doing in the dark, when I thought I heard my name being called.

"You going to share those sandwi…"

"SHHH!" I grabbed Dewey's wrist and waited. My heart was pounding against my ribs like it was trying to escape from my chest. It sounded like someone was swishing around in the grass outside the fort.

"Cosette?"

"It's Diana!" I stood up, so my head poked out of the moon roof, and spotted Diana pushing the tall grass aside with a long stick like she was parting hair.

"Psst! Diana. Over here." Diana heard my voice and looked around trying to find the rest of me. "Over here," I said, waving like I was lost at sea. Diana stopped right where she was and waved me to her.

"You better move your ass! Ken knows you're out!"

"I gotta go!" I yelled, not bothering to explain because I was about to get murdered for sneaking out. I headed for Diana, who had already turned toward the street.

"How does he know?" I asked, running beside her, moving my tongue over little bits of meatloaf still stuck in my teeth.

"He called and asked for you."

"What? Why didn't you say I was sleeping and cover for me?"

"Because Ma answered the phone, not me." Diana shot me a look like I should know better than to think that she would ever rat me out.

"Ma knows?"

"Yeah, and you better come up with a good reason for not being in your bed because she's pissed and waiting for you." I stopped running. What's the hurry if she was waiting to kill me? Diana slowed down with me, dug around in her pocket for her cigs, and lit up.

"Man, you're in deep shit girl." She passed her cigarette over and I took a long drag. The stars were thick and bright like a swarm of fireflies.

"No moon," I said, remembering what Dewey had said about the stars.

"What?" Diana asked.

"Nothing."

"What excuse are you going to give Ma, Cozy?"

"I don't know."

From half a block away I could see into the kitchen window. Ma was sitting at the table, just like before, except this time Ken wasn't around to throw stuff at me. Diana went in first and then me. I squinted across the kitchen and saw Ma heading for me. She wasn't yelling but she was moving fast. I fell backwards onto the floor and put my hands over my head, so she couldn't slap my face, and then I waited for hitting to start. But nothing happened. After a little while I peeked out and saw Ma's knees about even with my eyes. They had little wrinkles in them like mouths; frowns on the top and smiles on the bottom.

"I don't know what's gotten into you lately, but you better be prepared with a good excuse for Ken because he's on his way home and there's nothing I can do to help you. You made your bed..." I watched as her knees bobbed up and down with her words and then they walked away.

Diana took me into her room and sat me on her bed. It was like a different world in Diana's room with all her cool posters and smells, and her wordy music that talks to me and sticks in my head. Pulling my hair away from my face Diana said, "I wish Ma would throw his ass out." Her eyes were like Ma's, morning blue, and both hard and soft at the same time. I started crying because I knew Ma was never going to get rid of Ken and that I had to face the music on my own.

I went to bed and buried my head under the blankets to wait for Ken, wishing that Janice was in her bed so I could crawl in with her. After a while I heard Ken's tires crunching on the rocks in the yard, and his car door slamming. The kitchen door opened and shut and I felt the house shaking under his footsteps. My door opened, and more footsteps. Then the light clicked on making things awake and real. I stayed under my blankets and listened to him breathing through his nose while my heart beat in my throat. He ripped off my covers and smiled down at me like a hungry giant.

"I'll deal with you later," he said, and then he winked at me with his nasty little eye, and walked away.

I stayed frozen for a long time, listening hard to hear some fighting from Ma's room, but it was like everyone was dead except for me and the worms crawling around in my stomach.

The wind blew in through my window making the curtains snake up and down like long white Genie arms. If I had three wishes I would wish for Ken to be gone, me to be back like I used to be, and my real father to live with us. A car drove by playing loud music. It floated through my window like a friend to keep me company for a minute. I love my window. My window! I could climb out my window and sneak into Diana's room and sleep with her. That way when Ken comes around to teach me a lesson he won't be able to, because Diana will be right there next to me! I slipped out my bedroom window and spy walked to Diana's.

Whispering Diana's name through her window, I tap-tapped on the wooden frame, so I wouldn't scare her. The shade moved aside and she peeked out. Her eyes were moving around trying to spot who was there. I waved and grinned, hoping she wouldn't tell me to scram. But she didn't say anything and got busy letting me in.

I climbed through her window and got into bed with her, laying next to the wall right below her window. If Ken came hunting with his gun I'd jump out of it. I pulled the sheets up and sniffed. Diana's smell was pretty, like strawberries and Prell. I put my arm around her belly and counted backwards from a thousand until I couldn't count any more.

"Get your ass in your own bed NOW!"

"GET OUT!" Diana shouted, while I stayed put, hoping that Ken would go away. I knew he would come for me.

"Shut your friggen mouth or you're next." Ken said, yanking on our blanket, but Diana had a good hold on it so he couldn't pull it off of us.

"MA!!!" Poor Diana was calling Ma because she still thinks that Ma's going to come rescue her from Ken. I was helping Diana hold onto our blanket, and kinda hoping Ma would come in and tell Ken to beat it. Ken's bottom fangs were poking out, and his eyes were filled with fire. He gave the blanket a hard yank and Diana hit the floor. I let go of the blanket, jumped off at the foot of the bed, and raced into my room. I scooted under my bed, hoping that Ken would leave me alone, but I could already feel his thumpy footsteps coming across the house toward my room.

Ken's face was lying on the floor sideways trying to spot me under the bed, and his arm was swishing back and forth fishing around for me. He snagged my pants and pulled hard. I was holding onto the springs above my head while my legs went with Ken. He had me half out and now he was pulling with two hands. I could feel the metal springs biting into my fingers like hungry rats. "Ouch!" I let go with one hand, sucking on my finger, tasting my warm salty blood.

"What the hell are you doing?!" It was Ma's voice cutting into Ken's tug-o-war with my legs.

He let go and said, "She won't come out from under there!" He sounded like a big baby. I stayed put, waiting to see what Ma would do next.

"Well stop it!" She said, like she was talking to one of us kids.

"The little shit was in Diana's bed."

"So."

"So, she's punished and I want her in her own bed, not in Diana's bed having a friggen pajama party."

"I don't see what difference it makes as long as she's in bed." Ma said, sounding kind of weak, like she was leaving too much room for Ken to make a rule.

"Well, I want her in her room for two weeks. She snuck out for cripes sake. I don't want her in Diana's room or anyone else's room."

Ma didn't say a word, so Ken kept on yapping. "You don't even know what goes on around your own house. These kids are sneaking out and running wild while you're sleeping!"

"Cozy, get into bed." Ma said, and then I watched her lady feet, from under my bed, turn and walk away. I wanted to scream: "Stay with me in my bed Ma!" But I didn't because she wouldn't. Ken's square Flintstone toes were still there. He was waiting because he won again and he wanted to smile in my face because he got the best of me. I crawled out from under the bed, on the other side, keeping my eyes on anything but him.

"That's better." he said, like he had control over me, but I only came out because Ma told me to. I got into bed with my back towards him. I didn't want him seeing my loser face and smiling because he won.

Two weeks is a long time to stay in my room. But I know the real reason why Ken wants me to stay in here. I felt the tears coming, tickling my face on the way down. I stuck out my tongue and caught them as they slid down to my mouth. Dewey probably went home by now and I bet he's tired of me always having to go home early. I won't see him for two weeks and by then we'll be in school again. I bet there are lots of pretty girls in junior high and Dewey might decide to find a new girlfriend because I'm no fun anymore.

I want to get out of here and live with Dewey forever and I don't care that I'm only eleven and a half, because I'm way older on the inside, and age don't mean nothing to me. I kissed the angel ring that he gave me, then turned my pillow to the cold side and closed my eyes. The wind was blowing, making that low branch hit on the house. I listened, picturing the branch dragging its long fingers up and down like it was scratching my house's back. Up, down, up....

"Hoo, hoo."

"Huh?" I sat up and listened.

"Hoo, hoo."

It was Dewey! I crawled to the window, slid the screen open, and "hoo, hooed" back.

Dewey's head popped out from behind a tree and then he squatted and snuck over to my window.

"Are you okay?" he asked, putting his hand in my window so he could touch me. I touched his warm hand, swallowed the lump in my throat, and said, "Yeah. I'm alright. But I have to stay in my stupid room for two weeks." Dewey didn't say anything else and neither did I. We sat at the window with his arm hanging in like he was holding onto a floaty tube in the water.

"You want to come in?" I asked, feeling like a dare devil for asking.

"In there?" Dewey asked, like I was nuts.

"You can hide under my bed if somebody comes," I said, trying to make everything sound easy peasy. But Dewey stayed quiet so I dropped the subject. I didn't want to force him if he was scared. I was scared too, but not too scared.

"Get out of the way."

"Huh?"

"I'm coming in." Dewey popped the screen out then grabbed at the window sill with both hands, and climbed through.

"Shhh!" I said, because his shoes were banging on the side of the house. He slid in on his belly and his clunky shoes made a loud thud on the wood floor when he landed.

"Shhh!" I said, giggling because I was afraid of getting caught, but happy because he was here. We stayed still for a long time listening to the quietness that was not really quietness at all because there were all kinds of night time noises going on. I heard Crumbs clicking around in the next room and I was thanking God that she didn't bark. Then there was the tree scratching at the house, and little creaks and groans coming from the darkness somewhere.

I sat on the floor next to Dewey, snuggling up against him and sniffing for his smell.........meatloaf?

"Did you eat the meatloaf?"

"Ah, yup. I was starving," he said, looking sideways at me, grinning.

"Did you puke?" I asked, grinning back at him because I knew that he liked it.

"Almost,"he said, and then he ducked because he knew that I was about to smack him. I cuffed him off the head and he grabbed my arm and leaned in touching my nose with a little kiss. I closed my eyes. I was so happy that Dewey was sticking with me. He was even risking his butt by being in my room.

We heard a cabinet close in the kitchen, like somebody was digging around for something to eat, and we froze.

"Dewey, get under the bed!" I whispered. He was way bigger than me and parts of him were still sticking out so I crammed him under there with my feet until he didn't show any more. Then I jumped into bed and covered up.

"Ouch," Dewey whispered, because I probably just bounced the bed springs off of his face.

"Sorry."

We stayed still listening to the noises in the kitchen. Things got quiet for a little while and then the toilet flushed and a faucet turned on and off. I was praying to God that Ken didn't come in here to teach me a lesson with Dewey hiding under my bed. I couldn't even think of how horrible that would be.

Finally it stayed quiet for a long time, and I told Dewey that he could come on out.

"Man, that was creepy," Dewey said, picking dust out of his hair.

"You better go while the coast is clear," I said, pushing him toward the window. Dewey turned and stared at me. I could tell that he had something to say so I waited. He bent down and whispered in my ear, "I love you." Then he kissed me on the mouth, clacking his teeth against mine like champagne glasses. We both laughed while Dewey headed out the window backwards, smiling all the way.

"Where're you gonna go?" I asked, wishing that I could go with him.

"To the fort until it gets light out."

I felt a big empty space in my chest picturing Dewey at the fort without me in it. I imagined Dewey sitting up there all by himself, with the stars shining, and night bugs singing, and me laying here waiting for Ken to teach me a lesson.

"Gotta go." Dewey said, with his smile shrinking into a straight line.

"I love you, too." I said, but he had already turned into a shadow running up the hill.

Ken's been teaching me lots of disgusting lessons while I've been stuck in this room on punishment. He comes in once everyone else is gone off to have fun for the day, and slobbers all over me. He even brings cards so I'll play Pitch with him when he's done messing with me. I know I said I was going to scream and fight if he tried anything with me, but I can't because he'll just make my life torture, and everyone else's too. I decided to never go to confession again either. I figure what's the use if my soul is only going to get black all over again.

Ken says that I can get off punishment tonight because I've been so good. He's been Mr. Happy to everyone. He even gave Diana twenty bucks for her sixteenth birthday. Ma thinks he's changed. She said that to me yesterday when she came into my room to see me. She said, "If you just do as he says, Cozy, you'll see what a nice guy he really is. He just had a rough start trying to adjust to being a step-dad to all you girls and he's really trying to change." My mouth smiled at her when she was saying it, but my eyes were squirting out tears. She hugged me for a long time while I bawled my head off, soaking her dress through. All that time she thought I was crying because I was sorry for giving Ken a hard time, but I was really crying because my mother wasn't as smart as I needed her to be.

Diana turned sixteen and quit school like she said she was going to. And now she says that she's moving into the basement apartment at Gina's house with Gina. Ma didn't seem too upset about it, probably because she'll be glad that she won't have to listen to Ken and Diana argue all the time. Janice made sure she had first dibs on Diana's room.

I HATE that Diana is leaving. She's the only one who kind of understands me around this crappy house; plus she stands up to Ken for me. Janice is fun and stuff but she's in her own little Janice world most of the time. So, now I'll be all alone in my room, so Ken can come on in without worrying about waking up Janice, and I can stay awake all night worrying if Ken will be coming. I hate hate hate my life!

Ave Maria

I'm glad that summer is over because at least I have some place to go every day and I won't be stuck at home with Ken. Junior high is wild. I have about eight different teachers, mostly women, and I get to eat at the cafeteria where they have all kinds of food lined up and waiting for me.

Some kids say that school food is gross but I love it. I eat lunch with Cindy Diamond, she's short and has long frizzy brown hair like Janice Joplin. She's in four of my classes, plus home room. She has a big chin, kinda like a potato, but she's still pretty. I can tell that she comes from the rich side of town by how white her teeth are and all the cool jewelry and stuff she wears. She says that she hates her parents because they're too strict and don't let her do anything.

Cindy will be thirteen in March, but I'm only going to be twelve. I got to start school when I was four because of my birthday being in December, so I'm younger than most of the kids in my class. A lot of people say that I'm way more mature than most eleven year olds because I smoke and stuff. Anyways, I like Cindy because even though she has some dough, she's not a stuck up snob like a lot of the girls at this school.

Dewey's not in any of my classes, because he's in the eighth grade, but sometimes I see him in the corridors. It's weird seeing Dewey at school and not being able to stay with him, but we do get to ride the bus together. We always sit near the back of the bus, in a small seat, so nobody else can sit with us. It's not too noisy in the morning because of everyone still being too tired to stir things up, but on the way home its nuts. The ninth graders are the worst, picking on seventh graders, and spitting out the bus windows and stuff. Nobody picks on me and Dewey though because he'd clobber them if they tried it.

It's been weird not having Diana around all the time, but sometimes she lets me visit her at her new apartment. It's the coolest little apartment with beads hanging on her bedroom door, like Alex's, and a black light in the parlor that makes all the colors on the posters light up and all the lint on my clothes glow.

Gina is a little older than Diana and she quit school too. They both got jobs working the food counter at Kresge's but they said they didn't like it because they had to wear black hair nets like the cafeteria ladies at school. Diana said she only took the job for the money and that she doesn't plan on working there for long.

Janice is all snuggled up in Diana's old room. She won't allow me in her room unless I knock first, but she's always busting into my room, and when I tell her to knock she says that it's still partly her room because she still has stuff in my closet. Diana's room only has a coat closet and Janice can't fit much in it.

I still have two beds in my room, even though it's just me sleeping in there. Sometimes I take turns sleeping in the different beds just to make it feel like I'm someplace new.

I've been reading some of Ma's books since Janice left and took all her magazines with her. They're thick, and I don't understand some of the words, but they have good stories in them. My favorite so far is *The Pearl* by John Steinbeck. Ma said I should read *The Grapes of Wrath*, but its way too thick. I want to work my way up to being able to read *Les Miserables*. That's the one with my name in it. Anyways, I like reading as long as they're not too thick. I can't wait to help Dewey with his route tonight. He's bringing Tina so it ought to be fun.

Dewey's carrying Tina and I'm pulling the paper wagon. We're cutting through Middle Park where the trees look like they are on fire with color. It reminds me of Oz; the part where everything turns from black and white to Technicolor.

"Pig Pile!"

Dewey sets Tina down and the two of them race towards me. Crap! I curl into a ball on the ground waiting for them to hit. Dewey lays on me first then Tina climbs on top of him.

"Get off of me!" I shout from the bottom of the pile. But Dewey and Tina are laughing like clowns, and won't budge an inch. I like it, but I'm screaming like I hate it, just to make Tina feel like a big shot. I keep squirming and struggling, trying to get up, but its no use, so I yell, "UNCLE!"

Tina jumps off of me but Dewey stays put, sticking his mouth near my ear and whispering made up words, just because he knows that my ears are extra ticklish. It feels good and bad at the same time, but I can't take any more of it so I screech at him to stop! Dewey backs off but I stay there, in the leaves, all worn out. I can hear Dewey whispering to Tina, "Let's bury her." But I don't care because it's only leaves. I love the fall leaves. All that color on the ground makes it look like somebody tore up a Halloween rainbow and sprinkled it all around.

Pretty soon I was so covered up that I probably looked like a regular old pile of leaves ready for burning. I stayed still, because I was planning on jumping out at them when they didn't expect it. Dewey told Tina that I was dead and started humming the *Ave Maria*; a sad sounding song that we sing at church. I could hear them rustling around near my feet so I jumped up, like a zombie from the grave, and shouted "WHARRR!" I stomped towards them with my arms out straight and my fingers curled under like claws. Tina's face twisted up when she saw me, and she started screaming and running at the same time. Dewey scooped her up, and I went over to her making the nicest face I could, but Tina slapped my face, and pushed hers into Dewey's chest. Dewey was laughing but I wasn't, because Tina was fuming at me...not him. I rubbed her on the back while Dewey carried her over to the wagon full of papers and plopped her into it.

"Cozy's sorry," I said, digging through my coat pockets, looking for the Gumby that I was going to surprise her with.

I got him in my stocking a long time ago and never play with him anymore, so I figured I'd give him to Tina. I found Gumby and handed him over. Tina reached for him. I watched while her face changed from, "I hate Cosette" to "I love Cosette." She turned Gumby over and around, bending his legs, and laughing at his little surprised face. Pretty soon she was making him walk up and down the long metal handle of the wagon, and her mouth was jabbering, making Gumby say things that he'd never said before.

"You can keep him," I said, glad that she was happy, but just a pinch sad because I didn't have my Gumby anymore.

We got back to work delivering papers. Big clouds, all black and smoky looking, were swirling across the sky.

"It's gonna rain," I said, looking over at Dewey. He leaned his head back to look at the sky and said, "Shit." Then he looked at the wagon to see how many papers he still had left to deliver. Dewey doesn't know it yet but I have to go home early today. Well, I'm not really going home. I'm going to Marcia's house to baby-sit with Janice. Lately Janice doesn't like being all alone at night in Marcia's apartment because those cellar pipes running through the ceiling keep making all kinds of creepy noises. I feel bad having to tell Dewey that I have to go, but I promised Janice.

"I have to leave soon because I promised Janice I'd help her baby-sit. She's scared of being alone at night."

"That's okay," Dewey said. But I was looking at him and I could tell that he was trying to figure out how he was gonna beat the rain, and still take care of Tina. I wanted to stay with him more than anything and I wished I hadn't promised Janice.

"Go ahead and go. I got this," Dewey said, speeding up his walk to make up time. Tina started laughing because she was getting a thrill ride and I ran beside him trying to get a good smile out of him before I left.

"I wish I could stay," I said, waiting for him to look over at me. But Dewey didn't look at me. He just smiled with his face straight ahead.

"Dewey!"

"What?"

"Look at me."

"What?"

"LOOK!"

Dewey finally looked at me and I tossed him a quick blow kiss. He reached up, caught it, and then stuffed his hand into his pocket.

"Aren't you going to put it on your lips?"

Dewey just grinned and said, "I'm saving it for later, freaktard."

"Freaktard?"

"Freaktard?" Dewey said, mocking how I said it.

He was ticked. I kept walking because I couldn't leave with him mad at me.

"I thought you were leaving," he said, digging in his pocket for something.

"I can't leave if you're gonna be mad at me."

"I ain't mad at you Cozy. I'm mad at your stupid sister for being such a weenie."

Dewey pulled his hand out of his pocket, planted my blow kiss on his lips, and then blew one over to me. I caught it and put it on my lips right away. Now we were both smiling and I felt like I could leave without hurting his feelings.

"Love ya!" I said, instead of saying goodbye, and Dewey said, "love ya" right back, so we were even. I kissed Tina's curly top and watched while Dewey pulled away. He looked cute with his baby sister in his wagon. Some day he was going to make a good daddy...for our kids.

The rain was falling steady and starting to soak into my sweater. I should have worn a coat. I ran down the hill toward Marcia's, stopping to cross at Manchester Street. Marcia's was right across the street, but I had to go around to the side of her building to get to her door. I waited for a few cars to pass, looking over at the guardrail where I always meet Dewey when I'm helping him with his route. The coast was clear so I beat it across the street and down to Marcia's door. I leaned in the doorway, trying to stay out of the rain, and knocked. I could hear Jessica's little voice yelling, trying to tell Janice that there was someone at the door. I banged louder and waited. Finally Marcia came to the door wearing blue jeans and a tenty kind of shirt with exploded colors all over it. She was smiling out at me but I was wondering why she was still home.

"I thought my sister was baby-sitting?" I said, trying to look past her to see if I could spot Janice.

"Be cool, little sister," Marcia said, nodding her head and smiling. "Janice is on her way."

Marcia calls every girl she knows her sister, and the boys, her brothers. I don't know where she got that from but it takes getting used to. She stepped back and I walked past her, into the apartment. Jessica ran up to me, with her afro hair flying around her head like a messy halo, jumping up and down in front of me with her arms up. I picked her up and set her on my hip then I walked her into the kitchen. Kevin was sitting at the table, still in his fancy suit, eating a bowl of cereal. He looked up and smiled at me over his glasses.

"Hi Cozy. You baby-sitting for us tonight?"

"Nah. I'm just helping Janice," I said, plopping down on a chair because Jessica was starting to get heavy. Marcia went into her bedroom to get ready. I could hear her singing in French, and even though I didn't understand the words, I could tell that it was a gloomy song because it was making me feel sad.

I set Jessica on the floor, so I could unbutton my wet sweater, and tossed it over the back of the kitchen chair. My hair was wet too, but not dripping, so I figured I'd let it dry in the air. Kevin lifted his bowl and chugged down the last of the milk in it, and then he set it on the table. Stretching, he pushed his chair back, rubbed his skinny belly and said, "Nothing like a home cooked meal." We both laughed, and Jessica joined in too because laughing is catchy.

Kevin doesn't have an Afro. His hair is cut close to his head like he's in the Army. He's skinny, but handsome, and has the longest fingers that I've ever seen. Jess has his fingers too. Ma says that she should play the piano with those fingers.

Somebody was knocking at the door so Jess and me ran to answer it. Janice was standing there…soaking wet.

"MAN!" she yelled, shaking and stomping, trying to get some off the water off of her. She came in and took off her shoes, socks, and yellow rain poncho, and then set them on the tile floor in the hallway. Her hair was dripping wet, so she ran to the bathroom to wrap a towel around it. All the while Jessica was following her, with her arms held up high, begging for Janice to carry her.

I started thinking about Dewey and Tina out in this rain and my heart slumped down to my stomach. Dewey wasn't even wearing a coat and Tina only had a thin blue jacket on. I tried to picture them hiding in a building to wait out the rain. Dewey was probably reading the comics from one of his newspapers while Tina played with Gumby. Thinking this made my heart stand back up and I felt a little better.

We were all sitting around the kitchen table while we waited for Marcia to finish getting ready to go out. Kevin was showing us some card tricks that his father taught him when he was a little kid.

"Pick a card, but don't touch it," He said to me, holding out a fan of cards. I picked the King of Hearts with my eyes and waited.

"Did you pick one?" Kevin asked, staring at me for an answer.

"Yeah."

"Okay. Now don't forget what card you picked."

Kevin started shuffling and cutting the deck like a card shark. My eyes could hardly keep up with his fingers.

"Okay, now touch the top of the deck," he said, putting the deck down on the table and moving his hands away. I touched the top of the deck with the tip of my pointer finger.

SCREEEEEEEECH! CRAAAAAASH!!!

"What the hell?" Kevin said, jumping up and heading for the door. Janice and me followed right behind him. I didn't know what was going on but it sounded like a car accident. There were lots of them on Manchester Street because of it being so busy. Kevin yelled to Marcia to come get Jessica because she was crying and wanted to come with us. Janice was jamming her feet into her shoes telling me to wait for her. But I headed out with Kevin, slamming the door in front of little Jessica's face.

It was rainy, cold, and dark outside, so it was hard to see what happened. I should have worn my sweater. I kept on running toward a big white car that had stopped in the middle of the street. I didn't see any other cars so I figured it was a small accident and not worth seeing. But I kept on going because Kevin was.

There were little pieces of wood spread all over the road. I couldn't make out what it was but some of it was red. I kept walking, keeping my eyes on the ground, so I could solve the mystery. I kicked a small piece of wood away and my heart stopped beating. Gumby! I picked him up and saw the same little split between his legs that my Gumby had. The one I just gave to Tina!

I looked around searching for Tina and Dewey. Running forward, I felt a scream trying to climb up my throat. I stopped at a pile of clothes in the gutter…but it wasn't a pile of clothes at all… it was my Dewey! I swallowed the scream and stared. "Dewey?" I whispered, waiting for him to answer. But he didn't. He just laid there on his side in the gutter with his eyes half open…staring out at nothing. I heard myself calling his name. "Dewey!" Rain was falling on his face, running into his open eyes. His shirt was hiked up showing his soft white stomach to the world.

I heard Janice crying behind me and walked backwards towards her with my head floating and empty. I couldn't feel the rain, or the ground, and I knew I must be dreaming. I turned and looked down, my mind felt all scrambled up trying to figure out what I was seeing. It was little Tina in her baby blue jacket, lying face down on the sewer grate. Her arms were bent the wrong way and her shoes were gone too.

"OH MY GOD!!!!" I shut my eyes, trying to erase what I was seeing. My stomach turned over, filling my mouth with hot spit. I swallowed against it, breathing in the cold air. "They're all gone! ALL GONE!!!" I heard myself screaming. But it didn't sound like my voice. I screamed again, "DEWEY!!!!!!!!" and ran over to him. Somebody was holding onto my shoulders trying to steer me away from him, but I broke free. "HE'S COLD!!" I screamed, staring into Dewey's face, looking for the sparkle in his eyes. "I'm here. It's okay. Wake up DEWEY!" A black jacket fell over Dewey's face. I reached for it, crying, "He can't breathe under there! Get it off of him!" I heard a man's voice say, "Somebody get her out of here," and then a pair hands pulled me away. This time I let them. I buried my face into the stranger's chest while his hands rubbed my back. The tears came from my throat, choking and jerking their way out, making me howl like a wounded animal. Sirens screamed nearby and somebody was shouting for everyone to step back. All the noises spun together into a loud buzz until I couldn't hear anymore and I felt myself falling into a black hole.

I was being carried down the hill, away from the flashing police lights and crowd of wet shadows. I closed my eyes but Dewey and Tina were still there, broken to bits. I screamed "NO!" into the stranger's shoulder. His hand was on my head, patting me. I held my breath, trying to erase all the blood and horror, but the pictures in my head kept coming back.

I heard Ma's voice fussing over me. She took my hand and patted it, saying to put me on the couch. He set me down and I dropped to my side, crying and groaning with a voice I didn't recognize.

"Thanks Alex," Ma said, and then she covered me up with a blanket.

It was Alex.

Ken set me upright and Ma put a pill in my mouth then handed me a glass of water.

"Swallow," she said, studying my face to make sure I obeyed. I swallowed the pill, and looked out at the group of scared faces staring back at me.

"Dewey," I said again, trying to tell them all what happened, but the crying tied me up in a knot and I couldn't talk.

"Don't you dare wake her up!"

"I won't."

It was Ma talking to Tommy. I was still on the couch in my clothes. I knew something bad happened, but couldn't remember what it was, but then a picture of Tina's broken body flashed in my head, cracking my morning open, letting last night spill out of it. The crying started bubbling up again. I tried to let it out in little spurts, keeping it under the covers to myself, but it was like a disease taking me over and I couldn't stop it. I felt a hand on my shoulder and knew that it was Ma's. She was rubbing me quiet. I stayed still and tried to imagine that Ma's rubbing was erasing all the pictures in my head. Ma. Ma. Ma. I wanted to think of Ma.

"Sit up honey."

I pushed myself up, pulling the blanket off of my face so I could see. The light was too bright so I kept my eyes closed, looking through my pink lids. Ma gave me a good squeeze and said, "I made you some toast and tea. I'll go get it."

Once she left I opened my eyes. My head felt clogged and achy. Crumbs was sitting in front of me with her head tipped sideways. She stared at me with her chocolaty eyes, touching my sadness. I started crying again, hanging onto her soft neck, while she whined along with me.

I wasn't even hungry but Ma was making me eat. I tried swallowing a bite of toast but it wouldn't go down, so I sipped at my tea to help it along. I lobbed a piece to Crumbs, and then another, until all the toast was gone. I hadn't seen Janice yet, and I wondered if she was okay, because she saw the accident too.

"It's on the front page of the paper!"

"SHHH!" Ken spit at Tommy.

"Sorry."

I knew the accident would be in the paper but I didn't want to see it. Yet. I didn't want to see Dewey and Tina as the "dead kids." It was just too horrible. I started thinking about all the things that me and Dewey would never get to do again. I'd never taste his bubble gum kisses again, or talk to him under the stars. He'll never hold me down and tickle me, or take me for hot chocolates. He'll never marry me….

"I ran you a hot tub and put some clean clothes in there on the toilet for you," Ma said, picking up my breakfast dishes. Her voice pulled me back to the couch and the white light of the morning. I found my words and thanked Ma, and then I floated to the bathroom with my blanket wrapped around me.

The bathroom was foggy with steam so I couldn't see what I looked like in the mirror. I peeled my shirt off, then kicking out of my pants I heard something hit the floor, so I looked down. Gumby. I sat naked on the side of the tub staring at his little face, thinking that yesterday at this time Dewey and Tina were still alive and I hadn't even given Gumby away yet. My bottom lip started shaking and hot tears ran down my cheeks. I slipped into the tub, with Gumby and my tears, glad to be left alone.

I was unplugged from Dewey. The long extension cord was broken, and he'd never be in my tribe again. I tried to feel him near me, pretending that he was alive, but everything felt stuck and blank, and I couldn't feel anything except darkness.

I could hear voices coming from the kitchen, chatting and laughing, because they were still in their normal worlds, but I couldn't make out who they were. I felt like I was back stage and when I opened the bathroom door into the kitchen everyone would be waiting to see me.

The sun was slicing through the sides of the window shade, letting me know that it was still there, shining for everyone, but

Dewey and Tina. I wanted to climb out the window and not have to face the people in the kitchen. I scrunched my eyes shut tight and tried tricking my brain into making all those people disappear, and that I was only taking a bath so I could get ready to go collecting with Dewey, but my stomach wouldn't be fooled, because it knew the truth, and it was too knotted up to play the game.

I heard myself moaning with what happened, and I didn't want another crying jag with all those people in the kitchen, so I sucked some air in through my mouth, in and out, in and out, before the crying got too bad.

I finished dressing and sat on the toilet lid listening to the mix of voices. I could make out Ma and Ken, and Janice was out there too, but there were a couple of adult voices that I wasn't too sure of, so I pressed my ear against the bathroom door to listen.

"Steve said that those kids didn't even know what hit them. I'm sure they died instantly. He said that the cops didn't bother calling for an ambulance, seeing that they were already dead, and sent the Paddy Wagon to collect them instead. That's what Steve told me anyways."

I heard Mrs. Green's words and wanted to slap her for saying them. The Paddy Wagon was where they put drunks and criminals to carry them away to jail. I imagined the cops heaving Dewey and Tina into the back of the stinky wagon, their bodies landing on the metal floor like bags of trash, and the door thudding shut, leaving them in the dark.

"Dewey, Dewey, Dewey," I said in a whisper, looking for his happy face in my mind, trying to forget about the Paddy Wagon story.

Tap, tap, tap. "Cozy?" It was Ma checking on me.

"Yeah."

"You okay in there?"

"Yeah, I'm coming."

I collected my dirty clothes and walked out into the kitchen. The talking stopped and everyone stared up at me. I couldn't believe what I was seeing. Ken and Alex were sitting at the same kitchen table like they were best buds. Everyone was smoking and slugging down coffee like it was a regular day.

I said "hi" and headed to my room to toss my clothes in the laundry basket and get myself in a talking mood. I felt weird. Like I was filled up with mud and it was making me move slowly. I wanted the feeling to go away but I didn't know how to get rid of it. "Don't cry," I said to myself in the mirror, looking at my red eyes and stringy wet hair. I leaned in and stared at my eyes. They were brown, with little green specks, and red lines were running through the whites, like the roads on one of those folding maps.

I lay on my bed staring up at the cracked ceiling. Closing my eyes, I tried to think where Dewey and Tina were right now. Were they in heaven, or waiting in purgatory for a while? They should be in heaven, because they were just kids, and kids always belonged in heaven. I tried to imagine heaven but all I could come up with were golden harps and white puffy clouds. I think Dewey would get bored of heaven if that was all that was going on up there. It isn't fair that they had to die. Why couldn't it have been Ken? He's old and mean.

As soon as I thought it I felt ashamed, because I never thought I would wish anybody dead. "I don't wish him dead," I said out loud, so God would know I didn't mean it. I started thinking that if I'd stayed with Dewey and Tina last night I would be dead right along with them because we rode three to the wagon loads of times. I wish I'd stayed with them.

I could hear some laughing and remembered that the kitchen was full of people. I peeled myself off my bed, ran a brush through my hair, and smiled at myself in the mirror. It didn't look like an honest to goodness smile, but it was the best I had.

"Here's my girl." Ken said, slapping his knee for me to go sit on it. I didn't have any hate left in me so I went and sat crossways on his lap. I looked out at everyone and tossed them a ten cent smile. Mrs. Green started yapping about how dirty her floors were, and then made her getaway, but everyone else stayed put. I was glad that she left because she doesn't know anything about Dewey and had no right talking like she did.

I felt mixed up seeing Alex at our kitchen table, and I didn't know what to say, so I sat on Ken's lap and let things go the way they wanted to. Ma set a cup of coffee in front of me, like I was one of the adults, and said, "There's cream and sugar already in it."

I knew she was trying really hard to make me feel better so I thanked her and sipped at the coffee.

"Thanks for getting me home last night, Alex," I said, fidgeting with the little flashlight hanging off the end of Ken's key chain. Alex half-smiled, then he gave me a nod and took a slug of his coffee.

Janice came back into the room and plopped herself down on Ma's lap. Ma pulled Janice's hair back into a skinny ponytail, showing her pink ears. I could tell that Janice had been crying because her eyes were red-rimmed and her nose was blotchy. I was hoping that she wouldn't start talking about what happened, so I tried not looking at her so she wouldn't start up.

I spotted the newspaper sitting on top of the washing machine. I knew Dewey and Tina's pictures were on the front page and I wanted to see them. I needed to see their faces again before they got all blurry in my head and I forgot what they looked like. I'd snag it later, after everyone leaves.

Alex started talking hockey with Ken. This was good because Ken and Ma loved their ice hockey, but I wondered how Alex knew about it. He likes art, music, and hippie stuff, but he was blabbing on and on about hockey like a TV guy. Ken was full of it too, nodding and saying stuff before his turn, like he was afraid he wouldn't get a chance to talk. I watched Ma eyeing Ken and Alex, and then she looked over at me, and smiled. I knew she was glad that Ken was done hating Alex.

I wanted to talk to Alex, but I didn't dare, because I didn't want Ken to get jealous of him and then start hating him again, so I kept my head mostly down and let everybody else do the talking. I needed to go in my room so I could think about Dewey and Tina in private. It didn't feel right sitting out here laughing with everyone when Dewey and Tina's dead faces were in the newspaper on top of my washing machine.

"I'm gonna go take a nap," I said, hopping off Ken's lap and waving goodbye to the whole table full of people. Everyone said "Bye bye," at the same time, like they'd been practicing at it all morning. Snagging the paper off the washer, I headed to my room and crawled into bed. I waited, trying to work up the nerve to look at newspaper, and remembered the last time we all rode in the red wagon. We were done delivering papers, and were in a hurry to go spend some money. Dewey sat down first, then I sat on him, and then Tina sat on me backwards so that her legs hugged my waist. We shot down the hill, with Dewey using his feet for brakes, like Fred Flintstone, laughing all the way. It was the same hill they got killed on.

"Stop thinking," I told myself, unfolding the newspaper so I could get a good look at the pictures. Dewey's picture was on the top and Tina's was under his. They looked like dead kid pictures, shadowy black and whites with no life in them. I stared at Dewey's eyes, trying to find the real him, but he wasn't there. Dropping the newspaper, I closed my eyes, and let a big muddy wave of missing Dewey and Tina wash me away.

We all went to the funeral as a family and sat at the back of the church so I could leave if my crying got too bad. But I kept my crying to myself and made it through the whole thing. A lot of the kids from school were there, filling up the church so much that people had to stand against the walls and outside. The organ was playing the *Ave Maria* when a bunch of serious men in black suits carried in two pure white caskets dripping with flowers. They set them down at the front of the church for everyone to see.

I remembered Dewey and Tina singing that song after they buried me in leaves and that's when the crying hit me hardest, because I knew for sure that I would never, ever, see them again.

Those two white caskets looked like baby beds and Dewey's mom was hanging onto them, groaning into the happy flowers, and begging God to give her back her babies. I wanted to hug Mrs. Sloan, and cry with her, so we could feel all that sadness together. But I knew it wouldn't be right, so I turned inside myself and tried to find Dewey's smile in my head, but all I could picture was his body in that casket.

When I was waiting to walk outside the church, Father Bigglio stood beside me and put his hand on my shoulder. He didn't say anything to me but I could feel what he was saying through his hand. It was nice of him and all, but it didn't work, because I still felt mad at God… and all alone.

So now I'm supposed to act like it's all over with. Some of the kids at school point and whisper when I walk by them, and I know it's because I'm the girl with the dead boyfriend. They aren't mean to me or nothing, but I can tell they don't want to get too close or they might catch my bad luck. I sit alone on the bus, in our old seat, and won't let anyone sit next to me, because even though Dewey's not around, I still save him his seat.

Things are pretty much back to crappy normal around the house. Ma and Ken had a fight today because she let the dog get on their bed. Janice is making a skirt to wear to a dance that they're having at the YWCA this weekend. She tried talking me into going too, but I told her no. Janice is still pretty sad, but she's doing better than me. I guess it's because she wasn't his girlfriend and all. We talked about the accident a little bit but kept out all the gory details.

Tommy spends most of his time sitting in front of the TV and stuffing his face with food like he always did. He's been really sweet to me though, and for a little kid I think he's thoughtful. Diana's been letting me visit her more than she used to, but I stay mostly at home in my room thinking, or I head over to Alex's and watch him paint.

I'm on my way over to Alex's house. He's been really nice, letting me come over all the time and stuff, but I don't tell Ma and Ken about every little visit I have with Alex because I don't want them saying that I spend too much time there. Slipping through the hall door, I tip-toe up the stairs, so old lady Harris won't hear me, then I tap on Alex's door and wait. It always smells different in his part of the hallway; like a spicy forest baking in the sun.

Alex opened the door and his eyes got crinkly as he smiled big and wide.

"Little Chick! C'mon in."

"Thanks," I said, following Alex into his bedroom and plopping down on the end of the couch. I don't need to do any talking or anything when I'm here because I'm just glad to be here. I usually do whatever Alex does. Sometimes when he's painting he'll talk with his face, instead of words, so he doesn't interrupt himself. I know all his face signals by heart.

I remember when I first met Alex, I thought he was a loopy hippie, but now that he's grown on me, I think everything about him is cool. I like his eyes, his smooth tanned hands and long fingers; I even think his crooked front teeth are cute. One hangs over the other one a little like it's trying to cut into line.

"You want a Coke?" Alex asked, as he pushed through the beaded doorway heading for the kitchen.

"Sure!"

Alex returned with two icy cold sodas and handed one over to me. I took a long swig and felt the bubbles nipping at the insides of my cheeks like needles. "AHHH!" I said, smacking my lips like a beer drinker does when he guzzles a whole bottle. Alex laughed and then told me to shut my eyes.

"Shut my eyes?" I asked, wondering what the heck for. Cold soda and shutting my eyes didn't seem to go together.

"Yes," Alex said, with his back towards me, so I close my eyes and wait. I know he's putting on a record because of the noises he's making and I'm figuring he wants me to guess who it is. The music starts and the voice sounds kind of familiar.

"Who is it?" Alex asked, with a winning grin on his face, like he'd already stumped me. The dude singing sounded familiar, but I wasn't sure.

"Don't tell me," I said, squinting down at my soda, "I know I know it." Then the guitar part comes in and bingo! I know who it is.

"Donovan!" I say, smiling into Alex's eyes. Alex raises both eyebrows and says, "Very good!"

I was feeling proud because Donovan wasn't one of those singers that get played on the radio every day. He's kind of in the background and mostly hippies know about him.

We drank our sodas and listened to the music. I was lying on the couch and Alex was behind me on his bed. When I grow up I want an interesting house like Alex's instead of a stuffy house on Cherry Street. And I want a husband who likes to test me on music and makes me think about interesting stuff and isn't afraid to laugh like Alex. Besides Dewey, Alex is my next choice for a husband, only fat chance of that happening seeing that he's like ten years older than me and has a sort of fan club of girls always chasing after him.

I tried to picture what I'd look like when I was all grown up. I'd let my brown hair grow mermaid long and keep it shiny and brushed. I'd learn how to put liner on my eyes so that they looked slanty and sexy. I hope that I have more than a handful of boobs so that that little crack shows up when I wear low blouses. I bet I could win Alex over if I was all grown up.

"I'm going to work for a while," Alex said, heading out to his studio with his cigarettes and ashtray. I followed him out and plopped down on a pillow. He was working on hands. He had open hands, hands in fists, pointing hands, and praying hands. They all looked like mans' hands with thick veins and pudgy muscles. I looked at my hands; no nails, because I eat them as fast as they grow, a wart on the back of my thumb, and little blonde hairs growing out above my knuckles. I tucked them under my knees and pretended that they weren't mine. When I'm grown up I'm going to have nice hands like my Meme. She has beautiful hands because she rubs them in lotion and then puts lambskin gloves on them. She sleeps like that every night. She has nice rings too and they make her fingers look all dressed up.

Watching Alex made me tired so I pulled another pillow over and laid my head on it. I closed my eyes, just to rest them, and my mind took me to the fort with Dewey. It was the time when we were wrestling and he tried rubbing against me. I felt tingly down there just thinking about it. Part of me was wishing that I did go all the way with Dewey that night under that flashy diamond sky, instead of worrying that it was going to get snagged away from me by Ken.

Ken hasn't tried messing with me since Dewey and Tina died. He's always testing me though; grabbing my hand and putting it on his thing, or sitting me on his lap and doing a little wiggle dance under me. I always push him away and so far he hasn't thrown a fit about it.

"Time for a butt," Alex said, dropping his pencil on the floor like he was fed up with drawing hands. I went into the kitchen and sat at the table while Alex disappeared into the bathroom. I could hear him peeing. It sounded like somebody was emptying a bottle of soda into the toilet. One long pouring pee and then it stopped; except for a couple of extra trickles at the end. I could smell cigarette smoke, telling me that he'd already lit up, so I snagged a butt and lit up too. He came out smiling, but I could tell that something was bugging him because his eyes didn't smile when his mouth did. I didn't say anything and just kept dragging and flicking until he said something first.

"Have you ever smoked pot?" Alex asked, but I couldn't tell if he was asking because he had some, and wanted to smoke it, or if it was a test to see if I was a dope head. I decided to play it safe.

"No."

"Reeeeally?" Alex said, like he knew that I was a big fat liar and he was giving me a chance to fess up.

"Ah," I stammered, "I've seen it smoked before and smelled it." I figured inch-by-inch was better then diving in headfirst.

"Who?"

"Who what?" I asked, swallowing hard because he wanted all the details.

"Who did you see smoking it?"

"Bimini and Frank. Those people I used to baby-sit for. They smoked it all the time."

"And you never tried it?"

I felt like toothpaste getting squeezed out of the tube. I knew he was going to keep squeezing until he got it all out of me.

"Okay. I tried it."

"Ah-ha!" Alex said, pointing, and trying to look shocked. But I could see the twinkle in his eyes so I knew that he was just teasing.

"You want to smoke some?" He asked, opening his cigarette pack and pulling out a thin joint from the box. "It's supposed to be really good stuff."

I watched Alex sniff at the joint and put the tip of it in his mouth. I needed to get used to Alex and pot being in the same family. I hadn't smoked since Dewey died and I'd been wanting some really bad.

"Okay," I said, sitting up straight in my chair, getting all tickly in the belly thinking about getting high with Alex.

"We only need to take a couple of hits because this stuff is strong," he said, lighting the pointy end and sucking in. The end sparked like a firecracker fuse, and then he sucked in some more making it glare and glow. The smoke snaked up toward the ceiling, curling above Alex's head. He passed the joint and I took a good hit, inhaling until my chest was full, and then letting it out so I created my own little magic cloud of smoke. We each took another toke and then Alex snubbed it out and put the roach back into his cigarette box.

My stomach felt full, that's always the first sign that I'm getting high, and I felt slow, like everything my brain told me to do took me an extra long time to do it. Alex had his eyes shut and his chin was up, like he was waiting for a breeze to blow on his face. I wondered what he was thinking behind those closed eyes, so I stared up at him, waiting for him to come back.

His eyes fluttered and opened, and his cheeks piled up into a smile. "This is good shit," he said, in his whispery Disney voice, and then he looked down at me and grinned. His curly hair was shiny and soft looking, and I wanted to poke my fingers through one of his curls, pull it straight, and then watch it bounce back. His face looked amazing, all smooth, no pimples or scars, just nice tanned skin laid out like a new wooden floor.

"What?" Alex asked, catching me watching him. I felt my face heat up because he caught me staring.

"Nothing," I said, "I was just looking at how nice your face is. That's all."

Alex got up and looked into the little round mirror on the wall. He tilted his head this way and that, looking at himself, and then he said, "It is a nice face isn't it." We both howled, because he sounded so corny, and I had to head for the toilet because all this laughing was making me feel like I had to go. I closed the door, and then squatted to pee. Looking around his bathroom I could see a bunch of normal man stuff hanging around. There were shaving razors, blue toothbrush, a half used bar of soap for washing hands, and a small glass bottle of something brown sitting on the window sill. Hmmm. I flushed and headed for the little bottle. It looked important, like a love potion or something. Picking it up I tipped it and watched the liquid move slowly, like honey. Unscrewing the cap, I took a whiff. Hmm…yummy. It was that hippie after-shave that Alex wears. I spotted a little white strip of paper taped to the side of the bottle with the words "Patchouli oil" typed on it. Dabbing my finger over the top, I sniffed again. I loved it because it was like having Alex in a bottle. I wiped my finger under my chin and then I smeared some more behind my ears and on my pants and shirt. Now I could take his smell home with me. I put the bottle back where I got it and went into the kitchen.

Alex wasn't there, so I walked into the studio, but he wasn't there either. Parting the beads, I ducked into his bedroom where he was hunched over the stereo putting on a record.

"I thought you might have fallen in or something. Are you all right?" Alex looked worried. Probably because he gave a kid pot, and now he was afraid that I might be freaking out or something.

"I'm fine," I said, making a face that said, "Don't be stupid."

Alex put on a record and got on the bed next to me. We lay there, side by side, floating away with the music, and the smoke. It seemed like time was dragging and flying at the same time. Part of me wanted to yap, and the other part wanted to think. I peeked over at Alex and he was peeking over at me. Alex smiled and then he bit at the inside of his cheek and asked, "Has Ken been messing with you lately?"

My stomach flipped because I just got high so I could forget about stuff, and now I was seeing Ken pawing at me in my head. I answered Alex, trying to keep the shakiness out of my voice.

"A little, but not too much since Dewey…you know."

Lately I'd been trying not to think about Ken and me and talking about it now was making it all come alive again. So this is what Alex has been chewing on all night. It was weird talking about it out in the open, and sometimes I wish that I never told Alex, because I didn't want him picturing me and Ken doing nasty stuff in his head.

"Good," Alex said, pinching my arm and warming me up with his smiley eyes. "You let me know if he does. Okay?"

I didn't answer him, but it made me feel good knowing that Alex was on my side if I needed him, like Dewey used to be.

It got quiet again, and the music wiped out all our talking. It was the Beatles singing ..."You say goodbye, and I say hello. I don't know why you say goodbye I say hello." The words were cutting into my heart because of me having to say goodbye to Dewey and Tina. All that sadness was starting to pile up on me again, making it hard for me to breathe.

I guess Alex could tell that I was getting uptight because he said," Let's go sit on the roof." I was glad when he shut that song off, but I was still filled up with seeing Dewey and Tina all broken up and dead in the rain.

We grabbed our coats and I followed Alex out into the hallway where he pulled a ladder out of the ceiling so we could climb up into the attic. Alex flicked on a light, and walked bent over, because of the ceiling being so low, across some boards to a window in the roof. I followed Alex across the creaky boards, trying to get rid of my sad thoughts.

"I'll give you a boost out," Alex said, "but stay put until I get out there because it's slippery."

"Okay."

I made it out and looked around. The sky was fancy with stars. Alex held my hand and we inch-stepped over to a chimney and sat down, leaning against it. Some of the houses in the neighborhood were already decorated in twinkling Christmas lights. Thinking of Dewey out here with all these stars and happy Christmas lights made me feel like I was stuck in a muddy hole in the middle of a carnival. I told myself the story about him being in heaven, and how someday I'd see him again, and that made me start to feel a little better. But then I remembered that he was going to miss my twelfth birthday, which was coming up in a couple of days. I used to always be trying to catch up with Dewey, but now I'm not trying to catch up to anybody.

I didn't notice the tears, but I guess Alex did because he leaned over and wiped some off my face and asked,

"You okay, Little Chick?"

"Sort of."

"Dewey?"

"Yup."

Alex pulled me closer and put his arm around me. Then we both sat there, breathing and sighing, while we watched the neighborhood from the roof.

The house was pretty well lit up when I got home. Janice was standing on the pantry counter digging into the top cabinet, hoping to find some munchies. The TV was blaring from the parlor and I could see from here that Ma and Ken's bedroom door was already closed. Thank God. I didn't want to have to do any explaining about my bloodshot eyes.

"Want an Oreo?" Janice found Ma's stash of goodies and she was counting out some cookies. I wasn't hungry so I said, "No thanks," and trotted off to my room before she started gabbing at me.

Clicking on the lamp, I peeled off my coat, and then slid under the covers with all my clothes still on. I had a pile of Ma's books on the little table by my bed, but I ignored them and went straight to my Archie comics instead.

Archie wasn't that cute to me any more. He reminded me of a kid at school that I caught picking in his ear and then sniffing it. That was hard to watch. He's got red hair too. I bet Alex could draw a better comic. He draws stuff and makes it look real, like a photo. My eyes kept going crossed, from trying to read, so I shut off the light and lay on my side.

Ken hasn't been prowling around at night like he used to, so I've been falling asleep pretty fast. Usually I fall asleep thinking about Dewey and Tina, trying to remember everything that we did. I play it out like a movie in my head. Sometimes, when I forget a piece of it, it ties me in a knot, because I don't ever want to forget anything about Dewey and Tina.

I wrote Dewey's name on my forehead, hoping to dream about him, and rested my head on the arm that I dotted with Alex's love potion oil, so I could sniff at it while I tried to fall asleep. I still felt a little fuzzy from the pot so I let it pull me down into dream world where everything was dark, but nice.

Ma always knocks on wood when she says that something is going good. This is supposed to keep bad stuff from happening. Well last night, when Alex asked me if Ken had been bugging me lately, I should have found the biggest tree on the street and knocked on it.

In my dream last night I was letting Dewey touch me and it felt really good, but then Dewey's face twisted up and he yelled "SCREAM, COZY! SCREAM!" I woke up with my heart thumping and Ken touching me down there. I could still hear Dewey's words in my head so I opened my mouth and screamed at the top of my lungs. It was so loud that I scared myself. Ken jumped up and ran out of my room like a robber dodging a spot light. I stayed in bed, listening to my heart pound, waiting for Ma to come and ask me what I was screaming about. I was going to tell her that I had a nightmare. But she never showed up.

The way I see it, compared to seeing Dewey and Tina dead, Ken doesn't seem so scary anymore. So, I'm going to scream like that every time he tries messing with me, even if he makes my life a horrid hell. I'm not worried about Ken messing with Janice either, because she's toughened up a lot since she's been in Jr. High, so she can take care of herself. With Dewey being dead, I figure he can see what's going on down here and he's helping me take care of myself. I think that dream gave me some of his courage or something.

I'm working on a plan to get away from Ken forever, even if that means leaving Ma behind. I've been writing it all down in my diary. Right now I have Alex in my tribe, and my sisters and

Tommy, but that's not enough, because people die. I'm hoping that some day Ma will finally see the real Ken, and dump him, and then she can join my tribe again. But even if Ma sticks with Ken, I'm still going to follow my plan on getting out of here, because she ain't never going to save me, so it's all up to me now.

I'm heading to the fort, even though my stomach has eels swimming around in it, to see it for the first time without Dewey. Janice offered to come with me but I told her that I wanted to go alone.

It's nippy out, and starting to get dark, so I pick up my speed and turn off into the field. Most of the leaves are off the trees and the grass looks forgotten, sticking up brown and stubbly, so ugly it's hard to look at. I spot the pear tree, and there are still a few pears hanging on it, but most of the leaves are gone. I move closer, to get a better look at it, and a chill bites into me, like the devil is pinching the back of my neck. The tree looks haunted; with its naked branches sticking out like dead mans bones, and the last rotten pears holding on like they're afraid to die.

My heart is pounding thinking of all that spooky stuff, but I keep walking until I get right up to the fort. It's a wreck, leaning over itself like it's about to faint. The roof is gone so I can see inside of it. It looks nasty, filled up with trash, leaves, and rotten pears all mixed in together.

I kick at the fort but it stays put. So I kick at it some more, mashing my toes until they sting, and a side comes loose. Grabbing onto it, I pull until the walls fold in like a card table, leaving nothing but a heap of old wood. I start crying, because of tearing it down; but I had to do it because I couldn't stand to watch it caving in on itself.

I hoist myself up into the haunted pear tree and climb. Branches are snapping, pears are dropping, but I'm getting higher and higher. I reach the top, sweating like its still summer, and breathing in hard steamy breaths. Things are different now. The world is different. Dewey is really gone. I'll never sit up here and spot Dewey heading to the fort again. No more making bird noises to each other or sneaking sticky Bazooka kisses on his paper route. I look over at the wall were we used to sit, all rocky and gray like a tombstone, and my eyes fill with tears, making everything blurry.

One part of the sky is getting dark, but the other side, where the sun is setting, is swirly with blue, pink, and purple. The sun is peeking out through the clouds in long white rays, so it looks like the door to heaven just got opened, letting all that God light escape. I close my eyes and pretend that I can see Dewey and Tina walking through heaven's door, and meeting God there. I can only see the back of God but I know it's him because of how he's hugging them.

He points to a golden road that winds around the clouds and I'm thinking it must lead to carnivals, candy stores, and other places that kids like to go to. Dewey takes Tina's hand and they run off together, to go live it up, and never have to worry about the stuff that goes on down here again.

I open my eyes and watch the light shrink back behind the cloud, leaving me alone, at the top of this dark tree. I know that they're in heaven. And I'm glad too; even if it does mean that I have to stay stuck down here all by myself. I twist Dewey's ring around so the angel's face is facing out. This way she can see where I'm going and keep me safe. I'm glad I have it and wonder if Dewey had some special powers and knew what was going to happen to him.

I start making my way down the tree and spot a good looking pear hanging right by my head, so I pluck it off and inspect it. No bruises or wormholes, and just the right softness and yellow color. I bite down and the sweetness of it squirts all through my mouth. As I eat it I can feel it filling my belly with all that sunshine that made it grow, pushing out the squirming eels. A smile surprises my face, so I whisper, "maybe good stuff can still happen," to myself and Dewey... if he's listening.

Leah Griffith was born in Worcester, Massachusetts - the birthplace of her creative spirit which, through the years, has been nurtured by her time spent living in Hawaii, St. Croix, and North Carolina. She currently lives in Florida with her husband, Mike; her cat, Bella; and her two Chihuahuas, Duchess and Kahlua. After raising three children, Leah now enjoys writing full time. *Cosette's Tribe* is her first novel. Leah welcomes your visit online at: www.cosettestribe.com.

CPSIA information can be obtained at www.ICGtesting.com
Printed in the USA
LVOW07s1330190115

423445LV00006B/198/P